The Secret of the Veil

Claudette Spencer Jones

I0662394

<u>*The Veil Books*</u>

The Secret of the Veil

The Spirit of the Veil: Prophecy of the 7

(Publication February/March 2019)

Thanks to mom, Marlowe and all the family and friends who have been patient during my journey.
I am most thankful to the Father for a time of glorious discovery.   *CJ*

TABLE OF CONTENTS

BOOK I

Boston, Massachusetts

Blessed is he that readeth,
and they that hear the words of this prophecy,
and keep those things which are written therein
for the time is at hand.
Revelation: 1:3

Chapter 1

Sometime during the mid-eighteenth century, the Pilgrim House Inn was built by, and was the home of a rather infamous sea captain.

These days the stately Victorian building is a home only in the sense that it is a bed and breakfast hotel that hosts endless streams of vacationers.

Unlike those other vacationers who may visit once every year or two, for reasons I can't explain, I seem compelled to return every few weeks. My attraction to Newport, Rhode Island is akin to a magnet drawing a nail. I feel a vague connection to the town that I can't explain.

I would like to believe that it is my love of old architecture and antiques, but that somehow strikes a false note. It is much more than that, and I am blissfully unaware that on this particular visit I will discover just how much more.

As I park in front of the inn, I wonder again at my preference for Newport to the exclusion of other possible vacation destinations, and once again chalk it up to the town's fantastic coastal beauty, its colorful history, and the intriguing mansions I find so addictive.

Newport is the perfect weekend getaway, and at the end of each visit I return to Boston with a marvelous sense of renewal and contentment.

What I find most charming about the Pilgrim House is its fragile elegance, which has managed to prevail despite the passage of time.

Its beauty is partly accomplished with lovely antique furnishings, profusions of freshly cut flowers, and the perpetual aroma of a New England countryside wafting through the air; I suspect in the form of fragrance de potpourri.

The bedrooms are large and comfortable with enormous, old four-posters however, my favorite part of the house is the rooftop deck.

There, on clear, breezy mornings guests are served a delicious assortment of home baked pastries, rich gourmet coffees and aromatic teas, all accompanied by a stunning view of the ocean.

Breakfasting on the deck and nesting there peacefully each evening has become a ritual on these visits.

"Please watch your step," the tour guide cautions the twenty or so people trailing behind her. At the moment we're touring the largest of Newport's mansions and as usual, I'm completely mesmerized by the extraordinary opulence.

That these immense palaces were used only several months of each year as summer homes is far beyond my understanding.

Even more difficult to understand is my fascination with them and the town.

"The servant's quarters and the wardrobe rooms were on the third floor," the guide says, as she points to a winding staircase that curves up out of sight.

The group hesitates, but she walks briskly on.

"We're not going to see the servant's quarters?" A middle-aged woman inquires irritably of the retreating figure.

The question succeeds in bringing the harried docent to an abrupt stop, and we're surprised when she turns back around.

"No, those rooms are closed to the public."

Then, possibly aware of her brusqueness, she offers a little more on the subject.

"Each morning the servants climbed those stairs to the wardrobe rooms and brought down the family's attire, which generally included several changes during the course of the day and evening; sometimes as many as four or five.

Actually," she adds after a moment's reflection,

"The servant's quarters took up very little space compared to the space reserved for the family's clothing – maybe an indication which was considered more important."

A tall man walking next to me leans down and whispers conspiratorially …

"I agree with the lady who wants a look-see up there." He jerks his thumb upwards.

I smile noncommittally as we hurry to keep up with the guide who is moving again.

Keeping in step with me he asks,

"Think we missed anything interesting in the wardrobe rooms?"

"I've never been in this particular mansion, but I'd be willing to bet that unless they have some authentic, period clothing up there – which I seriously doubt – it's just empty rooms," I answer.

"You're probably right."

After a brief pause, "I'm Chuck Jacoby," he says, extending his hand.

"Pleased to meet you; Alexis Ashley." We shake.n front of me now, Jacoby leans his tall, lanky frame down to pass beneath a low archway.

I smile as I think that except for the silver hair and casually expensive clothes, damned if he doesn't look a lot like Abraham Lincoln.

I wonder if he's singling me out for attention because I'm the only black person on the tour and he thinks I might be uncomfortable.

But, since the two of us are the only participants without companions, it's more likely that I'm simply the logical receptacle for his comments.

Unfortunately, my first thoughts turn too quickly to race these days.

Since moving to Boston it's been difficult not to notice that the response to racial differences are more 'in your face' than in my hometown of Chicago.

Not that Chicago's really any better, just different in that respect. But, like my Uncle Milt always said, it doesn't much matter where you go; there you are.

According to Uncle Milt, where we are right now in the late eighties seems to be somewhere between the struggle to hold onto previous advances, and deciding what to do next.

We're now in a lovely boudoir and the guide is treating us to vivid descriptions of the furnishings that's interspersed with salacious details about the life of the room's original, long-departed occupant; who would probably spin in her grave if she knew what was being revealed about her to a group of nosy strangers.

Leaving the bedroom we take a narrow, back stairway down to the kitchen and I'm about to share with Jacoby that the stairs were the old servants' route; a shortcut to the kitchen, but close my mouth as I wonder how I would know such a thing.

I am stunned by the size of the kitchen. It is a football field of a room.

Two gigantic stoves stand side by side, and a multitude of gleaming, outsized pots and utensils hang from hooks over a long wooden table in the center of the room.

The guide is giving her spill and we're listening attentively when suddenly I feel uncomfortably warm, and slightly dizzy.

Hardly ever sick, I'm wondering what can be the problem when the room starts spinning wildly.

In an effort to make it stop, I grab the table for support and close my eyes. When I open them again, the world has undergone a terrifying change.

A dozen or so people move rapidly about the kitchen in a sort of controlled frenzy. Steam rises from huge pots on both stoves, and the tantalizing aroma of cooking food fills the air.

With tremendous effort, I manage to turn my head a little to look for the guide and the group, but they have mysteriously vanished. What the fuck!?

I close my eyes several times, but each time I open them, the frightening scene is still there.

Then, as if someone has turned on a radio that is not quite on the station, I hear the static babble of their conversation. I strain hard, but whatever is being said is beyond my ability to hear.

My impulse is to run, but when I try to move, I'm solidly locked in place. I try to speak ... do something, anything, but I'm totally incapable of action.

I can't even scream.

So, I just stand there trying to not have a heart attack and trembling so violently my breathing has become erratic.

I really look at the people in the room and realize they are all oddly dressed. The women move rapidly about

In short sleeved, floor-length grey dresses worn underneath equally long, old-fashioned white pinafores.

Their hair is hidden beneath small, white puffed, cotton hats that cover their heads and hang down the backs of their necks like thick hair nets.

The men are wearing simple grey jackets, black trousers, and similar hats that only cover the front and crowns of their heads.

As they talk, bushy moustaches quiver above their lips while peculiar long, thick sideburns are reminiscent of Elvis. Some of the workers are black, but most are white, and not surprisingly seem to have greater authority.

They are all bent to their work with admirable concentration, but not without humour as I see them talking and occasionally breaking into laughter.

Judging from the huge joints of meat, vegetables, breads and other foods spread out in various stages of preparation on the table, they are cooking a feast.

I can't decide whether it's comforting or frightening that I can see *them*, while they can't see me.

Then as if someone has switched off the radio, the babble of conversation abruptly stops.

Except for the sounds of their toil, the room is suddenly silent. I sense their tension, and my fright increases several notches.

I understand the sudden silence when a woman comes sweeping into the room, her long, black dress swirling vigorously as she moves from one spot to another apparently examining their work.

Light brown hair is swept up in a pompadour style, and her only accessory, a large cameo pendant, is worn at the throat of her high-necked dress.

The woman seems to be giving instructions to the workers, so I assume she's the mistress of the house.

As she turns to say something to one of them, she pauses and appears to look directly at me. But, she can't see me, I think. None of the others can see me, so she must be looking at someone behind me.

She smiles slightly and cocks her head to one side while a questioning expression settles over her hawk-like features. Then she is walking straight towards me. When she gets close enough our eyes connect and I know with terrible certainty, she does indeed see me.

"Miss Ashley! Alexis! Are you alright?" Someone shouts close to my ear. And as quickly as the people appeared, they are gone.

I blink several times to assure myself they are truly gone. They are. I test my ability to move, and that has returned as well.

Slowly I realize that Chuck Jacoby is standing directly in front of me and is more or less supporting my body by holding onto both my arms; if he had released me a moment ago, I know I would be on the floor. As it is, my legs are still watery.

All eyes are glued to me, but I'm so filled with relief and joy at being back to normal, I couldn't care less. I struggle to answer Jacoby, but can't yet speak. My mind is working in overdrive to rationalize the bizarre situation.

Despite my confusion and fright however, I notice that everyone is still standing pretty much where I remember them standing before whatever happened to me happened - which in all probability means very little time has elapsed.

Although sluggish, my brain is still functioning and I quickly decide to make light of the incident.

"Are you all right?" Jacoby asks again, giving me a last hard shake.

"I'm fine," I find my tongue.

"I just got a little dizzy for a moment, but it's gone now." The words tumble out in a rush.

By this time the tour guide is clucking around me. "Are you alright? If you can't go on, I'll have someone walk you back to the front office and call a taxi to take you back to your car," she offers.

"No, I'm fine, really … just a passing dizzy spell."

"Are you sure?"

"Positive," I assure her.

Obviously relieved, she immediately starts to gather her chicks.

"Okay everyone, everything is fine; just some momentary dizziness. Nothing serious," she assures them.

"Let's keep moving. There's another tour right behind us."

And, with many a surreptitious glance in my direction, the group follows her out of the kitchen.

"What happened?' Jacoby asks softly as we fall in behind them.

"I was just going to ask you that," I counter.

Something about the way he's looking at me tells me he feels that whatever happened amounted to more than dizzy spell.

"Well, you seemed to freeze all of a sudden. You stood there for several minutes perfectly still ... except you were trembling.

You appeared to be staring at something; like maybe you were seeing something the rest of us couldn't.

Then, you gasped and started to sway. I thought you were going to faint, so I grabbed you. Forgive me if I was rough," he concluded.

I feel terrible doing it, but I lie again.

"I don't remember anything other than feeling a little light-headed and then you were asking if I was okay.

Thanks so much for your help. I'm sure if not for you, more than my feet would have a close acquaintance with the floor."

"Glad to be of assistance," he answers, sounding both totally unconvinced and definitely not amused.

We silently follow our guide through several more rooms, including an incredible library.

I think it is nothing short of miraculous that I don't feel any ill effects from my experience but still, all kinds of thoughts race through my mind.

I doubt I have suffered a mental breakdown, or I wouldn't be so completely lucid now. It was obviously some kind of hallucination, or delusion. But, caused by what? I've certainly never been prone to any kind of delusional episodes. Just the opposite; I'm considered a very solid, level headed person ... often to the point of boring predictability.

So, where had it come from? And why?

As we walk into a dining room that is roughly the size of a gymnasium – there's no dizziness, no warm sensation, or warning bells. The people are simply not there one minute, and there, the next ... apparently in the midst of a large dinner party.

I look frantically around hoping to verify that the group is seeing what I am, but the group is gone.

The dining table is so long, it's difficult to tell how many people are seated in the brocaded, mahogany chairs. In the background servants quietly move about with huge platters of food and draped bottles of wine.

Supervising the activity is the hawk-faced woman in the black dress. I irrationally wonder if this is the same meal they had been preparing in the kitchen. Then again, perhaps it's a different day and occasion, I think crazily.

At the head of the table with his back to me a young blond man with long sideburns is talking and laughing with the people on his right.

At the opposite end of the table is a woman that I assume must be his wife and the real mistress of the manor. Hawk-face is apparently a servant.

The woman has flaming red hair, and is strikingly beautiful in a daringly low cut dress with a tightly fitted bodice. The sparkle of her eyes, as she laughs, rivals the out-sized jewels that glitter at her ears and throat.

In mid-sentence she glances up and apparently sees me. She looks startled for a moment, but then, incredibly, she smiles and rises from her chair stretching out her hand in my direction.

I'm gripped by a suffocating panic and my already pounding heart begins hammering so hard, I feel I can actually hear it.

When the blond man abruptly stops speaking and turns to follow the woman's gaze, the scream bubbles explosively up in my throat as the floor rises up to meet me.

Chapter 2

I open my eyes and see that Chuck Jacoby is beside me on his knees, and the tour guide, also on bended knee, is dabbing at my face with a damp cloth while directing someone to an office where they can call an ambulance.

I manage to open my mouth which feels as if it has been vacuum dried and weakly tell her there is no need for an ambulance.

I'm so embarrassed I can't look either of them in the eye.

Although I am petite, a bullish constitution has always been a source of pride. I have never in my thirty-eight years felt even close to fainting.

They lift me from the floor, determine I can indeed stand and walk, and we finally leave the mansion amid the well wishes of the others on the tour.

Someone from the Preservation Society, the group sponsoring the tour, drives me back to my car.

I am strangely relieved when Jacoby insists on accompanying us. Somehow, I know his concern is genuine and I'm grateful.

Before leaving the mansion, it takes all my strength to convince them not to drive straight to the hospital.

More humiliation at the inn when the manager and his wife hear of my collapse; thanks to Jacoby who insist they are informed.

He practically carries me up to my room, then waits outside in the hall while I undress, put on a lounging gown and prop myself up in the big bed.

He declares his determination to stay long enough to assure himself that I am recovered.

The manager brings up two steaming mugs of tea, which I accept, but I decline the offer of a bowl of soup.

When the door finally closes, I thank Jacoby for his kindness, but he hardly seems to hear me.

"You saw something, didn't you?"

"What?" My head involuntarily jerks up in surprise. Then, averting his eyes, I ask,

"Saw something like what?"

"In the mansion; you saw something."

This time it was a statement. "Something the rest of us couldn't see," he added.

"I didn't see a damned thing," I lie again.

"I really don't know what you're talking about," I say, sounding more indignant than I feel.

"Listen, professionally I'm an architect, which is the reason I took the tour of the mansions, but I also have an interest in parapsychology. Do you know what that is?"

"Of course I do," I snap.

"Psychic phenomenon and that kind of thing," he says anyway.

I say nothing in response. As much as I like him and as sincere as I feel he is, he's still a stranger and I'm not about to admit to a complete stranger something that makes me sound certifiable.

"I think you saw something, and whatever it was must have been pretty frightening judging from your reaction.

Paranormal episodes aren't usually isolated incidents, which in all probability means whatever it is you experienced back there won't simply stop.

More than likely, today's incident might be just the beginning."

"Look Chuck, suppose I admit that something *did* happen, but I'm not ready to talk about it, or deal with it just yet. What would you say?"

"I'd say, take my card and call me when you're ready."

"That's a deal," I smile with relief.

He shakes his head to signify that he is giving up and pulls out his wallet. He removes a business card and begins writing on the back.

"Here's the name and number of the hotel I'm staying at here in Newport.

After Thursday you can reach me in San Diego at either the office number, or the home number, which is on the back," he said, placing the card on the nightstand when he finishes writing. There is something that's absolutely final about this move.

When he said the name of the city, I had looked up sharply. Now, I pick the card up and look for a long moment at the words, 'San Diego'.

"You've been so kind," I finally say. I'm so sorry I spoiled your tour."

"Not at all," he responded. "We'd seen practically everything anyway."

"No, not really," I pipe up without thinking.

"You missed the ballroom with all the mirrors and Italian marble, and the beautifully designed loggia, and the sitting room that ..." my voice trails off.

"I thought you said you had never visited the mansion we were in today?"

"I ... I read about it somewhere," I mumble.

He stands then, and placing the chair back against the wall says, "Call me when you're ready to talk about it." And leaning down, he kisses me softly on the forehead.

Just before the door clicks shut behind him, I hear myself say quietly ... "You're wrong, you know. Today really wasn't the beginning."

The door stops moving and without a word, he slowly comes back into the room, grabs the chair, pulls it close to the bed and sits down.

He crosses his long legs and sits looking at me with what I imagine is an Abe Lincoln expression on his long face.

When I don't say anything further, he prompts ... "Why don't you start at what you believe was the beginning. And, don't leave anything out."

I take a deep breath ... "Well, I really believe that it all started the day I left Chicago. I was relocating to Boston and I drove.

At more than one point during the trip, I wondered if I would make it to Boston alive. Everything just seemed to go crazy."

"Why did you leave Chicago?"

"Burn-out and bullshit. Oh ... excuse me," I say, realizing that one of what mom calls my 'gutter' words has slipped out.

"A bad habit I've never been quite able to break I explain with some embarrassment.

"Anyway, I have a seventeen-year old son who believed that because he was a foot taller than me, he was head of the household ... by default.

I'm divorced, you see. Jason was staying out hours past curfew, hanging with the wrong crowd, and was one step away from flunking two of his classes. As for me, I hated my management job with a fortune one hundred company, and had nothing even remotely resembling a social life.

Between the two of us, we were pretty messed up," I said, recalling those hellish days when nothing seemed to be going the way it should.

"When my doctor diagnosed a problem I was having with fatigue as a case of mild depression, I figured what the hell, something had to give.

I never bought the pills he prescribed. Instead, I quit my job, sent Jason to my ex-husband in Colorado for some father-son therapy, loaded up the car and left. I had never been to Boston, but based on what I'd read about the city, I felt I'd like it okay."

I stop and take a sip of tea. I'm remembering the day I left Chicago and how mom had stood in the driveway smiling bravely, waving good-bye and looking as if she wished I was still the little girl a sharp word and raised brow could influence.

It had been a sunny morning with just a hint of the coming summer's heat in the air, and no suggestion of the foul weather I would soon encounter. A perfect day for new beginnings, I'd thought.

Except for mom's sadness everything would've been perfect; we'd always been close, so even when I had gone to college downstate, I'd been back home every other weekend.

While I packed the car, her eyes had followed my every move. She was worried about my driving such a long distance alone.

Frankly, so was I, but didn't let her know it. I promised to keep in constant touch during the drive to Boston, which had made us both feel better.

True to my word, I was only several hours outside the city when I'd pulled off the road to call. To be honest, I was more surprised than she was that I had actually left.

I glance at Jacoby who is waiting patiently for me to resume. I don't know why I trust him, but I do.

23

I have recently become a great believer in signs and omens, and I know that learning his home is in San Diego, the same as a friend who I dearly love, is somehow a sign that he is trustworthy. If he can shed some light on these weird events, I think, please Lord let him.

"It's a long story," I warn.

"I have nothing but time," he answers, settling back comfortably in the chair.

I begin …

"Some of my family said that my leaving Chicago the way I did was either a case of mid-life crisis or I was just plain nuts. But it wasn't and I'm not.

I think I was compelled to leave Chicago and move to Boston. I just don't know why. I do know things went badly from the beginning.

Chapter 3

"*H*i mom."

"Alexis! Where are you?"

"Halfway through Indiana," I answered proudly.

"Good heavens! I thought you were still driving around Chicago looking for that compass you mentioned."

"Nope. Found the compass, and I'm really on my way."

"Are you all right? I mean, I know it's a little late to still be asking, but you're sure you can really drive all that way by yourself?"

"I'd be in a helluva lot of trouble if I wasn't sure at this point. I'm just fine. Stop worrying. Go watch Oprah or something. Oh, and thank Cliff again for helping me move the rest of my junk to storage.

Anyway, I'm just checking in like I promised; gotta run, but I'll call again later."

The confidence in my voice belied the tension that had my stomach twisted in knots.

"Alexis!"

"I'm still here."

"Oh, I thought you were hanging up. Call me tonight when you come off the road.

You really are coming off the highway tonight aren't you?"

"That's still my plan. I wouldn't try to drive straight through by myself, anyway. Listen, I really do have to go mom, someone's waiting for the phone. I'll call later. Love you."

"Love you, too!" She said, still sounding worried.

My hand trembled slightly as I replaced the receiver.

I'd been driving steady since mid-morning and had made only the one stop when I called mom, answered the call of nature, and bought a bottle of water. It was now around five and the sun was riding low in the sky.

I was approaching a little town called Strongsville, Ohio when I decided to take the off-ramp at the urging of a sign that read … *Rest Inn.*

"Hello!" I called to get the attention of a little, old man sitting in a room behind the front desk.

The old geezer was so immersed in his television program he hadn't heard me enter, although the front door had banged noisily behind me.

"Hi de do," now came the rustic response followed by the television being turned off.

He pulled himself up out of his chair and shuffled to the desk while smoothing down the ten or so white wisps of hair on his otherwise smooth head.

Liquid blue eyes cynically sized me up while slack, soft lips chomped down hard on the soggy end of a cigar. Apparently deciding I was harmless, he pushed the register at me.

"Thirty-four, ninety-five plus tax," he said, tugging at the faded overalls hanging loosely from his gaunt frame.

His tone wasn't unfriendly, and since he appeared harmless as well, I bent down and signed the book.

"Which way ya headin?"

"East to Boston."

"Well, they's predicting a heck of a snowstorm tonight, ya know; a real blizzard, all the way from here to Pennsylvania."

"A snowstorm? But, it's April!" I wailed.

"Don't matta. A real doozy 'cording to the forecast. It is kinda strange for this time a year, but it's still coming," he said.

I tried to think. Should I attempt to drive as far as possible before the storm hit, or call it a night and hope for the best?

I was tired and my body was cramped and achy after the unaccustomed hours behind the wheel. I decided to stay the night.

I was paying the old guy when a young blond woman, who might have been his granddaughter, or in a long stretch, his daughter came slouching in from the back room with towels over her arm.

One look at her face and I quickly turned my head to hide my pity.

Despite a dishevelled appearance, she still might have been reasonably attractive except for a disfiguring harelip scar that looked the possible outcome of corrective surgery gone horribly wrong.

As she walked up to me, I noticed she was the model of dejection. With slumped shoulders and eyes examining the floor, she thrust the towels in my hand.

I felt the sadness and hopelessness surrounding her like a thick fog, and my heart ached.

When I reached for the towels our hands touched.

Impulsively, I took her hand and smiling, said hello. She hesitated, then lifting her head and looking

27

directly at me she smiled shyly and returned the greeting.

Her voice gave me goose bumps, and I thought in surprise … why, a voice like the sound of music.

As I looked into her eyes, I felt a curious communication between us that seemed to make looking away, or letting go of her hand impossible.

We stood there for … I think for just a moment. But, looking back, I was never sure.

The little innkeeper startled me by loudly clearing his throat and plunking the room key sharply down on the counter.

With his eyes suspiciously narrowed, and his little lips screwed tightly around the cigar, he told me the room number, hustled the girl into the back room and closed the door unceremoniously in my face.

I walked outside feeling as puzzled as he had looked. What, I wondered had that been about.

I pondered the peculiar exchange between the young woman and me but, when I found my room the incident was sidelined in favor of more pressing concerns.

I certainly hadn't expected the Ritz, but this I thought, was ridiculous. There was no telephone or television in the room. Not even a radio. It was bone bare, and chilly to boot.

For nearly forty dollars, this was pure shit. But, I was tired and couldn't bear the thought of confronting the old man and having to find another motel.

I found a pay phone outside, and called mom. I assured her I was okay, and was careful not to mention the blizzard.

Returning to the room, I barricaded the flimsy door with a chair and fortified it with my suitcase and carry bag.

I lay down fully clothed on top of the bed because the room was freezing, and the blankets, though clean, were threadbare. I didn't have an appetite, so hadn't bothered going out to eat. I figured if I went to bed early and got an early start, I just might beat the storm.

A little while later, I was deep into a novel when I realized everything was ominously quiet outside.

I couldn't hear the traffic on the busy boulevard in front of the motel any longer, so I got up and went to the window to investigate.

Pulling the dusty blinds apart, I saw that the snow had started to fall and had already deposited a layer thick enough to muffle the sounds of the cars.

My stomach tightened nervously as I wondered about this unusual storm and for a few seconds a feeling of such intense dread settled over me, I could barely breathe.

With some effort, I shook off the feeling figuring it was probably just residue from the horrendous scene I'd had with my sister, Sylvia about my relocation. Everything she'd had to say was negative and had upset me more than I was willing to admit.

"Are you mad?!" She'd shrieked.

"I don't think so," I had answered.

"Then why are you doing something so stupid?"

"Obviously, because I don't think it is stupid."

"Well, it's the dumbest thing I ever heard of; I mean nobody moves someplace they've never even been. It's just plain stupid, Alexis."

And on it went until I totally lost it.

"When was it that I asked for your opinion? And, I certainly don't need your permission … So Bug the Fuck Off!" I yelled before slamming down the receiver.

I was sorry the moment I hung up, but Sylvia was so damned bossy it made me crazy; besides I was nervous enough about the move without any help from her. I would have called her back, but I didn't want to start arguing again.

We'd made up before I left, but I could tell she was restraining herself … probably at mom's request. The air between us was heavy with disagreement.

I would have loved to call her now and confide my fears about the storm, but I knew better. She was so eager to prove that she was right about my move, she would have been on the phone scaring the hell out of mom the second I hung up.

Back on the bed I noticed that the temperature in the room had taken another plunge, so I pulled on my jacket, cap and gloves, and snuggled back down.

I gave up on the novel, closed it and laid it on the nightstand. The feeling of dread was still with me, but I was determined to keep it in check.

Before dropping off to sleep, I remember thinking that this was definitely not starting out as the fun, leisurely trip I had imagined.

The snow swirled around the car borne on winds that knocked it around like it was light as a feather. Visibility was so bad, I could only see a few feet beyond the hood, and the few souls brave enough and still on the road were, like me, reduced to moving at a mind-numbing twenty or so, miles an hour.

The going was rough, but I was determined to make it as far as possible in case the highway closed down at some point.

I had left the motel at around six that morning, and was close to exhaustion after three hours of slow, cautious driving while practically blind in the wind and snow.

As a late model Volvo inched its way down the ramp beside me, I noticed the passenger was a teenage boy about Jason's age.

I slowed down so they could get on the highway ahead of me. The woman driving didn't glance my way, but the boy leaned past her and gave me a little salute and a pleasant smile. I waved back.

As I crept along behind them, I thought of my own son and my decision to send him to James, my ex-husband. When I had finally put Jason on the airplane to Colorado, I was numb.

I was so shook up I couldn't function and had called in sick on my job three straight days. But, I knew

Jason needed something I couldn't give him. He needed his father. I hoped the move would be good for him, and prayed that James would rise to the occasion.

Of course when James found out I was moving to Boston, and realized he couldn't just send Jason back if things got rough, his voice was added to a large chorus of dissention.

Nobody could believe that I, who had always been so sensible and so responsible, was doing something so nonsensical and so irresponsible. I loved it. Now here I am on my way, I thought as I strained to see the road ahead of me. Well, almost.

Suddenly, the Volvo in front of me began to lurch erratically before going into a terrifying spin.

My heart jumped into overdrive as I frantically tried to force my panic down, and began pumping the brakes.

"Damn!" I cursed my bad luck as I struggled to turn the wheel away from the car ahead; and at the same time being careful not to jerk it.

Gradually, I was aware of a loud keening noise and honestly didn't know if the noise was coming from the car or from me.

I was truly terrified when I realized that the more I fought, the closer the two cars seemed to slide towards each other.

Finally, giving up the struggle, I braced for impact.

Chapter 4

*T*he Dunkin Donuts was packed with people wandering around looking shell-shocked.

Everywhere I turned the topic of conversation was the surprising April blizzard and whether or not the highways would close.

When a handsome young state trooper got in line behind me at the counter, I tried to get some information about the roads ahead.

"Hi," I said with a big smile.

"G'day ma'am," he returned. I half expected him to tip his hat, but he didn't.

"What're the roads like up ahead?" I asked.

All conversation within the sound of my voice stopped as everyone listened for his reply.

"It's bad all along the way and worst as you head east," he answered.

"If it gets much worse, they'll be closing the highway."

Great, I thought. The direction we're all travelling. There were moans and groans up and down the line.

After getting a bowl of soup and a cup of coffee, I looked around the crowded room for a place to sit.

I finally found a table next to two men who were deep in conversation. I should say one was talking while the other one listened.

The older, white guy was holding forth on the difficult business of trucking, his income and his friends.

His listening audience was a handsome black man who looked to be in his early to mid-forties and had a body I couldn't help noticing.

His short-sleeved shirt did nothing to hide the muscles that flexed slightly whenever he moved his arms. When he stood to get sugar from a neighboring table, I glimpsed a slim waist and long legs that ended in a pair of highly polished cowboy boots.

When I had left the counter looking for a seat, I'd seen the improbable grey eyes following me.

Although he was definitely a hunk, I wasn't even remotely interested; especially in anything of a fly-by-night nature, so when I'd seen him looking at me, I'd been careful not to make eye contact. Now, ironically, I was sitting right next to him.

My head was buried in my road map when I heard the talkative one mention Boston. I perked up immediately.

Apparently he was on a run to Boston and was complaining about staying on schedule with the bad weather. I figured truckers are more in the know than the average traveler, so I decided to ask them a couple of questions.

I patiently waited for a lull in the conversation. When one came ...

"Excuse me, but I'm trying to get to Boston. Do you think they might close the highway?"

They both started shaking their heads at the same time.

"Are you taking Interstate 80 … through New York?" The older one asked.

"Yes, I am."

"80 through New York's one of the worst highways in the country. When it snows it's even worse than normal because there's no systematic cleaning. The 90 Tollway would have been a better route for you to take."

My heart sank. I glanced at the brother silently asking his opinion.

"Yeah," he said. "You sh-sh-shoulda taken 90, the P-P-Pennsylvania Turnpike. When it snows, the turnpike is ca-ca-ca-constantly salted and plowed. It would have been a much ssssafer route for you."

Good heavens, I thought, understanding now why he was so quiet. I hadn't heard a stutter that bad in years, and was almost sorry for making him speak.

"Now, what do I do?" I asked aloud.

"I don't know how you feel about this, but probably the best thing to do is reroute to the turnpike," the old guy said.

"I'm not sure I know how to do that. My cousin mapped out my route from Chicago to Boston and I'm afraid I'd just get myself lost if I try to make a lot of changes," I explained.

"Well, I gotta get crackin, but Bo here can help you out." He turned to the younger man and said,

"Can't you Bo?"

"Be happy to help," Bo answered, with a smile and no stutter.

"I don't want to put you to any trouble."

"No trouble," he said. "We're sss-supposed to help each other."

"Well, I'll leave you guys to it. Good luck little lady. Don't worry, Bo'll straighten things out for you jus fine. Catch you later, man," he said getting up.

"Yeah," was the sum total of Bo's goodbye.

"Thanks a lot!" I called after him.

Bo left his little table and came around and joined me at mine.

"My name is Alexis, and I can't thank you enough for taking the time to help me," I said extending my hand.

"Benjamin. B-B-Benjamin Tucker, but most everybody ca-ca-calls me Bo," he said taking my hand.

"Mind if I use y-y-your map?" he asked.

"Be my guest."

And for the next half hour Bo marked out my new route, then went over it a couple of times to make sure I understood where I would change highways.

The new route was taking me out of my way, but rather than arriving quickly, I decided I was more interested in arriving in one piece.

Out of politeness, I sat a while longer and chatted with Bo about his job as a truck driver, his home in Virginia and the crazy weather that had caught everyone by surprise.

I recounted my near miss that morning with the Volvo, and he listened intently.

As I talked, I remembered the woman's distorted face visible through our windshields as she did the right thing by turning her wheel into the spin.

But, her efforts seemed useless and a collision unavoidable. I had actually closed my eyes and braced myself when my car suddenly and unaccountably slid to a smooth stop mere inches away from her car – that she suddenly seemed to have under complete control.

I released the breath I'd been holding and slumped over my wheel in shock and relief.

"I don't know how the car stopped," I said.

"W-w-what do you mmm-mean, you don't know ha-ha-how it stopped?" Bo asked.

"Just what I said … I even had my foot off the brake when it stopped."

"That's not possible. Unless you he-he-hit a pothole or something and that sss-stopped you."

"There were no potholes, and I didn't just roll to a

35

stop. I shouldn't have stopped at all … but I did. I can't explain it, except to say maybe divine intervention.

Anyway, I refuse to stare down the mouth of that gift horse," I laughed nervously. "Still …"

Later, when Bo and I walked out into the cold, soggy day, the snow was still coming down hard. I thanked him again and we shook hands and went our separate ways.

As I was leaving the first Toll Booth and entering the turnpike, I realized a trucker in a big eighteen wheeler was trying to get my attention. It was Bo. I waved, blew him a kiss and took off.

After a while, I realized he was following me. I felt he must have wanted to tell me something, so I came off the highway at the next exit.

Once he had extricated himself from his big rig, "Man, I'm glad you sss-stopped. I've been th-th-th-thinking about you crossing the George Washington and I don't like it. Lord, help you if you t-t-take a wrong turn and get lost.

Some pretty awful things have b-b-been known to happen to sss-strangers in New York."

"Well, I'm from Chicago, and I can take care of myself, Mr. Tucker," I said humorously with exaggerated offence.

"I kn-kn-know you can Alexis, but I can't h-h-help it. I just don't like sss-sending you that way."

"Is there an alternative?"

"I'm going to ss-send you the long wa-wa-way round."

"Aw shit! Excuse me. This already *is* the long way … longer than my original route. Does it have to get longer?"

"Yyy-yes. I'd feel b-b-b-better."

"Oh, all right," I said with real exasperation. "I know you're trying to look out for me, but damn."

"What's the new plan?" I ask, trying not to sound ungrateful.

"Tell y-y-y-you what," he said. "You're going th-th-through Harrisburg, Pennsylvania, and like I told y-y-you, that's where I'm he-headed. You could stop there too and I'll p-p-plot it out for you."

We decided to meet at the hotel where he always stayed when in Harrisburg. If I arrived late, I would spend the night. That decided we parted again.   It wasn't long before I realized Bo and his friend had been right about the turnpike. The going was almost smooth.

The salt trucks and snow plows were out in force and doing a great job. The snowfall had gradually slowed around mid-afternoon, and although it was still coming down, I was making excellent time.

An hour or so after my meeting with Bo, I had lost him, but since he'd given me such good directions, I knew exactly where I was going.

Harrisburg was charming and different from any city I'd seen. The Susquehanna River ran right through its center, which kind of reminded me of Chicago, but was still undeniably unique. The hotel when I found it was a disappointment.

It was at the opposite end of the city from where I'd entered and sat right next to the river. It had formerly been part of a huge chain and was large, intricately designed and slightly dilapidated. It had definitely seen better days.

After checking in I had contacted Bo, who had already arrived. A while later we met for dinner in the large, empty dining room where I discovered the river rats were so bold and unafraid they never stopped scurrying. Several of them came right out into the floor and stared at us as if we were the intrusion.

I hated rats and these had piercing red eyes that seemed to follow mine. They made me feel like they were watching me. It was spooky.

Suddenly feeling full, and slightly nauseous, I cancelled the dinner I had ordered and while Bo enjoyed his in sweet, masculine oblivion, I found a telephone and checked in with mom.

She had heard about the snowstorm and was a little pissed that I hadn't shared the information, but I talked her around.

After dinner I pulled out my map ... that was getting slightly dog-eared and went over the new route with Bo. It was definitely a long haul.

The plan had me going through a portion of New York before picking up Interstate 95 through Connecticut, Rhode Island and on into Massachusetts.

We went over everything a couple of times to familiarize me with the route, and I could see that Bo was sincerely relieved that I would by-pass New York.

He would lay over in Harrisburg for a couple of days before heading out on a new run, and I would be leaving early the next morning.

We were a little sad at saying goodbye, so we prolonged it by talking in the bar long after I should have been in bed. By the time he walked me to my room, it was late and I was hoping he wouldn't get amorous.

"P-p-promise me you'll call me he-he-here at the ho-hotel if you have any problems b-b-b-between here and B-Boston. And ca-ca-call me as sss-soon as you get there so I'll know you me-me-made it," he said, as we headed back to my room.

Reaching the door, I took the key out of my purse.

"I promise. Hopefully I won't have to call until I get to Boston. You'll be the absolute first person to know when I arrive," I said.

"But remember, I'll be coming off the road at night, and because of the rain it'll still take me awhile to get there."

The snow had stopped falling somewhere in Pennsylvania, but here in Harrisburg there was a light rain.

According to the news the rain would get heavier as I continued east, and was supposed to last the next few days. I wondered at my rotten luck. It was the worst spring weather anyone could recall.

"Here, take this," Bo said reaching for his wallet.

He handed me a card with a Virginia telephone number.

Looking at the card I wondered if maybe he hadn't been telling the truth when he said he was single. Despite all that, I felt like playing it safe.

"If I've checked out of here when you ca-call, leave a mmm-message on my answering me-me-machine in Virginia. I'll be on the road, but I'll get it."

"Bo, I really don't know what to say. You've been so kind. I feel I've truly made a friend.

When you're in Boston again, I want you to promise you'll stop by to see me. I want us to keep in touch," I invited.

"You bet. You know, I ne-never mentioned how much you remind me of my ya-ya-younger sister. It's something."

"Really?" I said totally surprised.

"Yeah. You're both, you know, on the sm-small side. You have the same smooth, brown complexion and you even w-w-wear your hhh-hair similar; kinda long and fluffy and turned up at the ends.

When I saw you this mmm-morning in Dunkin Donuts, I couldn't help st-st-staring," he concluded.

I was totally undone by the flattering comparison, and was about to thank him again, when he asked,

"May I have a goodbye hug?"

"What could I say? After all he had done for me, I could hardly deny him a hug, so I opened my arms and he sort of slid into them.

He pulled me close. Then closer. I admit he felt damn good.

He leaned back and tilting my face up kissed me lightly on the lips. I didn't resist.

By the second kiss our lips just seemed to melt together of their own accord ... tongues gently entwining ... barely conscious of my arms wrapping themselves around his neck.

Then I felt him smoothly sliding the key from my hand and backing me slowly up to the door, which jerked me sharply back to my senses.

Oh no, I thought. I brought the kiss to an end and pulled away from him with my key still in my own hand.

No point letting things get out of hand, I decided.

"Well, if I'm going to get an early start in the morning, I had better turn in," I said with a huge yawn.

"Thanks Bo. I'll be calling," I said, still slightly out of breath.

Accepting the inevitable with no sign of resentment, he gave me a quick hug.

"You be ca-ca-careful," he said chucking me lightly under the chin. I guess I had reverted to sisterly status.

Once in the room, I closed the door and leaned against it.

"Hot Damn."

I fell back on the bed laughing so hard tears stung my eyes. If I was right, I had come real close to being seriously 'played'.

When we first started kissing it had been with a lot of pity for Bo because of his speech problem, but also with a lot of gratitude, and hell yes, I admit it, with a lot of attraction. Bo wasn't a fool though, and probably knew exactly how I felt.

What's more, he apparently was fully prepared to use the knowledge to his advantage. And that bit about his sister ... whether true or not, it was perfect.

Things had started off heading in one direction, but had ended up going in quite another, which was probably the plan. Mr. Tucker had been well on his way to helping me right out of my little black, lace panties. Or, so he thought.

All things considered, I figured over the years, Bo had probably gotten more pity pussy than he would ever remember. Turns out, he was a pretty crafty operator, which I found hilarious.

The humorous situation with Bo was a great tension reliever, and preparing for bed, I felt more light-hearted than I had since starting the trip.

A bad storm had been safely averted and I had made a new friend who, despite his attempt to get in my pants, was a very nice man.

Yes, things were definitely turning around, and I was feeling pretty damn good about that.

That feeling would not last long.

Chapter 5

*I*t's been three days since I left Chicago filled with excitement and anticipation about moving to Boston. Three days. It seems like ages.

Enthusiasm has long since given way to a depressing drum beat of dread. So much has gone wrong. And after each new ordeal, foreboding settles around my shoulders like the bad weather that's settled over most of the country the last few days.

So far there's been a blinding blizzard, a close shave with another car, and torrential rain that's still pouring down in nearly impenetrably thick sheets.

As if all that weren't enough, now the car is giving out on me.

Despite everything though, I'm making reasonable time having made it as far as Connecticut, but in the last few hours every time I have to climb a hill, the car gradually loses speed until I feel I'll have to get out and push.

Then, just when I'm thinking I can make it to the next town and find a mechanic, I see another huge hill up ahead. Great, I think.

Since I can't fly over it, I accept the inevitable. Pushing my hair back from my face, I lick dry lips and press down hard on the accelerator to give myself a boost.

Reaching the hill, I start up at around eighty, but only a third of the way to the top, I'm back to sixty and still going down.

Perspiration dampens my face as I vigorously pump the gas. My motivation is double-edged. It hasn't escaped my notice that mine is the only vehicle I've seen in well over thirty minutes, which makes this the most deserted stretch of highway I've been on.

Suddenly, I hear a dog wildly barking somewhere close. I drag my attention away from the car long enough to wonder what a dog would be doing on such an isolated stretch of highway, but I'm too caught up in my private struggle to dwell long on the question.

A few minutes later, I'm shocked to realize the dog is running right alongside me.

As I turn my head to glance out of the passenger window, where I last heard the barking, the animal leaps almost all the way up on the hood directly in front of me. I can't stop the scream.

"What th …..!"

As he hangs precariously half on and off the hood, he's snarling, barking, and staring at me menacingly through the windshield.

My shrill scream, magnified in the closed car, scares even me. How had he done that? Wasn't that a really high jump for a dog? When I get a good look at the beast, I bite down on a second scream.

I glimpse eyes that appear to glow a smoldering red in the gathering dusk, and an enormous out-sized head. Long, sharp teeth strings saliva while scraggly brown hair hangs dark and heavy with rain.

Although I'm down to around thirty miles an hour, and the dog is all the way back down on the ground, he's keeping up, which still seems pretty frigging fast for a dog, even a big one.

Not only is he keeping up with the car, I think he's trying to bite it.

I'm just wondering where the crazy son-of-a-bitch came from and why in hell he's chosen me to kill when I see that not just saliva, but foam is dripping from his jowls as he barks insanely.

"Oh Father," I whisper, understanding at last. "Rabies."

Now, I'm terrified. I try to get a better grip on the wheel while continuing to work the gas pedal … willing the car to keep moving.

"Please, God don't let this car stop," I plead.

Suddenly the dog stops barking, but I'm not fooled. I know he's still there. He knows there's something wrong with the car and all he has to do is to wait. It's barely moving now. He can walk and keep up.

I try to calm down and plan an escape route because the car will soon come to a complete stop. When that happens I imagine the dog throwing himself against the windows until one of them breaks and he can get me.

Suddenly I remember the iron bar my cousin, Cliff placed beneath my seat before I left Chicago. For protection, he'd said.

I'd laughed at the time, but I'm not laughing now. I'm deadly serious. Leaning over I keep one hand on the wheel and feel around under my seat with the other.

When I brush against the cold, hard iron, I pull it out and loudly thank Cliff, God, and everybody. Laying it on the seat next to me, I feel better prepared for a confrontation with the maddened dog.

He circles the car quietly for a while, but as I near the top of the hill, he resumes his frenzied barking and running back and forth in front of me.

I'm so busy praying, I don't notice I've crested the hill until I'm headed down the other side and start to pick up speed.

When I do notice, I'm so excited I give a loud whoop of joy.

Losing his prey, the dog tries to keep up for a while, but slowly the barking recedes in the distance.

I blink back tears of relief. As my heart rate slowly returns to normal, I look for the town I feel must be ahead.

I try not to dwell on this latest in the string of disasters, but in the back of my mind, I add car trouble and rabid dog to the list. I also add the words 'divine intervention' with a question mark.

Not for the first time since starting this journey, I wonder about signs and omens.

If I believed in that kind of thing, I would have to believe that perhaps I am being warned not to continue – to turn back.

The thought has crossed my mind many times in the last two days, but whatever it was that compelled me to begin this journey will not allow me to turn around. So, I push on.

This room at the Comfort Inn is the best I've had in the last three days. It's modern, clean and best of all, has a large color television that actually works and unlike some other places, working heat.

I find a mechanic down the street and he quickly diagnoses the problem with the car as the Timing Chain.

He promises that a simple adjustment will hold it until I reach Boston and can have it changed.

I talk to him about the dog and he calls the police department so I can make a report.

That feeling of dread again when the police officer behaves as if I have a loose hinge; nobody else has seen a rabid dog in the area, which according to him would be

45

highly unlikely if one was on the road. I am too weak to defend myself. I simply give the information and hang up.

After having dinner at a restaurant suggested by the mechanic, I return to the hotel, take a shower and after resting a while, call mom.

"Alexis!" She starts off at a high-pitched screech. "I'm so glad you called. Where are you?"

"I'm in Connecticut. What's the matter?" I'm already upset, and I haven't the slightest idea why.

"Thank God! Did you hear about the bridge?"

"No, what bridge?"

"Honestly, Alexis if you hadn't told me about changing your route, I'd be in the hospital right now."

"Mom, please. What bridge? What happened?"

"I'm sorry, dear. I'm just so …"

"MOM!"

"Oh, I'm sorry. A bridge somewhere in New York washed out because of the rain. Several people were killed … a couple in a pickup truck and a woman in a car.

They don't know how many others. Honey, they were just swept away down the river, vehicles and all. They're still searching for them.

I thought about you and how you were originally supposed to drive through New York, and they said a woman alone. Well, it near scared me to death," she said tearfully.

"When did it happen?" I ask.

"This afternoon; I can't remember what time exactly, just that it happened on Interstate Eighty … the one you would have been on.

I'm sure it'll be on the news tonight. It's been on several times already."

I'm quiet for a moment as I digest news of the tragedy. I wonder if it's a bridge I had been scheduled to cross.

"You know mom, I just left New York. I drove a coupla hundred miles across the lower tip of the state, from Pennsylvania across New York to Connecticut. But, I was never on I80."

"I'm just so glad you're okay. How is everything going? Is it still raining?"

"And how. It feels like the forty days and nights. Otherwise, I'm good. The car's acting up, but I have a mechanic working on it now, and he said it should be ready in the morning, which is when I hope to make it into Boston, by the way. Well, at least by late afternoon."

"What's wrong with the car?"

"It's not anything major."

"Well, I certainly hope you do make it tomorrow. I didn't know it would take this long. I'll be so relieved when you get there. "

"So will I; believe me, so will I.

Well, I'm going to catch a little television and hit the sack. I'll talk to you tomorrow … from Boston. Love you."

"Goodnight dear. I love you too. Be careful."

I turn on the television and after a while the late news comes on. The bridge washout is the top news story. I listen to all the details then pull out my map. I definitely would have had to cross that bridge had I stayed on I80.

I try to calculate when I would have reached it in view of the snowstorm and the rain. The answer is … today. The only thing I can't calculate is the exact time.

Turning the television off, I suddenly feel hot and clammy and my breathing is shallow and fast. In fact, I seem to be gulping air rather than breathing it.

My heart is pumping and my legs are starting to go numb. I immediately know what's happening. It happened to Sylvia once at a funeral.

I call down to the front desk … "Would you happen to have a paper bag handy?" I ask, feeling foolish. They don't. I thank the desk clerk and hang up.

I'll just have to control the hyperventilation on my own, I think. I stretch out on the bed and concentrate on thinking beautiful thoughts. I don't think of blizzards, rain, snow, rabid dogs or people being killed on ill-maintained bridges.

I don't wonder why all these things are happening to me at the very time that I have chosen to change my life: a time when everything should be fun and exciting.

I don't wonder about deeper meanings, life changes, choices, or omens.

I think only beautiful thoughts and somewhere in there I remember to thank God for watching over me. After all, I could have been on the bridge the same time as the couple, and the woman in the car.

My own car could have stopped on the highway leaving me vulnerable to a crazed dog, or I might have had a horrible accident in the blizzard.

When I finally sleep, it is the sleep of exhaustion. I dream of life back home and of Jason and my job.

In the dream, everything is perfect.

Chapter 6

"**Y**ea, Boston!" I yell out the car window as I pass the city's welcoming sign. It's seven in the evening on the fourth day of what has been a long, long trip, and I'm positively giddy with joy at having finally reached Boston.

The deluge that has poured from the skies through parts of Pennsylvania, and all the way through New York, Connecticut and Rhode Island, as predicted has continued into Massachusetts. I drive through the city with my window down, getting a little wet and not caring.

I stop and ask directions to the YWCA on Berkley Street. I made a reservation there weeks ago, and called ahead to explain my delay while still on the road. The rooms are difficult to come by, so I didn't want to chance losing my reservation.

Even in the downpour though, I have no trouble locating the beautiful old ten-story building.

The front desk is located to the right of a spacious lobby and as I approach, an attractive brunette looks up and smiles pleasantly.

"Good evening. I have a reservation. I'm ___ "

"You must be Miss Ashley", the woman interrupts."

"How did you know that?" I ask, surprised.

"Because I received notice that you called and said you'd be here sometime late today. Actually, you're our *only* check-in today."

"Well, you're right, I am Alexis Ashley."

"Welcome to Boston. Is this your first visit?" She asks while busily jabbing away at the computer keyboard.

"The first," I answer.

"Well, enjoy your stay. Now, we have you down for seven nights. Is that correct?"

"Yes, that's right. Actually I'm relocating here. Would you know the best place to start looking for an apartment?"

"Just the newspapers, and there's a bulletin board on the wall behind you.

People sometimes come in and post rooms and apartment vacancies there," she said.

"Thanks, that's a start."

After checking me in, she points me in the direction of the elevator and wishes me a pleasant evening.

Once past the lobby I enter a large room with a mezzanine that is clearly the heart of the building. It is a lounging and greeting area with institutional, but comfortable looking furniture, a television, and a row of picture windows facing Berkley Street.

A huge magazine rack covers nearly half a wall and a row of pay phones are lined up across from an elevator that looks alarmingly antique.

A number of desks occupy the center of the room while a separate space at the back serves as a dining area equipped with a long table, chairs, a microwave oven and a small sink. Even from where I stand, I can see that the mezzanine contains a dusty looking library. Women are everywhere. All shapes, sizes and colors … and they all seem to be getting along, I note with satisfaction.

I take the elevator to my third floor room, which turns out to be little more than a utilitarian cell that's so narrow the only walking space is a skinny aisle down the center of the floor. With the door closed I feel like a monk.

A twin bed and closet take up one wall and a desk and chair, a small dresser, a mirror and a washbasin take up the other ... period. No pictures grace the walls, or rug the floor.

After unpacking a few things, I find the communal bathroom down the hall, and take a shower ... with my shower shoes on.

Returning to the room, I get dressed and go downstairs where I head immediately for the telephones.

"I'm heeerrre," I say, when mom picks up.

"Oh Alexis! You're actually there? In Boston?"

"I'm here in Boston," I assure her. "Checked into the YWCA and I'm on my way out to my first Boston meal."

"When did you get in?"

"A couple of hours ago."

"So, what's Boston like?"

"Exactly as I expected with old, old architecture and really clean.

As for what they say about New England's springtime beauty, it's all true."

Even in the rain, the countryside I passed through was absolutely lovely," I say, with no mention of all the dreadful things that happened on the long drive. Now that it's over, I realize I will probably never tell her.

"Well, honey I'm so glad you're there. And the place where you're staying looks okay?"

"It's great, but I'll still start looking for a permanent place tomorrow."

"I know you want to get to dinner, so I won't hold you up."

I realize she doesn't want to hang up, but I am starved. "Yes, I'm pretty tired and hungry, so I'd better go and eat before I fall asleep on my feet. Thanks for hanging in with me, mom. I felt like I had the Lord on one side and you on the other."

"Well, that's exactly what you had," she said, laughing.

"You know it's strange, but since starting the trip, I somehow feel closer to the Lord. There's been times I can actually say I felt his presence," I say, thinking of the near-collision and the rabid dog.

"Well, that's a good thing," she said, sounding a little surprised.

"Anyway, would you do me a favor?"

"Sure. What?"

"Call Jason and let him know I made it okay."

"I'll call as soon as we hang up. Listen, stay in touch. Call collect if you want. And, I Love you."

"Love you back," I said.

I hang up and call Harrisburg. The hotel verifies that Benjamin Tucker is still checked in, but doesn't answer.

I leave the message that I have arrived safely in Boston and leave the number at the Y with a promise to call again the following day.

I have dinner at an Italian restaurant in the neighborhood then go back to the hotel and crash. It's still raining.

After being out in the bad weather, I look at my little room with new eyes. Although cramped and unattractive, it's also clean, warm and I feel safe and secure. I count my blessings.

The next morning I'm anxious to see the city. Finally, it has stopped raining and my optimism and excitement, as well as my old sense of adventure have returned. I feel that all the bad situations are behind me and that I have at last hit a positive vibe.

Selecting some brochures from the rack downstairs I go in search of a restaurant. I find a great little deli around the corner and map out my sightseeing strategy over a rather lavish breakfast.

Then it's off to start my new life.

The city doesn't disappoint me. It is beautiful and charming. Dozens of sidewalk cafes add to that charm, and offer such an attractive array of foods, I want to stop and eat at each one. And the architecture, I grudgingly admit, actually comes close to Chicago's.

Most of the day is spent on a walking tour checking out all the marvelous Victorian buildings, but by mid-afternoon I'm bushed. I give in to the fatigue, but before heading back to the Y, I buy a newspaper.

When I get back, there's a message at the front desk from Bo saying he's happy that I made it okay, and asking me to try to reach him when I return. I go straight away to call hoping we'll connect before he gets back on the road.

"HH-Hello," he stammers, and I smile at the familiar voice.

"Hi there. It's your damsel in distress."

"Alexis, you made it!"

"I made it thanks to you."

"I di-didn't drive the car, you did. What do you think of Boston?"

"It's everything I hoped it would be and more. It's wonderful."

"Yeah, it's pretty nice; a little ca-cold for my taste, but nice."

"I can't thank you enough for everything you did for me, Bo. I'm sure the trip would have been a total disaster without your help."

"That's all right."

"I have your telephone number in Virginia and as soon as I get settled I'll call and leave you my permanent number."

"Good. When I get a run to Boston, I'll le-let you know."

"That's a deal. Take care of yourself, especially

on the road."

I replace the receiver and stand there for a minute thinking about my new friend.

I don't doubt that Bo harbours some hope of scoring romantically one day, and although I've lived long enough to never say never … I don't think so. It's strange that even after so brief an acquaintance, I oddly feel a sisterly love for him. Then, it hits me.

Bo had hardly stuttered during our conversation. How weird. It was puzzling because the stuttering had been so bad before. Well, maybe he has good days and bad days, I think, wishing him the best.

I cross the room, sit down at a desk and shuffle through the newspaper until I find the classifieds.

Although there's some coming and going, it's fairly quiet and I can concentrate quite well.

A short time later, I'm deep into the rentals and wondering how I will manage to pay the stratospheric rents when suddenly someone behind my left shoulder says …

"Girlfriend, as deep as you are in that paper, they gots to be giving away something in there."

Surprised, I spin around and find myself face to face with one of the loveliest women I have ever seen. She's one of those tall, willowy beauties that remind me of those extra pounds; fifteen to be exact – I've been hoping to lose.

Displaying a wide smile of white, perfectly even teeth, she extends her hand and says matter of factly …

"Hi, I'm Brenda."

"Here's a toast to your new life in Boston. May you be successful, happy and … find the man of your dreams," Brenda exclaims.

"Here, here!" I say. We solemnly touch our beer mugs, drink deeply and break into laughter. As I look at her across the table, I think of what mom always said about something or someone of great beauty …

"God was in a mighty good mood the day he was working on that."

To me, Brenda is the embodiment of the term, 'Nubian Princess'. She has eyes that twinkle when she smiles and skin that is as dark and flawless as a moonlit night.

Sooty black hair cut in a pixyish style perfectly complements her oval face while a short knit dress reveals an hourglass figure that appears free of even an ounce of excess fat.

Of all these wonderful attributes, her best I think is her total nonchalance about her beauty – as if she is either unaware of it, or doesn't consider it important.

Brenda, I discover is earthy, refreshingly outspoken and honest, which goes a long way toward explaining how we met. We had clicked immediately.

"Alexis Ashley," I'd responded to her introduction.

"Mind?" She'd asked before sitting down at the desk in front of me. "What're you reading with such intensity, the want ads?"

"No, I'm apartment hunting," I had answered. "Any suggestions?"

"Nope. I wouldn't have a clue. I've only been here about a week, and will only be here for a couple of months.

"Where're you from?" I asked.

"San Diego. My job sent me here for a computer-programming course."

She shrugged her slim shoulders. "I know, it seems a long way to come for a class, but this school is supposed to be the best."

"Beauty *and* brains huh?" I'd teased, and she had actually blushed.

"Well, let's wait to see if I pass the course."

We laughed at the same time.

"Anyway, where do you hail from?"

"Chicago. I just relocated here."

"Wow! Now that's deep. You mean you moved out here all by yourself?"

All by myself," I echoed, actually feeling equally impressed.

After a moment's reflection, she'd said …

"Well, you're not by yourself any longer; at least, not as long as I'm here."

Her sincerity had been surprising and touching, and had the effect of softening the sharp edge of being alone in a new city. I was grateful for the support.

We're at Chelsea's Seafood Restaurant on Brenda's recommendation. It's located somewhere on a wharf and is a cheerful, noisy establishment where blue jeans and T-Shirts make just the right fashion statement.

At least my purple cotton jumpsuit and Brenda's knit dress are casual enough to pass muster, and not scream 'tourist'. Of course she would look stunning in a barrel suspended by wire, I think.

When I agreed to come to dinner with her I planned on working on the extra pounds by having a small seafood salad, but once in the restaurant and seeing … and smelling the steaming platters of food that passed our table, I had weakened.

Finally, I changed my mind and ordered the combination platter with shrimp, crab legs, oysters and lobster tail deciding to worry about those extra pounds some other time.

Brenda had the same, with an appetizer, and had ordered dessert. I looked at her plate, then at her figure and shook my head in wonder.

"How did you find this place?"

"One of my professors told me about it. He had wanted to bring me here himself, but I didn't think that was such a good idea.

I figured it could make for a bitch of a situation if we dated and things didn't go well between us … him being my teacher and all."

She might have been young, only twenty-four, but

she certainly wasn't stupid, I thought.

"If by 'not going well' you mean if you got involved and he wanted a little piece of ass and you refused, then you're right; things probably wouldn't go well atall," I agree, laughing. Then added,

"What the heck. Sometimes shit just happens; you're alone in a strange city and might figure, what's the harm?"

"The harm could be ending up failing because of some jerk's ego," she replies.

"There you go! I'll drink to that," I tease. We laugh, and click our mugs together again. Like I said, she wasn't anybody's fool.

"Have you ever been in a situation like that?"

"Similar. Not exactly the same, but close." I thought back to my college days.

"It happened in my junior year of college. The class was in my major, so of course I was shooting for all A's. Well, it was the end of the semester and I was about half a point from an A, so I really needed to pull one on the final exam.

Since the exam was essay and the professor could be as subjective as he wanted, our final grades were pretty much his call. On the last day of class, he was telling us where we could pick up our finals after he'd finished grading them. The school would be officially closed by then. He named the administration building as the pick up location then, turned to me and said …

"Oh Alexis, you don't have to worry, I'll personally drop your exam off at your home."

Every eyeball in that class was trained on me. I could have just died."

"*Oh, no he didn't*!" Brenda was indignant.

"He most certainly did. As if we already had something hot going on. It didn't help that I was the only black person in the class."

"You know he was just asking for some."

"Sure, but in front of the whole class?

57

I guess he thought I wanted that A pretty damn bad. The answer would have been no in any case, but it was a triple N-O after his behavior."

"What did you do?"

"Didn't let his skuzzy ass get away with it; I answered back as sweet as you please.

"'That'll be just fine Mr. Durham, however *whenever* you come, I won't be home, so please leave it in my mailbox'."

Several people snickered while he was busy turning practically every shade of the rainbow."

"Cool," Brenda laughs. "Did you get an A?"

"An A?" I whisper fiercely.

"Are you nuts!? That asshole was so pissed with me, I was lucky I didn't get a fuckin D!"

And we break completely up.

We're pouring the last corner of the pitcher into our mugs when Brenda asks why I came to Boston. I'm honest. I admit that I don't really know.

I tell her the standard story about Jason and sending him to Colorado, and about my job and the decision to resign and try something different, but I leave out the gory details. I also leave out the hell I had gone through getting to Boston, and the questions I now have about my sudden decision to relocate.

She tells me about her family in California, her boyfriend, whom she plans to marry at some point in the near future, and the promotion that has led her to Boston and the training program.

By the time we leave Chelsea's, we're more like long-lost sisters than new friends, and I marvel at meeting two people as sweet as Bo and Brenda in the space of one week. I almost feel that there is some special connection between us.

But, of course, that's ridiculous.

Chapter 7

I turned left on Commonwealth Avenue and followed the street to the Boston University Bridge, which is commonly called the BU Bridge.

Once crossing the bridge into Cambridge, I slowed down to glance at the rest of my directions to Pleasant Street.

I was on my way to look at a room. After seeing how high the rent was in Boston, I had decided it made more sense to start out by renting a room rather than an apartment, which would give me time to learn my way around, find a job and find the better housing deals.

Driving slowly so I wouldn't have to backtrack also gave me time to check out the area. I was pleased with what I saw.

This would be the third room I had looked at in the last couple of days and I was hoping for better results this time.

The first room had been in Arlington, which was farther out from the city than I wanted to live, so I scratched that one. The second was in Boston in a nice area with the right price.

The woman had seemed nice enough, but when she said she and her young daughter rose very early, was in bed by nine o'clock in the evening and wanted the house quiet by then, I passed.

If she had been deliberately trying to discourage me, she had succeeded.

The room I was going to now was across the bridge in Cambridge. The advertisement had asked for a mature female, and although the price wasn't great, I could make it work. I was hopeful.

Since arriving in Boston, I had often wondered where the black people were hiding. Downtown Boston, unlike Chicago, was the whitest place I'd ever seen, and not one of the apartments or room vacancies in the newspaper appeared to have been placed by anyone black. Where were they, I questioned.

It didn't occur to me that they had their own areas, like Roxbury, and apparently was happy to stay pretty much in them.

I found the peach frame house with no trouble. It was lovely.

The house was not really Victorian, but was close enough. Jessica, the woman I had spoken with on the phone answered the door and led me up narrow, curving stairs to her second floor apartment.

Bracelets on both arms jangled furiously as she walked would have made it easy to follow her with my eyes closed. An older Jewess, she seemed friendlier and more at ease with me than people at the other rentals.

At the top of the stairs was a small foyer with a room on the right, and another one on the left with the door closed. The living room, which was full of healthy plants was straight ahead.

"Why don't I show you the house first, then we can sit and talk," she said smiling.

"That would be fine," I replied.

She started with the room to the right of the stairs, which was the bedroom she was renting. It was so small the bed took up three quarters of the space, but it was pleasantly decorated and had a nice size closet.

The room was furnished with a double bed, a dresser with mirror and a chest of drawers.

Two large windows looked down on the street, and unlike the Y, colorful throw rugs covered the hardwood floor, pictures hung on the walls and the windows had nice curtains.

Leaving the bedroom we passed out of the foyer into a spacious, sunny living room with a high ceiling, a lovely old chandelier, and lustrous hardwood floors.

We walked through a spacious dining room, then through a small pantry that ended in a large kitchen with an enclosed back porch.

To the left of the kitchen were a huge master bedroom and another hallway leading back to the front of the house.

Next to the bedroom was a bathroom with an old-fashioned claw foot tub and next to that was the third and final bedroom. The hallway ended back at the foyer, the stairs and the room that was for rent.

Walking through the house behind Jessica I tried to guess her age but couldn't; she could be anywhere from early fifties to a well-preserved seventy. She was tall, six feet or close to it with a slim figure that a more uncharitable description would call 'skinny'.

Unnaturally black hair was cut short, worn with bangs and framed lively, dark eyes. She wore blue jeans with an oversized cotton shirt knotted at the waist and leather sandals with socks.

The bracelets on each arm clanked in time to her movements and long, silver earrings with turquoise stones danced against the lean, scrubbed face.

Jessica had the slightly irritating habit of hitting the back of her right hand into the palm of her left for emphasis when she talked, which sent the bracelets into a frenzy, and made it difficult for anyone to ever ignore her. I thought she was the essence of an aging Hippy.

In the living room she pointed me to a seat. As I walked to the chair an oil painting on the wall above it caught my eye. It was an abstract with bold colors and a bewildering design.

There wasn't time to determine its subject if there was one, but that one glance left me with such a feeling of discomfort, I stumbled.

When I reached the chair and turned my back on the painting to sit down, it was the last time I would look directly at it, or even think about it for months.

As I sat down I caught Jessica watching me with a peculiar expression, but then she smiled, the look disappeared, and I thought I had imagined it.

"What is it that brings you all the way from Chicago to Boston, Alexis?"

"Like I said on the phone, I wanted to make a change, take on new challenges, see what it's like to live somewhere other than where I was born," I answered.

"To tell the truth, probably a bad case of mid-life crisis," I laughed.

"I hardly think so," she said. "You're not old enough for that drama yet. But, isn't it wonderful that we live in an age where a woman can choose her own life and lifestyle and can change that lifestyle at will?" She said, slapping her palm.

"Yes, wonderful," I echoed.

"It wasn't always that way. Oh, no. We've had to fight long and hard for what so many take for granted today," she said, sounding like an original Suffragette.

"Absolutely," I said, totally lost. What was she talking about? She sounded like women had only gotten voting rights yesterday and that she was there when it happened.

"And, you moved here alone, without any family?" She asked, changing the subject so fast I was caught off-guard.

"Yes. I mean no. No family. At least I didn't move out here with any family, or friends."

"I'm curious. Why did you choose Boston?"

"For many reasons … it's just full of wonderful, rich history that I happen to love; it's close to both New York and D.C.; and the climate is relatively mild, at least compared to Chicago," I laugh.

"It just seemed an interesting place to live."

"You're right about how nice it is being close to New York and Washington, but we're close to lots of other wonderful places like Cape Cod, the Hampshire's, Newport, the list goes on," she said, leaning forward in her chair and slapping her palm.

"I'm ready to go," I smile.

"What type of work did you do in Chicago?"

Another quick change brought me to attention.

I gave her some history that I concluded by handing over a list of personal references complete with a few telephone numbers and addresses. After glancing at it she said, "I'm impressed. Have you looked at any other places?"

I confirmed that I had seen several rooms, but didn't go into detail.

I was surprised when she spent the next ten minutes stressing the merits of her room over the others. She seemed anxious for me to take it, although I felt certain that she would have had little difficulty finding some nice Jewish woman to rent the room.

I asked her a few questions as well, and she told me she had been a registered nurse for many years, but now only did private duty nursing in the homes of her patients.

She used the fact that she was away so much, sometimes a week at a time, as a selling point for the room.

Seems I would have the house to myself almost all of each week.

Divorced for many years and childless, she said she spent quite a lot of time in New Hampshire where she owned a farm with friends. She didn't elaborate on the friends or the farm.

Jessica concluded by going over the room rate and additional charges, such as the telephone and utility bills, and what she called the rules of the house, which was mostly about cleaning and that kind of thing.

I was fairly certain I was going to take the room, but told her I would think about it and call her the next day.

As soon as I reached the Y however, I called and cancelled an appointment I had lined up for the following day. I had found my home; at least for the next few months.

There was no ominous sense of foreboding, no second thoughts, no dèja vue, no warning bells at all the day I moved into the house on Pleasant Street.

Everything seemed quite normal; at least, at first.

I had told Brenda about finding the place, and although she was happy for me, she was sad that I would be leaving the Y.

We hadn't had another chance to go out, but we would meet downstairs in the sitting room for a visit and a little television many evenings after her classes.

The morning I moved was a school day for Brenda, so she couldn't lend a hand, but she promised to come by and see the place after class.

As I carried boxes in from the car, I was a little disappointed that Jessica didn't offer to help.

I had a good-sized television in the trunk of the car, and was a little concerned about getting it up the stairs, but in the end I managed okay without her.

I couldn't help noticing that she was a lot more reticent than she had been the day we met.

As a matter of fact, other than our greeting, she had nothing to say. I chalked it up to moodiness and figured the house was large enough for us to live together but separately if it came to that.

After I had gotten everything inside, I found her reading in the living room and explained that I had several boxes I didn't plan to unpack, and asked about a little storage space.

"I wish you had mentioned that you would be needing storage space," she snapped.

I didn't answer. I was too stunned. I just waited. She would never convince me that in the huge apartment, she couldn't find a nook or cranny for a few boxes.

"There's a floor above this one, sort of an attic, but larger. You can put them there," she finally said.

I wondered why it upset her that I needed a little additional space if there was space available.

I was beginning to feel slightly uncomfortable. Why would she work so hard to get me here then treat me so badly? Had she changed her mind about renting to me? If so, it was just too damned bad, I thought.

Following her with the first box, she went into the kitchen and taking a key ring out of her pocket, opened a narrow door that looked like it might be another pantry.

The short stairway just inside the door was dark and a little dank, but when we reached the top, the room we stepped into was surprisingly large; although it had an uncomfortably low ceiling.

Since this was the back of the house, I was surprised at the amount of sunlight streaming in from two small windows.

The space had been divided into three rooms, as if there had been plans at some point to use it as another apartment. Maybe for a little person I thought, wryly. Now, it appeared to be a catchall for boxes, odd pieces of furniture and assorted junk.

For the first time I wondered who actually owned the house. Jessica had never said, and I hadn't asked.

She indicated a space for the boxes and suggested I take out anything I would need.

I explained that I wouldn't need anything from them, and brought up the remaining boxes while she waited. There were six in all.

When I finished she promptly relocked the door. I wondered what could be so important that it required keeping the space under lock and key.

Mine not to reason why, I thought. In short none of my damn business.

I was on my way back to my room to unpack my luggage and a couple of boxes when Jessica asked, "I suppose you'll be job hunting soon?"

"No not right away. After all these years with my nose to the grindstone, I think I deserve a break. I'm okay financially, so I think I'll take a few weeks off and enjoy my new home."

She frowned slightly and said … "Well, that's nice if you can afford to do it. I wish I could."

I didn't like the slightly antagonistic comment, but chose to ignore it, and with some effort, kept my voice light and pleasant.

What I did or did not do with my time was none of her business as long as it wasn't unlawful and I met my financial obligations.

Brenda came later that evening as promised. Happy to see a friendly face, I ran down to greet her.

Before showing her around the house however, I stopped in the living room so she and Jessica could meet.

Their response to each other was less than cordial. In short, it was a disaster. Jessica was aloof, almost to the point of coldness and Brenda, sensing this immediately responded in kind.

To keep the encounter brief, I hurried Brenda away on the pretext of a desire to show her the house. The minute we were in my room with the door closed …

"I don't like her," she uncharacteristically stated.

"I know, I know. I don't understand what happened. She was as friendly as a puppy when we met, but that seemed to dissolve the minute I moved in."

"Maybe she doesn't like black people," Brenda reasoned.

"Brenda, I was black when she met me. That wouldn't make any sense."

"Oh Right. Maybe she just wanted to get the bucks and she doesn't have to pretend any longer."

"Maybe," I agreed. "But, that would be some pretty deep shit to find myself in," I lamented.

"The one thing that keeps me from moving right back out is the fact that she's almost never home, and when she is, I can make it my business not to be."

"Maybe she's just having a bad day, or week, and once things straighten out, she'll be the nice person you first met," Brenda said with an optimism I knew she didn't feel.

"Anyway, girlfriend, let's get out of here. It's … oppressive or something," she said with a frown.

"Have you eaten?"

"No, this is the first time I've been still this long all day," I said.

"Well, let's go have dinner; my treat."

Dinner at a little Italian restaurant on the North End was just what I needed.

During the meal, we talked about everything *except* my unpleasant roommate. Determined to enjoy my evening, I pushed the mystery of Jessica from my mind.

"You know, during the time I was apartment hunting I really became familiar with this city.

I mean I'm a devoted tourist. I've been almost everywhere."

"Like, where?" Brenda asked between groans over what she said was an amazing Shrimp Linguini with clam sauce.

"Like everywhere. I've been to Faneuil Hall Marketplace, where I tried to sample food from every restaurant; I've walked The Black Heritage Trail, the Freedom Trail, and of course, I checked out Beacon Hill. Amazing history everywhere you turn," I replied.

I spent some time hanging out on the Common, and … oh yes, nearly went berserk in Filenes' Basement. You know, the store where they keep marking expensive designer clothes down until somebody buys the item."

"Oh, you're kidding? I've been here all this time and still haven't made it to Filenes'. Did you find anything?"

"A silk scarf for six dollars and a silk blouse for ten; but, I've got my eye on this fabulous Chanel suit.

As soon as the price tag meets my wallet, I'm going to snatch it up. If nobody beats me to it, that is. Maybe I'll get there this weekend. Damn, I always have so much homework, it's hard to get some free time."

"That's okay. You'll go if I have to drag you, homework, or not."

"I know. I can't go back to San Diego without getting something from Filenes'. That would be just crazy."

After we finished eating and the table was cleared, Brenda asked … "Have you changed your mind about not going to work right away?"

"No, I haven't. I deserve some time off and I'm taking it. I know this may sound like a catch phrase, but I'm suffering from some serious burnout. I can't face a real job right now. I wouldn't be at my best."

"What're you going to do?"

"See something of New England. Rest." I paused a moment. "To be honest, that's kind of bothering me. I'm usually so goal-oriented … you know, always got a plan no matter how fuckin crazy it is; but since I decided to move, it's like I haven't been in control," I smile self-consciously.

"It's hard to describe. I don't know, Brenda, I just have this feeling of being outer-directed, which is so unlike me.

I feel like I'm *waiting* for the next move instead of *making* the next move."

"You just sound a little unsure about what you want to do. It'll come. Anyway, who was it that said we have to be in control every damn minute."

"I know, and you're right," I agree, still with the weird feeling that something more significant than my physical location has changed.

"That's why I'm going to take a little time and decide what it is I really want to do. I've talked to several temporary agencies and think I've found the one that's right for me. It's the only one that will guarantee me short-term assignments and accept my working no more than two or three days a week."

"Temping is a great idea. You'll keep some money coming in, as well as put your finger directly on the pulse of the job scene."

"So, what about you Bren? How're the classes coming? And what's doing with the amorous instructor?"

"Everything's fine. The classes have gotten a lot tougher, but I don't mind. And, Mister Brennan has cooled his jets. I turned down two more dinner invitations and he finally gave up. I hope my refusal won't affect my grade."

"It won't," I say with confidence.

I think about what Jessica said about today's woman having come such a long way and smile at the irony of Brenda worrying about her grade in light of that statement.

One evening several weeks later, I'm propped up in bed trying to watch television, but what I'm really doing is listening to the house creak. Jessica hadn't come home, so I'm alone.

Despite my love for these old buildings, I have to admit they can be pretty scary.

There's a couple about my age in the first floor apartment, so I'm not totally alone in the house, but judging from their friendliness, I wouldn't want to have to count on them in a crunch.

It seems I get along with the other neighbors better than the people with whom I share living quarters.

Now that I think about it, Jessica and the Glenns, the couple downstairs – seems kind of aloof with everyone.

I've never seen them really converse with anyone on the block or, do anything other than speak and keep moving.

Is it my imagination, or does everyone keep their distance? Now, that would be odd.

Maybe it would be in my best interest to snoop around a bit. Get to know some of the neighbors, and see if any of them will share their opinion of my housemate.

I'm beginning to feel that Jessica and her friends downstairs are a little peculiar.

Then turning to happier thoughts, I pull out my road map, and look again at the route I'll take the next day to Newport, Rhode Island. I'm going on one of my little getaways and can't wait.

I've been to Newport a couple of times already and find its natural beauty, and the history surrounding the little town enchanting. But, most of all … I'm fascinated with the mansions.

The mansions were built by the Vanderbilt's, the Astor's and others of this country's outrageously wealthy around the turn of the century.

They were replicas of European palaces, and unbelievably extravagant and incredibly beautiful. If I could visit them every weekend, I probably would.

I put the map back in my purse, turn off the television and pick up my dinner plate and glass from the TV tray to take it to the kitchen.

There aren't any lights on other than the one in my room and the kitchen, so the foyer is fairly dark.

I'm on my way to the kitchen when suddenly I bump into something …or someone in the middle of the dining room. When they grab my arm, I drop the dishes and hear them break as I let out a blood-chilling scream.

"Hey … hey, calm down, it's just me!"

My arm is released and seconds later, light floods the room.

"See, it's just me," Barbara Glenn says.

"Barbara!" My terror fizzles.

The terror however, is immediately replaced with anger.

"What are you doing here?" I ask through clenched teeth.

"I thought I heard a noise, so I came up to investigate."

"You thought you heard a noise? Came up to … how did you get in?" I demand.

"With a key. Jessica gave Ralph and me a key a long time ago so we could keep an eye on the place when she's away."

"But, you didn't come in the front door?"

"Yes, I did. How else would I have gotten in?" She asks.

"You tell me. I know how you *didn't* come in. You didn't come up those stairs by *me.*

I've been in my room with the television turned down low and the door open. Nobody could have come in the front door and up the stairs without me noticing," I insist.

"I don't know what to tell you. I *did* come in the front door."

I was livid.

The woman was lying, plus why wouldn't she have assumed I had made any noise she'd heard?

"My car is parked downstairs right in front of the house, Barbara. Didn't you think it might be me?"

"Oopps, sorry, I didn't see it."

She knew I couldn't prove she was lying, and it nearly killed me to stand there and watch the bitch smirk.

"In the future, if you think you hear a noise, rather than creeping around in the dark and nearly giving me a heart attack, just pick up the telephone," I snap.

"Sorry I scared you. I'll be more careful next time," she threw back at me while walking down the stairs; her air of nonchalance was more than infuriating.

I planned to give Jessica a piece of my mind. If people were walking around with keys to the house, shouldn't I know it?

As I clean up the mess, I wonder how Barbara had *really* gotten in. She definitely hadn't come in the front door, and the back door opens with a key that always stays in the lock.

It was a mystery that added to a growing discomfort and a deepening sense of vulnerability.

Chapter 8

"*T*he incident with Barbara happened last night. I drove down this morning, took the tour, and here we are."

It had been mid-afternoon when I'd begun telling Jacoby my story, now it is late evening.

I had pretty much bared my ass, and hadn't realized that recounting everything up to this point would be such a relief.

The only thing held back was the part about Bo getting lovie at the hotel. I didn't think he needed to know that.

Finally, I glanced over at Jacoby who was disturbingly silent.

His chin rested on his chest, and his hands were folded across his stomach. He seemed asleep.

He had interrupted me to ask questions a couple of times, but it looked like he had succumbed to a bored slumber during my long monologue.

About to reach over and gently rouse him, I jumped when he said …

"Let's see. During the trip here, there was the blizzard, the accident, or near collision, the rabid dog, car trouble, torrential rain and a washed out bridge.

Since arriving there's the problem with your roommate, and the strange episodes or visions you experienced today."

He rubbed his chin thoughtfully. I waited.

"Well, you're right," he said. "It didn't just start today at the mansion. Of course, some people might say you've simply met with a series of unfortunate, even weird coincidences.

I, on the other hand don't believe in coincidence. Particularly after what happened today, I believe that something's definitely going on, and it appears to be escalating."

"Yes, I feel that too," I agreed, with intense relief. I hadn't known how he would respond to my story and wouldn't have been surprised if he had laughed outright.

It was so good to feel that someone understood … or at least believed *something* was going on.

As badly as I've wanted to talk to mom about everything, I couldn't.

It would worry her to the point that she would insist I return to Chicago. I couldn't talk to Sylvia because she would use the information as proof of my lack of judgment. So, just sharing the situation with someone made me feel a thousand times better.

"Have you noticed that you've never been harmed by any of these narrowly averted disasters?"

"Believe me, I've noticed and just hope like hell it continues."

"I think that's important." Then added, "I'll be honest, Alexis I don't know what's going on. I mean the things that are happening … they're all over the place, which makes it difficult to get a good grip on anything. I don't even know what to warn you about because it's coming from so many different directions.

Although I believe I can say with some confidence, you shouldn't worry. I don't believe it's by chance that nothing's happened to you."

He thought for a while longer and added,

"I would like to take this back, discuss it with some of my colleagues and see what they can make of it. Would you mind?"

"No. It actually would make me feel that I'm not alone." After all, I thought, I don't know them and will never meet them, so what if they think I'm nuts.

We talked a while longer about the institute he was associated with in California, and about my plans, or lack of plans for the future. By the time he left that evening, I knew I had made another friend.

Some pretty awful things had happened to me in the last few months, but some great things had happened as well – I had met some wonderfully kind people.

I hadn't planned on leaving Newport until Monday morning, but the fun had gone out of my little vacation. I still loved the town and viewed the vision or whatever it was as an aberration that wasn't likely to recur, but this particular trip was definitely over.

Instead of on Monday, I decided to leave the following day. Jacoby tried to talk me into staying a few more days so he could get a better handle on everything, but I just didn't want to be there any longer.

I called Jessica at the house just to touch base and let her know I would be coming in earlier than planned, but there was no answer. I didn't bother leaving a message since she normally was up at the farm on the weekends anyway.

I arrived back in Boston about six on Saturday evening and was surprised to see Jessica's car parked in front of the house.

I took my bag out of the car, went up the walk, unlocked the door and went upstairs.

I left my bag in the hall and went directly to the kitchen for a glass of water. But before drinking, unlike Barbara Glenn, I decided to say hello, so Jessica would know I was in the house.

I took a step into the hallway and stopped. There was something off-key. Her door was pulled almost closed.

She never closed her door, not even at night when she went to bed. Then, I noticed a strong smell, like musk, in the air.

The smell of sex, I thought. Just then I heard the bed creaking furiously and a loud, long drawn out feminine sigh followed by a series of deep-throated grunts.

Damn, I thought as I clapped my hand over my mouth and slowly backed up.

I had on my gym shoes so they hadn't heard me come in – then again, with all that was going on in there, it might be the same if I were wearing combat boots.

I slowly crept back through the dining room and the living room and picking up my bag went back downstairs. Once outside, I gave them a little more time by busily puttering in the trunk of the car arranging and rearranging boxes while being very tickled by the discovery that Jessica had a fella.

I thought it was great, but wondered why she had never introduced us; had never brought him to the house while I was there; and had never even acknowledged his existence.

Maybe they were just getting together. In any case, it was obvious that the only reason we would meet today is because she thought I wouldn't return until Monday.

I gave them about ten minutes then went back inside making as much noise as a Mack truck. I called out a greeting then went directly to my room.

A few long minutes later, Jessica called …

"Hi Alexis, is that you?"

"No, it's a burglar!" I joked.

"Yes, it's me! I came back early. How are you?"

"Great."

A few more minutes passed and she called to me again.

"Say, com'on in the kitchen, I'd like you to meet a friend of mine from the farm."

Well, here goes, I thought. Let's just see what trips her trigger. Exactly what floats her boat, I gloated.

When I walked into the kitchen there was only a young blond woman sitting across the table from Jessica.

I actually looked around for the man before it dawned on me there wasn't one.

Chapter 9

*I*t was a warm, sunny summer day as I crossed the Charles River on my way to the temporary agency in Boston. Corey, the personnel consultant had sounded extremely excited about a new assignment for me.

Everything in my life seemed to have fallen into place and settled into a predictable and comfortable pattern. I didn't take that for granted.

I had come to love Boston, which was still new enough for every errand to double as a sightseeing tour. Even after several months I was still discovering and enjoying new facets of both Boston and Cambridge.

I found the old world atmosphere and charm in the midst of big city, contemporary lifestyle really cool.

I had visited many of the tourist attractions, but what I loved most was simply walking around without a plan enjoying whatever happened to pop up.

I had visited Beacon Hill taking my time wandering down narrow, cobblestone streets through neighborhoods that looked, with the exception of the clothes and cars, exactly as they must have looked a couple hundred years earlier.

That day, while standing on a street corner under an old-fashioned type of gas lamp, I had closed my eyes for a moment and imagined that by-gone era.

I could almost hear the rumble of the carriage wheels; feel the stinging wind of a cold, blustery day, and smell the pungent odor of burning coal mixed with horse manure.

Suddenly remembering the mansion, I had been afraid to open my eyes, and had only mustered the courage when I'd heard a car horn blow shrilly a few streets away in the shopping area.

I had breathed a deep sigh of relief, and promised myself I would be more careful in the future.

There had been no more visions since the mansion, but tempting fate was incredibly stupid.

After a number of unsuccessful attempts, I had finally lured Brenda away from her studies. One Sunday we had gone to Faneuil Hall where we loaded up on moussaka, Brioche, Baklava, egg rolls, cheesecake and other goodies.

We'd spread our eclectic picnic out on one of the wooden tables on the Rotunda, and made pigs of ourselves.

Afterwards we had gone to Filene's basement where Brenda had become the proud owner of two designer business suits.

On the whole, life couldn't be better, I thought. Not only did I love Boston, but everything I had seen of New England, and was beginning to actually feel a part of the community.

I found a parking space close to the agency, parked the car and took the elevator up to the ninth floor.

When I first started working for STAR Temps, they had tried getting me to accept longer assignments, but I had adamantly refused.

Finally, they had stopped trying.

When I walked into the office, I was happy to see that Corey didn't have any other clients, and when she looked up and saw me, beckoned me over to her desk right away.

"Hi Alexis, how's our number one tourist?"

"Still busy giving this town a thorough going over; seriously, I'm great," I answered returning her contagious smile.

I sat down and waited patiently while she rummaged around in the mess on her desk frantically searching for something. Finally she extricated a file from the stack of papers and waved it triumphantly.

She slung geometric, precisely cut rustic hair from over the one eye it covered, and fixed big brown eyes on me with a look that said ... 'have I got something for you'!

Although she was, nobody would ever have described Corey as just average in looks; basically because what she lacked in that area, she more than made up for with panache.

She was never still, rarely quiet, and her colorful, sassy wardrobe made her petite frame difficult to overlook, even in a crowd. She was the personification of stylish.

When asked her age, she would say ..."Somewhere between twenty and eighty. When you find out where, you win the prize."

She was truly a riot.

I personally thought she was probably somewhere between thirty-five and forty-five, but her age seemed as indeterminate as it was inconsequential.

Corey reminded me of an exotic bird that despite constant motion and loud noises was really quite delicate and rare.

I found her frank, friendly personality quite lovable, and considered her a friend.

"Listen," she said, grabbing my attention. This really great assignment came in and it has your name all over it. I swear it was *made* for you! It's at one of the city's oldest and largest banks; and the salary – hell, I still don't believe it."

She paused, all excitement, energy, and exaggeration, I thought.

"What's the catch?" I asked warily. She ignored my question.

"See, because of your experience and credentials, I was able to negotiate a really great rate.

I let them know that in our *entire* agency, you're tops and will do an unbelievable job for them, and could back that up with your references," she said. Then quickly added,

"I mentioned that you insist only on short-term assignments."

"And?"

"They said fine. They'll only need you for about three months," she said, in a rush.

"Three months! No way."

"Now Alexis, three months isn't forever. And look what you'll have earned by the time its over."

She wrote a figure on her note pad, tore it off and handed it to me. I looked at it for a long moment, thought of my dwindling savings and gave the assignment further consideration.

"So," I said with resignation. "Tell me all about it."

"Thata girl!" She cried enthusiastically, clapping her hands in gleeful victory.

According to the information sheet, I would be filling in for the executive assistant to the vice president of real estate. The job would begin the following day.

After leaving the agency I had waited for Brenda to finish class and we went to a movie and had dinner. By the time I got home, it was late and the house was shrouded in darkness.

I hadn't expected Jessica to be there and she wasn't. I had finally grown accustomed to being in the house alone, but still didn't like it.

I walked into the hall, turned the light on at the bottom of the stairs and went up.

Reaching the top, I turned to go into my room, but a slight noise somewhere in the house stopped me. I stood perfectly still ... straining to see if I'd hear it again. I waited.

There it was again, a sort of tinkling.... no, a jangling. It was a familiar sound, but I couldn't quite place it. The sound was coming from the back of the house, so I eased my purse onto the floor, slipped out of my shoes, and tiptoed through the living room and dining room.

As I moved toward the rear of the house, I stepped on a floorboard that creaked loudly.

The sound abruptly stopped.

Once in the kitchen, I waited. While I stood there in the dark it suddenly hit me where I'd heard a sound like that before – it was like the jangling noise made by Jessica's bracelets.

But it couldn't be Jessica. She wasn't home.

I waited. Nothing. Finally I called out ..."Jessica!" I listened. Still nothing.

Then, what seemed like a slight, scurrilous movement above me. I went to the little door that led up to the third floor and slowly turned the knob; locked.

Exactly what is going on here, I asked myself. I waited a couple of seconds and called again. No response.

Finally I shrugged, went into the bathroom and turned on the light. Maybe, it's just my imagination.

Or, maybe some small animal from outside had managed to get in up there. Maybe a lot of things, I thought.

I had wanted to take a shower, but the thought of closing myself up in that little space with the running water blocking out all other sounds was too much. I settled for quickly washing my face and brushing my teeth.

As I walked back through the house, I thought about how sounds could play tricks on you.

It's entirely possible, I thought, that the noise was coming from downstairs, and only seemed to be above.

Back in the hall I picked up my purse and shoes and went into my room. I closed the door, and for the first time realized there was no lock.

Looking around I saw two boxes full of my belongings. I picked them up one at a time and stacked them against the door before climbing into bed.

There.

"Good morning," I said to the young woman at the desk.

"I'm Alexis Ashley … the temporary assistant to Mister Metcalf'."

"Good morning," the woman replied, smiling. I'll let him know you're here. Please have a seat."

She indicated the chairs around the walls of the large room. I walked over to one and sank down so far into the soft cushions I had to pull myself back up.

I had never been in the executive offices of a bank, and it was a real eye-opener. Talk about plush. The bank's real estate division, on the thirty-second floor of the skyscraper was high above the areas where customers routinely did their business.

After a dizzying ride to that upper floor, the doors of the elevator opened and I had fallen out with relief, but was then practically sucked up by the deep carpeting as I walked to the receptionist.

Everything was mahogany, brass, gilt, and the greenery of a few strategically placed plants.

The word *money* seemed to seductively whisper from every corner. It was all quite lovely and I think, deliberately intimidating.

Presently, another woman, this one older and even more sophisticated than the receptionist came to greet me.

To my surprise, she introduced herself as Metcalf's secretary.

Well damn; one thing is certain, I thought as I followed her through a maze of offices, I wasn't likely to spend the next three months typing.

But it was when I met Michael Metcalf that I got the real shock. He was an extremely handsome black man. When I walked into his office and he stood to greet me, I had to remind myself to close my mouth

At least six feet and well built, he sort of unraveled from his chair. A face that was interesting, as well as handsome broke into a dazzling smile while dark, piercing eyes that I could tell missed very little, gave me a brief but penetrating look.

Although the milk chocolate skin was baby smooth, I guessed he was probably somewhere around mid-forties. I also noticed that brother was dressed to the bone, and with a well-aimed glance of my own determined that his left hand was free of jewelry.

We shook hands, he indicated a chair and I sat down.

"I understand from Mrs. Johnson that your services were difficult to acquire. I'm glad you decided in our favor," he began in a nice baritone.

"Well, when I began with the agency, I requested only short term assignments, and that's how I've worked since arriving in Boston.

Although this one is longer than I prefer, Corey, my consultant at the agency felt that I would find this assignment both interesting and challenging. I thought she might be right, so I committed to staying the length of time you'll need me," I finished.

"Great!" He said, as if I had passed a test.

Then giving his watch a quick glance, he surprised me by adding, "Let's get down to business then, shall we?"

Over the next twenty minutes, he personally outlined the type of support he would need from me.

There would be several reports I would be expected to generate each month; report analysis; occasional presentations; property assessments; and other duties. He made it clear he understood that real estate was new to me, and assured me his expectations were set accordingly.

I was both grateful and relieved to hear that, as it definitely raised my comfort level.

"Do you have any questions, Alexis?"

"Not right now," I answered, "But I'm sure I'll have quite a few as we go along."

"I'm sure you're right. Just always feel free to ask. Mrs. Johnson is available to you as well.

And, don't worry … I won't bring you along too fast. Now, Mrs. Johnson will orientate you to the area and your office," he said.

"Oh, by the way, do you have plans for lunch?"

"No, I don't," I replied.

"Good, I'd like to invite you to lunch in the executive dining room. There'll be a few people there you should meet."

Mrs. Johnson appeared at just that moment to show me to my office. I had to admit things were starting out really well.

I actually liked Metcalf. It seemed he was a fair and probably easy person to work for, and the surroundings certainly wouldn't be a hardship.

I especially appreciated the lunch invitation and his obvious desire to make me a player of sorts, even during my brief stay.

To my relief I had worn my navy blue and grey suit, a powder blue silk blouse with pearls, and grey and navy pumps.

I looked every inch the part, even if I didn't quite feel it.

I was relieved that there was no chemistry between Metcalf and me; at least none on my part. No chemistry, no complications, I thought.

After lunch I called Corey to check in. She always liked her temporaries to call with impressions of a new company, its management and its staff. I suppose she filed the information for future use.

Normally that might have bothered me, but with the money I was earning on this assignment, it seemed churlish not to give the woman what she wanted. After giving my impression of the bank, my employer, and describing lunch in the executive dining room, I thought she would jump right through the telephone she was so excited.

I admitted that the assignment was not as bad as I had anticipated.

After a time, Brenda finished the computer course and began preparing to return home to San Diego. She had intentionally extended her stay in Boston by taking additional classes, but her time had finally run out.

She had done extremely well in the program, and I felt as proud as a mother hen.

As I dressed for our final dinner I tried so come to terms with the loss of my friend.

I considered her leaving a loss because I knew that 'keeping in touch' wasn't actually being there.

I remembered reading somewhere that everyone you know in your present life is someone you knew in a past life; supposedly you run into the same people over and over.

If true, it would certainly explain why Brenda and I had actually met as friends ... which only made our parting that much more difficult.

"Here's to friends never saying goodbye, but 'till we meet again'," I said raising my wine glass in a toast.

"Here, here," Brenda said, touching her glass to mine.

I had treated Brenda to her favorite dinner of broiled lobster and it was a pleasure watching her do justice to the meal. As always I marveled at her ability to to eat with such abandon, never exercise and still maintain such an awesome figure.

I had given her two framed photographs of us taken at different times and places over the last few months as a goodbye gift, and she had been as happy as a child on Christmas morning.

I was totally surprised by her gift of a box of stationary with my name embossed under the Boston skyline. It was so perfect I had to swallow the tears.

"So, you like the new gig? Has the boss put any moves on you yet?"

"Of course not! Don't be silly. Metcalf has a wife; *his job*.

Seriously, I've told you, there's nothing like that between us. I feel we could work harmoniously for years and never have to worry about that kind of stuff," I said.

"You tryin to convince me of that or yourself?" Then, laughing at the face I made …

"Okay, okay, just kidding! Really, it's great you like it – the job I mean."

"I'm surprised at how much I do like it," I answered.

"So, if they offered you something permanent after Metcalf's assistant comes back, would you accept?"

"No. At first, I thought I might, but no.

I really enjoy the work and I've learned a lot, but I'm not even close to being ready for the corporate milieu again. Not yet, anyway," I replied.

"Well, at least you like working with him. What's he like?"

"Really nice. Professional. He knows exactly what he's doing. I watch him in meetings, and he's so good, I'm like, mentally taking notes. They don't know how to handle that dude."

"When you first told me about him, I was afraid he might turn out to be a little bit on the slick side," Brenda said.

"Not at all. Just the opposite; he's actually a serious and very generous person who's affiliated with several charities.

He's even a Big Brother. I believe he really wants to give something back, and I can definitely respect that," I said.

Brenda looked at me over the rim of her wine glass with an annoyingly speculative gleam in her eyes.

"And you're not attracted to him … just a little? She teased.

"Not even a little," I said. "I did find out that he's married – *really* married but, has been separated from his wife for several years.

That, my dear, is dangerous territory. Somebody in that twosome is still real interested and real attached, and I don't intend getting in the middle of it to find out which one. On top of which, there's just no C.C.," I joked.

"CC?"

"Crotch-chemistry; you know, the kind of chemistry that makes your twat twitch whenever he's around."

"So, what you mean is that no C.C. means, no T.T.?"

"There you go!"

"Oh, you hussy!" Brenda laughed. "You're shameless!"

"Just honest," I said. "And, there isn't any of either; no chemistry and no twitching."

We laughed until the diners around us frowned in disapproval, which only made us laugh harder.

The same day Brenda left Boston, Sylvia called with some surprising news. She and mom had talked about it and decided to visit Boston. I knew immediately that Sylvia had talked, and mom had gone along.

She and Damon, her husband, had been planning to take a few days off, she said, and since they'd never been to New England, Boston seemed a great choice.

I had described the countryside and all the places I had visited with such picturesque detail, it had piqued their interest, she said.

Translated this meant that she was being a nosy-assed busybody. But, I refused to let it bother me. If they wanted to come and check me out, they could. I had nothing to hide.

They would see that I was doing just fine. We talked about the dates, but she needed to get back to mom before she could tell me that.

Sylvia thought mom could stay with me while she and Damon stayed at a hotel. I agreed to the plan not mentioning that there was a spare bedroom in the house so they could probably all stay with me.

I needed to clear it with Jessica first, but I figured she'd only be too happy to make a few extra dollars off the unused room.

Jessica came in on Friday and was her usual aloof self. After we exchanged greetings, I told her the news about the family coming for a visit and her reaction was immediate. With a menacing frown, she asked, "And where will they be staying?"

"Well, I thought mom could stay here with me, and I wanted to ask if my sister and her husband could stay in the spare bedroom. They would be more than ..."

"I would rather not have *anyone* here," she said brusquely.

"Not have anyone here? What does that mean?" I ask.

"I'd prefer not have anyone use that room," she changed the statement.

"Well, I was going to say, they would be happy to pay you for the room."

"No, I'd rather not!" She said, slapping her hand in her palm, bracelets jangling. No explanation, no apology.

"No problem," I managed through a haze of anger.

"They can afford a hotel," I added.

I stayed in my room the rest of the evening.

I didn't want to create any more tension as a result of the anger it was difficult for me to hide. The next morning when she left for the farm, I called mom.

"What bothers me," I told her, "Is that she wanted to tell me you couldn't stay here either, but she knew better.

I pay rent on this room, and if I want to have a guest for a few days, she can hardly stop me ... short of changing the locks and kicking me out."

"But, I just don't understand that. Why would it upset her that we're coming for a visit? You would think she'd be happy to meet the family of someone living in her home," mom said. "It just doesn't make sense."

"You'd think. But, you know, the bitch is weird. She seemed okay when I first moved in, but that didn't last long."

"Alexis."

"Oh, sorry, mom ... the *woman* is weird."

"Maybe we shouldn't come."

"You *better* come. You think I'd let that crazy heifer dictate whether I have company or not? No way. I've never disrespected her home in any way. In fact, Brenda is the only person to ever even visit me here."

"Obviously she wants to keep it like that."

"Well, she can want all she wants. It just *ain't* gonna happen."

Before hanging up, I made mom promise that she would still come to Boston.

By now I was looking forward to the visit pretty much like a drowning woman seeing an anchor floating past.

If Jessica's attitude had been sour before, it was completely funky after I told her about the family's visit. I tried to rationalize her behaviour, but couldn't.

Pretty soon I gave up trying to figure it out, and was just thankful that her job and the farm kept her away so much of the time.

When we did happen to be home at the same time, we were cordial, but the relationship was definitely strained.

After the episode with her friend, or lover or whatever she was, I had gently questioned her about the farm. I mentioned that I would like to come for a visit one day, and she had visibly stiffened.

"Well, we'd have to plan for it," she'd replied.

Then she started making excuses.

"It's a working farm and we allowed a group of people to come visit once before, and they were asking questions and getting in the way while we were trying to work. We haven't had anyone out since."

"How were they getting in the way?" I asked innocently.

"Well," she seemed to be searching for something to say ... "It's just that everybody is busy working and we don't have time to give tours and entertain," she said.

"I see," I said. "Well, when I come, I'll be careful to stay out of everybody's hair and I certainly won't expect anyone to entertain me. As a matter of fact, I'll probably pitch in and help."

She didn't invite me to the farm during that conversation and never brought it up again. Now, if that wasn't strange.

They had a large farm evidently run as a kind of cooperative, yet they couldn't have a couple of visitors stop by now and then? It sounded very much like they had something to hide. Maybe she was out of the closet up there, but not in Boston.

Maybe she didn't want her friends and acquaintances in the city to see her with her lover. Maybe she felt they'd guess what was going on and what? Give her a spanking? If that's what she felt, then it would really be stupid for a woman of her maturity to feel that way.

. She was more than grown and could do what she pleased.

Who gave a serious fuck, anyway? Plus, she didn't seem to have that many friends. At least, very few of them called or came by to see her. So, who were all the people who would disapprove?

Whatever the case was, I was sorry for having involved myself by moving in with her. After her response to my having guests at the house, I had known it was time to start looking for my own place.

The problem was that by now I'd learned just how difficult it would be for me to get my own apartment without going back to work full-time.

And, I didn't particularly like that as an option. I decided I would get through the visit with the family and deal with my living situation immediately afterward.

A week after our conversation about the family's visit, I told Jessica the exact day they would arrive. She hadn't said one word; just turned and walked away with bracelets jangling.

She hadn't turned away, however before I saw the strangest look in her eyes. It was a look of cold, hard rage.

I felt the most peculiar tingle of fear as I finally acknowledged that there was something terribly wrong here.

Chapter 10

*S*ylvia, Damon and mom had arrived from Chicago and were in the car chattering like magpies while I struggled to drive from the airport in rush hour traffic. It was horrendous, but I was the only one who seemed to notice.

Finally arriving at the Copley Plaza where Sylvia and Damon were staying, we got them squared away and mom and I continued on to Cambridge and Pleasant Street.

We had the house to ourselves, but when we entered the hallway I noticed mom hesitate and frown before starting up the stairs ahead of me.

When we reached the top, I asked her if anything was wrong, but she said that she was just a little tired after the flight.

I know her well enough to know that something was bothering her, but I didn't persist.

After a bath, a cup of tea and some conversation, mom wandered by herself through the house.

She went through all the rooms, but didn't comment on whether or not she liked the house. That was also unlike her.

Generally she had an opinion on everything, but on this she was strangely silent.

Soon it was time to dress and pick up Sylvia and Damon for dinner, and I couldn't help noticing she seemed relieved when we left for the Copley.

We had dinner at a Victorian restaurant on Beacon Hill with fireplaces and long-skirted waitresses.

Afterward, I drove around the city pointing out various areas of interest. I wanted them to love Boston as much as I did, and was rewarded by their interest.

We decided to turn in fairly early because the next day we were going to Newport for a couple of days. I looked forward to sharing that little piece of my world with them, as well.

Back on Pleasant Street, Jessica had not come in, which was unusual for a Friday. Normally, she at least stopped at the house before heading to the farm, but apparently she was making it clear as crystal she did not wish to meet my family, which was fine with me.

Sitting in the living room, mom and I talked later than intended, mostly about Jason. She said that after getting off to a rocky start, he was finally settling in and making friends in his new home.

Because of the move and already low grades, he had indeed failed two classes, which I knew about. He had signed up for summer school and was making the classes up, she said.

According to mom, at one point, Jason and his dad had almost come to blows.

Fortunately Jason had realized he wasn't dealing with me, but with someone who could and would actually whip his butt – only she didn't put it quite that way.

James had him on a short leash and only planned to lengthen it as Jason improved his behaviour and his grades. She said he had already improved in both areas.

As mom talked, I said a silent prayer of thanks at having made the right decision after all. Jason had needed his father.

I didn't talk to him as much as mom because I didn't like putting a lot of long distance calls on Jessica's telephone.

Plus, I didn't want to interfere with James' attempts to deal with him the way he thought best. We would talk more when I got my own apartment. By then, I felt his father would have him firmly back on track.

One thing mom told me was a real surprise. Lately, it seemed Jason was more in touch with what she called "his spiritual self".

She said his conversations were peppered with references to God, and a sudden desire to "do the right thing".

He didn't seem quite sure what that meant, but seemed serious about it nonetheless. When she mentioned it to James, he confirmed that he'd noticed this new attitude, and told her that Jason was also attending church more.

"Well, he *was* raised in the church, mom."

"That's true. It's just all rather sudden, and dramatic. Come to think of it dear, you mentioned feeling a new closeness with God too.

It's just kind of funny that both of you should feel the same way at the same time," she said.

Then, changing the subject and with her face screwed up with a frown, she asked,

"Aren't you nervous being here all alone?"

"Nope," I lied. "I know the neighbourhood is perfectly safe and the doors are all locked ... so, what's to be afraid of?"

"I'd be scared to death in this big, old house all by myself in an unfamiliar city, and what area is perfectly safe?"

"Well, there you are. I don't feel as though I'm in an unfamiliar city and the neighbourhood *is* safe."

She didn't look convinced, but before she could continue, I suggested we turn in. The next two days promised to be busy I explained, and we would need our rest.

When we arrived at the Pilgrim House Inn we received a special little welcome from the manager and his wife. I had been there often enough that I guess they felt I was a special guest and welcomed mom with a small, beautiful bouquet of flowers.

"Now, that's what I call great customer relations," Damon whispered.

"Isn't it wonderful," I agreed. "That's one of the reasons I keep coming back here. I had intended trying some of the other hotels in the area, but why?"

"Oh, I just think its lovely," mom, who was impressed with the antiques, the flowers and the atmosphere said, "It's small, but that just seems to make it more ... intimate, I guess."

"And romantic," Sylvia said throwing a meaningful glance at Damon that even I could interpret.

I was pleased they liked the Pilgrim House. It was part of the reason I felt so comfortable when visiting Newport. It was one of the best aspects of coming to the town.

I hadn't told them about the fainting spell on my last trip, and when making the reservations had asked Brian and Kathy, the husband and wife managers, not to mention it either. They assured me their lips were sealed.

I had never told anyone, not even Brenda about what had happened on that last visit. What would have been the point?

Nobody could offer a logical explanation. There wasn't one. I'd decided to just let it be. It was over and not likely to happen again.

Truthfully, I was worried about exactly that; the possibility that it might happen again, this time in front of the family.

In an effort to prevent it, I had lined up a tour of two of the mansions, omitting the one where I had the visions ... or whatever they were.

I thought of Jacoby, and wished he could be with me. We had talked several times after our meeting and the incident at the mansion. The first time, he'd called to tell me his colleagues couldn't offer any additional insight into the visions, except to agree that there was some kind of occult phenomenon at work.

I hadn't been surprised that they were stumped. But, since nothing else had happened, I just tried to forget the whole thing. He'd called a couple of times after that just to check on me, he'd said.

After settling in, the three of us left mom to rest while we went exploring. Damon, a boating enthusiast, headed straight for the marina.

Sylvia and I followed along enjoying the pleasant walk and the beautiful day.

Later, after Damon had described every detail of every boat in the marina until Sylvia and I begged for release, we had gone back for mom.

We had lunch at a restaurant close to the inn on Thames Street then, it was on to the tour.

"My goodness," mom exclaimed as we approached the first mansion. "These were actually private homes? Where families lived?"

"Absolutely," I said. "The tour guides are going to explain that they were actually patterned after the great palaces of Europe."

"The old ... 'if they can do it, we can do it better' syndrome," Damon said. "That's us; typically American," he added, with barely disguised pride.

"Actually you're right. The wealthy Americans considered themselves the closest thing this country had to royalty, and determined they would live the part.

"Well, they had to spend that money on something. Why not lavish homes?" Mom interjected.

As the first tour began, I held my breath. I had decided that if I saw any kind of vision, I would calmly watch until it was over. Nobody need know what I was seeing.

When the tour ended without mishap, I took my first deep breath. Everything had gone fine: no visions, no ghosts, or delusions. I was ecstatic.

Sylvia, Damon and mom all felt that learning about the mansions was an educational experience, and although I knew they didn't find them nearly as fascinating as I did, they had at least found them interesting and enjoyable.

We had a great time. We went to the beach, which was my first time in Newport; enjoyed excellent seafood, including the popular and delicious Lobster Roll; we went sightseeing and shopping; and of course, visited the mansions.

Everyone agreed that coming to Newport had been a grand idea, and although nobody said so directly, I knew they were impressed by how well I had found my niche in my new home. I was pleased that there was even discussion of returning for the popular annual Newport Jazz Festival.

Driving back to Boston late Sunday afternoon, ours was a festive group. We discussed New England and my move, the temporary job assignment I was currently working on, and my plans for the future.

It was when we reached the plans for the future that the conversation slowed down.

I tried to explain that I was taking a breather by working for the temporary agency, and renting the room on Pleasant Street, and would soon decide exactly what I would pursue as a new career, or at least something more substantial and stable.

Since I had always been so goal oriented I knew they were concerned about what appeared to be a new attitude; and from their viewpoint, not a very good one.

After my brief explanation, mom had the good grace not to pursue further discussion about what was so obviously *my* business.

Sylvia, on the other hand, indifferent to such diplomacy, plunged right in. By the time she was really on a roll, we were close to Boston, so I just tried to endure.

I didn't want to spoil everyone's day by losing my temper. I reached my boiling point however, before we reached our destination.

I eventually had to explain to Sylvia that it was my life, my business and even if I screwed up, it was my right. On that joyous note the conversation came to an abrupt conclusion.

By the time we reach Boston, the sun has set and the beautiful lighted skyline gives us an illuminating and marvelous welcome.

We decide to stop in Cambridge so mom and I can drop off our luggage and freshen up a bit before heading on to the Plaza and then out to dinner.

It will be the first time Sylvia and Damon have been to the house, and I'm a little anxious to show it off.

I'm still a little put out by mom's lack of response to what I consider – despite Jessica's funky attitude, a lovely house.

When we step into the hallway and I flick on the light, Sylvia immediately looks up and draws in a sharp breath.

Everyone turns to see what's wrong and we follow her eyes up to a little star shaped decoration. It is hanging on a long string from the high ceiling; made of a colored aluminium it is quite pretty.

"What?" I ask.

"Alexis!" Sylvia snaps.

"For Pete's sake, what is it?"

"Don't you know what that is?"

"Yes," I answer, looking up.

"It's a decoration. It's a star; probably the Star of David, or something."

"That's not the Star of David, you Ninny! That would be a six-pointed star.

That," she says pointing, "Has five points. It's a pentagram!"

"A what?" Mom asks with a look of inquisitive fear.

"A pentagram," I answer. Then ask Sylvia, "How do you know that's what it is?"

"I just finished reading a novel about a woman who was a witch, but nobody knew it."

"A witch?!" Mom practically yells.

"Calm down, mom. What Sylvia is saying is that the decoration happens to be a pentagram, which is something associated with witchcraft," I explain.

"But, let's not jump to any hasty conclusions. It's probably some little trinket that Jessica unknowingly picked up and hung there. In her mind, it's just an innocent decoration.

And even if she does know what it symbolizes, she could have hung it there on a lark. She's that kind of person," I conclude, although my stomach has convulsed nervously.

There is something very disturbing about hanging such a symbol at the entrance to your home. Even more disturbing is that I have never noticed it. I knew *something* was hanging there, but hadn't paid it any attention.

"Well, I for one think it's very strange to hang something like that in your house," mom says with agitation.

"I'm with you, mom," Damon adds his voice. "Damned spooky if you ask me."

"Okay, everybody, let's take this meeting on upstairs," I say attempting to take charge of the situation.

"Go on up, Sylvia while I lock the door."

They file up the stairs with me bringing up the rear. Ahead of me they move on into the living room. Just as I place my foot on the last step at the top the stairs, a picture on the wall to my left catches my eye. I pause.

The hairs, not only on the back of my neck, but all over my body stand on end as I catch the little scream just before it is expelled, then shake my head to clear the sudden dizziness that threatens another fainting spell.

Finally, leaning down for a closer look, I realize it's just what I feared ... a painting depicting what Satan presumably looks like, or of something closely resembling that.

The wood framed painting is small, about four by six and is in a peculiar place on the wall. It is just below eye level before taking the last step up into the foyer.

Anyone taller than me, and most people are, would miss the painting altogether. As often as I've come up the stairs I have never seen it.

The subject of the painting has reddish brown skin, pointed ears, severely arched eyebrows, dark lips, sharp teeth, and long black hair.

Other than that he is dressed like, and looks like a normal man. My heart races as I struggle to get a grip on myself. I don't want anyone to see how upset I am by the discoveries.

"Alexis, what's happened to you?" Mom comes out of the living room with her garment bag slung over her arm.

"I'll just hang this in the clo ... honey what's the matter?" She asks in alarm.

"I ... I ... nothing, mom," I finally manage as I move to take the bag and block the picture.

"Here, I'll hang this up for you."

But her eyes move past me to the picture that she'd obviously seen me looking at. She walks over, leans down and studies it for a moment. When she straightens up, she's frowning and clearly disturbed.

She looks at me, shakes her head and put her finger to her lips. Getting her message I go into the bedroom to hang up the garment bag, and she returns to the living room. When I join them I casually ask if anyone wants a beverage. Nobody does.

"Let's just stay here long enough for mom to change before we go on to the Plaza and to dinner," Sylvia says. "This place gives me the hebe gebes!"

"All right now, let's take Alexis' advice and not overreact to something we're not even sure of," mom cautions.

"Who's not sure? Maybe you're not, but I am.

This is, after all, Massachusetts and the home of all those witches. How far are we from Salem, anyway?" Sylvia asks, making me want to go for her neck.

"Sylvia, cut it out! Alexis has to live here. No point in scaring her," Damon reasons.

"She'd better be scared! She could wake up one night playing the lead role in somebody's ritual."

"Stop it!" Mom commands angrily. "You're not helping anything."

"Wait just a minute! Why is it that everybody's trying to shut me up?"

Somebody needs to say *something*. Somebody needs to be honest and tell her she f__," she glances at mom, and finishes with ... "screwed up.

Alexis, you could be in a dangerous situation here with madam ... who knows what? And, why hadn't you noticed that thing, anyway?"

Good question I think. I wish I had an answer. Quiet throughout her little tirade, I'm struggling with the shock of our findings.

"Maybe because I didn't read the same book you read," I say sarcastically.

My life suddenly seems to be flip-flopping from one horror to the next. This one however, is worst than the mansions ... it's literally come to meet me where I live. Now, Sylvia is busily and happily pouring salt on my wounds.

"Okay, Sylvia," I finally respond.

"I appreciate your clarification of the situation, but it's hardly needed, thank you very much. Yes, I could be living in the same house as a practicing witch, but then again, finding one questionable item in someone's home hardly justifies burning them at the stake. But, if it eases your mind, I had already decided to move. I'll just do it a little faster now. Okay?"

"Hey, as you so recently pointed out miss smarty pants, it's your life. I'm still wondering though, if you're so smart, why hadn't you noticed that little item?

And, about moving, instead of doing it a little faster, I'd do it a hell of a lot faster if I were you ... like tomorrow."

"Advice duly noted. Now, let's go to dinner," I said, loathe admitting that she's right.

My dinner stuck in my throat, but I managed to eat every bite. I'm determined not to spoil everyone's last evening in the city by showing the extent of my distress.

Still, Sylvia uses every opportunity to hint at how foolish a move this had been. By the time I drop them off at the Plaza, I'm uncharitably ready to stick my foot in her mouth; shoe and all.

Chapter 11

*W*hen Mom and I return to Pleasant Street we're unusually quiet. Neither of us feels particularly comfortable in the house at this point.

Again, we wander into the living room, and sit down to talk. I'm sitting in the chair that Jessica had sat in that first day, and mom is in my seat.

As we talk, my eyes drift up to the painting over her head, and my body goes cold. I rise, walk over and quietly study it for a moment.

It is an abstract; a weird jumble of unidentifiable objects, except that within the mixed-up mess I can make out what appears to be faces.

Then, suddenly I see the faces clearly. Simply put, they are demons; monstrosities cleverly hidden in a crazy quilt of confusion.

I can see bulbous eyes; suppurating knots and bumps; snakes slipping and sliding in and out of scenes; and feel a nearly uncontrollable urge to laugh … hysterically.

Instead, I take a deep breath, swallow hard, and walk back to my chair.

Mom takes one look at my face and without a word, stands and like before, examines the painting. When she sits back down she says sternly ... "I want you to come home."

"I can't, mom. Just because I've happened upon something unpleasant, I can't just give everything up and run home."

"Unpleasant? You call this unpleasant?" She nearly shouts.

"Sylvia is right. You could get hurt in this ... this ... lunacy. Please, please come home, Alexis."

"I'd give just about anything if you hadn't seen this, but you did. I can't change that. I am asking you to understand that although this situation is pretty awful, and scary as hell ... sorry, bad choice of words ... I can't come running home like a scared rabbit. I do, however need to move out of here."

"Well," she sighs, knowing my mind is made up. "At least do that. Tell me, you really never noticed any of this stuff?"

"Never noticed any of it; I could have sworn that little picture was never in the hall before today, but when I moved it aside a little, it left a light spot on the wall. It's obviously been there quite a while."

"Oh Lord, that's what worries me. It's as if she's done something to cover your eyes. You're generally so in touch with your surroundings, I can't believe you didn't sense something. I felt it the moment I walked in the door the other day. I couldn't explain it, of course. It was just a vague feeling that something wasn't right."

"Just like I didn't see the pentagram, I didn't feel anything out of the ordinary," I explained.

"I had started to suspect something was wrong because of Jessica's behaviour ... and a few other things," I said, recalling the sounds in the house and Barbara Glenn's mysterious appearance that night.

"But not because of anything concrete. And, let's look at it this way," I continued, "If they wanted me for any reason, they've had ample time to do whatever they want, yet nobody's bothered me.

So, at least we know they're not after *me*," I theorize.

"That's not necessarily true. Perhaps the right time hasn't come. Maybe they're waiting for something?"

"Waiting for what?" I ask.

"I don't know. If I did, I'd know what we were up against."

"Well, I'm not going to stay here and worry. I'm just going to move.

"Soon!" She says emphatically.

For a couple of moments, we don't say anything; just sit immersed in our own thoughts.

"Alexis?"

"Yes, mom," I glance up. "What is it?"

"There's something I never told you, and I think it's time I did. All these years, I rationalized keeping it from you. Like that would make it go away. Now, you need to know. You need to know everything that might have some connection with your being here … and you need to know anything that might help you."

"What on earth are you talking about?

You're scaring me, you know." I added.

"You know the old folks have a saying …"

"The old folks have a million sayings," I interrupt with a nervous laugh.

"Let me speak, Alexis."

"Yes ma'am," I answer, chastened.

"The old folks have a saying … that when a baby is born with a veil over its face, that baby will grow up to have second sight." She pauses.

"You were born with a veil, Alexis.

I actually laugh.

"I've heard of the veil," I say, humoring her.

"Mom, that's just a myth."

"No, it's real. It's rare, but it really happens. A few babies are born like that each year. It's some kind of tissue that grows over a baby's face and head while it's still in the womb. When it's born, it has to be removed."

She pauses another moment as if gathering her thoughts.

"You know, you were my last child, and the day you were born I knew something was wrong when everybody in the delivery room, including the doctors went, 'AAAAHHHHHHHH', when you came out.

They didn't lay you on my stomach, or let me hold or see you afterward like they had done with the others. I started crying and begging them to tell me what was wrong.

Finally, after raising a bigger ruckus than they could ignore, a nurse told me you were fine, but that you were born with a covering over your face ... a membrane," she said.

"And they were removing it. She told me not to worry because it was something that happened every now and then, but didn't hurt the baby.

I knew right away it was the veil that I'd heard about from the time I was a child, and I knew you were going to be a clairvoyant.

In the old days when women birthed at home, they kept the veil ... they said it brought good luck.

Anyway, a little later, they brought you to me, and I could see for myself that you at least looked okay.

I counted fingers and toes, checked eyes, ears and everything seemed fine," she laughs shakily.

"You're serious? I was born with something the old folks call a veil, and you believe the mumbo jumbo about second sight. Mom!"

"I'd really known all along – before that day that you'd be ... special somehow."

"Why didn't you ever tell me this? Not the myth part. I mean, about all the excitement when I was born?" I ask.

But she seems not to hear.

"Like I said, the old folks say that the veil or birth caul, as some folks call it, is a sign the baby will have second sight.

You know, able to see things other people can't, some of them can make predictions, or ... anyway the baby will grow up to have special gifts."

"Well, I guess you know by now they were wrong. The only second sight I have is when I put in my contacts," I say with heavy sarcasm. But, even as I speak, cloudy memories are struggling to surface.

"May the good Lord forgive me, but I didn't see it as a gift. As you grew up and things would happen, I'd try to stop them. I'd make you stop.

After a while I guess I pretty much succeeded. It all seemed to go away," she says with a bowed head, pitifully wringing her hands.

"I was wrong. But, I was afraid that the gift would hurt you somehow ... and I just wanted you to live a normal life. Now, I know I hurt you more by not letting you be your natural self."

"And, what *is* my natural self?" I murmur, more to myself than to her.

At a certain point in her story, I had really started to listen, and had begun to recall certain childhood occurrences.

Like, the times when I would play hide-and-seek with Sylvia, Cliff and the other neighbourhood kids. I never had to search because I always knew where everyone was hiding.

The kids found it more annoying than strange and eventually wouldn't let me play. I remember going crying to mom, and her teaching me to pretend I didn't know. Now I ask,

"What kinds of things did you make me stop doing, Mom?"

"Oh, a lot of things," she ambiguously answers.

"Like what?" I persist.

"Well, let's see. From the time you were small you'd tell your little playmates things you shouldn't have known. For instance, the day you got upset and told Jerry he needed to go home. You told him not to come back until his mother said it was okay.

I scolded you for being unkind, but later found out that Ruth hadn't given him permission to come over. She had discovered he was missing from their yard, and had been frantically searching for him at the same time you were sending him home.

You couldn't have known he didn't have permission … I heard him tell you his mom had sent him over to play, which she did sometimes.

Then, there was the time you told Doris she would win the spelling bee, and even knew her exact score.

Oh, there were so many things. I would scold you … even spank you," the guilt clouds her eyes.

"I just wanted to teach you it was bad to talk about things that hadn't happened yet. But, as bad as those things seemed at the time, they were far from the worst that happened."

"And, what was that?"

"It happened when you were around four.

Every night when I put you to bed in your room, you would start talking. Oh, you'd just be talking up a storm. Of course, it was mostly gibberish. At first your father and I … we just thought it was cute.

But, after a while I noticed you really acted like you were holding a conversation. You'd talk and then listen. I thought it was strange so I came in one night and asked if you were talking to someone.

You pointed at the ceiling and said, 'the man', and kept repeating what sounded like, 'Bic-tor'.

You were so serious and so sure about him that based on things that had been happening with you, I became convinced someone really was there – someone I couldn't see.

Your father, God rest his soul, thought I was nuts.

Finally, we questioned some of the older tenants in the building and discovered that someone had died in our unit a few years before we moved in, and that the person hadn't simply died – the man, Victor Snow, had been murdered.

We moved you into our room that night, and moved out of the building two weeks later.

We didn't fail to notice that moving you out of the room ended the conversations."

She stops, looks at me with concern and asks ...
"Are you all right?"

"Sure, I'm fine." And I am. As she talked, I'd felt an enormous sense of relief ... as if I'd been hiding from myself most of my life and all of a sudden a door had opened and there I was.

Tears stung my eyes, but I blinked them back. I knew what she was telling me was true.

"Then, there was the time when __ "

"That's okay, mom, I get the picture."

"I just can't believe you never said one word about any of this." I tried not to sound accusatory.

"Well, really Alexis, I felt there was no reason to. You didn't know about it, so how could you be bothered by it."

"And you're telling me now because ..."

"Because, for some reason, I think it's possible they may know you're special."

"They who? And, please don't say 'special' like that. Sounds like another way of saying abnormal."

"The woman who lives here and her cohorts, that's who. And you know very well you're not abnormal. That's not what I'm saying."

"What do you mean, they may know? And even if everything you said were true and they do know about it, what good would it do them?"

"I don't know. It's really just a feeling; a feeling that they might want to use it, or somehow use you."

I have a need to keep talking, dig deeper, learn more about this secret past, but glancing at the clock I see it's long past time to turn in.

They're leaving the next day, and I know mom needs her rest, plus, I realize that I am emotionally exhausted.

"I'm glad you told me," I said.

"Although I'm not sure how knowing will help, it's good to at least be aware of that part of my life."

I walk over, lean down and give her a big hug.

"I'm so glad you came, and please don't worry. I'm still not alone, you know," I say, glancing upward.

"And, that's my comfort," she fingers the cross at her throat.

"Alexis, I really am sorry I made you stop doing something that was natural. I didn't understand. I was wrong."

"Let it go, mom. You did what you thought was right at the time. That's all any of us can do. You were trying the best way you knew to protect me. I'd never blame you for that."

She smiles and with a small sigh of relief says ...

"You're a good daughter."

I couldn't see them off on Monday because I was due back on the job. I had told Metcalf in advance that I would be taking Friday off, but I knew taking Monday would be impossible because of several important meetings.

I dropped mom off at the Plaza early in the morning, said my goodbyes and continued on to work. They'd take a taxi to the airport for their noon flight.

I was both happy and sad to see them leave.

Most of the happiness had to do with Sylvia. Our relationship was like playing a football game in the Twilight Zone where I was condemned to play defense for all eternity.

The sadness had to do with mom. I hated the thought of her going home worrying about me like I knew she would.

I had wanted so much to demonstrate how well I was doing, and it had totally blown up in my face. If only I had discovered the satanic stuff before they'd come. But, I hadn't, and nothing could change what they had seen.

For the rest of the day, I tried my best to keep thoughts of Pleasant Street off my mind, but it kept creeping back.

Metcalf asked me twice if there was anything wrong, but I blamed my agitation on my family's departure, which was at least partially true.

That seemed to satisfy him, and I made an effort to behave normally, which was impossible.

At the end of the day I dreaded going home. If I hadn't been so tired I would have stayed out as late as possible, but the long weekend was taking its toll. I needed my bed.

When I entered the house, my eyes automatically went to the pentagram. I stood a moment watching it turning slightly in the air coming in around the window.

I loathed having to walk underneath it, and refused to even glance at the picture at the top of the stairs. And, the living room, with its horrid painting, was absolutely off limits from now on.

I had a newspaper and planned to look through the rentals, but first went to the kitchen to get a glass of juice.

Turning to leave, my eyes fell on the little door leading up to the attic. I walked over and placing my hand on the knob, turned it slowly. I don't know what I expected, but the door was, as always locked.

Giving it a closer look, I realized the lock would probably be easy to pick, then chided myself for thinking what could be dangerous thoughts.

Since I would be leaving soon, the less I knew about this place, the better.

After going through the rentals and finding nothing, I stacked the boxes against the door and slid under the covers. I wanted to go to the bathroom, but the thought of the darkened house and those horrible paintings I would need to pass, discouraged me.

Instead I thought of the conversation with mom.

Her revelation had released a flood of memories both from my childhood and more recent years.

Obviously, I had learned my lessons of suppression so well; I could deny the reality of the episodes by conveniently forgetting they ever happened.

I remember a particular incident that happened one day while in college. I was standing on the quad talking to friends when suddenly my mind had gone blank. I mean totally blank ... I couldn't even remember my name.

Then, something had started to materialize in front of me. I can still feel my fear, and the tremendous force of will I had exerted to stop whatever it was from forming.

After a few seconds it passed, and I apparently forgot about it ... until now. Many such incidents, some more dramatic, were now rushing through the floodgates.

As much as I hate to admit it, the veil thing would go a long way toward explaining what had happened at the mansion, as well as all the past incidents that I am now remembering so vividly.

Which begs the question, why now? Were the details of my birth all that was needed to bring the memories back?

Maybe I simply can't suppress these things any longer. Perhaps, I have simply grown beyond a desire to conveniently forget.

However, in view of everything that's happened to me recently, I believe There may be forces capable of over-powering my efforts at control, as well as mom's efforts to keep her secrets.

I think back to my impulsive decision to leave Chicago and move to Boston; so unlike me.

I recall the long drive, all the things that had gone wrong, and how I had wondered at the time if the incidents were an omen warning me to turn back. Was I being cautioned to go back home where I was safe and secure.

Could there really be some outside force dictating my life, now? If so, is there more than one? And, are they at odds with each other; one that wants me here, and one that doesn't?

One that's benign while the other is malevolent? And the biggest question … why me?

The questions trip over each other in my mind, but there are no answers. Each question simply leads to another. I feel that something is definitely going on, and admit to myself that I am afraid.

It's like a puzzle being pieced meticulously together, and this overwhelming feeling that now that construction on the puzzle has begun, completion is mandated and will require large doses of fortitude and patience … and faith, I add remembering the narrowly averted disasters.

Slowly, I'm drawn back to the present by the persistent need to use the bathroom. I dread the thought of going through the house, but have no choice.

I get up and remove my pitiful barricade, but instead of going through the living room, I cunningly go through the spare bedroom across the hall. That way, I only have to pass the picture at the top of the stairs.

I am as quick as possible using the bathroom, and just as I am about to turn out the light and race back to my room, suddenly, like before, the noise sounds above. I stand still and listen.

After a long while, it comes again, this time accompanied by the sound of something being moved or dragged – like a box. And, could that be whispered voices?

Then the jangling sounds; closing my eyes and seeing the bracelets on her wrists and hearing the noise they make each time she moves is somehow terrifying..

I get back to my room in record time, replace the boxes and jump under the covers. Why hadn't I listened to everyone and left the house immediately, I ask myself as I lay trembling.

In a room with no lock on the door, and only a couple of flimsy boxes as a barricade, I am a sitting duck.
I begin a serious conversation with The Father. Then, my eyes fly open as the sound comes again; this time louder, and not from above, but much closer.

Is it my imagination, or is it coming from this floor?

At some point, I must have drifted off because some time later I awake to the sound of distant, muffled singing.

I dig my knuckles in my eyes to try to wipe away the sleep and realize that what I'm hearing isn't exactly singing, but more like many voices joined in some kind of chant.

Chapter 12

"*G*ood morning, may I please speak with mister Jacoby?"

"Mister Jacoby is in a meeting right now. May I take a message?"

"Yes, would you tell him that Miss Ashley called … from Boston."

I gave her my telephone number at work, and asked that he return the call. From the moment I had awakened that morning, Jacoby had been on my mind.

Although I really wasn't hopeful, I wanted to believe that he might somehow be able to help me. I wasn't even sure what I would tell him if he called back and decided I would deal with that when and if the time came.

About an hour later, he was on the phone. When he'd seen my message, he said, he knew I needed help.

He had asked his secretary not to disturb him and had called me back right away.

"How can I help you, Alexis?"

"Honestly, I don't know. I'm not even sure why I called," I said in confusion.

"Why don't you just tell me what's happening," he urged.

Throwing caution out the window, I tell him about the devilish discoveries in the house on Pleasant Street.

"You are having a tough time, aren't you? Are you sure you haven't had any experiences in the past that were ... could be described as psychic experiences? I know you said you hadn't, but are you absolutely sure? "

I told him about mom's recent confession, and about some of my earlier memories, but left out the specifics about the veil. I didn't feel comfortable discussing that with him. It sounded too mythological.

"That's more like it. Now it's beginning to make sense," he said, sounding elated.

"We figured you must have had some experiences with the paranormal, somewhere in your past. Have you ever talked with anyone, other than me ... someone like a professional about your experiences?"

"No, I didn't remember them until all this started with the mansion, and the Satanism, and mom and I had that conversation. I'm hoping that maybe nothing else will happen, and that I'm overreacting to everything," I said.

"I wouldn't count on that," Jacoby replied.

"I'll tell you what I don't like ... I don't like you living in the house with this woman. I must say I particularly don't like the part about her not wanting your family to come and visit.

I'm thinking that she might have thought, or hoped that your moving to Boston alone meant that you were estranged from your family.

I totally agree with your mother that there's most likely a connection between your psychic abilities and her desire to have you there and *keep* you there, alone."

"But, this just all seems so ... ridiculous," I said.

"Yes, it may seem ridiculous, but do take it seriously, Alexis.

I'm going to give you the telephone number of the Institute for Parapsychology there in Boston. I suggest you call them."

Even as I wrote the number down, I knew I wasn't likely to use it. It had taken enough courage just to call him.

"Have you given any thought to returning home?"

"Yes, but somehow I know that going back isn't the answer."

I paused, and then said, "It'll just follow me."

"Well, at least move out of that house as soon as possible."

The urgency in his voice compelled.

"That's what I plan to do; as soon as she gets home from her job. She's supposed to be a private duty nurse who stays on the job all week.

I have some belongings stored in a room she keeps locked and as soon as she gets back, I'll get my things and leave.

I'm paid up for two more months, but I don't care about losing the money."

"Well, if you're going to be there for a few more days, it would be to your advantage to do a little reading about witchcraft. Maybe you'll learn something useful."

He gave me the name of the person at the Boston Institute and the names of what he said were some good books on the dark arts. He suggested I check the library.

I thanked him for his help and told him how glad I was that had decided to call him.

He, in turn, apologized for not being of more help and had me promise to call him if anything else happened. Regardless of the distance, he said he would find a way to help me, even if it meant hopping a plane to Boston.

I assured him it wouldn't come to that. At least I hoped it wouldn't.

After work I went to the library and wasn't the least bit surprised at the amount of literature available on witchcraft.

When I found one of the books that Jacoby had recommended, I settled down at a table and in no time was deep into an almost clinical discussion of the subject.

I felt as if I had left the real world, or at least the world, as I knew it.

If I hadn't been frightened before, by the time I finished reading about witches' covens, Sabbaths, rituals, and even sacrifices, I was terrified. I thought of the farm, and wondered at its real purpose.

Finally I turned to the chapter on protection, and avidly read how one might survive close encounters with witches.

The author suggested wearing a crucifix. Not a cross, but a crucifix, and advised praying with a rosary. If a rosary wasn't available, he suggested using any long strand of beads.

He was very specific in detailing how and when to pray, and even for how long. The subject was treated with the kind of gravity that only a week or so before, I would have thought humorous.

After I got home, or after arriving at the house I lived in, I hurried through a shower and dinner, and rushed off to the refuge of my room.

Carefully stacking my boxes against the door, I turned on the television and tried to watch, but kept catching myself listening for sounds upstairs.

The night before, I'd been badly frightened by them. They had seemed to be moving around more than ever and worst of all, had at one point seemed to be coming from my floor.

Then, later I had heard what sounded like chanting.

I had lain in bed shaking under the covers and feeling like a coward when I suddenly remembered something mom had taught us.

"If ever in a situation where you need something to hold onto," she had said, "The Good Book makes a pretty firm anchor."

I had quietly gotten out of bed, turned on the light and found the bible I had kept on the seat beside me on my drive to Boston.

Clutching it close, I got back in bed and settling back on the pillows, randomly opened it; the pages fell open on Psalms.

I had quickly skimmed the page and my eye inadvertently stopped on the thirty-fifth chapter.

I read verse one through eight and was stunned. When finished, I read it again.

The words fit my situation so precisely it seemed prophetic. I read several of the scriptures a third time.

> *Plead my cause O Lord, with them that strive with me: fight against them that fight against me.*
> *Psalm 35:1*
> *Let them be confounded and put to shame that seek after my soul: let them be turned back and brought to confusion that devise my hurt.*
> *Psalm 35:4*

Tears filled my eyes, and wiping them away with the back of my hand I continued to read. The next two verses spoke so clearly to me they left no doubt that my remembering the bible had been no accident.

> *Let them be as chaff before the wind: and let the angel of the Lord chase **them**.*   *Psalm 35:5*

> *For without cause have they hid for me their net in a pit, which without cause they have digged for my soul.*   *Psalm 35:7*

I smiled through my tears as I closed the bible, turned out the light and went peacefully to sleep feeling well and powerfully protected.

§§§§

120

"Have I mentioned how lovely you look tonight," Metcalf asks.

"Yes, you have, and thank you again," I laugh, my hand automatically moving to the small gold crucifix at my throat as if seeking help staying grounded.

Today was my last at the bank and Metcalf had totally shocked me by inviting me to dinner. For one stupid moment I had considered refusing, but common sense prevailed and I accepted the invitation.

After all, I figure it is more than appropriate to be treated to dinner after the great job I had done for him. But, I must say, I am surprised that he is interested in me, since he never once indicated an attraction.

Now, we're sitting cozily in a charming, Italian restaurant on the North End where the food is so delicious, I have to remind myself I'm on a date and to behave accordingly.

After dinner we get better acquainted over our coffee. His life is a fascinating story, and I'm not the least bit surprised to learn he has a military background.

When I ask what he had done in the service, he answered, 'Special Forces', period. I want to know if that meant what I thought it did, but when I try for more information, he skilfully moved the conversation on.

After leaving the military he had returned home to Boston and opened a real estate business and is the sole proprietor of Metcalf Realty ... all five of them.

"Why," I ask, "Are you working at the bank when you have your own successful business?"

"I came on at the bank close to a year ago as a favor to a friend. I was asked to restructure the real estate division, which was in pretty bad shape. I admit it's taken longer than I anticipated, but it's going well."

"Of course, I still don't know a great deal about real estate or banking, but from what I can tell, your division seems to run pretty much like a well-oiled machine," I respond.

"Well, thanks," he laughs. "It's taken quite a bit to get it to that point and to the point where it's showing black instead of red on that bottom line."

"If you don't mind my asking, who's the friend you're helping out?"

"Robert Pierson," he answers.

"Oh, just the bank's president," I say.

I realize there are layers to this man that would probably take years to unpeel.

"Robert's an old college friend," he replies.

"Oh," I say simply.

I thought it wonderful that he was well positioned in life, yet hadn't let it go to his head and was still so down to earth.

The conversation soon turned to more personal matters, and Metcalf freely admitted that he was separated from his wife of ten years, but not divorced. There hadn't been children.

I want to ask why no divorce, especially since there are no children, but hold my tongue.

When finished he asks about my life, and I am honest ... to a point. After hearing what I have to say, he comments:

"It took a lot of courage to make such a drastic life change. Most people would opt to stick with the familiar, whether or not it's satisfactory to do so; you know the status quo thing.

I admire the strength and conviction it must have taken to do otherwise."

I am a little embarrassed at the compliment.

"Thank you, but like I told a friend, it would have taken more courage to stay and work on a job I had learned to dislike, and live a life that was totally unsatisfying until I retired from both a bitter old woman."

He looks at me for a moment, neither of us speaking, and finally smiles. "I think we have a lot in common," he says quietly.

I didn't know where to take that so I leave it alone. We linger talking, surprisingly comfortable with each other, and enjoying ourselves immensely.

When we realize the restaurant is empty except for the staff that is eyeing us impatiently, we laugh and prepare to leave. Metcalf promptly pays the bill.

He walked me to my car and surprised me again.

"I don't know about you, but I hate to see the evening end. I'm really enjoying our conversation. Listen, I don't live far from here, why don't you stop by for a nightcap?"

I hesitated a moment while warning bells clanged loudly in my head. But, I wanted to go, so I ignored them.

I was enjoying myself on a date more than I had for a long, long time.

Oh wait, I was *on* a date for the first time in a long time, which was something of a phenomenon these days, I thought chuckling. He interrupted my reverie ...

"Share the joke?"

I hadn't realized I'd laughed aloud. Instead of answering though, I agreed to accompany him home for a nightcap, and as if reading my thoughts, he added,

"Just a nightcap, and more conversation."

"Lead the way," I replied laughing, but relieved.

To my amazement and complete delight, I followed him to a Beacon Hill townhouse furnished with lovely antiques, but it was the architecture that I found particularly exciting; beautiful Parquet floors in the small foyer, marble fireplaces, high ceilings with curlicue corners, bay windows, and a mahogany staircase.

I insisted on a tour of the first floor before settling down with a glass of wine.

Later, as we sat on the comfortable sofa sipping chilled Champagne, I cautioned myself to go slowly, which makes it all the more remarkable that I still ended up only moments later, in his arms.

One minute we were talking quietly, the next I was wrapped up in his arms and he was devouring my lips.

Locked in a tight embrace with his lips crushing mine felt for all the world like the most natural thing in it.

My body leaped in response as his tongue probed and caressed with strong, sensuous strokes … building a fire in me so swiftly, it swept my breath … and my mental faculties completely away.

For the briefest instant my head cleared long enough to appreciate that the sea of passion I was swimming in could have a serious undertow.

Somehow that thought gave me the strength to swim against the tide that was rolling over me in dangerously sensuous waves.

I pulled away and tried to stand, but before I got completely up, he pulled me back down and recaptured my lips.

When he gently guided me back on the sofa and covered my body with his, I forgot everything and clutched him even closer as our bodies fit into an amazingly natural groove while moving together with passionate abandon.

Almost to my regret, the fog started to clear again. I tried to ignore the intrusive thoughts, but it didn't work.

My body was ready … actually was on fire, but my mind was shouting, 'Moving too fast!'

My mind won.

This time when I pulled away and attempted to stand, he seemed to sense my resolve and released me.

I stood shakily and moving over to the lifeless fireplace, leaned my head against the mantle while struggling for composure. For a while the sounds of our ragged breathing seemed enormous in the sudden stillness.

I had really known better than to come, and now accepted responsibility for our awkward situation.

"I'm sorry. I … I'm sorry I let things to get out of hand," I said.

"Well, I'm not sorry. Let's face it ... we're good together, or we could be. I can't think that's a reason for either of us to be sorry," he said, with an infuriatingly relaxed smile.

He walked over to me and pulled me tenderly into his arms.

"If you need to take it slow, that's no problem. We can do that," he whispered against my hair.

Damn, damn, damn, I thought in total frustration.

His strong arms and his body felt so damn good, I felt myself heating up again. I reluctantly moved out of the circle of his arms.

A couple of life times ago, I remembered telling Brenda how he didn't move me physically. Right, I thought. She would love this.

But, my horny emotions aside, there was something else that was nagging at me. There was a question burning my tongue; one that I needed answered.

"May I ask a question?"

He looked for a moment as if he would come after me to try and finish what we had started, but seemed to change his mind. Instead, he leaned back against the mantle next to me, and crossed his long legs nonchalantly.

I couldn't help thinking he made a pretty picture.

"Go ahead," he said finally. "Shoot."

"I'm curious about your wife?"

Just like that, something in his face slammed firmly shut.

"What about my wife?" His annoyance was apparent.

I continued more courageously than I felt.

"I was just curious to know why haven't you divorced after all this time?"

After a strained moment he replied,

"Jennifer and I can't live together. We simply don't get along up close. But, we do care about each other, so we've just never seen the need to divorce.

I admired his honesty, but no thanks. Metcalf and his wife had clearly not given each other up; possibly never would, and I certainly didn't intend to test the strength of their commitment.

I didn't fool myself for an instant ... I could really fall for this man. Hard.

I've known women who have literally grown mold waiting for attached lovers to make a promised break. Some even settled for sharing. I never found either of those circumstances attractive.

"So, what you're saying is that you and Jennifer have an open relationship. You do your thing, she does hers, and when you both feel like it, you do it together."

"No, that's not what I'm saying." He frowned threateningly.

"We're legally separated and we're ... we're also still ... friends."

"Uh huh," I said, mentally reaching for my purse. Okay, *friends,* I thought. Let me outta here.

"Well, thanks for being honest with me. And, I'm sorry if I seemed to be prying," I said sincerely.

"It's just that I have a habit of looking before I leap. Listen, it's late," I said, stifling a yawn and standing,

"And I have to drive all the way over to Cambridge. I'd better call it an evening. Thank you for a really wonderful time."

"You don't *have* to drive to Cambridge tonight," he said still frowning. I didn't doubt he understood that my abrupt departure was related to our conversation.

"Oh yes, I do," I laughed.

"All right, if you must. Hold on. Let me get my keys. I'll walk you to your car."

Before leaving, he took me in his arms again and asked, "When can I see you again?"

"Just give me a call," I said, too tired and disappointed to prolong my departure. And as we walked out into the cool, velvety night, I was totally surprised at the depths of that disappointment.

126

Chapter 13

"*H*ello, Jessica, I'm sorry to bother you at the farm, but I guess I missed you here yesterday, and I wanted to speak to you."

"You didn't miss me," she said dryly, "I didn't stop at the house. I came straight off the job to the farm. What's the problem?"

Had I said there was a problem?

"I know you had asked for at least a two week notice if I wanted to give up the room, but something's come up, and I need to leave in the next couple of days."

What she said next sent a chill down my spine.

"We're not keeping you here."

Whoa … we?

The statement seemed to acknowledge that she wasn't alone in whatever was going on, and seemed to be letting me know that she knew that I knew something.

"I know you're not keeping me here, I just wanted to let you know I was leaving, and ask if there's a key to the rooms upstairs so I can get my boxes?"

"No, I have the only key."

I waited. When nothing further was forth coming, I asked,

"How do you suggest I get my belongings, short of driving to New Hampshire?"

"Is someone in your family critically ill?"

"No, nobody's ill," I replied.

"Then, I guess you'll have to wait until I come home." My anger was the color of bright red. I tried to harness it before I spoke again.

"Maybe the Glenn's have a key. They seem to have one for all the other doors."

I had spoken to Jessica about Barbara Glenn walking in on me that day and she had informed me indirectly, but clearly, that their having a key was none of my business.

"No," she answered, "The Glenn's don't have a key to that door. If it's not an emergency, why is it necessary for you to leave so fast? I'll be home in a couple of days."

"I didn't say it wasn't an emergency. I said nobody's ill."

Suddenly she became suspiciously cordial. "Listen, I'll be home Monday … Tuesday at the latest, and I really would prefer to see you before you leave so we can settle up the bills and your advance rent."

"I figured we could do that over the telephone."

"You have to agree, Alexis, it'll be easier to sit down together."

Although the last thing I wanted to do was sit down with her face to face, I had to admit, we did have financial business, and it probably would be easier to take care of it before I left.

"If you'll wait until I get there, I'll overlook the fact that you're not giving me notice, and reimburse your advance rent. How's that? Can you wait?"

"Oh, okay. I'll wait, but I definitely need to leave by Wednesday morning," I said, caving in.

"Good. I'll probably be home by Monday, but definitely no later than Tuesday. I'll see you then, dear."

'Dear?' I hadn't been a dear in months.

After hanging up the phone, I sat and stared at it in deep thought. Something about the conversation bothered me; something other than her intimation that I was on to them.

It was there in the back of my mind, it just wouldn't come to the front.

After worrying over it for a while, I gave up and tried to decide on my next move. I didn't intend hanging around any longer than necessary. I'd give her until Tuesday. After that, I'd vacate the premises.

I still didn't have a place to stay, but figured if push came to shove, I'd just try to get a room at the Y or, failing that, go to a hotel.

My thoughts turned to my date with Metcalf the night before. I hoped I was gone before he called and asked to see me again ... if he ever did. I knew if I was available, and he was persistent, I might weaken and the last thing I needed was a dead-end relationship.

I walked to the window and looked outside. It was a Saturday and the traffic was heavy on the residential street. It was always like that on Saturday.

I had things I needed to do, but I didn't feel like getting caught up in the traffic. And, I guess I was moping.

More because of Metcalf I thought, than because of the sick situation I was involved in at this house.

I sat in a chair by the bed and stared out the window feeling morose, and as usual, uncomfortable simply being in the house.

I thought of the sounds I heard at night and wondered if it was Jessica, or some of what mom called, her cronies. If so, what were they up to in the attic, and how were they getting in? Suppose the house had a secret passage, I thought.

With Barbara's sudden appearance that night, I knew they couldn't be coming through the front door.

Not through the back door in the kitchen either.

That rusty door made enough noise to wake the dead when opened, plus the key always stayed in the lock.

That reduced the probability of anyone opening it from outside with a second key.

Since I knew for sure that at least for the next several hours, Jessica was a long way from home, I decided it might be a good time to do some investigating.

I found a flashlight in the kitchen, and going back to my room, I opened the closet and pressed and knocked around to see if there might be a hollow wall or something.

Not finding anything, I moved on to the extra bedroom. Nothing. I went into the dining and living room and checked the backs of all the cupboards. I did the same in the kitchen.

Finally, there was only Jessica's room left. I hated invading anyone's privacy, even someone like Jessica. But, I did it anyway.

Opening her closet, I was amazed at how few clothes were there. There were a couple of wool jackets, some shirts and sweaters, and several pairs of jeans. Lined up on the floor were boots, walking shoes and gym shoes. It looked more like she was visiting rather than living in this house.

Not for the first time, I wondered about those weeklong nursing jobs. Where did she really disappear to every week? I had never had a telephone number for her on any of these jobs.

When I first moved in, she'd given me the number at the nursing agency that sent her on assignments. In case of emergency she said I was to call them. I realized the number could belong to one of her friends, and could be a ruse.

Pressing the walls and floorboards I came up empty again. I moved the flashlight up to the ceiling, but didn't see anything up there either. After a long hesitation, I opened her dresser drawers one by one. No photos, no papers, few personal items.

I left her room a lot more puzzled than I had been when I entered. I was really curious now.

Going back to my room I took a credit card from my purse and went back to the kitchen. Years ago, Cliff had shown me how to trip certain locks this way. I'd never had a need for the illicit skill ... until today.

I came back to the door that led to the rooms upstairs, slipped the card between the lock and door panel, and worked it. I was soon rewarded with the feel of the tumbler sliding back. I turned the knob and opened the door.

I stood a moment and listened, but there wasn't a sound. Slowly, I went up the stairs.

I had been worried about having enough light because this was a back room, but the sun shining in the small windows, provided all the light I needed.

The large room was filled with old furniture, broken appliances, old magazines, a busted television and assorted junk.

My boxes were just as I'd left them, neatly stacked against a wall.

I went through a doorway to a middle room, one I hadn't seen the day I'd moved in. Here, boxes were scattered all over the place. Because there were no windows, this room was much darker than the first.

I could see that most of the boxes were open, so I got down on my knees, and juggling my flashlight, started going through some of them. More junk.

Moving on to the front room I found more boxes, dozens of them in all sizes, but these were sealed.

On closer inspection, however, I saw that the boxes had tape across the tops that at some point had been pulled loose, re-taped, and was now barely sticking.

There was just enough light from several small, high windows for me to see without the flashlight, so I put it on the floor and squatted down to one of the boxes and peeled away the tape.

I opened the box, looked inside and was stunned.

Even with all the suspicions I'd attached to my sleuthing, I hadn't seriously expected to find anything. Now that I had, my insides chilled to an icy cold.

The box was full of candles; mostly black ones. There was actually quite an assortment: long, short, fat and skinny ones. There were candles shaped like demons, and some that were shaped like strange, vile looking beasts and others shaped in basic human form.

Some of the candles were partially burned and still stuck down into intricately designed silver candleholders, while others were new and unused.

A second, larger box contained a number of folded long, black and grey robes with cowls. Yet another box was filled with old, old books, and some drawings ... all based on the dark arts.

I pulled out one of the books and read the title. It simply said, "The Coven". I put it back and picked up another one that said, "Ancient Practices". The drawings inside were sickening. I dropped it like I would a bag of live snakes.

The last box I decided to open contained glass jars and vials filled with putrid looking, unrecognizable liquid substances of various colours and consistencies. I closed it without further investigation.

Suddenly, I felt like I was going to throw up. I sat down on the floor and put my head between my legs and took several deep breaths.

With the exception of my heart trying to pound its way through my chest, I felt better after a while.

Finally, standing up, I tried to decide what to do next, and then nearly fainted when I heard a sudden noise downstairs.

I froze. Straining ... listening ... but I didn't hear anything else.

When I could force my legs to move, I tiptoed out of the room, through the middle room to the top of the stairs where I listened for a few minutes more. Then, what sounded like a door softly closing. I kept listening.

`

Nothing. Had I imagined the sounds?

I tiptoed back to the front room and with hands trembling so badly I could barely control them I re-closed the boxes trying to leave everything the way I had found it.

Before leaving, I even checked the floor to make sure I hadn't left new and visible footprints in the dust.

I went back downstairs, closed and locked the door and went to my room, but not before checking every room on the floor.

Finally, convinced I was alone in the house and back in my room, I collapsed on the bed. So, now I knew for sure, without a doubt, it was true. I was living with a real, live witch.

I had heard that there were good witches and bad witches. Something told me there was nothing good about Jessica.

I must admit however, once I hear the word 'witch', I don't plan to stick around to determine whether there is good or bad attached to it.

Of all the places I could have chosen to live, how had I ended up here? Had I come to this place by accident, or design?

As I thought about it, I had that vague feeling of inevitability. Unsure what else to do, I took out my beads and began to pray.

I opened my eyes and stared into darkness. My heart skipped a beat as I jumped up and turned on the light. I must have dropped off while saying my prayers.

Turning on the television, I went through the house and turned on more lights.

Although trying my best to behave normally, I didn't kid myself … I was scared shitless. I didn't know exactly what I was afraid of, which only made me more afraid.

Realizing I hadn't eaten anything since that morning, I went into the kitchen to fix some dinner.

Although I wasn't very hungry, I took a chicken I'd baked earlier, out of the refrigerator, sliced some and popped it into the microwave.

I took fresh broccoli out of the vegetable pan and prepared it for steaming with new potatoes.

A little later, while eating, Atlanta, Georgia kept coming to mind. I still loved Boston, but with my negative situation, I was feeling less enthusiastic about the city.

Sylvia had repeatedly asked me why I had chosen Boston instead of Atlanta where she said black people were doing such positive, progressive things.

I hadn't particularly wanted to go south, but now it kept popping into my thoughts.

My heart was heavy at the thought of leaving Boston … or Newport, or any of the great places I had discovered in the past months, but for the first time, I realized I might eventually move on.

After dinner, I cleaned the kitchen, turned the light off, and took a quick shower before heading to my room. I kept sticking my head out of the shower just to make certain nobody was sneaking up on me. I'd seen "Psycho", and was absolutely in the know.

I had never been more miserable.

I was leaving the bathroom when the telephone rang. It was Metcalf.

"Hello, there. How are you?" He asked, his voice eliciting emotions that pulled me in different directions.

"Just fine. And you?" I said, keeping my back to the wall.

"Great. I really enjoyed last night. Do you think we can do that again … soon? Like tomorrow? I know a great little supper club with live jazz that I think you'll enjoy.

The food is great and the music equally good," he said.

"I don't think so, Michael. You see, something's come up and I'll probably be leaving Boston soon," I said, surprising myself.

"Leaving Boston?!" He practically shouted, sounding shocked.

"Yes, looks like I'll be leaving in a day or so. Uh, it's sort of a family emergency," I added.

I figured, what can it hurt to make him think I was leaving the city and not just moving to another apartment? The chance of us running into each other on the street in the future was slim.

"After all you went through to get here, you're turning around and going home?" He asked.

"Well, not exactly. I'll be going to Atlanta," I said, shocking myself again.

"Atlanta? I guess I didn't realize you had family there," the surprise still in his voice.

It wasn't a question, so I didn't bother to comment.

"I can't believe it. This just seems so sudden. Can't you go take care of whatever it is and come back?"

"No, it's ... it's just too complicated," I stammered.

"I'm sorry; I don't mean to browbeat you. It's just that I'd be lying if I acted like I don't hate to hear you're leaving," he said.

"I feel the same way," I said. "It's a shock to me too," I truthfully replied.

"Will you promise to get in touch with me when you get settled? A little distance doesn't mean we can't still be friends."

"I promise," I said, knowing he was wrong. Long distance relationships are rarely sensible or successful.

When we hung up a few minutes later he still sounded dazed. I wished I hadn't promised Jessica I'd stay.

Since waking up, I wanted badly to leave immediately. But, I tried to calm down. I've been here this long a few more days certainly won't matter.

I was in bed watching television when the telephone rang again. I jumped up and ran into the hall to catch it before it stopped.

"So, what're you doing home on a Saturday night, beautiful?"

"Brenda!" I cried. "How the hell are you?"

"Great. And you, girlfriend?"

I sighed. I hadn't burdened her with my problems while she had been in Boston because I hadn't wanted to distract her from her studies. Now, it really didn't serve any purpose to tell her. What could she do to help?

"Oh, I'm okay. Can't complain. So, tell me how the job is going, and have you had a chance to apply all that knowledge yet?"

"Have I?" She said, with obvious satisfaction, and launched into a description of just how she was utilizing what she had learned in her classes in Boston.

Things were going well for her. She was glad to be back at home with her boyfriend whom she had worried about leaving for so long. Their brief separation hadn't placed any undue strain on the relationship, she said, and they were closer than ever.

I was glad. I looked forward to attending a wedding in San Diego one day.

"I do miss our little get-togethers," she said.

"I didn't realize just how much our little outings meant to me until I was back here."

"The same goes for me, Bren. I miss you too. But, we'll get together again one day soon. Either I'll come out there for a visit, or you'll come …," I cut myself off.

"Okay, I guess I might as well tell you, I'm leaving Boston."

There it was again.

Now, I was telling Brenda the lie.

"You're what?!" She screamed so loudly in my ear, I pulled the telephone back.

"I'm leaving Boston," I repeated.

"Why? To go where, and do what?"

I was about to fabricate some story of why I was leaving, but decided I might as well be honest about the circumstances surrounding Pleasant Street.

I told her the whole story, even about the mansions, which was punctuated by sharp intakes of breath and, "No's" and "Aaahhhhh's".

In the middle of the story, I insisted that she hang up and I called her back so I could absorb some of the cost of the call. When I finished, she angrily jumped all over me.

"How *could* you have kept this from me for so long?"

"What could you have done if you'd known?"

Nothing, but you still should have confided in me," she said accusingly.

"Well, maybe so," I agreed. "But, then you'd have been as worried and helpless as me. Plus, Sylvia finding the witchcraft stuff happened right after you'd left."

"I'm glad you're getting the hell out of there. I just can't believe this shit! Yes, I can," she contradicted herself. "The world is full of nuts and you were unlucky enough to find one," she said.

"Not just any one. I'd say I happened upon a major case."

"Alexis, do you remember how we talked about how few black people you see in Boston?" Not waiting for an answer, she asked …

"Do you think things might have been different if you had found some nice black family to stay with?"

"Who knows," I answered.

"Maybe instead of pictures of Satan and pentagrams, there would have been Voodoo dolls.

Evil doesn't have much to do with demographics. Evil is evil, and where it finds a weak or willing vessel is where it can make its home. I could've run into this anywhere. Of course, I'd never be able to sell that one to my sister."

"Damn, this is just too deep," she said quietly. "Really scary.

"If it's scary to you, think how I feel."

Then, not wanting her to feel any worse about my

situation, I changed the subject.

I told her about my date with Metcalf, and she was so excited, she forgot to say, 'I told you so.'

She felt it was foolish to leave Boston when there was such a great chance for a relationship.

"Brenda, the man is married," I reminded her." There's no chance for a real relationship. Some pretty good nookie, maybe."

We laughed, and it was like old times.

It was like there wasn't some anonymous danger lurking in the shadows around me.

"You might have been the woman to change that," she said.

"That's what women usually think."

Which is what the men count on; more to the point, I might not have been the woman … then what?"

I tried to explain that Metcalf had as good as told me his wife was in his life ... period. Obviously any other woman he got involved with was simply supposed to quietly accept the arrangement.

Brenda urged me to tell him what was going on, but I refused.

There was no point involving him in my life. Finally she saw it my way and gave up.

At her questioning, I told her I planned to move to Atlanta and promised to get in touch with her as soon as I got there.

I had no idea why I kept saying that about Atlanta. I hadn't decided any such thing. Or had I?

Such a move was a possibility sometime in the near future maybe, but not right now. Yet, every time I opened my mouth that's what came out. It was the damned craziest thing.

When I awoke, it was the middle of the night and my stomach was heaving and churning. I jumped up and ran. I made it to the bathroom just before everything I'd eaten that day ejected from my stomach at an awesome speed. I couldn't believe I was so sick, out of the blue. Every time I thought I was through vomiting, more would come up.

Finally, too weak to stand, I lay on the floor beside the commode and just sat up every time I had to throw up. When there was nothing left in my stomach, even from previous days, I kept on heaving and gagging.

I couldn't recall ever being this sick, even from past viruses. When it over, I pulled myself up to the basin, washed my face and sloppily brushed my teeth.

Slowly going back to my room, I used the walls for support. I lay down, but was soon bathed in perspiration and writhing in pain.

I wondered if I had been poisoned.

I had eaten chicken, so it could have been Salmonella; except I knew it wasn't.

Salmonella normally didn't work that fast. I also knew how to properly handle fowl to prevent illness.

I had cleaned my utensils, work area and hands with hot soapy water after preparing the chicken, and had made sure it was well cooked; I generally over-cooked it a little just to be on the safe side. And it had been fresh.

But, if it wasn't the chicken, then what, I wondered.

The answer seemed to just drop into my spirit with absolute clarity. Something had been put into my food, not to kill me, but to make me sick.

They wanted to delay me ... stop my leaving. I would be so caught up with the illness, I wouldn't ... couldn't leave as planned.

But, when had they done it? I had taken the chicken from the freezer to thaw out in the refrigerator on Friday after my date with Metcalf.

I hadn't left the house from that time until I had cooked it Saturday morning, and eaten it that evening.

Then, with horror, I thought back to earlier that day when I had been in the upstairs rooms, and had heard a noise from below.

I had baked the chicken that morning, cooled it on the stove for a while, and put it in the refrigerator.

It was there for anyone to see ... and tamper with. The next question was who had done it?

I knew Jessica was out of town. Again, the answer just seemed to drop out of nowhere; it was the couple downstairs.

A witch and a warlock, I thought. They were buddies with Jessica. As a matter of fact, the couple was often away on the weekends, as well. Probably at the farm or whatever it was.

I wanted to believe I was being paranoid, but every time I doubted what I thought, the certainty of it would hit me with a nearly physical force.

Now, I knew for sure there was a way into the house - probably, leading from their apartment below.

I simply hadn't found it. My next thought was that as quiet as I had been, they had known I was up in the attic. Somehow they had known.

They hadn't known how soon I planned to leave, or if I really planned to wait for Jessica. They might have thought I had gone up to get my boxes, and was going to sneak out.

And, even if I did wait for her, she couldn't do anything short of knocking me over the head to keep me here.

They also had to figure that I might have seen the contents of the boxes.

While I was upstairs, they had used that opportunity to put something in my food.

I had a sudden vision of the stuff in the jars upstairs, and the thought that I had ingested some unknown filth made my stomach lurch sickeningly.

I thought about going to the hospital, but there wasn't much they could do at this point.

There was no need to pump my stomach, it was already empty, and I didn't want to take the time it would take for them to do any testing because I knew something else now.

It was time to go. Not in a day or so.

Right now.

Chapter 14

*T*he voice inside is urgent. It is telling me to get up and prepare to leave.

Although sick and weak, I obey because it finally dawns on me why there had been something disturbing about my telephone conversation with Jessica.

To say she is frugal is a kindness, so why is she – someone who counts every penny and has never given me a break of any kind suddenly willing to reimburse me two entire months rent when she doesn't have to; which is so uncharacteristic I should have been alerted immediately.

She badly wants or needs me to stay … possibly until a certain date.

I take my garment bag and suitcase out of the closet and start to pack. When that's finished, I drag myself into the kitchen, throw out all open food, and pack my few utensils and appliances in a box.

By this time the sun is long since up. Finally, I Jimmie the attic door again and start the slow process of bringing down my boxes.

I am scared nearly out of my wits. Every time I come downstairs, I expect to find someone waiting for me.

My next problem is that the car can't hold all my belongings without pulling a U Haul or putting a carrier on top. I don't want to leave the house, but there is no other solution.

I decide to head out early, like I'm going to the store or something, get the carrier attached and come back and load the car. I thank The Lord that U Haul is open seven days a week.

Outside, I notice the Glenn's car parked in front of the house. I hope they won't enter the apartment while I'm gone and see how close I am to leaving. I make a lot of noise at the car, and make an issue of holding my stomach and grimacing in pain.

I figure, if they look out and see me leaving, maybe they'll think I'm either going to the hospital or the drug store for medicine.

I am back in about an hour with the carrier attached to the car. My stomach is cramping again, and I am so weak I can barely stand. I stopped at a drug store and picked up supplies that I hope will help.

Once back inside the house, I check the rooms and take some of the medicine before stretching out on the bed to rest. In fifteen minutes I'm up again, but before I start to load the car, I make a couple of calls.

I leave a message for Corey at the agency telling her I have to leave town unexpectedly. I tell her I will be in touch to tell her where to send my last check. I call Metcalf and leave a brief, goodbye message on his answering machine at the bank.

I explain that I don't have a forwarding address, but leave mom's telephone number and address in case he wants to get in touch at some point.

I call mom, last. I don't tell her I'm sick, and struggle to keep my voice sounding vigorous and strong. She expresses her surprise that I'm leaving so suddenly and even more surprise that I'm actually leaving Boston and moving to Atlanta.

It is at that exact moment I understand that Atlanta is indeed where I am going.

It's a total surprise because I don't even know how to get there.

"But, why do you have to leave Boston when you love it so much?" She asks. "Why can't you just move to another apartment?"

"I don't know. I can't answer that. I just know it's what I should do ... just like I know that leaving today is the right thing. I just don't want you to worry."

"Well, that's nice, but I am worried; and why Atlanta?"

"I don't know that either. Just seems a ... logical place. Sylvia's always going on about it like it's the best thing this side of heaven," I say.

And, since when did you start listening to Sylvia?"

"Good question. Look, I have to go, I want to get an early start and I haven't even mapped out my route yet. As a matter of fact, I think I'll do that once I get on the road."

"Alexis, I don't understand this rush, or your decision to leave Boston, but ... be safe."

"I will be. You know I have you on one side and —"

"The Lord on the other," she finishes.

"Yep."

A little later when I'm loading the car, both the Glenns come out on the porch.

"Are you going somewhere?" Ralph asks, his voice tinged with belligerence.

I'm not afraid now. I'm leaving.

"Good morning," I say pointedly. "I certainly am going somewhere," I answer sweetly.

"Oh how nice. Where're you going so early on a Sunday morning?" Barbara asks.

"I can't tell you. It's a secret," I say, and laugh as if it is a big joke. But, their expressions tell me they're not joking.

"So, you decided not to wait for Jessica to get back?" Then, thinking about what he'd said, he changes it slightly.

"I mean does Jessica know you're leaving? She might want to see you before you go?"

I pause for a moment and look at them. Their attitude and questions confirm everything I suspected about their involvement with Jessica ... and my illness.

"Jessica will find her house intact."

I don't answer whether or not she knows I'm leaving. I'm sure they know the answer to that already. On top of which, none of this is supposed to be any of their business.

I walk past them back into the house for another load. Once inside I glance out of the window to make sure they don't go near the car. When I come back down, Barbara is inside her apartment, probably talking to Jessica on the phone.

When finished loading, I walk slowly through the house carefully checking to make sure I haven't left anything.

In the living room I glance at the painting and wince. It will be so good to get out of this house once and for all.

I leave Jessica a note explaining that I can't wait for her return after all, and have managed to retrieve the boxes from the attic.

I tell her that I will call about the rent and send a forwarding address so she can mail my balance. But, even as I write, I know I will never contact her again.

Downstairs, the Glenn's are still on the porch and are actually blocking the steps. I try to go past, but Barbara stands menacingly in my path.

"You know, we don't think it right for you to leave and Jessica's not here," Ralph says.

"Well, she's not here, and I *am* leaving," I reply.

"Since we look out for the place when she's gone, and we don't know what you're moving out of her house, we're asking you to stay until she gets here.

She's on her way now," Barbara hastily adds.

"I don't think so. She'll just have to trust me. And, I'll ignore the implication of what you just said."

At this point I am both frightened and angry. These are the sick people who put something in my food to control me.

I could have died. Still could.

I look at them and they are narrowly eyeing me like they're daring me to make a move … or like they're about to make one.

Suddenly I see them clearly, without their masks of civility. Evil incarnate.

Now, I am simply frightened.

As if I can hear their thoughts, I know they're planning to over-power me and force me back into the house. It's early and nobody's outside. They're going to take the chance they won't be seen.

The time for conversation is past. Barbara opens her mouth to say something, but I gather what little strength I have in me, and jab her as hard as I can in her stomach with my elbow.

She grunts and falls back against a startled Ralph who almost falls, which would have sent them both over the porch banister.

The move takes them totally by surprise.

I rush down the steps and jump into the car, and before they can recover well enough to stop me I'm pulling away from the curb.

When I look back a couple of seconds later, they're on the sidewalk staring after me with amazement on their sinister faces.

They hadn't figured I had that in me, I think groggily.

"Too damn bad you assholes!" I shout just to relieve my tension.

I can see them now trying to explain their failure to detain me to Jessica, the High Priestess. I catch myself. Where'd that come from?

As I turn the corner at the end of the block, I look back for the last time knowing I have seen the last of the house on Pleasant Street and the evil that lives there. I'm nearly overcome with gratitude and relief.

For the first time in a long time, I draw an easy breath. But, I also feel a deep sadness and regret at the loss of a city that I had come to love. I will always remember beautiful architecture, delicious seafood and the awesome history. But time to go means just that.

As I pick up speed and move onto the highway, I think back over everything that has happened to me since leaving Chicago and wonder why I have been chosen for whatever this is, and if I will ever understand what *it* is all about.

More to the point, I wonder if it is over.

BOOK II

Marietta, Georgia

"And He said, Hear now my words: If there be a prophet among you,

I the Lord will make myself known unto him in a vision,

and will speak unto him in a dream."

Numbers 12:6

Chapter 1

*G*ood, I think, as the jumble of signs for Cracker Barrel Restaurant, Quality Inn, and a myriad of restaurants, stores, and hotels come into view. This looks as good a place as any to come off the highway and ask directions.

It's late on my second day of driving; the sun is close to setting, and I'm trying to make it to Atlanta before that happens. I take the off-ramp and see a service station almost immediately. Pulling in, I line up in a self-serve gas lane. After pumping the gas, I follow the instructions posted on the pumps and go inside to pay.

"Hi," I greet the young attendant.

"Hey. That'll be 'leven even ma'am," he answers with a drawl as long as any country mile.

I refuse to let the threatened smile loose. After paying for the gas and a bottle of juice, I ask ...

"Can you tell me how far it is to Atlanta? I thought I'd be there by now," I add in frustration.

"This here's Mayretta, Geoja. Atlanta's back down the road that way," he says, pointing in the direction from which I had just driven.

"Bout fifteen or so miles."

As well as the fact that the 'road' he mentioned is Interstate 75, a busy, eight-lane highway, and Mayretta is really Marietta, I hope he's also wrong about Atlanta's location.

I'm sorry, but that's the direction I just came from, and I certainly didn't pass Atlanta."

"Did you come in on 85?"

"Yes, I did."

"Well, right there where it kinda merges into 75 is 'roun the time you was passing Atlanta."

"But, there were no signs," I reply in total exasperation.

"Weelll..." he says, shrugging his bony shoulders, his attitude clearly implying my going off-track is my own fault and not the lack of proper signage.

"Welcome to Atlanta," I say aloud. I was about to ask him about a place to spend the night, but thought better of it.

No telling where I'd end up. Just then, the woman in line behind me asks....

"Were you supposed to be goin to Atlanta?"

The words poured from her mouth like a stream of thick molasses. If I thought the service station attendant had a drawl, this woman gave new meaning to the word.

Yes, but apparently I've missed it."

"Well, Abe's right, it's just about fifteen miles back. Won't take ya long to drive. It's a straight shoot."

"Thanks," I respond gratefully. "But, I'm not feeling well, so I'd rather find a place to stay the night and head back in the morning. "

"Could you possibly make a suggestion?"

"Sure," she drawls.

"There're all kinds of places 'round here. Let's see, there's the Sheraton, a Quality Inn, and a Motel 6 nearby.

But, if you want something a little different, there's a coupla bed and breakfast hotels up off Marietta Square," she advises.

"A bed and breakfast would be great. Can you give me directions?" She'd pronounced Marietta correctly.

"You kin folla me. I live just a coupla blocks off the Square.

"Thanks. You're very kind to take the trouble."

"No trouble. No trouble at all," she responds.

I figure a bed and breakfast probably won't cost much more than the regular hotels, and should be a lot more interesting. When the woman leaves, I follow her outside.

"I'm in that truck there." She points to a red, late model pickup.

"By the way, my name is Alexis Ashley," I say, holding out my hand.

"I'm Gail. Gail Mathis."

"Pleased to meet you," I say as we shake hands.

"Same," she replies with astonishing economy.

She pulls out of the parking lot with me close on her tail. Only then did I really notice my surroundings.

There are dense pockets of trees everywhere along the highway and back off the streets, behind and in between new looking apartment complexes; just about everywhere. They're beautiful, if just a bit much.

I note the cleanliness of Marietta and the gorgeous landscaping. Prettily designed lawns with riotous flowers and a multitude of attractive complexes and condominiums line the streets.

I have the feeling that Marietta is something of a boomtown. Almost everything looks new, and there's construction going on just about everywhere.

Soon we're driving into a quaint little area with narrower streets and older buildings. Then we pass what must be the town square, which is wonderfully picturesque.

After a few turns, Gail pulls into a small paved driveway behind a large three-story, pink and white frame house that is pure Victorian.

The classic gables and dormers are intriguing and make me anxious to see the interior.

I park and get out of the car while Gail stays in the truck with the motor running. I walk over and thank her again.

"Aw, stop. I'm just being neighborly. You'll be all right now?" She asks.

"I'll be just fine. If I decide not to stay here, I can find my way back to I75 and some of the other hotels."

"You sure?"

"Positive."

"Well, welcome to Georja," she drawls as she backs the pickup out. "Bye-bye!" .

"Goodbye!" I call back, waving to her as she leaves.

I walk around to the front door of the house and ring the bell. I'm surprised when a rather slovenly looking young blond woman finally opens the door.

"Hi," she looks at me suspiciously. "Can I help you?"

"Yes, I'm interested in a room."

"Oh." She looks surprised. Finally …

"Com'on in." I notice she looks behind me to make sure I'm alone.

"Thank you," I reply, trying not to get an attitude.

I follow her into the hotel's lobby. A long time ago, the lobby had been the foyer of a beautiful home.

On my right are mahogany sliding double doors that are closed; and on the left, the same type of doors, partially open and through which I can see a parlour with a highly decorative cathedral ceiling.

The entire place is filled with the most marvelous antiques, although most of them appear in desperate need of both repair and a delicate, but good cleaning.

The woman goes around behind the registration desk, which is a contemporary piece of carpentry in sharp contrast with the rest of the furnishings. It stands against the wall close to a beautiful mahogany staircase. She passes the registration book to me asking... "How many nights?"

"I'm not sure. I only intended staying one, but now that I've seen how lovely the house is, I'll stay an extra night."

The girl, who is mid-twenties moves at a snail's pace. She is about a head taller than me, but straw thin with long, stringy blond hair, blue eyes and a bored expression.

Had she been more animated, I thought, she might have been pretty.

Her name I learn is, Bobbi (with an i), and she's the manager of Stanford House. An unsettling turn of events, I can't help thinking.

I want to take a look around, but I'm too weak and tired. The weather has been cooperative on the drive from Boston, so I made fairly good time, but the push to get to Atlanta has taken its toll.

My illness has improved since leaving the city, but whatever it is that ails me has by no means passed. I am still having occasional, but slight bouts of nausea.

Bobbi leads me to a room on the ground floor, right off the lobby. I'm so tired I don't get a good look at it, but have a brief impression of a rather smallish space with a high ceiling.

The room does have its own bathroom, although it's kind of cruddy.

The building is beautiful, as is the antique furniture, but it's all tottering on the brink of shabbiness and is positively screaming for attention.

Although I badly want a bath, I'm not about to sit my naked ass in the bathtub before giving it a thorough scrubbing, and since there's no shower, I make myself content with a quick sponge bath in the basin. Then, I fall over in bed.

The bed is big and comfortable, but when I lie down I can't sleep. There's this mysterious odor that's awful. When I stand up, it disappears, but the moment I lie back down, it's stifling again.

I get up, turn on the light and examine the sheets. They look clean enough, but on a hunch I pull them back, and gasp.

Apparently there has been more singles in the room than doubles, and you can actually see the filthy imprint of numerous bodies on the cotton mattress pad. There's matted long hair sticking to it and the funk, once the sheet has been pulled away, makes my head swim.

I realize with disgust that the mattress pad has probably been on the bed for years, but has never met soap and water.

The fact that anyone could have changed the sheets continuously and left the filthy, disgusting pad on the bed is unbelievable. Then, I think of Bobbi (with an i), and nod my head with understanding.

Nearly feverish with fatigue, I pull on a shirt and jeans and go out to the car.

Once there, I take a box out of the trunk and go back into the house. Inside again, I strip the bed of everything, including blankets and comforters, and replace them with my own linen, which I had also used at Jessica's. I place the reeking pile of linen from the bed outside my door.

Mom had insisted I pack some sheets and towels of my own, and I had crankily complied. I was glad she had insisted, and that I had listened.

I got back into bed and must have passed out because that's the last thing I remember.

I wake up to the aroma of percolating coffee and bacon and feel myself practically salivating with anticipation, until I remember the dirty linen, and realize there is no way I can eat anything cooked by that girl in this house.

Taking time to lie in bed and reflect, I realize that for the first time since Boston, I feel normal. I don't feel sick and I'm not afraid.

It's like a new lease on life, like I'm starting over for the second time in the space of a few months and feel positive this time will be the charm.

I'm grateful to have been spared whatever premeditated malice had awaited me in Boston, and eagerly look forward to this new beginning.

I yawn and stretch lazily feeling self-satisfied. Then, touching my crucifix, I say a prayer of thanks.

Finally getting up, I pull on a pair of jeans and a sweatshirt, catch my hair up in a ponytail, and finding a baseball cap in my carry bag, put it on. I feel like being comfortably casual, unaware that for some time to come, the outfit will be like a standard uniform.

I hear voices coming from one of the rooms and the unmistakable sounds of china and silverware colliding.

Following my nose, I come upon two people having breakfast in the dining room. They are a middle-aged white couple immediately on guard at my presence.

I remind myself that I'm in Georgia, but not Atlanta, and need to be on guard myself. Determining the racial climate of the town is a priority.

"Good morning," I say politely. "Is Bobbi around?"

"G'maw'nin," they reply in unison.

"She's in the kitchen," the woman answers. "Down the hall on your left."

I notice they have full plates of bacon, eggs, and biscuits. Much more than the usual B&B fare, I think, as my stomach gurgles in greedy betrayal.

"Thank you," I say, smiling, but thinking, they probably think I'm the cleaning woman.

Following the direction the woman pointed me in, I walk down a long hallway, and the first room on my left is indeed the kitchen.

It is a long, narrow affair that is basically all counters and cupboards. I know instinctively that the room is less than half its original size and that at some point its beauty had been sacrificed for the sake of economy.

What a pity, I think as I try to imagine the original design.

Suddenly, I can clearly see a room that is as wide as it is long with shiny hardwood floors instead of the current aged linoleum, and beautiful cabinets made of real wood.

The image fades, and I force myself to not question its origin.

Bobbi is pouring juice, and while the room looks reasonably clean, I still decide against eating breakfast.

"Good morning," she greets me. "Did you sleep well?"

"Like a log," I answer.

"By the way, I hope you don't mind me using my own linen on the bed. It's a habit of mine," I say laughing.

"No, I don't care; as long as you're comfortable."

And, I knew she didn't care ... about much of anything having to do with the hotel.

"I'm wondering if I can look around. Victorian architecture is one of my passions, and this house is a treasure.

"Sure. Look around as much as you like. You and the Brents are the only guests right now, and they're going in town for a while before checking out later. So, take your time.

There're some brochures on the registration desk that'll give you a little history on the house," she said. "Would you like some breakfast?"

"Thank you, no. My stomach has been a little upset lately, so I'm taking it easy," I answer, as my stomach loudly and mutinously growls in contradiction.

I follow the hallway back to the dining room where the Brent's are still engrossed in their meal. I'm crossing the lobby to my room when out of the periphery of my eye I catch a movement on the stairs. I turn quickly to see who's there, but the stairs are empty.

I stand there for a moment totally baffled. There had definitely been a movement on the stairs and a glimpse of something long and white, like maybe a dress.

Continuing on to my room, I figure it was just a trick of light.

I plan on going out for breakfast as soon as I finish touring the house, so I take my purse and head down to the first floor where I plan to start.

I slide open the doors and go into the room that was on my right when I entered the house the evening before.

It's a sitting room with a mish-mash of furniture and a lovely old fireplace.

In a small windowed alcove that looks out on the front porch and the street beyond, I imagine a cushioned window seat rather than the Georgian sofa that now fills the space; so much the better to stealthily gaze out on unsuspecting pedestrians, I think. I can practically see the window seat that had surely once been there.

Although thin layers of dust cover everything, it is still a bright and pretty room that was undoubtedly well used in its time.

Next to the sitting room is a contemporary conference room with a long table and chairs that jerk me unceremoniously back to the twentieth century.

Across the hall, the parlour is probably the largest room in the house. Big bay windows with stained glass tops offer an uninterrupted view of Clancy Street, while a huge fireplace framed by a marble mantle adds what must have been just the right touch of genteel wealth to the turn of the century home.

What is probably an unused and out of tune Steinway fills the corner by the window creating a perfect party setting. Like people passing on the street must have heard, I imagine that I too can hear the sounds of music, singing and laughter echoing back through the years.

More sliding doors separate the parlor and dining rooms where the primary distinction is a sparkling glass chandelier hanging over a massive Renaissance Revival dining table. I don't go into the room because the Brents are still there.

So far, the house seems to contain an eclectic mix of furniture that ranges from American Empire, which was popular in the mid 1800's to Renaissance Revival, more popular in the latter half of the same century.

It is like a wonderful museum, and I'm enjoying studying the furniture as much as the architecture.

Finally, my cramped bedroom completes the tour of the first floor.

I wander up the beautiful, wide staircase to the second floor where I discover four more bedrooms.

There is a sixth on the third floor, which I later learn belongs to Bobbi. Each room has its own fireplace and private bath.

The prettiest of them all is the powder blue and cream honeymoon suite with its huge bathroom, canopied four-poster, and private balcony.

The one that totally captures my fancy however sits on its own short corridor with the bathroom directly across the hall. The spacious room has a mahogany four-poster, a colossal wardrobe, the requisite fireplace and towering ceiling. A locked door connects the room to another bedroom on the front of the house. It is exquisite.

Each room has a distinct personality, however the general lack of cleanliness clouds their beauty; the windows need washing, the unused fireplaces need cleaning, the Venetian blinds could use a good scouring, and I don't have to wonder about the state of the bedding.

Returning downstairs, I'm shocked to see a cleaning woman fumbling with a vacuum cleaner in the lobby.

It's all too obvious that Bobbi doesn't know how to utilize the woman or herself in maintaining the large property and I feel sympathy for both her *and* the house.

I go in search of Bobbi and find her washing dishes in the kitchen.

I approach her about the possibility of changing rooms.

"Bobbi, the house is simply beautiful. While wandering around upstairs, I fell in love with one of the bedrooms, and wondered if it's available tonight."

"Oh. Which one?" She asks in her monotone.

When I describe the room, she tells me it is available and if I want, I can take it.

Excited at the prospect of sleeping in that lovely room, I immediately go to move my things.

Chapter 2

*W*alking around for awhile, I found an attractive little restaurant on the Square that served the traditional southern breakfast of country fried ham, sausages and bacon; grits with either redeye or white gravy, or cheese; eggs and omelettes; homemade biscuits either with or without gravy; and pancakes and waffles.

Since grits had never been a favorite, I ordered a western omelette and biscuits with white gravy on the side, and coffee. When finished, I almost licked the plate.

Afterwards I took a walk around the Square, which consisted of restaurants, bars, retail stores and second floor offices, all of which form a four-block rectangle around a grassy little park with a band shell in its center.

A number of wooden benches, a statue of General Robert E. Lee and several water fountains complete the park. I was sure it looked very much as it had a century before.

I left the Square, crossed some railroad tracks and ran into another street of stores. Beyond that street I could see a residential community and thought of Gail, the woman who had helped me the day before.

Gail was everything I thought people described as 'redneck' would sound like, and to some extent would act like, yet she couldn't have been kinder to me, which is why stereotypes are always, always just plain stupid. Something told me though, in this community, she just might be an exception and not the rule. I hoped not.

On impulse, I went back to Stanford House, got the car, found my way to I75 and drove the fifteen miles to Atlanta. When I reached the downtown area, I was a little disappointed. It seemed really small for a city the size of Atlanta. I drove around a while then headed back to the heart of town and parked in a parking garage.

I wandered into one of the large hotels and asked the concierge for literature on the city. She handed me a packet thinking I was a guest, and I didn't correct her.

Looking over the information, I discovered I was close to an indoor mall called Peachtree Center and easily found my way there. The Center had a food court with a dozen or so restaurants and a slightly higher number of retail stores and shops.

A glass of iced tea at one of the restaurants while reading the literature and a newspaper I had purchased was delicious and refreshing. By the time I finished reading, I had a fair idea what was happening in Atlanta.

I was totally open to the city however, my reaction was far from my love-at-first sight experience with Boston. One of the reasons was the architecture.

Unfortunately, unlike Chicago and Boston Atlanta had not preserved many of those beautiful, character-laden buildings and mansions from earlier centuries.

This wasn't as much because of the burning of Atlanta during the Civil War, as it was due to The Great Fire of 1917, a conflagration that destroyed thousands of commercial buildings, mansions, and shanties in the city.

Today, there is little sense of the city's history and past. Of course, the residential communities away from downtown might be a different story, so in the interest of fairness, I tried not to rush to judgment.

After seeing Atlanta, I decided to hang with Marietta for a while. When I was better acquainted with everything, I could look for something permanent in the city. But, even as I thought of putting down roots in Atlanta, I strongly suspected I would never consider it home.

"Do you ever rent a room long term, Bobbi?" I asked after returning from my excursion into Atlanta.

"Sure, we get businessmen that stay for a few days, sometimes as long as a week or two. Although in the last year, fewer of them have wanted to deal with the traffic between here and Atlanta, so they opted to stay in the city."

"Well, I was thinking of staying a little longer than that ... maybe a month or two."

"A month or two?" She squeaked.

I had never seen her so animated.

"Yes, just to give myself time to learn my way around and find a job."

"So, you really are moving to Georgia?"

"Yes, just like I told you I was."

"Well, I don't know. We never had anyone to stay that long. I wouldn't know what monthly rate to charge."

"Couldn't you ask?" I said, feeling a twinge of impatience. "Who owns Stanford House, anyway?"

"A group of doctors; they call themselves a consortium, or something like that," she said.

My eyes briefly sought the ceiling.

"Will you ask them, Bobbi?"

"Yeah, I'll talk to their lawyer, my contact person. He'll talk to them directly. I'll probably know something in a few days."

"Great. I'll just continue paying the daily rate until you get back to me."

That done, I felt more productive and more relaxed.

"How long have you been managing Stanford House, Bobbi?"

"A little over two years," she answered.

"Do you mind me asking how you came to find such an interesting job?"

"They advertised in the paper, and I answered the ad. I'm really a singer you know," she stated proudly, while flipping her limp hair out of her eyes.

"No, really?" I was genuinely surprised.

"Yeah, I sing with my sister. She lives in Norcross. We both play guitar and sing in some of the local clubs. Sometimes we sing in other cities, too. Like, Macon. We even performed once in Memphis."

This was as full of life as I had seen her. On a scale of one to ten, she was cruising around seven ... a real breakthrough.

"Here let me show you," she said, breaking into my uncharitable reverie and delving into a drawer underneath the counter.

She pulled out a promotional photograph of the dynamic duo, and they actually looked really pretty.

There were yards of black lace with satin trim, upswept hairstyles, and actual make-up. The caption read ... *'An Evening with Satin Velvet'*.

"You two look beautiful! And that's some name," I said.

"Thanks. You like it?" She was now nearing ten on the Richter scale.

"I do; I think it's great. It sounds real classy.

What kind of music do you sing?"

"Mostly Blues," she said, startling me.

I couldn't imagine this girl singing any Blues I was familiar with. Then I took another look at the long face and bored expression, which could possibly be misconstrued as sad, and thought, well, maybe.

"I'd love to catch your act sometime," I said with sincerity.

"Well, I'll let you know the next time we have a gig around here." She was actually smiling.... broadly. I was happy to become acquainted with Bobbi's alter ego.

Stanford House didn't have television sets in the rooms. The owners felt they detracted from the hotel's charm, which I thought reasonable.

They would however, provide one if it was requested. I was still riding mine around in the car trunk and didn't plan to take it out until I had a permanent residence.

I had asked Bobbi for one before I left that morning, and planned on going up to bed and watching myself to sleep. But just as I was saying goodnight to her, a man I had seen earlier in the backyard entered the room.

"Hey, Jim," she said. "Were you able to fix it?"

"Took a while, but I finally found the problem. It's working now," he answered, his eyes directly on me.

I couldn't believe his voice; a deep, rich baritone, that sort of vibrated over you in waves. Astonishing.

"Alexis, this is Jim Blalock, our caretaker. He lives in the apartment downstairs."

Which was a surprise; I hadn't even known there *was* a downstairs.

"Jim, this is Alexis Ashley. She's from Boston. Alexis may be with us for a while."

There was a slight rise of one brow before Jim said,

"Pleased to meet you, Miss Ashley."

"Alexis. And same here."

"Jim," he said in response.

As imposing as his voice was Jim's size.

Tall and impressively muscled for a man of middle age, he had a full head of pepper and salt hair that topped a ruggedly lined, deeply tanned face; a face and body that bespoke years of outdoors work. Jim seemed likable enough except for one thing ... his eyes were anything but warm.

"The grounds, the plumbing, electrical problems ... Jim's our resident expert. And," Bobbi paused, "He's also a musician. He plays the guitar," she concluded.

"That's me," he said, "Jim of many trades."

"That's fascinating," I said, wondering if everybody in town had two occupations, and if the second one was always as a musician.

"Do you play in a band?"

"If you want to call it that; we play mainly for special occasions."

"Well, you seem to have the best of all worlds," I said, smiling. Then, stifling a yawn, I decided to make my exit. "If you'll both excuse me, I think I need to find my bed and get in it. Goodnight, see you both tomorrow," I said, heading for the stairs.

"Goodnight," my two new, decidedly edgy ... and slightly weird neighbours responded.

When I got to the room, I didn't bother turning on the television. Still a little drained from the drive and the illness, I put away my things, changed the linen on the bed then fell over in it dropping off the moment my head hit the pillow.

When I opened my eyes I was disoriented for a moment. The windows were dark, so I knew it wasn't morning, yet the room was strangely bright. I glanced at the clock and it was three in the morning. What was it that woke me? I lifted my head and was startled to see a man standing by the fireplace.

He was leaning on the mantle staring into ... a crackling fire? His area of the room was totally different than when I had gone to bed.

The man was average height with a beard and sideburns and wore clothing similar to some I had seen fairly recently. The suit jacket nearly reached his knees, but I couldn't see the front, or his face because he was half turned from me.

I had a sinking feeling in the pit of my stomach. Not again. Not here. Oh please, no. I simply won't see it. I refuse, I thought.

Luckily, I could move enough to lay my head back down on the pillow and close my eyes tight.

I decide I simply won't look.

And I didn't.

Chapter 3

I had walked up to the Square to get something to eat, but couldn't make up my mind what I wanted. Standing on the street in front of an Italian restaurant, I was trying to decide whether to go in when I heard a voice behind me calling...

"Hey, uh ... Miss. Miss!"

I looked around and there was the woman who had helped me my first day in town. I remembered her name was Gail. She was double parked, and in the same red pick-up truck.

"Why, hello," I said, walking over to the truck.

"Hey," She answered in return. I knew by now that 'hey' was the standard greeting in this part of Georgia and wondered if I'd ever get accustomed to it. I thought not.

"You still here? I thought you'd be in Atlanta by now."

"Yes, still here and settling in; I really like it here."

"By the way, I'd like to thank you for taking me to Stanford House. I like it so much I've decided to stay there for a while."

"Well, that's jus great!" She said every word soft and long. It was a funny thing about drawls; not everybody had them; while on the other hand, some were so much more pronounced than others.

I guess it depended on the area of the South a person grew up in, or how their parents spoke. I found her speech charming.

"Headin to dinner?" She asked.

"Yes, if I can make up my mind what I want. I really don't think it's Italian," I answered.

"What about barbeque? I was jus on my way to dinner. My husband's workin late, so I thought I'd go over to The Depot. Why don't you come with me? They have the best barbeque in Georja," she said convincingly.

Although I wasn't in the mood for barbecue either, at least accompanying her would mean having someone to talk to.

"Where's The Depot?"

"You mean you ain't been to The Depot, yet? Well, that's about as much a part of Marietta as that Square there."

"Where's your car?"

I pointed down the street.

"It'll be fine, there. Why don't you ride with me?"

I walked around to the passenger side of the truck, and pulled myself up beside her.

As it turned out, The Depot was only a few blocks away. It was next to the same railroad tracks I had crossed that first day. It was for a fact, a piece of Americana, and absolutely delightful.

I learned that the train tracks the Depot sat on ran the length of Marietta, and was said to have once been a loading point for Confederate soldiers.

As a matter of fact, General Robert E. Lee had reportedly spent a night or two in Marietta and had come into town at that very same station.

That was the one thing about the town I found peculiar; the place was full of memorabilia from the war.

In fact, so was Atlanta. It gave one the feeling that on some level, it wasn't really over for the residents. Maybe, never would be.

There was a sense of loss that was still sadly palpable in these memorials: loss of brother, father, friend, neighbor and loss of a war where the psyche had grown a scab, but still many decades later, wasn't completely healed.

From outside, The Depot looked like any other small town train station, except for the big sign on the roof with the name of the restaurant and the promise, '*Best Bar-B-Q in Georgia*'.

On the tracks next to the building was a train car. When we got closer, I was amazed to see it was set up with booths, tables and chairs and was part of the restaurant.

The first room we entered was a cheerful little pub, which led to a second room with a small restaurant containing five or six round, wooden tables and chairs and a stairway that led up to the train car. The car had booths and tables just like a real dining car.

Of course I opted to eat upstairs and since it wasn't busy, the waitress even let me take a look around.

She proudly explained that the train car was an authentic L&N dining car and that along with the dining compartment, there was also a kitchen where cooks had once prepared complete meals for the passengers.

The kitchen was the size of a small closet. On a wall plaque I read that cooks had prepared food for an entire trainload of people out of the space, which couldn't comfortably hold two people.

I was fascinated with the teeny sink, a teeny stove and oven and the teeny cupboards. They must have been magicians, I thought.

Although difficult to believe, the plaque emphatically stated that the food back then had not been prepared ahead of time, and was famous for its goodness. What!?

Stairs at the back end of the dining car led down to The Depot's kitchen, which was a part of the building. It, thank heaven was much larger, and spotlessly clean. I went back to my seat totally intrigued with the historical setting and prepared to enjoy my meal.

Gail, who had declined the tour saying she was interested in the dining car only in so much as what turned up on her plate, was reading the menu when I returned. While she studied it, I really looked at her for the first time.

She was a chubby young woman ... not really fat, just chubby, with one of those pretty faces that made her weight inconsequential.

She had shiny, long, brown hair that I later learned she rinsed with beer to give it body and that shine. Bright brown eyes smiled when she did, and she had a peaches and cream complexion that was similar to Brenda's; they were both disgustingly flawless.

What I found most interesting about Gail wasn't her looks, but something in her manner that suggested a sweetness that was encased in steel.

I seemed to recall something about southern women's deceptive gentleness. I couldn't quite recall the saying, but somehow I knew Gail fit the bill.

She had a huge heart, would help anyone she could, but wasn't in the habit of taking any shit from anybody.

After turning my attention to the menu and considering the ribs, beef, chicken and pork plates, I settled on the beef plate and Gail chose pork.

While waiting for our meals I learned that she was in her early thirties, had been married for six years, and had a five year-old daughter whom she clearly adored. Tonight, Baby Girl, as she called her, was staying overnight with Gail's in-laws.

Gail worked as a secretary for a company that was between Marietta and Atlanta and although she had never made it to college, she said that the lack of higher education wouldn't stop her from reaching her goals. I heard the steely determination in her voice and believed her.

When I told her about my traveling around to different places, she had a hard time relating to me leaving a good paying, secure job like the one in Chicago to go some place where I had no guarantee of work.

I think she thought I was a little addled, but was too polite to let on. She cautioned me about Atlanta.

"Atlanta ain't … isn't exactly an easy place to live. Everybody hears it's such a great place, but it can be damned hard to make a living here. Hell, most people have to hold down two or three jobs jus to pay their bills," she said.

I thought about Jim and Bobbi, and their different streams of income and mentioned that to her.

"That," she said, "is the norm."

"I've only been here a few days," I agreed, "but I can already see something of what you're talking about."

"Don't get me wrong, I'm not sayin Atlanta's not a good place to live, I'm sayin it can be … hard.

People from other places don't usually find that out until they get here."

She wanted to know how I came to stay long-term at Stanford House, and I told her how it had happened and that I had only found out earlier in the day that the owners had approved the extended stay.

"I think that's smart of 'em. The place is like a ghost town durin the week. They get more traffic on the weekends, plus they rent out the big rooms for special occasions like parties, receptions and anniversaries."

I smiled wryly at the word 'ghost', but only said … "Oh, great."

I hadn't considered that aspect of living there. But, then, I didn't believe those types of functions would really bother me."

She asked, "Do you have kitchen privileges?"

I nearly choked on my Coca-Cola.

"Yes, but I don't think I'll be doing much cooking."

She didn't ask why, and I didn't volunteer.

"Well, you're welcome to come over and eat with us anytime," she said.

170

"Jus call to make sure I'm not workin late and that I'll be cookin."

"Are you serious?" I asked, surprised. After all, she hardly knew me.

"Sure. You're a nice person, aren't you? You're in a strange, new place and you don't know nobody, so I'll be happy ta help out if I can."

I stared at her thinking suddenly of Brenda. She saw me staring and said …"Where I'm from, everybody was pretty poor. We had to stick together to survive. You don't think about it, you jus do it. It's jus what's expected; how I come up."

At that point the food arrived and I was grateful for the distraction because I was too choked up to talk. I was to learn Gail meant every word. I had been adopted.

This of course, made me think of Brenda. She and this nice woman somehow seemed close to both of us; somehow it seemed we all knew each other. Imagine that.

The food was even greater than the promise.

The beef plate consisted of thick, juicy slices of slow cooked beef covered in a barbecue sauce that had just the right bite. As side dishes I had chosen corn on the cob and Coleslaw.

The meal was served with a small plate of Jalapeno Cornbread; something I had never tasted. Stuffed with kernels of corn, chopped onions and Jalapeno peppers, the buttery bread was deliciously flavorful and spicy.

When I finished eating, my plate was as clean as a shiny new quarter. Every morsel had been consumed down to the last little crumb.

"That food was cooked with love," I said to Gail. "Who owns this place?"

"I really don't know. There's a little old guy who's on the bar a lot. I think he's the owner."

As with Brenda, when Gail and I left the restaurant, we were already friends. She drove me back to the Square and we exchanged numbers. As I got in the car I smiled at the incongruity of the new friendship, and was pleased.

§§§§

Maybe it's the heavy meal I ate earlier with Gail, but I can't sleep and decide to read for a while. The house is quiet. Bobbi and her boyfriend, Mark, are upstairs in her suite on the third floor.

The nights Mark don't spend here with Bobbi she spends with him at his apartment. Often, I'm the only person in the big house at night, but unlike the house on Pleasant Street, I adjusted quickly to being alone.

Although it's after midnight, I feel like a cup of tea, so pulling on my slippers I head down to the kitchen. I don't bother putting on a robe. After all, who will see me?

In the hall I flip on the stairway light. When I reach the bottom of the stairs, I turn to go down the hall to the kitchen, but just as I turn, I catch a movement out of the corner of my eye.

It looks like someone turning to go into the dining room. I run down the hall into the dining room and turn on the light. There's no one there. I run through the dining room into the parlor and then across the hall into the sitting room.

Nothing.

I don't feel it is a trick of light as I had that first night. This time I definitely made out the figure of a woman ... a woman in a long, dark dress.

I think of my second night in the house when I'd seen the man at the fireplace. After a time, the light had faded, and never opening my eyes, I had actually gone back to sleep ... with the covers over my head.

The next day when I remembered it, I told myself I'd just been dreaming. But, I can't tell myself that this time ... I haven't been to sleep.

I had seen it for only a fraction of a second, so it was more impression than anything, but seen it I had.

"Oh Father," I moan aloud. "Will this ever end?"

I stand a moment deciding whether to run back up stairs or go on to the kitchen. I go on into the kitchen and although frightened, and constantly looking over my shoulder, nothing else materializes.

When I finish, I walk back down the hall and into the dining room carefully balancing the hot contents of my cup. Suddenly, I get that nearly forgotten woozy sensation. I remember swaying slightly and trying not to spill tea all over the floor.

The next thing I know, the room is bathed in light. I look up in surprise to see daylight streaming in the windows. I know what's happening, and wrestle with my panic.

I look around but there's nobody in the room, which is quite a switch. It is the first time I have walked into an empty vision. I check the furniture, and except for the chandelier and the basic design of the room, it is totally different from the one I so recently walked through.

There are several layers of curtains at the windows, the color scheme is completely different, and there's a lot more furniture.

Then, a movement at the front of the large room catches my attention. I look down and there she is. She'd been there all the time ... on her knees, scrubbing the floor. I know it's the woman I glimpsed earlier, only this time I'm looking directly at her.

She's a black woman who's perhaps around thirty, maybe a little younger or older. She has on a plain, floor length rustic dress, and a wrap on her head that's knotted in front.

With a pail of soapy water at her side she's scrubbing the floor with long, slow strokes of a brush. Her dress, covered in front by a long apron, is damp but she doesn't seem to notice. I try to get closer for a better look, but as before, I can't move.

Even at a distance though, I can see she's crying. I can't hear anything this time; no voices in the background, not even birds singing outside. Still, I see tears flowing in relentless streams down her distorted face. Clearly, something has broken her heart.

Suddenly, another woman enters the room. She is white, and I can tell by her imperious manner she is the preverbal '*Miss Ann*'.

Unlike the woman on her knees, she wears a flowing light green dress of a shiny, heavy material like taffeta. The dress has a square cut neck, a fitted bodice, and sleeves that puff out below the shoulder and taper snugly from elbow to wrist. The full skirt is trimmed at the waist and bottom with a deeper shade of green. It is quite elegant.

She wears a bonnet that ties under her chin, and is carrying a large straw basket on her arm.

I get the impression she's either just entering, or leaving the house. She leans down to the woman on the floor, and speaks rapidly, her gestures and slowly reddening face signifying anger. The woman on the floor cowers and begins wiping her face with her dress.

The white woman suddenly raises her hand as if she might strike her, but the black woman quickly scoots backward out of her way.

Apparently either changing her mind or feeling assured that the threat was effective, the woman lowers her hand and seems to issue some type of order before turning and striding from the room.

The woman on the floor is still for a moment with her head down. Then, visibly restraining the anonymous grief, she dips the brush in the water and continues scrubbing the floor, as if the enormity of her anguish precludes any greater emotion, even rage.

When I come to myself, I'm standing in the dining room that's dark again except for the moonlight flowing in the windows. The teacup and saucer I'd been carrying are on the floor in pieces at my feet, and the front of my gown is soaked. Tears drench my cheeks as I whisper over and over ... "She was a slave."

I stumble to the table and sink down in a chair, my body shaking. Overwhelmed with sadness I lay my head in my arms and give in to the hard, wrenching sobs.

I cry for unknown places across divisive oceans; for people different, yet the same as me; for rites and rituals at once familiar and unknown. I cry for lost seeds of origin, and for a pain and suffering so profound, it stretches across the seas of time.

Finally, completely drained, I drag myself up, clean up the mess, turn out the lights and slowly climb the stairs. As I walk, I wonder how I had known the black people at the mansion in Newport hadn't been slaves, but that the woman tonight was one.

It occurs to me that different time periods made each situation plausible or implausible; the mansions weren't built until slavery was over. Stanford House on the other hand, had been built and existed at the height of slavery.

I wonder if my awareness of the different periods had made the difference, or had everything so definitively pointed to a master-slave relationship between the two women, it had been an easy determination.

Back in bed I've lost interest in the book, so I put it away. The sorrow I witnessed downstairs is clinging to me like dew on grass. I can't shake it off.

I've read about slavery, seen films about it, written college papers on it and discussed it, but until tonight, I had never *seen* … never *felt* slavery. Now, it's real in a sense that's nearly impossible to comprehend.

The episode has even taken on a surreal quality; like I'm not *relating* to the woman's pain as much as I am actually experiencing it; as if we have changed places and I am the one scrubbing the floor, helpless to prevent some recent or imminent disaster.

Somewhere down the corridors of my past I must have known similar heartbreak and tragedy, which condemns me now to relate to the woman's fear and grief far beyond normal empathy.

I try to reign in these emotions, but to no avail. As amazing as it seems, there is a clinging residue of guilt regarding the woman's tremendous need and my complete impotence in the face of that need.

There is also a sense of sadness relating to the responsibility that some historians have tried to place on Africans regarding their enslavement; which to some degree is justified, yet in another sense isn't justified at all.

I know better than to be swayed by revisionist history. The truth is that Africa is a huge continent, not a country and at the time of the slave trade it was a world of vastly different peoples: tribes separated by geography, language, culture and societal systems.

Not only were these tribes different from one another – in many cases they warred against each other.

When warriors were captured, they were usually enslaved by the victors however, their slavery wasn't generational; wasn't intended to last forever.

In the span of the captives' own lives after some period of servitude, they either managed to escape, or assimilated into and became a member of the captor's tribe … most commonly through marriage.

Africans knew nothing of the kind of slavery that lasted from one generation to the next into infinity; or the kinds of atrocities and inhumanities characteristic of European slavery. And when assisting with the slave trade, Africans certainly didn't turn over their own tribesmen to the slavers.

Of course, there were those Africans who didn't know, or care how others would fare. All they cared about was what was in it for them.

You had those individuals in African societies back then, and you have them in every society in the world today. Unfortunately, moral corruption is an age old human condition.

So, for the most part, Africans simply hadn't known the true extent of their betrayal. And as much as some historians attempt to reposition blame, the actions of some of the greedy, weak and ignorant will never absolve slavery's real perpetrators; the truth is … there's enough blame to go around.

Another truth is … it's time to move on. I tell myself to never forget the past, but caution myself to not become shackled by it, which as it turns out is just another form of slavery.

I also firmly tell myself that whatever it is that happened in this house and in Africa so long ago is long past and far beyond my reach. It can't be changed; only studied and remembered to prevent it from ever happening again.

But when I turn off the light and try to sleep, it won't come. I find myself plagued by questions regarding the woman.

Why was she   so unhappy? Had someone died, been killed, or severely punished? Was she tormented by some horrific, impending tragedy?

As foolish as I know it to be, I am totally intrigued and long to return to her world just long enough to obtain the answers to those questions.

Chapter 4

*S*ince coming off the highway in Marietta, I've learned to move in step with the rhythm of life on the Square, which includes accepting my status as something of a community oddity.

I can tell by their looks that those who live and work in the area have, I'm sure, discussed to the point of boredom, the black woman living at Stanford House. In response, I simply try to keep a low profile – as if that were possible.

As in Boston, I talked with a number of temporary agencies in Atlanta about work, and was shocked at the low pay scale. When the first consultant I spoke with told me the average rate of pay for assignments, I had laughed and said the rate couldn't possibly be for adults ... adults didn't work for that kind of money.

She had tersely replied that adults did indeed work for that kind of money, and so would I if I came to work for them. Needless to say, I didn't.

I thought of Gail's warnings about the city. It was the same everywhere, but I knew that working for such low wages would call for a serious attitude adjustment on my part that could only be caused by something drastic; like running completely out of money, or my mind.

So, I was still contemplating what to do, including whether to leave or to stay in Georgia.

I had spent quite a bit of time in Atlanta and had found pockets of the city I really liked, but staying in Marietta for the present was still preferable.

Although I hadn't had any more visions, I think my decision to remain at Stanford House was partially influenced by the hope that I would. I wanted to know what had happened to the slave woman.

Eventually, I had grown weary of watching television and reading as my only sources of entertainment, so one night I had bravely decided to check out the nightlife on the Square.

I had gone into two different bars, neither of which was very welcoming. I tried a third and knew immediately I wouldn't stay; the clientele was a little on the rough side.

Then, I remembered The Depot. I hadn't been back since the dinner with Gail, but remembered it as a nice, friendly place.

It was still early, only about eight o'clock, and when I walked in, there were only three people on the two bars ... and all of them turned to stare at me.

The bartender was the little old guy that Gail had mentioned and was the only one that didn't stare or act surprised at my presence. I hoped this meant he felt I had as much right as anyone of drinking age to sit on his bar.

When I sat down, he ambled over with a big smile and asked ... "What's it going to be little lady?"

"I'll have Chablis," I answered.

He poured my drink and sat it down in front of me. "Don't believe I've seen you before ...you just passing through, or visiting?"

179

"I live in the area," I answered. Then, deciding to identify myself, added ... "At Stanford House."

"Ah yes," he said, knowingly. "Well, welcome to the Square."

"Thank you."

"I'm Charlie, by the way." He extended his hand.

Taking it, I said, "Alexis Ashley."

"Are you the owner of this lovely and unique establishment?" I asked.

"That's me. Evelyn and me ... that's my wife, have owned The Depot for about eight years now," he said.

"It's fascinating. I've eaten here before, and I felt such a sense of history in the dining car. I mean ... the thought of all the people who all those years ago sat in that very dining car enjoying their meal while the world passed by outside ... it's just ... I think it's pretty exceptional," I said.

Then added, "And the food is excellent; absolutely delicious."

Without a word, Charlie pulled out the wine bottle and poured me a second glass of wine although I hadn't finished the first.

"For that glowing testimonial, you just earned yourself a drink on the house."

Laughing, I assured him I could think of something different to say every night, and he laughed along with me.

Just then, a lovely blond came in from the restaurant, went behind the bar and sat on a stool next to Charlie.

"This is my wife," he said, and introduced us.

Evelyn and Charlie were about as opposite in appearance and personality as was possible.

Charlie was a short, little guy who, despite bundles of energy, was probably in his mid-to-late sixties.

With a nose that was much too big for his small face, ears that stood out from his head like an elf, and steel grey hair thinning on the crown, few people would describe him as handsome.

He was however, extremely charismatic, gregarious, knowledgeable on multiple subjects, and as I would discover, a shrewd businessman who had a gruff exterior, but was something of a softie.

Evelyn was a blue-eyed blond. Tall and statuesque, she was at least twelve to fifteen years younger than her husband. Thirty years of marriage and two adult children however, had done nothing to diminish her knockout figure, or her obvious adoration of Charlie.

When Charlie retired from the Marines, he had started a successful contracting business that he still operated. The Depot, which came years later, was never revenue driven, but was a labour of love that allowed him to share his secret barbecue sauce and his award winning recipes and cooking with the world, he said.

I would learn that although he employed a full time cook, he himself did a lot of the work.

After a pleasant evening of conversation with Charlie, Evelyn and some of their customers, and after three glasses of wine, I was moved to do something incredibly impulsive.

Charlie had just finished describing how he'd renovated the building, purchased the dining car and remodeled it, and turned the whole thing into a huge success.

It was such a great story, and they were such nice people, I suppose I got carried away.

"Do you need any help here? I originally wanted to do temporary office work, but the pay is too low. Maybe you could use me here," I said.

Charlie looked totally surprised. But, I must say, he was cool. "Well, now that's a thought, although the pay here might not be a whole lot better. Tell you what, I don't need anybody right now, but you never know. Give me your number before you leave. I gotta warn you though, the only thing I would have is a waitress job."

"Oh, that's just fine," I said, already wondering why I had offered to do something so bizarre.

"You ever waited tables?"

"To be honest no, but I'm sure I can do it. I can do anything anybody else can," the Chablis responded.

"Alexis, waiting tables is a different ballgame from any kinda office work. It's damned hard."

"Hard work? No problem."

"Okay, if anything opens up, I'll let you know."

Sylvia had gotten my telephone number at Stanford House from mom, and called me. For the last few minutes she had waltzed around the 'I told you so' about Boston that was waiting to rear its ugly head.

"Mother told me you chose Atlanta based on what I'd said about it. Listen, don't go blaming anything you're doing on me."

"I'm not blaming anything on you."

And I didn't come to Atlanta because you suggested it. Like the big girl I am, I came entirely on my own," I said, already struggling with patience.

"Mother tells me you're living at some kind of hotel. It's going from bad to worst. I'm hoping we don't look up one day and discover we have a bag lady in the family.

And anyway, what happened at your last residence that made you leave Boston in such a hurry in the dead of night? Were the witches after you?"

I silently counted to ten and answered …"I didn't leave Boston in the middle of the night. It was actually early in the morning. And, if I thought you really cared, I'd tell you what happened, but since I know better, I won't.

Listen, I have to go. Talk to you later," I said, before throwing out a quick goodbye and hanging up. Counting hadn't helped this time.

Then, it suddenly dawned on me that I hadn't been cursing as much as usual. It seemed odd. Cursing was something that nothing inspired in me more than Sylvia, yet I hadn't gone there.

I had been trying to break the habit for years, now all of a sudden it seemed to be going away on its own. Cool.

I had talked with mom the night before on a three-way call with Jason. He had whined and complained about Colorado, but I knew my son well enough to know he was yanking my chain – trying to create some guilt. I wasn't buying, so he finally gave up, and we talked about what he described as my new 'digs' at the B&B in Marietta.

Even Sylvia had agreed that conversation about the witch I had lived with in Boston wasn't in Jason's best interest. I felt dishonest at his confusion over what he described as my sudden decision to leave Boston.

He knew I loved the city, so it didn't make sense to him. I wished I could explain, but how could I? It was something I didn't understand.

As Gail rocked in the recliner, I took in the white, skin, thought of her origins, and tried to feel some resentment at her as the living representative of her ancestors, but couldn't, and smiled.

I was relieved that my experience hadn't clouded my judgement or my perspective about people, or the human condition in general. I would still take people one at a time just as I always had.

"What're you over there grinnin like a Cheshire cat about?" She asked, noticing my private musings.

"Oh, just thinking about some things from the past," I replied.

Just then, Gail's husband, Bill, came into the room with five-year old, Melanie, who was the real boss of the household. She sat down on the carpet near my feet playing with one of their two cats.

When Bill stretched his long form out on the sofa with the day's newspaper, Gail caught my eye and winked. We both knew that in a matter of minutes, he would be asleep with the newspaper still in his hands. It was his evening routine. He would sleep about half an hour and wake up refreshed; most of the time, totally unaware he'd been asleep.

We had eaten dinner earlier. Although Gail was fantastic on a grill, she wasn't the world's greatest cook.

I had selfishly volunteered to bring potato salad and fresh broccoli to add to the menu of grilled steaks and chicken. I had taken Gail up on her dinner invitation one day when I had felt particularly homesick for my family and friends. Now I spent at least one evening a week at their house. If she made her world famous strawberry Daiquiris, I would even stay over.

I usually spent the night on the sofa, but now and then, Gail insisted Melanie give up her bed. We all got along remarkably well, and Melanie treated me as if I was just another aunt.

Sometimes I wondered if she and Bill had me come around so that Melanie would be exposed to someone black on a social level. If so, I was more than happy to be used for something so positive.

"Gail, I hope you don't take this the wrong way, but how is it that you grew up in a truck stop of a town in Georgia, yet from what I can tell, you don't seem to have gotten caught up in the racism that had to be all around you?"

She looked up in surprise then, thought a minute before answering, "I don't really know.

It's just that no matter what went on around me, where that kinda thing is concerned, I always knew better.

Oh, I'd listen to what was said about black people, but I just always knew it was chicken shit.

The Klan even used to come into the schools every now and then to recruit."

"Get out of here!" I said in stunned disbelief.

"No kidding. They used to come and give talks on how great it was to belong to such a fine organization, and would give us literature to take home to our folks."

"Damn, that's deep."

"Yeah. I just always felt all of that had nothing to do with me."

By that time Melanie had drifted back to her room with the cats in tow and Bill was snoring gently.

"Ya know, I went through a lot of shit when I was

184

younger," she said, apparently in a reminiscent mood.

"And none of it had anything to do with black people. I knew they weren't my enemy. I was."

"Why would you say that?

"Well, when I was in my late teens I got caught up in drugs, and was livin pretty fast," she confided.

I came to full attention. Gail and drugs?! I couldn't picture it. She was too solid, too grounded.

"No way. That's impossible to believe."

"It was really bad for a while. I even started some lightweight dealing to pay for my habit; it was on a small scale, mind ya, but it was bad enough."

I was struggling to hide my incredulity.

"What turned you around?" I asked.

"Saw a pusher beat near to death once 'cause he got carried away and used a bunch of the shit instead of selling it. That kinda woke me up."

"What were you on?"

"Cocaine, but I'd take whatever was available," she explained as if talking about the weather.

"I hate to think about the amount of money that went up my nose durin that time."

"I'm glad you came through. I know you're strong, but damn. It must've taken a superhuman effort to turn your life around the way you have."

"It wasn't easy, but I wanted to get somewhere in this world.

I didn't jus wanna live and die and not have accomplished nothin. I've always felt there was something I needed to do. Plus, now that I have Melanie I'd like her to grow up in a nice home, and have all the opportunities I didn't," she said with vehemence.

"She'll have them. Hell, you're her ma, right?"

I had an even greater respect for the determination I had already seen in her.

"Well, there's a lot of self improving I still   need to do," she sighed.

"And that is?" I asked, perplexed.

"Well, for one thing, I've heard myself on a tape recorder, and I sound awful. I couldn't believe the hick I was listenin to was me."

"That's ridiculous. So what if you have a drawl? It's where you came from. It doesn't have anything to do with your intellect, or anything else for that matter. It's just the way you talk. Personally, I think it's charming."

"You know that's true about the intellect, but everybody ain't ... isn't as intelligent as you. Anyway, I'm workin to clean it up."

"Well, if you feel uncomfortable with that part of who you are, I admire your determination to change, although I think it's only an issue in your own mind."

"Talkin about who I am ... have you heard that new song that tells you how to recognize a redneck?"

"No, I don't believe I have," I laughed.

"Well, it's a hoot. When the singer gets to the part about a redneck woman, I swear it sounds just like he knows me.

First time I heard it I nearly choked when he said redneck women know how to change the oil, not only in trucks but, in motorcycles.

I never knew how much of one I was till that song come out," she said, laughing.

I reminded her of the day I had come over and she'd been changing the oil in their truck. She had laughed at me because I hadn't even known where the oil was located in the vehicle.

"Hell, I thought *everybody* knew how to change oil!" She had screeched, and we howled with laughter.

Bill woke up frowning and irritated. "What in the name a hell's wrong wit yawl?"

We fell out all over again. Bill took his pillow and shaking his head, went to bed to escape our idiocy.   It was an evening like many others at their home ... warm and caring.

I thought Gail was a pretty remarkable woman, and she didn't even know it.

———

Chapter 5

"*A*lexis Ashley, please," the caller said.

"This is Alexis," I said frowning at the unfamiliar voice.

"Hey, Alexis this is Charlie, down at The Depot."

"Oh hi, Charlie," I responded, really curious.

"What's up?"

"If you're still not working, you can come on down to the restaurant and work for us," he said.

A puff of smoke could have knocked me over. I had forgotten all about my offer to work for him. Hadn't he known I was under the influence, of both alcohol and stupidity?

I had never done that kind of work, and wouldn't know what to do first.

"Thanks Charlie, but I seriously rethought that idea. I know I said I really wanted to do it … and I do, but I know you need experienced people."

"Yes, but Evelyn will train you. Com'on down in a little while and we'll talk about it.

You're not working anywhere yet are you?"

"Well no, but __"

"We'll be at the restaurant in about an hour. Let's just sit down and see what we can come up with."

Before I could say another word, he said, "See ya later," and hung up.

"What have I gotten myself into this time?" I asked aloud.

I'm not quite sure what happened that day at the restaurant. Somewhere between Evelyn's soft coaxing, and Charlie's conversion back to a drill sergeant issuing orders to a new recruit, I ended up a waitress at The Depot. I was to report for work the next morning for training.

Evelyn told me what I already knew ... that the uniform consisted of black slacks, white shirt, and white sneakers. They would issue the red apron. Luckily, I already had the needed items.

She planned to rotate me between the lunch and dinner shifts, just as she did the other waitresses, most of whom were college students. I would be the only, let's say, mature woman on the staff.

I agreed to do it figuring I would enjoy it as a new and different experience for a couple of weeks before moving on to Atlanta and settling down with a real job.

The rest of the week was a blur. I learned to carry plates; three in one hand and two in the other; how to pour beverages, serve tables, write ticket orders, do side work, set up trays, and most important of all, how to hustle for tips.

I was exhausted both mentally and physically at the end of each day, and it felt great. I learned an enduring respect for a line of work that was by no stretch of the imagination easy.

Still, I had a ball. It was an incredibly liberating experience. When I finished work at the end of my shift, I was really finished. No evaluations to take home and work on; no reports to analyze and act on; no training programs to design and implement. In comparison, waiting tables was actually fun.

My first two weeks were rough, but I gained a new respect for myself because … I could take it.

During this period, I had no idea that I was something of a sensation on the Square. All I knew in those first weeks was that at the end of each shift, I had made it.

There were some bad times, like when customers got up and walked out after learning I was their waitress.

More upset about Charlie losing the business than about my own feelings – since I knew they were asses anyway – I had gone to him after the second time, and offered to quit.

He had laughed and said he wasn't worried about those dumb crackers. "They'll be back, cause they can't get this kinda barbecue anywhere else 'round here."

He was right. All of them eventually came back, and I waited on them many times.

My worst day was the time I spilled iced tea down a woman's back. She had on a sun-back dress and with the air conditioning going full blast, when that ice hit her back, you could hear the howl a block away.

I cried over that one. What did Charlie say?

"Well, I won. We took bets on just what your initiation would be and I hit it right on the head.

I could tell that was your weak spot and predicted you'd spill a drink on somebody, and today's the day I collect. Welcome to the profession."

I cried harder.

Evelyn smacked Charlie and tried unsuccessfully to console me.

Then, there was my feet … swollen for two solid weeks; but there was good news in all of this, which was that after a couple of months, I had lost the extra weight that had always obstinately refused to budge.

I had never done much hard physical work in my life, and surprisingly found there was something about it that was liberating, cleansing; not to mention honourable.

I also learned that waiting tables was addictive. I never figured out why. Maybe it was the element of hustle and having money in your pocket everyday; perhaps not taking any part of the job home; or, maybe it was simply because it was fun. Whatever it was, I loved it.

Working at The Depot changed me in so many ways … all of them good. One of those ways was with music. I had always been a music lover, with the exception of Country and Heavy Metal.

In the restaurant, country music tapes played continuously and in the bar customers played country on the Jukebox.

At first it was maddening, but gradually, imperceptibly, I began to find it more tolerable.

Then, I began looking forward to hearing certain songs. Before I realized what was happening, I was a country music lover, and a big fan of Lee Greenwood who had a song on one of the tapes called, 'I.O.U '.

I thought that song was so beautiful, and expressed such love that every time it came on, I felt like crying. It really touched me and I usually wound up surreptitiously wiping away tears while trying to serve the customers.

After a while the regulars knew how I felt, and got a big kick out of seeing me make a fool of myself.

To avoid their teasing, I learned to make myself scarce whenever I knew it was time for the song to roll around on the tape.

Years afterward when I'd hear 'I.O.U.', rather than my mind turning to thoughts of love and romance, my wet eyes were the result of slippery memories of golden days on an old L&N dining car in Georgia.

Before long, I had regular customers and everybody knew me. They'd come in and holler, "Hey Lexis, what's doing?" Gail said they were all just a bunch of rednecks, but I was oddly at home with them.

There were no pretensions, no superficialities … just everyday folk struggling to get by every day.

They were people who enjoyed the simple things in life. I didn't feel at all out of place on the Square, which taught me a ton about myself.

We had an unexpected crowd one night and the restaurant stayed open almost two hours later than usual. It seemed people were never going to stop coming. I made more money than I ever had in one night, but truly worked for it. Now, home at last, I only wanted to relieve my feet of their burden and stretch out.

After showering, I went to the kitchen, made a cup of tea, came back upstairs and sipped it while trying to finish the novel I'd been reading off and on for several weeks. By the time I read the last page, it was almost three in the morning. Before turning in I ran across the hall to use the bathroom.

On the way back to the room, I caught the movement out of the corner of my eye. My heart skipped several beats then accelerated to the point that I pressed my hand over it in an effort to slow it down. I had hoped for this for weeks and it hadn't happened.

Now, here it was, and I was excited at seeing more of what had happened with the slave woman.

I didn't even mind the slight sickness that usually heralded the episodes.

The figure had been heading toward the stairs. I turned on the stairway light and rushed down, but when I got to the first floor, it was gone. Turning quickly around, I caught another movement at the end of the hall by the backdoor. Of course there was nothing there when I reached the area.

Remembering the other episode where it had disappeared then later re-appeared in the dining room, I thought I would hang around and see what happened. But, I kept looking at the back door. Maybe, just maybe, I thought, it had actually been leaving the house.

I went outside and looked around. Nothing. It was scary being out there alone at that hour, but I went down the back steps and took my bearing.

There was nothing to see but the parking lot, a small garden with benches for the guests, and the tool shed.

Wait a minute; the tool shed.

I really looked at the shed for the first time and realized it was as old as the house. It was well maintained, and freshly painted, but it was quite old. I wondered if …

I walked down the brick path to the shed and stood there a moment making sure nobody was around. I didn't hear or see anything, so I inched up to the door and turned the knob. It was locked.

Then I remembered the key ring in the kitchen. I retraced my steps to the house, slipped into the kitchen and grabbed the ring. Bobbi would definitely need keys to all the doors, so the tool shed key had to be there.

Running back down the steps, I nearly fell and tumbled to the bottom. I slowed down. Walking briskly back to the door, I tried several keys that looked as if they might fit. The fourth one was the charm. I turned the knob and slowly pushed the door open.

Chapter 6

*T*he room was dark and smelled faintly of oil and old leather. Only a dim light fell over my shoulder courtesy of the streetlight a little ways down the block, so I really couldn't see a thing.

Well, this made sense. I didn't have a flashlight and couldn't see anything. Brilliant. I figure there's nothing here anyway. But just as the thought crossed my mind, the room suddenly illuminated.

There wasn't any nausea or dizziness, but when I saw the woman sitting at a table, I knew I was there. She wasn't crying this time, but the look of sorrow now seemed permanently etched on her face.

She was occupied with placing items in a small knapsack, some of which she would stop to lovingly caress before placing it inside.

Suddenly, she turned as if there had been a sound, then rose and hurriedly walked over to a cot against the wall. There was someone in the bed that I couldn't see because they were covered.

Just then, the woman pulled the covers back to reveal a small child, a little girl of about five or six. I immediately connect the knapsack and the tears.

They're selling her baby, I think with a sudden, crushing clarity. They're selling her child.

I don't know how I knew, but I did … and was devastated.

The little girl appeared to be crying in her sleep, so the woman gathered her in her arms and began to sing and rock.

Two shadowy figures entering the room caught me by surprise since I was standing in the doorway; I had to remind myself that I wasn't really there.

The new arrivals, a man and a woman, were also Africans and slaves and by the way they moved around putting things away, this cramped space was apparently all of their living quarters.

Laying the child gently back down, the woman covered her again and moved back to the table where the others now sat.

As soon as she sat down, she covered her face with both hands and with her body rocking back and forth, shook with sobs.

The others, whose features I couldn't really see in the dim light, stared morosely at the floor.

The next thing I knew, the light was gone and I was standing in the doorway of the tool shed staring into darkness. I stood there a moment longer until I could move, then realizing I still had the keys in my hand, backed out of the room, closed and locked the door.

I was hurrying back along the path when I bumped into …

"JIM! Uh, good morning."

The only thing I could do I decided was act as if nothing was wrong.

I was grateful for the darkness as I put my hand with the key ring in it down by my side.

"Are you lost?" He asked. I didn't miss the sarcasm in his voice and wondered had he seen me in the tool shed. Then, decided he hadn't, or he would be all over me by now.

"No, just couldn't sleep and thought I'd take a walk."

"Well, I don't mean to scare you, but it might not be safe to wander around down here at this hour of the morning. As a matter of fact, I thought I heard a noise around the tool shed. We would hate to lose any of the equipment stored there.

Did you see anything?" He inquired, the deep voice rumbling.

"Not a thing," I said. I had decided long ago that Jim Blalock gave me the creeps; with his cold fish eyes, and his apparent distrust of me. Clearly he didn't agree with my living at Stanford House, but fortunately for me it wasn't his decision to make.

Once when Sylvia had called and he'd answered the telephone, she said his voice reminded her of the inside of a tomb.

"Well, I would advise __"

I cut him off ... "Yes, yes, you're absolutely right. I'll be more mindful in the future. Good morning," I said curtly and walked on down the path leaving him staring after me.

Returning to the kitchen I quickly replaced the key ring before he could sneak up on me again.

Back in bed I thought of the little girl and the woman who was so devastated at the impending separation. Somehow I felt certain it was a separation and that they were selling the little girl and could barely contain my rage.

But, rage against who? Everyone involved in this was long since dead.

The more I thought about the situation the odder it seemed. Everything I'd read about slavery indicated masters didn't particularly like to sell children because they didn't bring a very high price.

They weren't strong enough for the fields, and were too young for any serious housework, so it was usually more lucrative to wait until they were older before selling them.

After mulling it over a while longer however, I saw the flaw in my reasoning. Waiting until the slaves were older before selling was probably more practical at larger plantations, which had greater numbers of what the owners thought of as their chattel.

It was maybe less true at a small residence with only three or four slaves used to cook, clean, maintain and tend grounds. In that scenario there would be little to gain from feeding and clothing a child for fifteen or so years before they were old enough to either make a contribution, or fetch a good price.

I deeply felt the woman's pain. Who wouldn't? She was giving up her child to an unknown fate – maybe even death, or giving her up to an existence more horrible than death, and never really knowing. My heart broke for them.

Now, that I had gotten my wish and had seen what was happening to the slave woman, I decided I didn't want to see anymore. It was too painful.

I slept late the next day, but as soon as I got up, I went in search of Bobbi. I found her in the laundry room. Seems the cleaning lady hadn't shown up.

"Good morning, Bobbi. Do you know if there's a more extensive history of this house? You know … something with information about the original owners.

"No, I don't think so; at least, nothing that I know about." She shook her head. "Why? What's up?"

"Well, it just dawned on me that there's a possibility slaves actually lived and worked on this property.

I think the tool shed might even originally have been a slave cabin. I thought it would be great to find out for sure," I concluded.

"Sorry, I can't help you. I wouldn't know where to look."

"That's okay. It was just a thought."

I was disappointed.

I politely spent a few minutes more talking to her about happenings around the Square before leaving.

I knew I could probably go to the courthouse, the library and even the town newspaper to learn more about the house and past occupants.

In the end though, I decided against doing any of those things. I decided that the more I got involved with the lives of the slaves, the greater my frustration and pain.

And, since no amount of my heartache was going to help them, I'd do myself a favor by not getting in any deeper.

That afternoon, I got to work a little early as I often did lately, so I would have time to talk to Sammy, the cook.

Sammy, who had worked at The Depot for five years, was from the Caribbean and although he had been in the states for over ten years, he still spoke with that musically, lilting accent. He was a wonderful storyteller who offered fascinating accounts of life on an island.

After finishing my side work and setting up my station, I would go sit on a stool in the kitchen, and while Sammy seasoned the huge rounds of meat, turned those in the smoker, and chopped vegetables, I would listen to his stories of island life.

Sammy's wife would pick him up each night with their son and daughter asleep on the back seat.

Some nights after work, I'd leave out with Sammy and leaning against the side of the car, the three of us would talk quietly so we wouldn't wake the kids.

They described the beauty of waters so clear you could see the pebbles on the ocean's floor; year round sun cooled by soft trade wind breezes; rolling hills, dense foliage and beautiful flowers.

I never tired of hearing about Carnivals, Steel Pan music, Calypso and Reggae music and the Calypsonians who told satirical, humorous and bawdy stories in song.

I felt familiar with the narrow streets and paths, colorful painted houses, and tourist-laden cruise ships docked in the harbour.

I promised myself that one day, I would visit Sammy's home and see for myself the place that sounded so much like paradise.

As soon as the dinner crowd started coming in we knew it was going to be a busy night. I was running from the start.

By the time I'd get one table's order to the kitchen and get them set up with their beverages, two more tables would sit down. And since I had tables in the dining car and one on the main floor, I was in a frenzy of motion.

One of the bartenders, a woman named Betty had sent her family up, and I had waited on them.

Betty was one of those Georgians I knew harbored something other than love for me, but outwardly was congenial enough … most of the time. I felt that as long as she treated me decently, I would treat her decently.

After my experience in the slave cabin however, I was rarely in the mood for her occasional bad mood and attitude, which always seemed directed at me.

I figured the only reason I had gotten her family was because the other waitresses just couldn't take them. There was her jerk of a boyfriend Jake, her two kids and a man that turned out to be Jake's brother, Richard.

I didn't think about them after I had served their dinner other than to check on them a couple of times to refill coffee and drinks.

After serving their dessert and presenting the check, they were a done deal.

A little later, I ran down to the kitchen to get the food for another two tables, turned around and there was Jake's brother, Richard.

"What can I do to help?"

I hesitated only a second. "You can go to the bar and get vodka and tonic and one Heineken and bring them to me upstairs. Tell the bar it's for Alexis."

He took off while I set up several orders on my tray. I went up on the train car and was dropping the appetizers for one of the tables, and there was Richard sitting their drinks down right on time.

While I dropped the second table's dinner, I asked him to go check on appetizers for still another table. Richard worked alongside us for the rest of the evening as an expediter. I didn't have time to wonder or ask why … I just accepted the help.

Evelyn had shown up dressed in an expensive pantsuit and wearing a ton of jewellery that looked like the real deal.

She had been ready to enjoy the evening by meeting and greeting friends and patrons, but when she saw we were in the middle of a 'hit', she had put on an apron and gone to work. You really had to love these people I thought as I ran past her at one point.

At the end of the night, after I cleaned up my station, did a reconciliation of order checks and money, counted my tips, and turned everything in, I went up front to the bar for a good stiff drink.

No glass of wine for me tonight, I thought, wearily wondering why in the world I was doing this. While it could be fun, this work could also kill you.

I was so tired, putting one foot before the other was an extreme effort.

Richard was sitting at the bar. I had already figured his tip-out and was about to hand it to him when he asked …

"What's this?"

"It's your tip-out for expediting. I can't thank you enough. You were absolutely wonderful. We would never have made it through the night as well as we did without your help," I was genuinely pleased that this stranger had pitched in to help.

"Well, I didn't do it for a tip. I just wanted to lend a hand."

"That's all well and good," but you deserve some compensation for your hard work. Plus, we wouldn't have made the great tips we did without you. So, you made us money."

I tried to stick the bills in his shirt pocket, but he grabbed my hand.

"If you keep this up, you're going to insult me."

I stopped. I had learned that when the people here offered help and didn't look for compensation, it was best not to force the issue. They really would become offended.

"Well, at least let me buy you a drink," I said.

"That would be nice. Won't you join me?"

"Sure," I said sitting on the stool next to him, and noticing for the first time that he didn't have a drawl.

It was Saturday night and the bar was crowded. I decided to have just a glass of wine after all and ordered from Jimmy, the bartender on our end. I was so tired, I was afraid anything stronger might knock me out.

"What made you jump in like that?" I asked.

"Just saw that everybody needed help, and since I wasn't doing anything in particular, why not."

"I've never seen you before. Do you live around here?"

"Nope, saw this town for the first time a week ago. I'm from Cleveland," he said.

"Well, welcome to small town America."

We laughed and he said, "It's not so bad."

"True. I'm here. Can't quite figure out why, but, here I am. No, it's really quite charming, and I feel very much at home here."

"And, you're from…?"

"Chicago," I answered.

Richard's easy-going manner made him easy to talk to, but underneath the quiet calm, I sensed a well-contained nervous energy.

He was tall and thin; around six feet with blue eyes and blond hair streaked by the sun and worn a little long in the back. A full moustache that looked like it didn't quite belong to his face rested above sensuously full lips; a really handsome man.

He was a curious mix of big city sophistication and down home country, and although he wore his attitude, his jeans and boots country, he talked in big city lingo.

I planned to have one glass of wine.

One glass, go home and collapse was the plan, but conversation on the bar was interesting and before I knew it, I had several drinks lined up in front of me.

I found myself lingering and arguing local politics with Charlie, Evelyn, some of the bar's regulars and Richard.

Soon we had the entire bar involved in the conversation and it got pretty hot and wild. Richard, I noticed, was a big joker. Always out to get a laugh, especially when he thought the atmosphere might be getting uncomfortably tense.

Much later, after everybody except a few of the customers were gone, Charlie and Evelyn left asking Jimmy to close up for them.

Richard and I were finishing our drinks when after a lengthy, but comfortable silence he said;

"Something tells me waiting tables is temporary for you."

"Well, that something would probably be right. Is it all that obvious?"

"It is to me. And not because you're not good at it; you're a natural. It's just that I can tell you've probably held positions with big responsibility."

"What makes you think that?"

You delegate like its second nature. Must be a long story how you wound up working in a redneck restaurant and bar in Marietta, Georgia," he said curiously.

"Well yeah, but I'm too tired to tell it. Just take my word ... it's a long and twisted tale. What about you?" I asked curiously.

"Your story must be pretty interesting, as well. I get the feeling you've come a mighty long way in more ways than one.

Let *me* tell your story," I said, and proceeded to do something I hadn't intended.

"You'd like us to believe that you're a pretty simple guy, and a big joker," I said.

"But, we'd be wrong on both counts. 'Cause you're neither. You're really very intelligent and very serious. I see deep pain in your eyes, and a lifetime of struggle and heartache.

Your pain and suffering began as a child and you still carry the scars. Few people know the real Richard; the sensitive and caring Richard that's so skilfully hidden."

I closed my eyes for a second and floated over the hills and valleys of his life. The valleys were deep enough to qualify as canyons, and his hills and peaks were woefully few.

"The scars *will* heal. Trust me," I whispered, passionately. "In time, they'll heal, and the pain will only be a memory. Life has many wonderful surprises in store for you, Richard. You'll find your way, and it'll be your turn for happiness."

When I stopped talking, I was stunned. I could have kicked myself.

I had no idea what I'd been talking about. Didn't understand why I had said those things and was so embarrassed I didn't know how to act.

The silence lengthened. I was trying to think how best to phrase my apology, when he said quietly ...

"Right on every score; how did you know?"

I didn't know what to say. But I looked into his eyes and the pain looked back at me, totally exposed.

Hiding had been his defense and for the moment, I had stripped him of that.

"I'm so sorry. Don't mind me. It's just the wine talking. I'm really sorry," I repeated.

"But how did you know?" He asked again.

"That's the point, I don't know. That was just some senseless, alcohol induced rambling."

He looked at me with the question still hanging

in the air between us.

He was waiting for the truth. Finally I gave in and replied, "It was just f a vibration I picked up on.

Doesn't make anything I said worth a grain of salt."

He stared at me for a moment longer, then said, "It's worth a whole lot more and you know it. Don't try taking it back. It's too late. I guess all this confirms what I felt when I first saw you tonight."

"And, that was?"

"That there was something special about you."

Then, he blushed charmingly, and said something that would endear him to me forever.

"Something different … and I don't mean different from other black people. I mean different from any people … from anybody I've ever met."

He paused and seemed uncertain how to continue.

"Whatever it is," he added, "It's what attracted me to you. That's why I couldn't stand by and see you struggling so hard tonight. I was compelled to help you. Like I didn't have a choice," he concluded quietly.

I didn't know what to say. His little speech was so sweet it was almost painful.

The bar had almost emptied out by then, but neither of us made a move to leave. Betty, Jake and the kids were long gone.

"So, how long will you be here?" I asked to change the subject.

"I don't really know. I'm trying to decide if I'll be staying in Georgia or going back to Ohio."

"Oh, I thought you were just visiting."

"No. Well, in a way. It started out a visit. You see, this is the first time I've seen Jake since I was seven."

"Seven? Wow! How were you two separated … if you don't mind my asking," I said, damning my nosy nose.

"There're eleven of us all together, and we're originally from Tennessee. I remember a pretty nice farm ... nothing probably that special, but as a kid, I remember it as being great.

And even though there were so many of us, they tell me we were doing well. Mom and Pop made us all do chores, and one of mine was feeding the chickens.

I used to love doing that," he said, staring into space as if he could see the farm, the chickens and himself as a little boy.

"Then, there was the accident with the truck, and just like that, mom and pop were gone. I remember the older kids wailing and carrying on, but I couldn't quite grasp what had happened.

They kept telling me the folks were never coming back, but at seven, I didn't get it. We didn't have any relatives close to us, so in the end they farmed us out to different relatives and acquaintances around the country.

A short while after the funeral, almost every one of us ended up with a different relative." The tragedy of it was still clearly in his voice.

"How awful that must have been for you," I said, feeling what felt like every bit of his pain.

"Yeah, it was pretty bad. I'd finally understood at the funeral what everybody had been trying to tell me, and cried every night for weeks; until it finally dawned on me that crying didn't help. Nothing was ever going to be the same again so I figured I might as well stop being a baby."

"Were you all right after that?"

He paused ... "I think I would have been, but the uncle they sent me to live with was abusive. He abused his kids, his wife, and me; me, worst of all.

He never let me forget that I was an orphan, and that I owed everything to him. The saddest part of it all is that he was a highly respected member of the community."

"Did you ever tell anyone?" I didn't ask what form the abuse took. Somehow I knew it was beating and not feeding him.

"Naw. When I was twelve I couldn't take it anymore and left."

"You're kidding?"

"No, I'm not. I was on the street for almost a year before I got caught stealing and was placed in a foster home. I did time in several foster homes," he said with an agonized smile.

"And, you never knew what happened to your brothers and sisters?"

"Not until I grew up. I managed to talk to my uncle's wife without my uncle knowing. She gave me a couple of phone numbers.

I didn't use them for years. I guess I was afraid. After all, I didn't really know these people any longer. I hardly remembered them. So, I just carried the numbers around in my wallet."

"What made you finally call?"

"I got tired of being alone. The telephone numbers were in Tennessee. One day I just called. The bottom line is that I got back with all the kids who had either never left or had moved back to Tennessee.

I went there first, but in the last few months I've been to Alabama, Louisiana, and now Georgia meeting them all."

Richard was seeking the connections to his past. I admired his wisdom in understanding that our futures are built on the foundations of the past, and for a fleeting moment thought about the visions.

"They all ended up in the south?" I asked.

"Everybody but me," he laughed. I'm the only Yankee in the bunch."

"Boy, that must gall them," I said, and we both laughed.

At that point Jimmy made it clear he was closing up.

We laughed self consciously, and I did something that amazed me. I invited him to the house for coffee.

He accepted with alacrity and I found a diplomatic way of making it clear that the invitation was only for coffee.

I saw Jimmy's eyes follow us out of the bar and knew the drums would be beating out the message before we pulled out of the parking lot. Oh well, I thought, if they hassle me about this, I'll just quit.

I felt comfortable taking Richard home at this hour of the night only because I knew that Bobbi was spending the night and probably the rest of the weekend with Mark, and Jim and his band were playing some gig in Atlanta and wouldn't be back until Sunday. I was alone in the house.

Richard followed me and when we pulled up in the parking lot behind the house, I remembered that with the house empty, I'd intended investigating the tool shed more thoroughly with a lantern. I'll just do it another time, I thought.

Richard followed me into the house. I showed him into the parlor and went to the kitchen to make coffee. When I came back I found him at the piano. He was looking down at the keys and I knew he could play. I assured him we were alone in the house and encouraged him to play something.

When he started playing a popular tune that I really liked, I was shocked. Richard was definitely full of surprises.

The playing went well until he hit a sour key, and we laughed. He closed the piano confirming my suspicion that it was seriously out of tune.

I brought the coffee into the parlor and sat on the sofa beside him. At his urging I told him a little about my background and how I had come to be both a temporary resident of Marietta and a waitress at The Depot. As usual, I refrained from any deeply personal revelations.

We talked close to an hour, but finally beyond tired, I told him I was going to have to turn in.

When I discovered he had to drive all the way out to Kennesaw, an area north of Marietta, I invited him to stay the night. He insisted on leaving, and I insisted on him staying.

Finally, he relented and we walked through the house together turning out the lights before going upstairs.

I gave him the honeymoon suite, which was on the back of the house, so his light wouldn't be seen from the street.

After bringing towels for his bathroom, I was leaving when he pulled me into his arms and leaning down, softly kissed me.

His lips lingered on mine. Then, he slightly lifted me off my feet and moving slowly, pressed his lips harder against mine while softly parting my lips for a more passionate, yet still a sweetly gentle kiss.

Everything seemed to move in slow motion during one of the longest, most romantic kisses I'd ever experienced.

Gently setting me back on the floor, we held each other for a moment longer, but not wanting it to go any further, I disentangled myself and we said our goodnights.

I went to my room and for the first time since moving in, it felt empty and cold.

The next morning I was up first, and after showering and dressing, went downstairs and made coffee. I would have made breakfast, but I hadn't ever bought anything that had to be refrigerated.

The first time I had opened the door of the refrigerator, I had closed it in disgust. It was filthy. If the people who ate at Stanford House could see it, they'd sue all those doctors.

Just when I was bringing the tray into the dining room, Richard came in. He folded me into his arms and gave me a proprietary kiss.

"Good morning," he said.

"Good morning. Did you sleep okay?"

"Like a top," he answered. And as he sat down, I apologized for not cooking breakfast quickly explaining that I usually ate out.

"Then, let's go out," he said.

"Well, I don't know," I responded, imagining the good citizens' response to me being escorted by one of their fair-haired boys.

"I do know. I'm hungry, and I hate eating alone. I've done enough of that in my life, so get your purse, or whatever it is you women carry and let's go."

Put that way, I couldn't refuse. I asked him to wait while I made up my room, but what I really wanted to do was clean his room in case Bobbi or Jim returned earlier than expected.

I changed the sheets and blankets, quickly cleaned the bathroom and took the linens and towels downstairs and threw them in the washer.

Finally ready, we took his car and drove to a restaurant off the Square that he said he'd discovered only a few days before.

Aside from the fact that we were stared at from the moment we walked out of the house until we got back, we had a great time.

Before leaving, he kissed me once more and asked me out that evening. I accepted.

Since I was off that day, and we were both movie lovers, we decided to take in a movie and have dinner. He would pick me up around six.

When I closed the front door I walked past a mirror in the lobby and stopped to look at my reflection.

I looked big-eyed and wondrous. Staring myself sternly in the eyes I asked aloud.

"What in the name of heaven are you doing? Trying to get your self lynched?" I shook my head and walked on.

No matter how hard I tried, I couldn't think of Richard as a white man. To me, he was just a man; a gentle, sweet man who deserved a break.

And although I knew I wasn't that break, I hoped he would find what he was looking for one day.

I hoped we both would.

Chapter 7

"*Y*ou're a what?"

"A waitress ... a food server ... Oh hell, I'm a waitress."

After a pause that was too long to bode well.

"Alexis, you know I try to support what ever you decide to do ... but this?"

"I know it sounds strange," I agreed.

"*Sounds* strange? Do you know how many people wish they could have your education and background? How many people pray for an opportunity to do something other than wait on tables and sweep floors for a living?"

"It's ... it's an experience, mom; the chance to get to know how different people live differently.

Probably the reason I enjoy it so much is because I *can* do something else."

"I don't agree with a lot of the stuff Sylvia has to say about a lot ..." she stumbled, and I interrupted her.

"About me; a lot of the things Sylvia have to say about me. You can go ahead and say it. It's okay."

Anyway, I don't always agree with her, but this time, I'd have to go along with what I know she's going to say about you taking a job as a waitress. What you're doing is just plum nonsense!"

"You're allowed to your opinion, the same as Sylvia. But, regardless of what you think, in the final analysis, what I do with my life is my decision. Your understanding … at least your support has meant more to me than I can ever tell you. I can't complain if I lose that now," I said.

"Look mom, I wish I had an explanation for some of what's happening to … with me, but I don't. I just know that I need to keep moving ahead, and even if the choices I make seem strange, good or bad, they're the ones I'm making."

There was a long silence on the other end.

"You don't have to get an attitude. You know I'm always there for you.

It's just that you're not twenty-one anymore. This is the time you should be building for a solid future, not playing at being a waitress in some town in Georgia."

"How do you know I'm not building my future?" I sighed, despairing of ever finding peace while being confronted with the things I was experiencing.

For one wild moment I thought I'd just tell her everything and get it over with. I thought of her reaction, and the moment passed.

I'll settle down. I promise, I won't be moving round like this and doing things that seem weird forever."

"I hope you're right, honey."

I wanted to ask her something, but didn't want to freak her out.

I had to be careful because if she had any idea what I was going through, she would be on the next plane to Georgia, and I definitely didn't want that.

Listen, about the veil … uh, can I ask you something?"

"Sure, but I don't know a whole lot about it."

"What happens to people born with the veil? How do they usually end up?

Are they treated like weirdos, you know, like the village idiots? Do they all have strange experiences? Do you know anyone else born this way?"

Once started, I couldn't seem to control the questions. They shot out one after the other with the speed of bullets.

"I've heard of a few people who they say was born that way, but other than you, I've only known one personally."

"Who was that?"

"Eva."

"Not your *friend*, Eva?"

"Yes."

"But, she's normal," I said with relief.

"Well of course she's normal; except, she can tell things about the future. But then, few people know that. She never wanted to be treated like she was different, probably the same thing you're worried about right now, so other than her family, I'm one of just a handful of people that know.

I hadn't known Eva when you were born; otherwise I doubt I would have had the reaction I did to your being born with the veil.

If you're worried about other people …you and I are the only ones who know since your father passed.

I think it should stay that way."

"Sure. You're right."

"What's the matter, Alexis? Are you having strange experiences?"

Strange was an understatement, I thought wryly.

"No, I'm fine. I was just curious, that's all." I hadn't answered her second question. Luckily she didn't notice. By the time we hung up, I felt she was a little calmer about my new lifestyle.

Unfortunately my own frustration and confusion wasn't at all appeased. I was growing more bewildered by the day and only managed to hold on because of the notion that at some point I would understand what was happening to me.

I prayed this would happen before I lost my mind.

Much to my surprise, Richard and I became a couple. Well, not in the intimate sense … at least not yet. We enjoyed spending time together. We'd take in a movie, go to dinner and sometimes just take long walks.

One of our favorite places was a river close to where he lived in Kennesaw. We'd sit for hours on the dock by his house hanging our feet over the water and talking about his plans to start a business, and his greatest goal, which was to one day have the family he'd never had.

At the beginning of our relationship, my co-workers had many dire warnings about how Richard was a drifter and no good. I thought that was funny. I wasn't a drifter?

Everything was a double negative. I'm sure he was receiving similar warnings about me.

The first time I brought Richard to Stanford House when everyone was there, I thought Blalock's eyes would pop right out and land on the floor.

Bobbi was so confused, she didn't seem to know whether to flirt with him, or hit him.

It might have been humorous had it been happening on a TV Sitcom, but unfortunately, it was real. Richard was embarrassed by it all. Poor thing, he tried to take personal responsibility for all of their bad behavior. In the end, we simply tried to endure.

Although he never elaborated, he said enough for me to know he was catching hell from his family.

These were the sons and daughters of the south. I'm sure they felt he was embarrassing them in front of the community and probably told him so on a regular basis. At the moment, though, we seemed to need each other more than we needed everyone's good will.

It was Richard who told me I was something of a sensation when I first started working for Charlie. It seems I was the first black person, man or woman, to work on the Square with anything but a broom and mop, or a skillet in their hands.

I didn't think waitressing was much of a far leap from cleaning and cooking, but apparently people on the Square thought so. At first I actually thought Richard was kidding, but he was dead serious.

He jokingly informed me that I was dragging the Square into the twentieth century kicking and screaming.

Although this information gave me an even greater respect for Charlie, I didn't flatter myself that I was really seriously changing things. I understood the psychology behind, "one or two, maybe so ... three or four, hell no!"

Time rolled by and neither Richard nor I made a decision about moving on.

Richard had gotten a job in construction working with Jake and I knew he was happier than he'd ever been in his life. He and Jake – a redneck in a negative sense – were nearly inseparable.

I knew that for Jake, I was the only fly in the ointment. Betty was so pissed about our seeing each other she had nothing to say to me aside from work, which I actually considered a bonus.

As for Richard's and my relationship, it was definitely bizarre. To think that I had met and started going out with him around the same time I was introduced to African slaves who had once lived, toiled, and probably died at Stanford House, was the ultimate irony.

Was there something in particular to be gleaned from the experience? I didn't have a clue.

During this period, I occasionally thought of Metcalf and our one evening together. Strangely, I still had feelings for him, but that relationship had been doomed from the start.

It was as hopeless as my relationship with Richard was beginning to feel. There were just too many obstacles to be ignored for long.

One day, I decided to do something I hadn't done since coming to live at Stanford House and since I'd started dating Richard; I planned to cook us a wonderful meal.

There were no parties planned and no guests registered for the weekend I chose.

Bobbi was spending the weekend with Mark and had left me in charge of the house, which I thought was a joke.

She had told me that there were no registrations, and the answering machine could catch calls if I wasn't there. I didn't bother to ask about walk-ins. If she felt comfortable leaving, I felt comfortable with her gone.

I wondered how they managed to keep the place open. Bobbi did very little to attract new business, which was one of her responsibilities, and the thin occupancy rates had dwindled even since my arrival.

Blalock too had gone off somewhere that I suspect had a woman attached, so I was alone.

Richard liked Italian, so I was cooking Lasagne, Caesar salad, garlic bread, and was conceding to our environment by making a pecan pie. It was a complete surprise. He thought we were going out to dinner.

When he walked into the dining room and saw the table romantically set with candles, and champagne cooling in the ice bucket, he was shocked. All through dinner he kept saying how great it was, and that nobody had ever done anything this special for him. It made me want to cry.

After dinner he helped me clear the table, but when he started to put the leftovers in the refrigerator, I stopped him. He asked why, and I told him I was sending them home with him because I refused to use the refrigerator.

He opened the door, looked inside and couldn't believe his eyes. I had cleaned the stove inside and out, had cleaned the counters, and had scrubbed the floors before cooking, but I refused to touch the refrigerator.

"Get me a pan of water," he said taking off his shirt.

"What are you going to do?"

"Clean this mother out."

"No, it'll just end up like it is now in a couple of weeks."

"Alexis, get me a pan of warm, soapy water. Do you have any baking soda?"

I got the soda, and he went to work.

As I helped him take everything out of the reeking fridge, I discovered foods that had grown colorful whiskers. Once he started cleaning in earnest, he tied a handkerchief around his nose.

He soaked, scraped and peeled, and in the end conquered the filth. After more than an hour, I was able to place my food inside a beautifully clean refrigerator.

When finished we danced around the kitchen like two nutty children. Then, we went into the parlor to relax and finish the champagne.

I took the opportunity to quiz Richard on how things were going with his family. I had noticed a certain strain the last couple of days; a preoccupation that was unusual for him. I had an idea what was wrong, but I wanted him to tell me.

"So, how goes it with the folks?"

"It goes," he said, his mood suddenly changing.

I was quiet a moment, but when he didn't continue… "You wanta tell me about it?"

"Tell you what?"

"Com'on, Richard, I can read you like a book. What's up? Spill it."

He laughed and said ... "Yeah, ya can."

"It's about me, isn't it?" When he didn't answer, I continued, "We've always been honest with each other. Let's not stop, now."

Then, when he told me, I was so shocked I almost wished I hadn't asked.

"You're right, you should know."

He cleared his throat nervously. I didn't push, and presently he said, "I've been told that if I continue to see you, I could end up with a bullet between my eyes."

The pain of the threat was written on his face, and told me he didn't feel it was idle. I had jokingly made reference to that kind of threat once, but I had been halfway kidding. I was stunned.

Then, after thinking about what he'd said for a moment, I felt there was something that didn't add up.

"Something about that threat just doesn't ring true, Richard." I paused ... "They didn't threaten to kill *you*. You're one of them.

They said they were going to kill *me*, didn't they? That's the only reason you're telling me. So I can be careful. I'm right, aren't I?" I pressed.

At first he wouldn't answer or look at me.

Finally, he took both my hands in his and looking directly into my eyes, said... "Let's get married. Let's get married and move back to civilization. We could go to Ohio or Illinois; it's your choice. We could probably even live in Atlanta in some peace."

"Don't count on it," I replied dryly.

"And, the answer is no. I wouldn't marry anyone under these circumstances. And running away certainly isn't an option. Leaving your family after being separated all these years is absolutely out.

I know how much you've come to love Jake. Well, maybe you don't love that one side of him we've discussed, but he's the big brother you never had and always wanted.

And what about the plans the two of you have to start your own contracting business? No Richard, I know exactly what you'd be giving up, and the price is much too high for me to ever live with."

Then it was Richard's turn ... "Listen, I love you, Alexis, and I have no intention of losing you. If we go ahead and get married, they'd have to come around in time; at least those close to us. They'd just have to learn to live with it."

"Boy, I think I know these people better than you do, and you're one of them," I said.

"Remember, your brothers and sisters didn't grow up with you. You only recently came back into their lives. If you left them now, I suspect they may be able to cut you out of their lives and just chalk you up as a misfit. They're never going to accept me ... not even twenty years down the road. I'd never accept them either ... now."

And on we went for the next hour until I finally put an end to the discussion.

"Richard, if we'd been together longer, or had made serious commitments to each other then, I might agree with you. I'd say to hell with them – I'd be your family.

But, it isn't like that. Sure, we're attracted to each other ... okay, we may even love each other, but our relationship is still at a point where we can let go. Let's do that.

Let's just let go before someone gets hurt. I believe if it's meant for us to be together, nothing will keep us apart in the end. Let's just let destiny decide if we'll be together."

"That's bullshit! I'm not going to be told what I can't __ "

"Okay, I'm not arguing anymore. If you don't agree that we should stop seeing each other, I'll just have to leave. I'll pack up the car and drive out of Marietta one day soon and you'll never see me again. I mean it, Richard. One day I'm just gone."

In the end he wearily agreed. He didn't have a choice. We talked a little longer, but tired and despondent, we finally turned the lights out and walked slowly, sadly up the stairs, arm in arm.

How could I have known that my lovely evening would turn into our goodbye; but, would I have rather not known?

Once upstairs, Richard kissed me and we clung to each other with mutual desperation. Then, he let me go and headed off to the room he always slept in when he stayed over.

I watched him walk away feeling more wretched with each of his steps.

"Richard," I called softly.

He turned around and I nodded my head in the direction of my room.

As he walked back to me his smile warmed my heart.

Chapter 8

*L*ife after Richard had no zest. I had known I would miss him, but the void he left was like a knot in my chest that painfully throbbed with every breath. The last night we spent together had definitely been a mistake. Richard had breathed life into a part of me that had been dormant for so long I'd almost forgotten it existed.

Afterward, it was harder than ever to turn away from him. But, I'd think about the threats, remember where I was, and held firm to my decision.

It nearly killed me. But, in my heart I knew that what we were doing was for the best.

If I was wrong, I felt certain that no obstacle would separate us forever.

I had been on the Square for over a year, and had lately found myself thinking more and more about making a move.

It seemed that my break-up with Richard had been the first in a series of downwardly spiralling events that seemed destined to lead to my departure.

The first of these had taken place shortly after we stopped seeing each other.

To my shock, Stanford House closed its doors as a bed and breakfast. It happened so quickly I didn't see it coming until it was almost over. I'm sure that Jim and Bobbi had known, but of course they hadn't told me until Bobbi, unintentionally I believe, let the cat out of the bag.

It was a Sunday and I had come in while she was cleaning up after a big anniversary party. I stopped to give her a hand. Maybe she was grateful, because out of the blue she blurted out …

"At the end of the month Stanford House is closing down."

"What!? Closing down?" I parroted. "You're kidding!"

"It's been on the market a while now, and the owners feel they're losing too much money trying to keep it open until they find a buyer, so they're closing."

"What does that mean for you?" I asked.

"It means I'm looking for a job," she answered.

"Hey," I said, thinking belatedly of myself.

"What does that mean for me?"

"Nothing. Unless you just feel like leaving. They said you could stay. Why not? It's revenue.

They're going to continue with the weekend parties and weddings, so the house will be open for that anyway, and your monthly rent probably pays a bill or two," she explained.

There was no discernible sadness, anger, not even relief in her voice or on her face. She was just as deadpan as ever, I thought unkindly.

"So, who's going to host the parties?"

"Jim," she answered.

"Oh, pleeze," I said, before I could stop myself. The maintenance man? It was going from bad to worse.

"Well, they thought he already knows the house and how the parties work, and has to stay to keep the house maintained anyway, so they wouldn't have to pay anyone else, plus I think he wanted to do it," she said.

"Good for him," I said dryly. I wasn't relishing the thought of living alone in the same building with Jim Blalock who had such total access to everything.

On the other hand, he had never bothered me in any way. So, I decided to see how things went.

That had been over a month ago, and things had gone well so far, except that Jim was beginning to throw off those signals that said, 'Why don't we get to know each other a little better?' Yuk!

At least he hadn't made any real moves. Just the same, I sadly acknowledged that my time at Stanford House was surely drawing to a close.

The second thing that happened was Charlie's heart attack. He had the attack about a week after Stanford House closed.

Although he was a slim bundle of seemingly boundless energy, and had the appearance of excellent health, all those pork and beef years had probably taken a toll on his arteries.

They had to do bypass surgery. Evelyn was frantic, and the whole Square was abuzz with the news.

After the surgery, and reports that everything had gone well, there had been some pretty serious celebrating at The Depot and on the square.

Thankfully, to everyone's relief, Charlie was expected to make a full recovery. If he ever doubted how everyone felt about him, he could rest easy.

I had been the assistant manager of The Depot for some time, so when Charlie's son took a leave from his accounting job to manage the restaurant, I familiarized him with everything ... except the books, which had always been Charlie's domain.

After a while, I began to wonder if Charlie was ever coming back. I knew he couldn't continue to run both businesses, and this one was by far, the most demanding, and perhaps, the least lucrative.

I suspected they were going to sell, but nobody had mentioned anything to me yet.

I had asked Richard not to come to The Depot for a while to give us a chance to adjust to the idea of our separation.

Of course, he ignored me; at least at first. But it was so uncomfortable with everyone watching to see what was going to happen between us when he came around, he finally did stop coming.

I stopped socializing at all on the Square. I figured it was more Richard's world than mine, and knew he would be going out with Jake and Betty and their friends, so I gave it up and began driving into Atlanta occasionally.

He still called me now and then, and we'd talk like old friends, but I knew the calls would eventually taper off.

Gail became my port in the storm. When I'd told her I wouldn't be seeing Richard any more, she had hugged me, and asked what happened. I replied that it had been decided by certain elements of our society.

She hadn't been surprised. She told me she had held her breath the entire time Richard and I were together, praying that nothing bad would happen.

"This whole thing is just really ridiculous!" I said, finally venting the pent-up anger.

Eventually calming down, I asked,

"Why didn't you ever mention your fears?"

"I don't exactly know."

Then, after thinking about it for a minute, she said ... "I guess partly because I was shame to be living in a place where people acted like that, and partly because you two were so happy, I hated to put a damper on it."

We never discussed Richard after that. She just stuck closer to me than before, inviting me over more often; on family outings, and doing what she could to help keep me occupied.

I hadn't seen any more of the slave family, and was hugely relieved.

I didn't want to get in the way of another heart-wrenching scene.

Except for a second brief episode in my bedroom one night, there were no more visits to times past for quite a while.

But, just when I was rejoicing and thinking maybe I could control the visions, it began to happen again ... and this time, I didn't just see slaves.

There was a whole new cast of characters.

Chapter 9

I was slowly learning my way around Atlanta. Sometimes I would drive in on my off days and stroll the shopping malls, or go over to Little Five Points, an area reminiscent of New York's Greenwich Village, but on a much smaller scale.

There were the usual weird sights and costumes, but also many talented artists displaying their work along the streets.

It was there that I learned about a nightclub on the south side of the city. Several people had recommended it to me, saying it was *the* place for mature, not to say old, folks to gather.

So, one Friday night I gathered my courage, drove into the city, and after losing my way twice, finally found the club tucked away on a dead-end street.

It was evidently so popular they had a parking attendant directing traffic in the parking lot.

After parking I went inside and was pleasantly surprised. The building was actually an old two-story house that had been converted into a clubhouse. There were rooms for different activities, like a billiards room; several small, intimate bars; a private 'members only' club; and the main nightclub with a huge dance floor.

Outside, near the swimming pool and patio a small restaurant in a separate little building sold some of the best fried fish I'd ever tasted. The club had a warm, easy atmosphere that I immediately liked.

Feeling a little self-conscious walking in alone, I quickly found a table and sat down. I was glad it was still early, and was relatively empty. But, only a short time later, the place started to fill. Before long I was sharing my long table with several friendly people.

I like this place, I thought. The music was R&B with some Caribbean and light jazz thrown in for good measure. When the disc jockey slid into some Whitney, followed by Patti LaBelle, I was in heaven.

A number of couples started to dance and the evening kicked into high gear.

I sipped a glass of wine while watching the dancers, the women's fashions, which was a show all by itself, and the good-looking guys in the crowd.

I had the long drive back to Marietta and was restricting myself to two drinks, which actually was about all I drank at one time anyway.

A short time later an attractive man passed the table, stopped and turned back around while scanning the room either for friends, or a place to sit down. Our eyes connected.

A couple of people called to him, both voices feminine I noticed, and he waved a hello.

He then came straight to my table and asked if he could take the vacant chair. I indicated that it was fine with me, and he sat down.

"I'm Simon," and extended his hand.

"Alexis," I said, shaking his outstretched hand.

"Nice crowd tonight," he observed.

"Yes, it is. But then, this is my first time here, so I don't have anything to compare it with."

"This is your first time here? You must be from somewhere else. Everybody in Atlanta's been here ... at least once, he said.

That was an exaggeration, I knew. Not everyone partied the same way.

"I live in Marietta, but I'm actually from Chicago," I responded.

"Why do you live way out there in the boonies?"

"Just happened that way," I said, not feeling like defending where I lived.

"So, did your job bring you this way? To Georgia?"

"No, it didn't. I just wanted a change."

"So, what do you do for a living? He asked, not skipping a beat. Well, that took less than three minutes, I thought a little disappointed. But, maybe I'm jumping the gun and he really is genuinely interested in knowing about me.

"I'm a waitress," I answered.

"I work at a restaurant in Marietta called The Depot. Ever heard of it?"

The look of shock that registered on his face couldn't have been any more horrified if I'd said I was a serial killer.

That was followed by a look most likely reserved for the hopelessly insane, who disguising themselves as normal people show up at places like this just to annoy people like him.

"No I haven't," he answered with a frown.

"Hey, it's good you're working," he continued, and patted my hand before turning his back to me. Before the next song came on, he was gone.

I was left to assume that admitting to being a waitress must be an inexcusable faux pas.

Well, so much for that; one jerk down, I thought.

After a while another fellow came over and leaning down said.... "As pretty as you are in that red dress, you should be on the dance floor showing it off."

There was little need for further coaxing. I love to dance, but hadn't been dancing since long before leaving Chicago. Once on the floor, I saw he was good and that we were well matched.

I was really getting into it when he suddenly sidled up to me, and leaning down whispered in my ear ... "So, what's your name?"

I told him, but not asking his, just continued dancing. I hated it when guys tried to rap while dancing. When I'm dancing, that's all I want to do. We can talk about the birds and the bees when we finish.

I moved a little away hoping he'd get the message. He didn't. Back he came.

"So, Alexis, what do you do?"

I ignored him and kept dancing. What was it with these people? I moved away again. He came after me. Obviously dancing was only a means to an end.

"Let's see if I can guess. You're a model."

When he got no response, he unfortunately continued, "I know, you're a businesswoman; miss corporate America. Am I right? Which one of those late model BMWs outside is yours?"

I didn't mean to do it; it just happened.

It seemed that of its own volition, my naughty foot rose up and came down on top of his foot.

"OOOUUUCCHHH!!!"

Everybody around us stopped dancing for a couple of seconds craning their necks to see what had happened.

"Oh, I'm so sorry. Did I step on your foot?"

"Ugggahhh," was his gurgling response as he limped back to the table.

"No, really, are you hurt?" I asked, knowing that his pride was paining him far more than his foot.

"Honestly I can be so clumsy sometimes."

"I think I'm okay," he finally said, as he wiggled

his foot around.

"No lasting damage? You sure?"

"Yeah, it's getting better already."

"Good, let's finish the song," I said.

He backed away mumbling something about going to the bar for a drink.

I had to stifle my laugh because people were still looking at us, but couldn't hold it in as I watched him make his way across the room *away* from the bar.

Later I saw him leaning over a woman at a table across the room. A sore foot obviously wasn't going to detract from his mission … zeroing in on a likely target.

I tried to feel remorse for what I'd done, but just couldn't muster any up.

Nobody else asked me to dance. I guess they were afraid that the same thing might happen to them that happened to the first guy.

But, I didn't mind. I knew by now this wasn't my scene. I enjoyed the great music and watching the dancers and after an hour or so, happily retreated to my more familiar world of haunts and time warps.

The time finally arrived when staying at Stanford House was no longer an option. The day of this revelation began like any other, except that I hadn't felt well all morning.

It wasn't anything in particular, just a feeling of malaise and occasionally a slight feeling of nausea.

I feared I was coming down with a virus, and stayed in bed a little longer that morning.

Later, I made myself a nice brunch, which I enjoyed. But, after eating, I felt a little sick to my stomach. I just need some fresh air, I thought.

Instead of going to sit on the front porch, I went out back, just in case I became ill and couldn't make it inside in time. I didn't want to upchuck in sight of the neighbors.

I sat on the back steps, and before long was engrossed in the lovely Georgia day. It was one of those times when the sun is so brilliant it seems to spread a magical glow over everything it touches.

Sitting there on the steps my mind wandered back to Boston, and what it had been like when I first saw it through the rain.

Suddenly, between one thought and the next, it started. The day changed from bright sunlight to overcast and cloudy and the yard, empty only seconds before, now seemed filled with people.

The yard was twice its present size reaching far beyond the back fence that now enclosed the property.

I tried my best to stop it. I could hear myself moaning with the effort to rise, but it was no use. As usual I was frozen in place, forced to witness until the end whatever was revealed to me.

A horse-drawn wagon with two white men on the driver's seat pulled slowly into the yard. Eight to ten slaves of different ages sat huddled in the back.

One of the men, with a rifle draped over his arm kept a watchful eye on the wagon's occupants.

A well-dressed man that I had seen in a previous vision and who looked to be in charge, had apparently been waiting in the yard with several other men.

The man, that I suspect was Stanford walked up to the wagon and began to converse with the two men on the driver's seat.

After a brief exchange one of the men jumped down and followed Stanford into the house. Everyone else waited in the yard.

After a moment, the slave woman came out of the tool shed leading the little girl by the hand.

No! I don't want to see this, I thought.

The child carried the knapsack the woman had been packing that night in the tool shed. The woman's face was a mask of pain, while the child simply looked bewildered.

Looking around, I counted four adult slaves in the yard, which was in keeping with my earlier projections regarding the number of slaves the family probably owned.

As they stood watching with grim faces, I could plainly see the rebellion and anger they felt, but even I knew that everyone there had weapons, but them. I hoped I was not going to see something more horrible than I could imagine.

The driver, who still sat in the wagon watching, abruptly jumped down, walked over and snatched the child from her mother's arms.

He quickly looked her over … I suppose searching for signs of disease or illness, and apparently not finding any, pointed her to the back of the wagon and walked away.

The minute he released the child she ran back to her mother, who breaking down, lifted her up and embracing her tightly sank to her knees.

I had read somewhere that selling slaves to slave traders was often worse than selling them directly to another slave owner or at auction. I remembered that part of the reason for that was their unbridled cruelty.

The driver reached the kneeling, crying woman and child in several long strides.

He grabbed the child's dress by the back and yanked her from the woman's arms.

At that, I could see the little girl must have let out a howl, which he met with half dragging, half pulling her to the back of the wagon.

The woman rose from her knees and before anyone could stop her leaped through the air and landed on the trader's back taking them both down in a cloud of dust.

The other slaves surged forward, but then stopped abruptly.

Glancing at the group of whites I could see several cocked pistols aimed at them. Yet, the pistol holders made no move to help the trader.

The two grappled on the ground for a couple of moments, and then disentangling himself, the trader regained his feet and backing up reached for something on his waist.

In one fluid motion, a small whip unfurled and snapped in the air. Almost instantaneously the woman's cheek split open and dark red blood spewed out instantly covering the ground and her clothes.

The other slaves grabbed her, and dragging her to her feet, began forcing her back toward the cabin.

She fought like a tiger, but to no avail.

The trader snatched the child up, walked around to the back of the wagon and literally tossed her inside as if she were a sack of flour.

"What's the matter with you? Hey!"

I felt a shake of my shoulder.

"What's wrong with you?

I jumped to my feet wiping my tears with the backs of my hands. I looked up into Jim Blalock's face, and with all the anger and sadness I felt at that moment, said with emphatic coldness.

"Don't touch me! Don't you ever touch me!"

I turned and ran into the house, giving in to the torrent of tears I couldn't hold.

The next day I profusely apologized to Jim, telling him that I had been remembering a distressing episode from my past.

He, of course watched me like he expected me to jump up brandishing a weapon and screaming like a banshee, which I could totally understand.

I told him I would be leaving Stanford House in a week, which was how long I had given myself to find somewhere else to live. He seemed relieved and to my surprise, concerned.

I wondered briefly if I could have misjudged him, but thought not.

He probably thought I was crazy as a loon and didn't want me to completely lose it there with him, so he was being uncharacteristically kind.

All things considered, I had to admit I appreciated his kindness. He could have responded just the opposite.

I was anxious to leave now because I definitely did not intend witnessing another of the visions, at least, not at Stanford House.

If memory serves me correctly, they severely punished slaves for the type of behavior I had observed.

If they didn't shoot the rebellious soul on the spot, then they whipped him or her to within an inch of their lives, or applied some other equally barbaric form of punishment. I simply couldn't bear it. I had truly had enough.

The final irony, I thought ... I can't bear to witness what my ancestors had actually lived.

I could only hope they would deem that having her face sliced open and losing her child was punishment enough for her errant behaviour.

Chapter 10

*A*s if in confirmation of my decision, the same day I told Jim I was leaving, I went to work and discovered the restaurant had been sold.

After meeting the new owners, a married couple, I knew I was out of there. They were some piece of work. They seemed to have some kind of love-hate relationship with each other that was frightening to watch.

She sucked up glass after glass of vodka gimlets, yet never seemed drunk, while he spent each day eyeballing the women, including me, with her constantly trying to catch him at it. I could see where this was going and it wasn't any place good.

They made pretty speeches and spoke to each of us in private.

They told me they were depending on me to stay on board as manager for which they would compensate me well ... once they were up and running with the business.

I could have laughed out loud. I cut my business teeth on seriously slick characters in the boardrooms of Chicago, and could recognize empty promises from a mile away. I thanked them and submitted my resignation.

I gave them two weeks' notice, but explained that I would leave earlier if they found a replacement for me. I actually planned to leave in a week.

Several others had chosen to leave as well. One of them was Sammy. I was sorry that his happy association with Charlie and Evelyn was coming to an end, but he surprised me by explaining that he would be returning to the Virgin Islands.

He said they'd never been really happy away from the island, and had already lined up a job at home.

He seemed about ready to burst with joy and I was happy for him. He gave me a telephone number where he could be reached on the island and invited me again to visit. I promised him I would shock them both by turning up one day.

I had decided to move on to Atlanta. My priority now was finding a place to stay.

I confined my search to an area called Virginia Highlands that wasn't far from Little Five Points. It was an area of big, old homes, some Victorian, some not, but all loaded with character and charm and were mixed in with apartment buildings clearly from the sixties era.

Only the facades were left on some of the buildings that had been mercilessly chopped up into apartments. Most of them, now a little on the run-down side, were still clean and well maintained.

After a search of several days I found a suitable place in one of the old apartment buildings that had large, sunny rooms. I would need to purchase at least a minimum of furniture.

Purchasing furniture made me feel bad because I was making that specific commitment to the city out of necessity, and not because it was something I really wanted.

My last week at the restaurant felt like a period of mourning. Everyday I said goodbye to little pieces of it. One slow afternoon when there was just a couple of us working, I looked up to see Richard coming in the door.

He was with a pretty brunette, and judging from the way she looked at him, I knew they were a couple.

He hadn't called me in quite a while, but I'd heard that he and Jake had started their own company, and right from the start had been doing well. That news alone was justification of my decision.

As I approached them I could tell she knew who I was. She tried to adjust her features to what she thought was appropriate, and finally giving up, simply looked away.

"Hey, Richard," I said, smiling to myself as I noticed the automatic 'hey' in my greeting.

"Hey Alexis."

They sat down, and Richard introduced us.

She turned to me and I looked deep into her eyes. Richard said he'd heard I was leaving and had come by to say goodbye and wish me well, but while he talked about he and Jake's new business, I was swimming around in his girlfriend's eyes.

I didn't know where their relationship would take them, but I knew for a fact that she was a good person and wouldn't deliberately hurt anyone, especially Richard.

It occurred to me later that for the first time I had consciously read a person. On some unconscious level I had been doing it all the time, but it hadn't been effective because those times I hadn't acknowledged that what I felt was real.

Later, when Richard was leaving, he came back over and gave me a big hug.

"I'll never forget you," he whispered.

"And, you think I'll forget you? Never," I said, meaning it. "Have a great life, Richard."

"You too, Alexis; and who knows, we could meet again."

"Oh, we will … we will," I said with an absolute conviction I didn't understand.

I watched as they left. One of the gentlest men I've ever known, I thought, as a solitary tear slid slowly, smoothly down my cheek.

The Friday night before I moved, Gail spent the night with me. She had volunteered, bless her heart, to help me move the following day.

The lunch shift I worked at The Depot that day had been my last. Theresa, the wife half of the new owners, hadn't given me a dinner shift since I'd resigned.

We made more money at dinner, so Charlie had always rotated it evenly among all the girls to give everybody an even chance.

Already she was giving more dinner shifts to the ones she liked personally; those who she thought were the least physically attractive to her husband.

I had only worked a week of my notice because Theresa hurriedly gave the management job to one of those waitresses. She had asked for my recommendation as to who to promote. I had given it to her, and she had done just the opposite.

Again, someone she liked rather than someone who would do the best job. I felt sad for what would surely be the eventual demise of a solid part of life on the Square.

I had said goodbye to Charlie and Evelyn over dinner one evening at their home. Charlie, still recuperating, had dinner in the living room on a bed tray while reclining on the sofa. Evelyn and I had sat in easy chairs and used TV tables for our plates.

They were surprised I had known about being the first black person hired on the Square to do the kind of work I did for Charlie. I told them I understood it had taken a great deal of courage to go against the grain and thanked them for so many happy memories.

Charlie was his usual salty self, saying …

"Oh, give me a break. I didn't think one way or another about the folks on the Square when I hired you, so you can forget all that courage nonsense. I hired you because I knew you'd do a great job."

Unfortunately, I had been the first and last black person to enjoy that particular community largess, but I knew that was going to change.

Despite the few people fighting it, the little community would continue to change and develop.

My last day, I was given a little afternoon party at The Depot, and many of my regulars came by to say goodbye.

I received many little keepsakes, although I would never need anything to remember them by.

When I left, they played 'I.O.U.' several times in a row and it was still playing when I walked out the door for the final time.

I was crying so hard, I could hardly see how to get down the steps and knew memories of my days on the old L&N dining car would be forever punctuated with the sounds of Greenwood spilling out his heart at high volume. Marietta, the L&N dining car, Gail and Stanford House would always occupy a special place in my heart.

When I got home I finished the last of the packing and cooked dinner. Gail loved steak, so I had cooked Porterhouse steaks, twice baked potatoes, spinach salad, and Butter Pecan ice cream for dessert.

I had taken the family out to dinner a number of times and it was always frustrating because she wouldn't try anything new and different; it was always steak.

And, since I wanted tonight to be her night, it was steak. The only thing I wanted her to do was make the strawberry Daiquiris.

By the time she arrived, I had everything in order. My boxes were ready to go. I had acquired a few things since moving in, like a rocking chair, a desk and a few more kitchen appliances. Otherwise, it was the same boxes and television I had brought from Chicago.

After dinner we sat in the parlor with our drinks trying with a sense of futility to freeze-frame our memories. I told Gail that one of the times I'd always remember was the night I almost got mugged or attacked.

She laughed and said, "Oh yeah," I don't guess either of us will be forgettin that night. I was madder'n hell."

It had happened one evening after I'd been in Marietta about six months. I had gone to pick up some books a waitress from The Depot was giving away. She lived in one of those nice, but huge subdivisions with the winding streets that formed a puzzling maze.

When I finally found the house, I'd had to park a little distance away, which bothered me because the area was pretty dark.

As was often the case in unincorporated suburban areas, the residents were responsible for street lighting, and many times I had found myself searching for someone's home in almost complete darkness, or with a flashlight.

When I got up to the house, she had left a note saying she had to leave unexpectedly, but had left the books in a bag on the porch.

I had picked them up and was on my way back to the car when suddenly a man rushed up behind me.

He grabbed me tightly by the arm forcing me to drop the books and pressed something that felt like it might be a gun to my side.

"Don't scream!" He fiercely warned, and began pulling me towards a wooded area behind the houses.

Don't scream? Was he nuts, I thought. Then, I totally surprised him by jerking my arm out of his grasp with all my might. Once free, I took off down the street screaming at the top of my lungs.

When I looked back, I saw a figure dressed in dark clothing and a baseball cap, running in the opposite direction. Luckily I was running toward the main road. Once there, I ran to a pay phone, called Gail and told her what had happened.

I told her I was afraid to go back to my car, and my co-worker wasn't home so I couldn't go there.

Gail drove all the way from one side of Marietta to the other in record time. When the pickup pulled up, I jumped in still trembling. But, instead of going directly to my car, she said ...

"We're goin to drive around and see if we can't find that sonofabitch. He wants ta hurt somebody huh? Well, let's see him deal with this." She patted something on the seat.

I looked down and there was the biggest rifle I'd ever seen ... up close.

"Gail, what are you planning to do?"

"If you spot him, I'll drive on past, park the truck and walk back down the street like I'm heading home. If he comes after me, I'm gon blow his ass up, that's what I'm gon do."

"Gail!" I was shocked. "You can't do that! It's wrong!" I had never met the angry, pistol toting, Gail.

"Oh, relax. I'm not gone kill him. Just shoot him in both legs, so we can hold him till the police get here.

Don't worry, I'm a great shot," she'd added, totally serious.

"Oh, well that makes me feel so much better," I'd intoned sarcastically. It had taken a bit, but I'd finally talked her into giving up the idea of finding the thug.

She had reluctantly consented to driving me to my car and waiting until I had gotten inside before we both left the area.

"Were you really going to do that if I hadn't talked you out of it?" I asked now.

"What, shoot him?"

"Yes."

"Damn straight. You know everybody's got to be involved in keeping the streets safe. If I could've done somethin to take one dangerous asshole off the street, I'd have considered it a privilege."

"You know you're a nut case," I said, laughing so hard the tears welled up.

"Well, we've always known that," she laughingly replied.

Gail and I stayed up half the night talking. We promised to keep in touch and vowed we would still get together on the weekends, but deep down we knew it wasn't true. With her job and Melanie and Bill to look after, she would seldom get into the city.

I knew we both would try to keep the relationship going, but even the best intentions would eventually succumb to job pressures, other commitments, like dating (I hoped), and just plain fatigue at the end of a long work week.

I thought about Brenda. Yes, we would keep in touch, but it would never be the same in terms of the closeness we now shared, which made me feel sad.

After Gail turned in, I walked around the house taking it all in for the last time; imprinting it on my brain so that years later I could close my eyes and call it all up.

I wondered what had happened with the slave woman all those years ago, and with the Stanford's and wondered what other stories these walls would tell us if they could talk.

I recalled an evening, not long before the last time I had seen the slave woman and child. It was an episode that had actually introduced me to the Stanford's.

The day had been a joyous one at Stanford House, which had been the site of a large, rather rowdy wedding reception.

I had been hired as one of the servers by the wedding coordinator, a woman who was a regular customer at The Depot, and had enjoyed myself as much as any of the guests, most of whom I knew.

When it was over, I helped Jim clean up, and then had gone upstairs to spend the rest of the afternoon and evening doing uninteresting things like my hair, straightening my room, and later, catching up on my laundry.

When finished, it was late and the house was quiet. Bobbi had long since moved out, and Blalock had returned to his sanctuary downstairs after we'd finished cleaning. I was putting laundry away when suddenly I felt the dizziness.

They appeared right in front of me. Sitting before the little fireplace was a man and woman that I felt were probably the Stanford's.

It was the same woman who had threatened to slap the slave woman that day and the man I would later see in the back yard with the slave trader.

The couple both wore dressing gowns, she with a satin nightcap on her head. A small fire was burning merrily, leading me to believe it must be either the fall or winter season.

They sat across from each other in matching wing chairs. While her hands were busy with some type of stitching, he read by the light of a lamp on the table between them.

I wondered why they would have this bedroom, which was by no means the largest in the house, then realized that the connecting doors were open. I realized my bedroom had been part of a suite of rooms.

Their bedroom was actually through the open doors while the room we were in, which was my bedroom, had actually been their sitting room. The two of them weren't talking, just sitting companionably. I studied them with interest.

The woman was younger than I thought when I'd seen her that day in the dining room. Without the bonnet and her face not screwed up in anger, she didn't look particularly cruel, or even mean. She just looked ... regular. So did the man. They looked like any couple you might see in any period of time, anywhere. They were just ordinary people.

I wondered if their treatment of the slaves stemmed from a conviction that the Africans weren't really human and therefore, didn't have feelings. I shook my head with sadness. How had intelligent people convinced themselves of something so ludicrous?

The answer of course was economics.

For the more humane among slave owners, that rationale promised an attractive, even moral expediency that allowed them to prosper, free from castigation. Of course, there were others who didn't require a rationale.

Like all the episodes, that one had lasted only a few moments. When it was over, I was racked with the questions that had become tiresome in their redundancy. What was this all about?

There was no doubt that there was reason to the madness ... but what reason? Would I ever learn the truth, or was I condemned to spend the rest of my life experiencing these vignettes from the past without a whit of understanding what it all meant.

Unable to sleep, just as this night, I had put on my robe and like a ghost myself, had drifted through the house. I had felt the heartache and tragedies endured by those like me within the walls of Stanford House through the passage of time.

It was clear that although reconciliation seemed impossible, at some point it would come; it would come because it already dwelled in the hearts of men.

That night I had slept fitfully and dreamed. I know I dreamed, but to this day cannot remember what the dreams were about.

I only know that when I awoke the following morning, I had received what I felt could only be divine confirmation of the reality of all I had seen and experienced; assurance that I was not in danger; and that further revelations would be forthcoming.

There was also the troubling confirmation that I had been right about feeling more than one force at work. In actuality, there were two forces, but I was not to dwell on that fact.

I understood that everything was indeed connected to the veil and that I was being directed to continue this journey leading to a specific destination.

There was also the pressing feeling that at some point something was going to be required of me; something important. I had felt my spirit bathed in the words, *"faith and patience"* and understood that both were important to my continued well being. I just had to have faith. And I knew I did.

I awoke crying with relief and new understanding. The dream had ultimately provided a measure of calm, as well as the capacity to continue my day-to-day existence without plunging into madness. I felt that I had been thrown a life jacket.

Now, as I remembered that night and the dream and thought of the visions I had witnessed, particularly since coming to Stanford House, I felt a tremendous sorrow.

I would never know what happened to the woman or her daughter, but knew that I could at last forgive myself for being unable to help them when they needed it so desperately.

After all, my response … nearly a hundred and fifty years after the fact would be irrelevant.

Chapter 11

I settled into my new home in Atlanta, and after spending much of the first day cleaning, slept the first fitful night on a pallet on the floor. The following day I went shopping and bought a bed, a small sofa and chair, a few dishes, some curtains and area rugs.

I told myself that in time, I would buy all the things that make a house a home. I never did. My apartment always had an, 'I'm just passing through' feel. I was always conscious of the feeling, and always anxious to disregard it.

The next week I went job hunting. Since I only knew what I didn't want to do, it was difficult finding something. Waiting tables was definitely out of the question. That special period had passed.

Eventually I got a response to an application I had submitted at one of the major convention hotels in downtown Atlanta.

The job was for a catering coordinator. During the interview a job description had been provided, and I'd known it was too clerical to hold my interest for long, but I had never worked in a hotel, and wanted to see if it was as glamorous as portrayed in the movies.

It only took a few days to learn that the glamour was strictly reserved for vacationers, conventioneers, and television programs. For the rest of us, it was a job.

I worked in one of the business offices, and for the first month or so, seldom even ventured into the rest of the hotel. I was much too busy trying to keep afloat in an overwhelming sea of work.

The catering department consisted of the director, three catering managers and me. So, in reality, I worked for all three managers. It was terribly unfair, as well as impossible, which made me wonder how the previous coordinators had fared.

I decided to reorganize the department. The sales department, in close physical proximity to catering, had a coordinator and two secretaries working with several sales managers, as opposed to catering which only had me. No way, I thought.

First, I did my research. For days, I went through old files, and reviewed past events.

I discovered exactly what I thought I would; a multitude of every conceivable mistake, and some pretty imaginative cover-ups.

I devised a workflow chart that would, to a degree, combine the sales and catering departments. Part of the plan involved creating a typing pool to service the two departments, and it continued from there.

I knew that lightening the clerical load would free me to live up to my title as coordinator of the catering department.

Lightening the workload would also allow me to change some long, outmoded procedures. In my proposal, I outlined what the new organization would mean in terms of efficiency, and increased revenue.

When I turned it in to Phillip Sawyer the catering director, I knew by the next day that he would try to make my life miserable. His expression had clearly asked, 'who the hell do you think you are'?

After that, he did what I pretty much expected, he held onto the proposal for a month, without comment.

I asked him about it several times, but he claimed he had been too busy to really examine it, but would get around to it soon.

After the fifth week, I submitted a copy of the report to the assistant manager of the hotel, Jacob Bell.

Three days later, we were all in a meeting. The plan was adopted two weeks after that.

It all turned out well, but I realized that might not have been the case. It could have failed miserably. Like Phillip, they might all have felt I was too big for my britches.

Had I really cared about the job, I probably would have been more cautious, but I figured if all their attitudes had been that they wanted me out ... I would simply have left.

Phillip was fit to be tied, but covered it nicely with smiles and patronizing, insincere compliments. Then, he set out to undermine as much of the plan as he could, but I had learned how to protect my back in the corporate trenches. He didn't stand a chance in hell of causing any real damage.

I also hadn't endeared myself to the women in sales. Their department head had tried to shoot the plan down, but in the end, even he had to admit it created a more effective, efficient operation.

Not the best atmosphere to begin a new job, and normally that would have bothered me a great deal. For some reason, it didn't. I was pleased to have done something to help the person that would come after me, which would probably be a woman.

As I suspected, I never fit into the fabric of life in Atlanta. With the passage of time, I doubted there would be any deep and lasting attachments like Gail and Brenda, and absolutely nothing resembling romance. None of which was surprising. After a point, I knew in my heart that I really was just passing through.

What *was* surprising was that I no longer had visions. No going back in time, no slaves, no masters, nothing. It was like a new lease on life. Apparently the visions had been triggered by location, and I had finally chosen someplace innocuous, someplace without the requisite history.

During the Atlanta period I simply marked time. Then, quite unexpectedly, all the bits and pieces of my life began falling into place in a way that would lead me to the next step of my journey.

It all started with a promotion.

I had worked hard to implement my new plan, and it had paid off. I was no longer chained to my typewriter, and had time to make other needed changes.

Phillip and I had settled into, if not a comfortable relationship, at least one that was mutually respectful. In short, we stayed out of each other's way.

As a natural by product of the plan, I had penetrated other areas of the department taking over some of the functions of the catering sales force. At first they had resisted, but it soon became apparent that they had more time to go out and make sales. More sales meant more clients and more money.

A few months later, one morning after our weekly staff meeting, Phillip asked me to wait after the others had left. I really became curious when Jacob Bell came in and sat down.

The upshot of the meeting was that they offered me a promotion to the position of catering sales manager.

I was flattered. After all, promotions are recognitions of good performance. The problem was I didn't want to get back into that rat race.

It had been bad enough dealing with the power plays that resulted from my reorganization.

The dust had settled from that after a few weeks when everyone's common sense had kicked in. But, to accept that sort of thing as a steady diet again ... I didn't think so.

I was diplomatic; I expressed my delight at being invited to move up, but made it clear that I was content with my present position. I promised to think about it over the weekend, and let them know that coming Monday, which was satisfactory to both men.

That evening I was in a quandary. I rocked in my rocking chair with the television on, and my mind far away. I hadn't expected to make a career out of my position at the hotel and had primarily reorganized to make my job easier.

Now that the offer had been made, however the financial factor made it impossible to simply brush it off.

The increase would almost double my present salary, and since much of the nest egg I'd left Chicago with had hatched and taken wing long ago, money was indeed an issue. But, even with all those considerations, I knew the promotion wasn't something I wanted.

I went to bed that night troubled. I knew Sylvia would blow a gasket if she knew I was thinking of refusing such an offer.

Mom, too, would be hard pressed to understand. I had to keep reminding myself that they weren't the ones that would have to live with my decision.

That was the first night I dreamed of the Caribbean. The next morning, I didn't have a clear memory of the dream, just an impression of warm, sugary sand, breezy palm trees and Caribbean music.

The following night I had a similar dream, only this time I remembered more when I awoke. I was on a Caribbean island walking down a lovely heart-shaped beach carrying my shoes in my hand and feeling warm, damp sand squish up between my toes.

Someone was with me. His face was in shadow, but he was someone I knew. He stood right next to me, and although I couldn't see his face, I had never felt happier in my life.

Suddenly, another man jumped in front of us blocking our path. The man stuck a folder in my hand and said ... "We expect a complete and thorough analysis of this report in the morning. Please include an action plan based on your findings."

He turned and walked away and I was devastated. For some reason this work meant I had to leave the island and the man at my side. I awoke in a panic.

As I showered the next morning, I knew I would not accept the new position. The dream had somehow given me the answer I needed and oddly, I didn't dream about the island that night.

At work on Monday, I requested a meeting with Bell and Phillip. In the meeting I again expressed my gratitude for the consideration, but declined the offer.

Phillip nearly went into shock. He half rose out of his chair then plopped back down. He was so surprised it took him several minutes to recover.

I knew he thought I was a 'climber', and that had been the motivation behind my changes. Now, he was confused.

I had expected turning down the promotion would somehow put an end to the island dreams, but to my surprise, it didn't. I still had them.

I dreamed of soft Caribbean nights, and warm, sunny days at least three times a week. Now, I was the one confused.

Finally, just to get information, I called the Tourism Bureau in the Virgin Islands, Sammy's home. I explained that I was thinking of visiting and asked if they could send information. I felt quite satisfied when I hung up, as if I had really accomplished something.

Then, a couple of days later, I did something that I thought was strange indeed. I called the Chamber of Commerce in the Virgin Islands and requested information on businesses and employment.

By the time I hung up the telephone, I understood my motivation clearly; the Virgin Islands was calling me. That realization, as bizarre as it was, brought a feeling of incredible relief and from that point, the dreams stopped.

There were times when I wondered if I had lost my mind while other times I felt that moving to an island in the Caribbean was perfectly sane.

I recognized that same compelling force that had drawn me to Boston, and later to Georgia was again at work. Slowly the picture gained definition.

I had sent résumés to all the islands' major hotels, and the responses I'd received were positive. Everyone wanted to set up interviews, if not for current positions, at least for future possibilities. I began looking in earnest for a place to live.

Whenever that fell in place I was prepared to move quickly. I had casually mentioned to Phillip that I was thinking ... just thinking, I told him, of relocating.

He had nearly become hysterical. In a matter of weeks, I had gone from being his worst enemy to his best friend. I told him that if anything happened to solidify my plans, I would let him know immediately.

Then I called Jason. His response to the news that I might be moving to the Caribbean was an attitude that implied ... so, what else is new? When I spoke with Mom, she had been a bit more outspoken.

"Are you crazy?" She had shouted, sounding exactly like Sylvia.

"No, I don't think so," I had replied.

"Alexis, you know I've traveled a great deal in the Caribbean ... Jamaica, the Bahamas, you name it. How many times have I said if I were rich I'd move to one of the islands?"

"Lots of times," I answered dutifully.

"The reason I said that, Alexis is because it's not easy living in those places. The cost of living is ridiculously high, and it's an entirely different lifestyle, not to mention a different culture.

The living is rough. This isn't like moving to Boston or Atlanta. You won't be able to get in your car and drive to a different city if you run into trouble."

"Mom, I know I'm worrying you sick with all this moving around, but believe me, I feel that every move has been the right thing to do." An explanation that sounded anemic even to me.

"Well, I'm through worrying," she said.

"This is it. I can't believe you're going to do something this … this … outrageous. You don't know what you're going to run into down there."

And so it went. I felt terrible.

I felt that I was being such a pain to everyone, but I didn't know what to do to change things except deny the intuitive feelings – and compulsions that now seemed to characterize my life.

The turning point, when I was forced to set aside all the angst and jump into action, came when I found a place to live.

I had called on a house-sharing situation, and spoken with Sarah, the woman who had run the ad. She was looking for a housemate to share expenses.

She lived in an area called Frenchman's Bay, which I didn't know from any other, but she assured me was a very nice area.

We sort of interviewed each other on the telephone. I noticed that she didn't have an accent, and assumed she was from the States, as well.

Sarah was concerned when I explained that I didn't have a job on the island yet, but when I told her some of my background, she seemed to relax. I assured her that if necessary I could wait tables.

She had laughed and said that with my experience, she was sure it wouldn't come to that.

The house had two bedrooms, each with its own bath, and a great deck, she said.

Then, she asked if I liked dogs. When I said I did, she was relieved because, she said she had a dog.

Picking up the vibrations through the telephone, I knew that I liked her and that she felt the same about me.

We went ahead and clinched the deal with my promise to send a deposit and references that she should feel free to check.

We ended our first conversation with my promise to call back with my arrival date.

After Boston I had promised myself never to live with anyone on a roommate basis again, but somehow I knew this was different, plus I seemed more capable of picking up on a good or bad vibe these days.

Maybe I always could, but had never paid any attention until mom had explained the veil. In any case, I was prepared to give it another try.

The next day, I put in my notice at the hotel and at my apartment complex. Then, I did what nearly everybody in that community does on Saturdays at one time or another ... I had a yard sale and sold all my furniture.

My television, unbreakable kitchen items and linen I was shipping by air. I sold the car through a newspaper ad, and it was like parting with a family member.

I thought of the drives to Boston and Georgia, and got teary-eyed. She had been with me through so much and had served me well ... parting was difficult.

Unbelievably, a little over two weeks after my first conversation with Sarah, I was on an airplane headed for the Virgin Islands. Again, I was full of anticipation and high expectations.

The difference between the start of my journey to Boston and now, I thought, is a conditioning to handle whatever comes along.

I was certainly more confident. I had been through a lot since the early days of my journey, but was glad that my spirit was just as open and receptive and as full of trust as ever. I believed that regardless of how crazy and scary things were, it would all work out in the end.

Later, I couldn't believe I had still been so naïve.

BOOK III

St. Thomas, U.S. Virgin Islands

Be merciful unto me, O God, be merciful unto me:
for my soul trusteth: yea in the shadow of thy wings
will I make my refuge, until these
calamities be overpast.
Psalms 57:1

Chapter 1

*F*rom the sky the ocean was a deep, mystical blue, but when the shoreline came into view before landing on St. Thomas, the water turned a translucent and beautiful shade of deep turquoise.

When the airplane landed and I walked down the steps into the bright sun, the heat hit me like a solid wall. For a few moments, I felt like I was suffocating and frantically wondered what I was doing on this island, but gratefully, right about that time, the trade wind breezes I had heard about kicked in and cooled me down.

When I reached the ground, I stopped and stood staring at Sammy's hills; green slopes chequered with colorful houses.

As people brushed past, I continued to stand transfixed by an eerie sense of familiarity with a place I had never seen and only recently had heard about. I had an odd feeling of inevitability combined with a peculiar sense of homecoming.

Of the four major islands in the Virgin Islands chain of St. Croix, St. Thomas, Water Island and St. John, I had chosen St. Thomas only because it was where Sammy lived. I hadn't a doubt it was the right choice.

I finally gathered myself together enough to move in the direction of baggage claim where Sarah, who had kindly volunteered to pick me up, and I planned to meet.

I had explained that I had about fifteen boxes that would be on the same plane with me. She hadn't felt we'd have a problem fitting them into her mid-sized car although I tried to tell her it wouldn't work.

As I watched the luggage pass on the carousel, I kept a watchful eye out for the cut-off jeans and white shirt she said would identify her. After collecting my bags and stacking all my boxes around me, I carefully counted them.

Everything was in order, so I settled down to wait. A little while later, I looked up and spotted a woman with cut-offs rushing across the terminal. Even from a distance, I could see she was gorgeous.

A knockout figure that was slim, yet curvy and a honey hued complexion added up to looks that could rival any high fashion model I'd ever seen. In fact, a little more height probably could have placed her on any runway in the world.

As she hurried towards me, a profusion of long, reddish brown hair bounced wildly around her head and face, in both a contradictorily childish and charming fashion.

Practically skidding to a stop at my feet, she said, "Hi." Her slightly slanted green eyes questioned.

"Alexis?"

"Hey," I returned. "Yes, I'm Alexis. How did you know?"

"The boxes. Who else would be sitting here patiently waiting, practically covered up by all these boxes," she said, flashing a perfect smile.

"Oh, I forgot about the boxes," I laughed.

"Well, I'm happy to meet you. Welcome to St. Thomas, Virgin Islands."

"Same here and I'm happy to be in St. Thomas."

We were comfortable with each other from the beginning. As I suspected, she was wrong about the car holding the boxes, so we hired a taxi to carry some of them and we carried the rest.

On the drive from the airport, we passed the harbor in Charlotte Amalia and it was pure majesty. Cruise ships lined up at a dock across the bay had disgorged thousands of passengers who filled the streets and the colourful shops to overflowing.

Once through town we were driving up and down hills so steep, I was light-headed and breathless, and more than a little bit afraid but, pretended not to be.

The island is so beautiful, colourful and exotic; I can clearly understand why it is called "The American Paradise".

The house, when we arrived, sat below street level so I couldn't get a good look at it when we first drove up. After parking, I had the impression of an unassuming, smallish white house with a bright red roof.

When the boxes were unloaded and the taxi paid, Sarah led me down the steps to a brick walkway that led to the front door.

When she opened the door, I was totally unprepared for the spacious, beautiful house we entered.

In the large foyer, the first thing I noticed was that the flooring was a beautiful white tile, which immediately brought to mind movies I'd seen in tropical climates where the homes and buildings always seemed to have similar flooring.

The second thing I noticed was that one vast open space contained the living room, dining room and a chef's kitchen with the work island in the center of the large space.

All of this was enclosed by floor to ceiling sliding glass doors that covered two walls and brought the outdoors right into the house.

A sensational wrap-a-round deck and a panoramic view of the ocean was postcard perfect. The bedrooms, on different sides of the house, were marvelously separated by the foyer, and true to Sarah's description, each had its own bathroom.

My bathroom didn't have a tub, just a shower, but Sarah said I could use hers anytime I wanted.

It was all so spectacular I couldn't believe my good fortune. I walked over to the sliding doors and opened them, intending to get a look at the ocean from the deck.

"No! Wait!! Sarah yelled too late.

With the door halfway open, I looked back to see why she was screaming, when I heard a low rumble similar to distant thunder.

It sounded like ... I turned slowly around and sure enough there was this huge dog with a bass growl, baring its teeth at me. My mind went to the dog on the highway and I felt faint.

To make matters worse, this wasn't just any dog, it was a Rottweiler for heaven sake. This was the pet? The dog rumbled again, deep in his throat.

"Okay, Buddy. It's all right, boy."

She came around me and going over to the pony-sized animal patted him on his big head. It may be all right with Buddy, but it's not alright with me, I thought. While she murmured soothingly to the dog, I began a slow retreat.

"No, don't leave. Come here and pat him."

"Pat him?"

"Come and make friends with him. He likes women, he just doesn't know you," she said.

I figured she could have told me the family pet was a Rottweiler it might have had a little to do with my decision to move in.

But, certain that she didn't want me dead, I did as she suggested and sure enough the brute turned out to be a sweetie.

Before long he plopped down and rolled over on his back, so I could give his massive belly a good rub. What a pussy I thought, completely won over.

Mollified, I finished bringing in boxes and went to my room to begin the arduous task of unpacking while Sarah made sandwiches for lunch.

When we sat down to eat, she told me she worked for an import company and hated it. The money was good though, so she said she was trying to be practical and stay put until something better came along.

I learned that Sarah was a curious mix of the old and new worlds; she was half Japanese and half Caucasian. Although born in Japan, she had spent many years in the States, had been on the island for nine years, and was intimately knowledgeable of all three cultures.

Sarah's boyfriend Don, on the other hand, was a third generation islander, and although of Irish ancestry, she said he didn't feel much connection to that distant homeland.

Sarah didn't really own the house; it actually belonged to friends who had moved back to the states after a pretty bad hurricane some years earlier. After repairing the damage to the house, they had arranged for Sarah to live there, pay some of the bills and look after the maintenance while they high tailed it to Florida.

With the help of a housemate to share expenses, she had managed quite well, she said, until the roommate had recently married and moved out.

I, in turn, told her about Jason, mom, Cliff and Sylvia, and about how I had left Chicago to move to Boston, and was still on the move.

"It's so beautiful here, perhaps this is where you'll put down roots," she said.

She had no idea how much I wished that would be the case.

Suppressing a yawn, I told her I'd been up half the night and it was catching up with me. At the moment, a shower and a nap was worth more than gold.

"Well, we take military showers here," she said sounding apologetic.

"Okay, I give. What's a military shower?"

"Turn the shower on and get wet then turn it off and soap and wash, and turn it on again to rinse off."

"And that's to … "I looked at her questioningly.

"Conserve water," she answered.

"And, water is that much of a problem?"

"Oh for sure. Most people here use cisterns for their water supply."

"And a cistern is a kind of underground container, right?" I was remembering some of what Sammy had told me about cisterns and how they worked.

"Right, except they can be built above ground as well. Anyway, the water in cisterns comes primarily from rain.

When it rains, the water that falls on the roof is guided down pipes into the cistern. When it doesn't rain for a long time and your cistern is low on water, or empty, you have to buy water."

"*Buy* water?" I had never heard of such a thing.

"Yep. Buy it from private water companies that come out in big trucks and replenish your cistern supply. It can get pretty damned expensive, so like most islanders, we're into conserving water."

"And, does this happen often? Needing to buy water?"

"Not really, but we've just come through a drought," she answered.

"Oh."

"I'll bet you're wondering why we have such a water problem when we have that big ocean out there, aren't you?"

"First, it's salt water, and also because it's full of bacteria?" I answered, like a good student.

"Exactly … which means it has to be desalinated and purified. It's an expensive process, so whether you get your water from a cistern or live in town and use the city's water supply, at some point you're going to have to pay."

"Oh," I said again.

"Wanna hear a cistern story?" She continued.

"Sure" I said, not really sure at all.

Going out on the deck, she said, "Come here."

I followed her outside with Buddy lugging along after us.

"You see that house down there with the blue roof?" She pointed down the hill.

"Yes, I see it."

"They found a dead body in their cistern."

"Oh stop. That has to be a joke," I said, as my stomach did a sickening lurch.

"No, no joke. The family decided to have the cistern water tested because they kept getting sick with infections and all sorts of stuff, and didn't know why.

Finally, they took a sample of the water to a lab, and sure enough it had an unusually high level of bacteria. So, they called out cistern cleaners who drained the old water out before cleaning it and refilling it with fresh water. That's when they found the body."

"That's disgusting. Tell me, does that kind of thing happen often?" I shuddered and involuntarily glanced at the kitchen faucet.

"If it did, I'd be forced to check my cistern every day. That was unusual, but it did happen."

"Did they find out who it was?"

"Not to my knowledge."

"Well, thanks for sharing that fascinating bit of island lore," I said.

She laughed, and added … "Oh, another thing … we don't flush the toilet every time we use it either."

"Come again? You don't flush the toilet?" I asked, idiotically.

"Not, every time … say like when you tinkle. It takes about five gallons of water to flush, so we don't flush for number one."

"Gotcha. Anything else?" I asked, revolted at the thought of not flushing a toilet after each use.

"Oh, and about doing laundry; follow the front walk around to the left side of the house and you'll walk right into the laundry room.

Try to limit doing laundry to only once a week."

"I know. Water, right?"

"Right, water.

"And that's about it." She smiled, seeming quite satisfied at having properly indoctrinated me.

I thanked her for the information, and went to my room with mom's words ringing in my ears: "Living there is rough. You don't have any idea what you're getting into," she'd said.

Okay, so it is rough. No problem. I can handle this, I thought. I had no idea at the time just how rough it was going to become.

On Monday I had several hotel interviews lined up. The first two properties I went to had me fill out applications, but there was nothing available.

I wasn't discouraged. There were plenty more hotels on the island, and if that didn't work, there were a few other options.

At the third hotel, I learned there was an entry-level position in the wedding department. It wasn't exactly what I had in mind, but it was work and a foot in the door of the local hotel industry.

The job involved working with couples planning to use the hotel's chapel to tie the knot. And if there was a reception, we'd handle that as well.

The chapel was outside on a little hill with an amazing view of the ocean and some of the out islands and was an idyllic location for weddings.

I filled out the application and the secretary explained that the assistant manager of human resources would be with me shortly. I thanked her and picked up a magazine.

A few minutes later I heard the door open and looked up. A lovely young woman entered the room wearing a nametag that identified her as the assistant manager.

She was about late twenties, fair complexioned with a short curly haircut. I smiled warmly and stood to greet her.

As she walked towards me however, my smile faded. There was something not quite right about the woman.

There seemed to be something lurking just beneath the surface of the friendly smile; something sinister.

I couldn't tear my eyes away from her, and as I continued to stare, the something that I'd sensed suddenly shifted and I could see it;

I recoiled in terror at the horror that stared back at me with both recognition and malice.

Chapter 2

*T*he band moved smoothly from reggae to the faster rhythms of calypso. After several months on the island, I flowed as effortlessly with the change in cadence as if I had been dancing island style all my life.

My partner, who had moved away, pulled me back to him and we cut a pattern across the floor that left me slightly dizzy as we turned this way and that, our hips swaying with the beat, our bodies moving in perfect unison.

When the music ended, we broke apart clapping, laughing and winded after a good half an hour of straight dancing.

Now here, I thought, were people who loved dancing purely for the sake of dancing. If there were other motives to be pursued, they generally took a back seat to the first order of business.

This Sunday afternoon beach party was my favorite thing to do since arriving on island.

It combined some of the best aspects of my new home: a beautiful beach; Caribbean music and dancing; happy crowds of tourists and locals celebrating the joys of life in a lovely environment.

The party was held at one of the Island's resorts under a covered pavilion that housed a small stage, a tiled dance floor and a sunken bar.

Partygoers moved back and forth between refreshing dips in the ocean and even more strenuous workouts on the dance floor to live band music.

One of the best elements of the weekly event was that it was equal parts visitors and residents.

My anonymous partner escorted me back to my table where Sarah, Don and two of their friends sat watching and enjoying the dancers while sipping on Bushwhackers, a delicious, but potent island drink.

"Say, you sure you weren't born here?"

Sarah asked laughing when I dropped into my chair almost winded.

"Sometimes I feel as though I were," I shot back.

As I picked up my own drink and thirstily sipped, I thought about the truth of my reply. I had adapted to the culture, the people and the island itself with an ease that was astonishing.

The unaccustomed hardships did nothing to diminish my absolute love affair with my new home: not the constant conservation of the precious water, the sky-high cost of living, and not even the mental adjustment required to live on a few square miles of land surrounded by water.

'The Rock', as St. Thomas is called is for all its good and bad points, my home.

A woman I had met several weeks earlier interrupted my reverie, calling …

"Good afternoon, Alexis!"

"Hey there," I called back.

"Glad to see you made it today. I missed you last week."

"Yes, last Sunday I went to a wedding. It was very nice, but I missed being here," she said, making her way to the table.

"I *heard* that," I answered, laughing. "Sit down," I invited.

"No, I'm with friends over there," she pointed to a table across the pavilion.

"I just wanted to say hello," she said already moving away.

"Glad you did. Enjoy!" I called, as she melted into the crowd.

"You too!" She yelled back.

Her name was Mina and I'll never forget how we had met. It had been several days after the terrifying incident at the hotel, and I was still in a state of paranoia about everyone and everything.

Actually, after that incident was the first and only time I had seriously felt I was on the verge of a breakdown. Afterward, I had taken to avoiding looking directly into anyone's face for fear of what I might see. I really felt myself coming unglued.

The evening I met Mina, I was eating dinner at a restaurant on the waterfront, and although the place was packed, I had lucked up and gotten a window seat with a view of the harbor.

While still savouring my good luck, the waitress had come over and asked if I'd mind sharing my small table with another person. She made it clear that I didn't have to, but how could I refuse? I agreed and thanking me she left and returned a few minutes later with Mina.

I realized that at such close quarters I could hardly avoid looking at the woman, so I had steeled myself and when she sat down, looked her directly in the face as we introduced ourselves.

Before she could reply though I gasped, clasped my hand over my mouth and half rose from my chair, knocking it over.

"What's the matter?" She asked in alarm, half rising herself.

Upon closer inspection, I realized that what I thought was something malevolent in her face, was only shadows created by the restaurant's dim lighting; just shadows. I had sat back down feeling foolish and embarrassed, and made some flimsy excuse to cover the gaffe, then quickly started a conversation.

We had enjoyed our meal and each other's company, but the incident had forced me to get a grip on myself. I had simply prayed for protection, and decided to never remove my crucifix.

Now, as I look around the beach at the many people I had met since that day, I was grateful to have learned to cope with this new aspect of what I now almost jokingly call, my third eye; a reference to something in one of the books Jacoby had recommended.

I excused myself from the group at the table, strolled down to the beach, plopped down in the sand and just quietly contemplated the beauty around me.

My mind drifted back to that day at the hotel ... the day that had me fearful to make eye contact with strangers; the day that would forever mark my time on the island as before and after.

It was the first day of my job search, and having a vision or encountering anything of an occult nature had been the last thing on my mind.

When the human resources manager, the person I would interview with entered the room and I looked up into her face, there had been no attempt at political correctness before I jumped up and bolted for the door.

Once outside, I was forced to wait for the elevator while struggling to catch my breath and trying to force my racing heart to slow down. I was shaking like a leaf.

Suddenly, the door I had just come through opened. I didn't have to look to see who was coming out – I knew it was the manager, and I knew she was looking for me.

I could actually smell her – an odor that came straight from the pits of Hell.

I forgot the elevator, and ran for the stairs.

Once back on the main floor, I must have looked positively maniacal as I dashed headlong through the lobby and out of the lobby doors.

One of the doormen saw me and hurried over and asked if I was okay. I assured him I was fine and asked if he could get me a taxi.

While I waited I kept glancing back, afraid that she ... it might have followed me.

The Bellman kept a wary eye on me. I could see how my behavior had alarmed him, but I didn't have the time or presence of mind to be concerned with that; my total focus was escaping; getting away from the horror that was possibly following me.

I didn't relax until I was in the back of the taxi moving away from the building. Only then did I allow myself to think about what I had seen.

Underneath the woman's pretty face and lovely smile had been something so ugly, so foul, it could only have come from the absolute belly of the beast. It was monstrous.

Rationally thinking, it didn't seem real, but like the dog I had encountered that night on the highway, I knew it was very real.

The poor woman was possessed of a demon.

The entity had resembled the things in the picture at Dana's ... grotesque and menacing.

And the feel of it ... "Ooohhhh", I moaned as I buried my face in my hands.

"You okay, Miss?" The driver asked, as he peeped at me in his rear view mirror.

"Yes, I'm fine. Just an upset stomach," I lied.

What had scared me most was that the demon had known I could see it and the anger directed at me was like a blazing pit into which I was being sucked. It was angry because I had found it out. That's why I had run ... like my life depended on it. The belief that nothing I saw could hurt me was temporarily shaken.

On the heels of the fright had come anger and frustration. I thought of the lovely young woman ... a poor lost soul whose circumstance I had the ability to see, but like the slaves, was powerless to change.

Unlike the slaves though, who were long dead, the woman was still alive – in a way. I sighed, and did the only thing I could; I prayed for her.

I couldn't help thinking that my experiences in the realm of the supernatural now seemed all over the place and wondered what new horrors still awaited me.

When I got home that day I had closeted myself in my room and paced back and forth for a long time. I decided to leave the island and put as much distance as possible between me, and the thing I'd seen.

At the same time, I instinctively knew there were more of them. Many more.

"Alexis!!" A voice called, breaking my chain of thought. I looked out into the water and Timothy, one of our neighbors was waving at me.

"Com'on in!" He beckoned. "Water's great!"

"Not right now!" I yelled back.

"Maybe later!"

He shrugged and adjusting his snorkel, headed out into deeper water. I watched until he was lost from view among some other swimmers. I smiled, satisfied at my final decision that day; which was to remain on the island rather than run away.

Just as knowing that the demons had been around all along, I knew that from that point on, I would be confronted with them wherever I went.

So, I had controlled my panic, reminded myself about the need for faith, and put away the clothes I had already packed. After that day, prayed a lot more. I knew I needed to stay as close to the Father as possible.

Sylvia called one day when I wasn't at home and talked to Sarah at length questioning her about everything she could think to ask.

I was furious, but gave my anger a few days to dissipate before calling her back.

"So, you did it again," were her first words.

"Did what?" I asked.

"Took off chasing another dream; this time all the way to the Caribbean."

"I'm real serious about this, Sylvia. Sarah told me you called the day before yesterday and quizzed her about me.

Don't ever do that again," I said sternly.

"She said you two talked for about forty-five minutes, and admitted after my prodding that you seemed to be digging for information.

"I'm basically a stranger in this woman's home," I continued, "The fact that you find it necessary to check up on me ... at my age, can only create doubt about my stability, or my credibility.   Don't ever do anything like that again," I reiterated.

She tried to double-talk her way out of the situation.

"I'm just concerned, that's all. I mean, how do we know you're really alright? Anything could be happening down there, how would we know?"

"You'd know because you'd ask me, and I'd tell you. Why would I lie? If I tell you I'm okay, and everything is fine, why can't you just accept that?"

"We were worried, and that's all I have to say on the subject," she snapped, clamming up.

"Don't say 'we', Sylvia, as if mom was involved in that with you. I know better."

"I wasn't trying to imply anything of the sort. Anyway, getting back to why I called ... how long are you planning to stay down there?"

"I've moved here. That seems to imply I plan to stay forever."

"You can't mean that! Think of what you're giving up. You can't really drive anywhere ... I mean, a few miles and you're at the end of the island.

As much as you love to drive, I can't imagine that. And then there's shopping and movies and restaurants and __" I broke in ...

"We have all of that here ... just not on as grand a scale, but then a person doesn't move to a place like this if those kinds of things are critical to their happiness.

I would think the average person that moves here, feels that the beauty of nature and the lifestyle are a tad more important than a movie or shopping."

"Why did you really move there?" She asks.

"To be honest, I'm not quite sure; maybe, because I didn't have a choice. I felt compelled to come. I don't know. It seemed the right thing to do and now that I'm here, I know it was right. It fits me like a glove. I'm ... I don't know, I feel content here."

"Alexis, do you think you're too young for menopause?"

"GRRRRRR," I growled into the telephone totally exasperated.

What's the matter with you? You have to admit you sound crazy as hell. And some women actually lose their minds at that time, you know."

"No, I don't think I'm going through menopause. So, now what?"

"I never said you were crazy or anything. I said you sound crazy. There's a big difference."

She paused for a few seconds and continued,

"You think you'd have had enough of this moving in with strangers after the episode with the witch in Boston, but nnnooooo... you're still at it. You'll learn."

She didn't know how close she was to being cursed out, and I certainly wasn't going to tell her.

"Don't worry about me. I'm fine. If at any time I'm not fine, you'll be the first to know," I said.

"You seriously need to get your shit together. And look, don't be calling me when it's too late."

"Okay, I won't. Did mom tell you about my job?" I asked, hoping to change the subject.

"Yes, she did. One bright spot," she conceded.

"What's the name of the hotel again, and what is it you do there?"

"It's called Ocean Pointe Beach Resort and I'm a sales manager."

"Now, that's great," she said, a smile in her voice.

"It is a great job for someone who can appreciate it, which doesn't happen to be me. But, it'll do until something I can really enjoy comes along."

"Oh, don't start that crap again!" She snapped.

"How's Damon?" I ask, changing the subject again.

Ocean Pointe was a lovely and popular oceanfront resort with two hundred and fifty rooms and suites.

The hotel was actually built on the slope of a hill above the ocean with amenities that boasted three restaurants; two nightclubs; a water sports center; a recreation center with tennis and fitness center; and an intricately interesting walking and biking trail.

The lobby, with its wide, curving staircase was said to be the loveliest on the island. During peak season the hotel was always full to capacity and busy.

The person that hired me was Angela DuBerry, a woman in her early-forties who was originally from Miami. She had been on St. Thomas for five years and made it clear that the only thing that could entice her to leave was a sizable promotion.

Ocean Pointe was one of a chain of about thirty similar resorts throughout the Caribbean and the states, and it had actually been a promotion from one of the mainland properties that had brought Angie to the Virgin Islands.

She was extremely successful as the sales director, and made it clear to everyone under her command that she intended to continue that trend, and if anyone proved a hindrance, out they went.

Reed thin and slightly hyperactive, Angie was an incessant smoker. What I respected about her though, was despite the blond, short cut hair and big, blue eyes, which she knew how to use effectively; nobody ever mistook her for a bubble brain. She was noticeably smart.

Regardless of the tropical climate she was always impeccably dressed in expensively tailored, lightweight and flawlessly accessorized business suits.

Her concession to make-up consisted of highlighting her eyes, and wearing a pale lipstick. The small amount of jewelry she wore was just as under-stated as the rest of her attire. She was definitely on the corporate fast track.

Perhaps the reason she and I hit it off so well was because we held totally opposing views of the corporate milieu. Whereas she thrived on the intrigue, power plays and the struggle for upward mobility, I abhorred those things.

During the interview I had not hidden the fact that the job would be just that for me ... a job; one that I could and would do well but not one that I had any desire or expectations of being a career builder.

I think Angie recognized that I had the experience and background she needed, but didn't represent any kind of professional threat either now, or in the future.

There were only three of us in sales: Angie, who was the department head, Marian, the sales coordinator and me. The work, as usual was more than plentiful but as in Atlanta, I met the challenge head-on with positive energy.

Like most communities, the hotel had a rhythm and a life of its own.

The employees formed a sort of transient, extended family, which created the usual melee and intrigue one would expect to find in such a setting. All told, it was a nice place to come to work.

I worked hard, but didn't marry the job leaving plenty of time for my solitary walks, swims at the beach, my Sunday afternoons and everything in between.

I was as content as my paranormal circumstances would allow.

Chapter 3

Since my arrival on St. Thomas, I had been promising myself I would take a tour of the island, which I felt would help me learn more about my new home.

Finally, one Saturday morning I had followed through on the plan and gone into town in search of a tour.

On Main Street the taxi drivers, with their multi-seat vans and open air Safari's, were busily hawking their tours. I listened to them describe the stops they would make, and after a while joined a group of excited tourists on a Safari with an itinerary I liked.

A couple of hours later, after a morning of going up and down hills, sometimes climbing down from the bus to walk through a particular location or attraction or take snapshots, I relished the stop at Magen's Bay.

The half hour at the beach would provide a much-needed respite, plus Magen's Bay was rightfully advertised as one of the world's most beautiful beaches.

When I had gotten on the bus in town, I'd found myself seated across from Clarinda and Kendall Freeman, the only other blacks on the tour.

The Freeman's were an attractive young couple from Jamaica that had recently moved to the Virgin Islands and explained that they wanted a formal introduction to some of its history and attractions.

It was interesting that the islands were new to all of us however, island life and most aspects of Caribbean culture had always been their experience whereas all of it was new to me.

Clarinda was petite with walnut colored skin and natural braids that framed her face and hung down on her shoulders. With her long denim skirt, colorful shirt and leather sandals, she was a living advertisement for Caribbean life.

Kendall was tall and stocky and wore beautiful Locks that were so long, he had caught them up in a ponytail, wrapped them around a couple of times and still they hung down his back. He too was dressed in jeans and sandals. A really beautiful couple, I thought.

After the safari parked, the three of us carefully made our way down to the water's edge and taking off our shoes, strolled along the shore. Suddenly my heart skipped a beat.

I stopped walking and took a long, slow look around. I couldn't believe it. This was the exact same beach I had dreamed about in Atlanta ... the night I had decided not to take the job promotion.

To my knowledge, I had never seen it in a photograph, or film and Sammy had never described it. Yet, here it was, big as life. It was the same beach.

"Is something wrong?" Kendall asked. They had stopped walking when I had, and now stood staring at me in confusion.

"No, no nothing's wrong ... except for a little dèja vu at finding my self on this particular beach."

Kendall picked up on that right away.

"Having the feeling that you've been somewhere, or seen someone, or said something before?" He asked.

"Exactly ... the feeling that I've seen this beach before when I know I have never been here," I answered.

"Yeah, I think we've all felt that; the feeling that you've been somewhere before, or knowing what someone is going to say before they actually say it. It's a little scary sometimes."

"Yes, it is. Good thing it doesn't happen often," I laughed nervously.

"Yeah, a good thing," he said, looking at me with his head cocked speculatively to one side.

Returning to the Safari, we headed back to Charlotte Amelia making brief stops along the way for snapshots of more breathtaking scenery. It had been an excellent, but rather long tour and I was tired.

In town we disembarked and the Freeman's and I walked a little distance from the crowd so we could exchange telephone numbers.

With that done, I was about to say goodbye and leave them when Clarinda asked ...

"Have you seen Market Square yet?"

"No, I haven't. Where is it? Better yet, what is it?"

They started talking at once, then stopped and laughed and Clarinda took over.

"It's an open air market where the few farmers here on St. Thomas and some other vendors come to sell their goods.

Some of them are here everyday of the week, but Saturday is the big day when everything from mangos, plants, and herbal medicines to jewelry are on sale. It's really great. Come on we'll show it to you."

Tired as I was, I didn't really feel up to any more sightseeing, but to refuse their offer would somehow seem impolite, so I hoped for a second wind and agreed to accompany them.

"I'd love to see it. Is it far from here?" I asked, trying to hide my fatigue.

"No, it's just down the street a couple of blocks. Com' on," Clarinda urged, and I followed dutifully.

We walked down Main Street and presently came to a section that opened onto a plaza jammed with pedestrian traffic.

It was a chaotic jumble of people where vendors stood and sat behind tables loaded with fruits, vegetables, herbs, flowers and plants. There wasn't a tourist in sight – this was strictly local.

The long street is divided down the center by a unique elevated structure; an open air market.

The market is made entirely of stone and runs almost the entire length of the street.

The last of many coats of paint is a dark, dreary green trimmed in what probably had once been a bright red. Wide stone steps lead up to the old, open-air structure, while an oddly sloped roof offers shelter from the sun and rain.

A raised section similar to a stage runs down the middle of the edifice and forms a sort of platform with a single stone speaker's podium made into the very center.

For some odd reason, I don't need to be told that what I'm looking at is simply referred to as the Bungalow.

The structure had obviously been built to showcase particular items of some sort. Now, numerous tables and stands loaded with intriguing natural and home made products crowd the stand and the street below.

"I'm going to get a snapshot," I excitedly tell Clarinda and Kendall. I had taken quite a few photos that day, but this is something really special; something with a flavor and atmosphere so historical and colorful, I want to see if I can capture it on film.

"I'll be right back," I say, leaving them and walking halfway down the block to the middle of the Bungalow. Standing on the street and jostling for position, I back up raising the camera l to just the right angle.

The dizziness sweeps over me so fast, I don't even have time to acknowledge its arrival. When I look up again, the beautiful day has turned to something at once compelling and horrible.

The African slaves stand in long, ragged lines. Their meager clothing tattered and soiled and all of them visibly weak; some to the point that they appear to be hanging on by the force of their will.

There are maybe fifty or sixty slaves on the platform that looks the same except that now it is unpainted, roofless and less aged.

Many of them stand with their heads bowed and eyes on the ground while others stand in their filth, fatigue and sicknesses with shoulders squared and their heads proudly lifted high. These particular slaves can also be seen staring boldly and in some cases, fiercely into the eyes of the whites.

A slave market; this is where they were sold. I somehow know that these particular Africans are recently off the ships.

They have remarkably survived the horrible, unspeakable agony of the Middle Passage only to end up in this ignoble, inhuman situation.

I think that these, men, women and handful of children are the ones emotionally and physically strong enough to have withstood the horror and misery necessary to make it here, but to what end?

Rather than receiving a reward for their survival, they can only expect further brutalities.

Why is this happening again? And why can't I stop it? As usual, I'm as much a captive of the moment as those I watch. At the moment I can only find solace in the fact that unlike Stanford House, I at least don't live here, and have no reason to return after today.

It was then that I notice her; small and delicate, she is at the far end of the platform with a group of female slaves. Unlike the men who are manacled at the neck, the women are bound together at the ankle.

she catches my attention when she moves defiantly when prodded by one of the slavers.

Her head had been down, but she lifts it now to stare at him with a burning hatred, and when I look into her face, my eyes widen in shock and I nearly strangle on my huge intake of breath.

"Oh, my Father!!" I moan.

Chapter 4

*I*t's like looking into a mirror. I recognize my oval shaped face, my eyes, and the high cheekbones.

Although her head is covered with a rag, I can see the hair escaping from the back and hanging past her shoulders in thick, kinky loops. The lips are fuller than mine, the skin is darker, yet nevertheless the girl is the image of me.

I want to run screaming, and at the same time, I want to stay and fight for her. My suffering feels no less than hers must have been when this was actually happening. My heart beats a heavy tattoo and I struggle to remain conscious.

The slave trader, irritated I guess by her defiance raises his hand and slaps her hard across the face knocking her down.

She hits the platform hard, but slowly, clumsily struggling with the leg irons she finally regains her feet.

Once up, she gathers in her cheeks and leaning far forward, spits in his face.

Oh No! I scream inside.

"Miss! Miss! 'Xcuse please," came the interruption. "I need to get b'hind you, so."

A heavy-set woman with a thick patois is glaring at me with one hand propped up on an equally thick hip, while the other one is pointing to the area she needs to reach.

I shake my head and look up at the platform. It has returned to normal. With a mournful sigh I stumble away from the woman's table.

It's been a while since I've had a vision, and I feel dazed and shocked. As I dry my tears and look behind me, the woman who asked me to move is still glaring. She thinks I'm a drunken tourist I realize, and I move further away.

The significance of the incident with the slave girl doesn't escape me. I know now that I am not on the island by accident. This is the home of some of my ancestors. For at least one of them this had been the first stop out of Africa.

But I am worried about the girl. She had been so young. No more than fifteen or sixteen. What in heaven's name had happened to her after she spit on the slave trader?

Regardless of her actions, I knew one thing for sure ... she had survived. I am living proof that she had survived and bore at least one child, maybe more.

"Alexis!"

I look up and Clarinda and Kendall are making their way to me through the crowd. I wave and start towards them.

When we meet, I can see from their concerned expressions that they witnessed at least part of my reactions to what I'd seen.

Are you alright? Why were you standing there staring at the platform like that?" Clarinda asks immediately.

"Oh, was I staring? I didn't realize."

"You lowered your camera ... did you get any pictures?" Kendall asks.

"Not really," I answer truthfully.

"It was too congested. I couldn't get a good shot."

In reality, I hadn't thought to take pictures of what I was seeing, but on the other hand, I knew instinctively they wouldn't have turned out.

"Well, do you want to walk around a bit? Maybe you'll see something you'd like to buy."

"I don't think so," I reply. "I'm kind of tired, so I think I'll head on home."

"Okay," they both answer at once.

But, before I turned to leave, I just had to say ... "I wonder why Market Square isn't included on the tour route as the old slave market? It's not in any of the literature I've seen of the island either."

They look at me in surprise.

"How did you know it was a slave market? You had never heard of it before today when we told you about it." Kendall is staring at me with the same speculation I'd seen earlier.

"Oh, just ... a guess," I stumble.

"The platform just looked like a spot where slaves might have been displayed. I saw a picture of one similar once," I conclude.

"I see," he replies.

"Well, from what we understand there's a dispute about whether it actually was a slave market. Seems it can't be authenticated for that use because there's simply no documentation either way.

The historical preservation folk don't want to acknowledge it without verification," Clarinda explains.

Kendall follows up with ... "They do know that it was a produce market after a certain period, so they just go with that. Then, here you come along and out of the blue recognize it as a slave market. Amazing," he says, still looking at me inquisitively.

"Goodness! It's an even luckier guess than I thought," wishing I had the ability to authenticate the site. It seemed such a historical loss.

"Well, it was really nice meeting you both, and let's stay in touch like we promised."

I'm already backing away.

"Same here," Clarinda responds. "I'll call soon."

I don't waste anymore time putting some space between us. I don't like the way Kendall is looking at me. He reminds me of Chuck Jacoby back in Newport, and I'm not up for that right now.

I cast one last glance back at the platform before turning the corner and heading towards Waterfront.

"How was the tour?" Sarah asked.

"Great. I really enjoyed it and learned a lot too," I was in a chair on the deck with my feet propped up on the railing and a glass of wine on the table beside me.

"How was work?" I asked.

"Don't get me started. I hate that place. Soon. One day soon it'll be adios."

"But, until then it's like Ocean Pointe ... helps keep the roof over our heads." I laughed.

"True," she sighed. "Listen, I'm going to take a shower and meet the gang out at the ballpark. The guys have a baseball game later. You wanna come?"

"Naw, I'm bushed. Listen, before you go, Sarah ... did you know that Market Square was once a slave market ... where they auctioned slaves?"

"What?! Are you serious?"

"I guess that means you didn't know either."

"Nope, I've never heard that before."

"Curious," I murmured. Cutting that part out of the island's history was like denying those poor souls their rightful legacy even if it was horrible.

"Wow, Imagine that. A slave market and I never

heard a word," she said, as she picked up the shoes she'd kicked off and wandered off to her room.

After she left, I lazily watched a motorboat cut a frothy swath through the glass smooth water, then picked out a couple of sailboats on the horizon and followed their paths while my thoughts traveled back to Newport.

I remembered when the episodes had first begun, and how the first visions had frightened me so badly I'd fainted.

Thank goodness, I'm beyond that kind of response although the encounter with the demon had been a serious setback.

I've seen many entities since that day, but because I know they can't harm me, when I see one, I simply go the other way ... fast. I always pray for the lost soul while on my way, but recognize that there is nothing else I can do for them.

I feel almost as bad for their families and loved ones who have no idea that the person causing chaos and confusion in their lives isn't the same individual they have always known and loved.

In fact, with the entities' presence inside of them, those who are possessed don't exactly qualify as a person.

As I continue to watch the boats, I acknowledge a strong feeling I've had recently that time is growing short, and that it won't be long before I understand why I can see demons, and have visions, and why a coven of witches found me so intriguing.

The insight however, will not come free of charge, but will come heavily attached with responsibilities. Of this I'm certain.

There is something purposeful in my experiences, which suggests if there is purpose there probably follows application. As much as I wish for it, I know there is no escape from whatever is behind all of this.

As surely as the sun rises and sets each day, the time of disclosure is fast approaching and I am both anticipatory and fearful.

§§§§

"Hey, I'm ready for those steaks!!" Don yells from the deck. I break off a conversation and hurry to take a platter of steaks and more hamburger patties out of the refrigerator.

As the self-appointed grill master, Don is in charge of cooking the ribs, chickens, steaks, burgers and hot dogs and is apparently ready to fill the grill with another round of meats. I rush to fill his order.

Bass booming Soca music fills the air on the deck where two couples are energetically dancing. Others sit talking around the large, mahogany dining table that always sits outside, and lounge in chairs placed around the deck.

Conversations range from a recent crime wave, that coming from Chicago, Boston and Atlanta I don't think much of, to the economy.

Other guests are in the living room, or hanging out in front of the house.

Sarah and I spent much of the day before preparing the potato salad, pasta salad, and fruit salad; the fruit dramatically presented in hollowed watermelon rinds.

Corn on the cob, baked beans and a green salad rounds out the menu with the exception of dessert which includes Sarah's specialty of three different types of crème pies, including chocolate and banana, and of course my specialties, rum cake and pecan pie.

A baker friend of Sarah's generously donated a sheet cake, which rounds out our sweet treats.

The food is set up buffet style in the dining room on two long folding tables that had been loaned to us for the party and as Don grills, he adds the meats to platters on the tables.

To keep things in order with the beverages, our neighbor and friend, Timothy George is serving as our Mixologist and is having the time of his life talking and pouring with equal parts dexterity.

The party is a celebration of my six months on the island. It started with me inviting a few friends over, but was extended to Sarah and Don's friends and finally escalated into this overwhelming over-flow of people.

We all agree that it's a good thing we went overboard on the amount of food we bought and prepared.

I invited Sammy and his wife, whom I had visited twice since arriving on the island; Mina, who had shared my table at the restaurant that night in town; Clarinda and Kendall, and a few others I've met over the months.

From work there is Angie, Marian, and anyone else who wanted to attend. I had posted a flyer on the bulletin board in the cafeteria.

Judging from the number of people that showed up from work, the free food and unlimited liquor has been a powerful inducement, or I have more friends than I know.

When I return to the kitchen after giving Don the meats, Angie follows me behind the counter swaying to the beat of the music.

"What can I do to help?" She asks.

"Just enjoy yourself. Everything else's covered."

"Well, that I can do," she replies, as she dances around the kitchen with an invisible partner.

I shake my head and laugh.

"Maybe, I should take that," I say, reaching for her glass.

"Try it, and you could get hurt real bad," she says before dancing away.

Most of the crowd is wearing shorts and T-Shirts, but not Angie. She's outfitted in crisply creased blue jeans; a short-sleeved white shirt trimmed with blue denim and the cutest little denim sneakers I've ever seen. No matter the occasion, Angie is always perfectly dressed.

Thanks to a collision with some barbeque sauce, I was forced to change from my own white jumper shorts to a pair of cutoffs, a T-shirt and sandals.

Now, I blend in with the crowd.

Finished with chores for the moment, I go out on deck and run right into Clarinda and Kendall.

"It's about time you took a break," Clarinda scolds.

"Yeah, we didn't want to bother you while you were busy, but, we'd like you to meet a friend of ours," Kendall says as he beckons to a man standing by the rail.

I had noticed the man earlier, but thought he was one of Sarah and Phillips' friends.

He apparently has been watching and comes right over. The man's name is Vincent, and he and Kendall are co-owners of a downtown gift shop.

After Clarinda and Kendall introduce us, we all talk for a few minutes before the couple conveniently drifts away.

I could pinch them both. Alone with Vincent, I self-consciously try to make conversation.

"So, are you from St. Thomas, Vincent?"

"Not originally. I was born in Jamaica."

"I've never been to Jamaica, but I hear ___ "

"I think you're as uncomfortable about this as I am," he's smiling broadly.

"I ... pardon me?"

"You didn't know about this little scheme of theirs either, did you?"

I laugh with relief.

"No, I didn't and might I add, they're about as subtle as being run over by a Mack truck.

"We laugh together, which breaks the ice.

"They mean well. Anyway, I was born in Jamaica, but I've lived here most of my life. What about you? Where in the states are you from?"

"Chicago, but I moved here from Atlanta."

We chat a few minutes more and I excuse myself to go over and check on Sammy and his wife.

I introduced them to a few people when they arrived, but I want to make sure they're having a good time.

They were so surprised when I let them know I was on my way to the VI. They'd had two small dinner parties in my behalf.

Sammy and I immediately get into a conversation about Marietta and The Depot, and I find that he has news received from friends.

He tells me that a woman purchased Stanford House shortly after we left Marietta, and immediately began lavishing it with some much needed attention.

With a thorough cleaning and painting, some repairs, and the installation of new fixtures, new appliances, and refurbishment of the furniture, she had returned the house to its former glory.

I was so happy to hear that the painted lady had gotten a facelift, I could have cried. Gail had told me earlier about the sale, and now I was happy to hear about the renovations.

Sammie said that everyone in Marietta was pleased to see the old house reemerge as one of the most stylish Bed & Breakfast hotels in the southeast.

The Depot, as suspected, hadn't fared as well. It was still owned by the same couple, but business had dropped disastrously.

On top of their own personal problems, they foolishly hadn't made it a condition of the sale for Charlie to release any of his recipes; and he didn't.

There were rumors that they'd been trying to sell, but couldn't find a buyer. In time it would probably just close and the community would be the loser; not only because of the history it had created, but because of the loss of what might be the best bar-b-que in that region, and maybe the entire south.

It is sad that the pair had taken a successful and profitable business and squeezed the life right out of it. I had known it would happen, only not so soon.

We talk until I really do start to get watery-eyed with memories, and excuse myself to go and speak to someone else before I'm bawling like a baby.

I see Marian and her boyfriend finish dancing and I head over to talk with them for a few minutes. They're a funny looking pair. Marian is much taller than Ken, but neither of them seems to notice.

When at work she is forever having whispered telephone conversations with him, and he takes her home from work each day. Their relationship is great because Marian has two little boys that Ken seems to adore.

I am still talking to them when I look up and Ron Baldwin, the general manager of the hotel is walking up.

"Alexis, this is some party," he says, as he juggles a plate of food in one hand and a wine glass in the other.

"I'm glad you could make it, Ron," I reply, trying to cover my surprise at his appearance.

Although he's quite friendly, other than professionally, we'd never had much to say to one another.

"Is Peggy here?" I ask, wondering about his wife, that unlike Ron is friendly, but in a vague, obligatory kind of way.

"She's off island for the weekend, so I'm just hanging out," he answers.

"Well, you've come to the right place to hang. You know almost everyone here so I don't have to take you around."

"You're right about that. It took me nearly twenty minutes to get through the crowd from the driveway to the house. Seems like everybody turned up, which makes me wonder who's minding the store. Say, you have one heck of a view up here."

"Thanks. It is lovely," I agree. I take a moment to look with satisfaction out over the trees at the ocean.

"Well, I think I'll go over in the corner there, dive into this great food and enjoy the scenery," he said.

"Help yourself to both. Have you seen Angie?" I ask, looking around for someone to keep him company.

"She and Ruth are getting plates so we can eat together," he replies.

"Enjoy." I leave knowing he's in good hands.

Ron is something of a maverick. He's from the state of Michigan, has been on St. Thomas for seven years and like Angie, doesn't ever want to leave.

He's that rare general manager who operates more by the seat of his pants than by the rulebook and has a 'hands on' style that's made him wildly popular with employees.

On my way into the dining room to check on the food, I run into our banquet manager, Freddie Monsanto and the front desk manager, Felicia Bryant, both Thomians who I am beginning to suspect are a couple.

If they are, I'm probably the last to know since I try to avoid the hotel melee as much as possible.

I talk to them for a few minutes and go on inside. I'm checking on the baked beans when someone behind me says ... "If you can tear yourself away from your hostess duties for a few minutes, I'd like to dance with you."

I know who it is before I turn.

"Sure, Vincent," I answer, turning to face him. "I'd be delighted," I reply with a smile.

He leads me out on the deck where a few dancers are gyrating to one of my favorite songs; a big hit by the band that was crowned 'Road March Kings' during Carnival that spring and is ironically named Jam Band.

No way to sit still when Jam Band's music is playing. The song is hot ... and fast. I pull on every ounce of strength I have left in my tired body to keep up with the rhythm, and with Vincent.

Before long, however I've forgotten the fatigue and the people and go with the music. When the dance is over some of those on the deck applaud, and I'm so embarrassed I cover my face with my hands.

The music starts again and a number of couples pile onto the dance floor. Vincent grabs me and off we go.

He is an excellent dancer, and since we've broken the ice, this time the dance floor is crowded. Don and Sarah join the throng and as Jason would say ... "It's on!"

Much later that night, or rather that morning, Don, Sarah and I bade the last of our guests, goodbye. Everyone is gone except Vincent.

The four of us are sprawled around in deck chairs tired, but giddy with success.

Don is all for planning another party on the spot, but the idea is nixed when Sarah takes him by the ear and pulls him off to bed.

After they're gone, Vincent and I don't seem to have much to say, but I find the silence perfectly comfortable. He sits quietly looking at the lights down below us while I study him.

I had read him earlier when we were introduced and know that he is a good man. He's average height with a brown complexion bronzed to reddish tones by the tropical sun; deep brown eyes,

nice lips and a cool, laid back attitude all add up to one handsome man. He told me earlier that he's forty-four, but with his wiry build and close-cropped haircut, he looks much younger.

I know I should be grateful to the Freeman's for the introduction, but my experiences with matchmaking have never netted success.

Vincent explains that he and Kendall are childhood friends from Jamaica and that their friendship fortunately survived the separation caused by Vincent's move to the Virgin Islands several years before him.

"I must say that for the first time with his matchmaking Kendall got it right," he said.

"Oh, so he's fixed you up before?"

"Absolutely. He and Clarinda are so happy together they're convinced that 'happily single' is a misnomer. They never give up.

I didn't know what they had in mind tonight and they knew better than to tell me because I'd have begged off.

I'm glad they kept it a secret."

"So am I," I respond.

After a brief pause, he asks ... "Would you like to have dinner this evening?"

"Yes, I would. I'd like that very much."

"What about I pick you up at five-thirty?"

I think selfishly of the beach party on Sundays and say, "That's fine."

"Five-thirty it is. I guess I'll be pushing off. It was a great party, Alexis. I'm glad for lots of reasons that I came."

"It was a great party, if I do say so myself. I'm glad you enjoyed yourself."

We climb out of our chairs and stand, but before I can turn to leave the deck, he takes my hand and cool and calm as you please, he slides his arms around my waist, pulls me into his arms and kisses me.

"No need to see me out. I'll talk to you later," he says, releasing me.

The kiss was totally unexpected and I stand there for a moment after he's left still feeling the pressure of his lips and wishing he hadn't felt it was necessary to leave.

Then I chuckle. "Down girl," I say aloud, "You just met the man."

As I walk through the house turning out the lights and checking the doors, I think about my feelings for this new man, and decide I like him. I like him a lot.

And most importantly, I think ... he's not married! Hallelujah!

But strangely, after going to bed with such beautiful thoughts of Vincent, I suddenly wake up from a dream bathed in perspiration, my heart pounding and my mind completely befuddled.

Almost as shocking as the dream is who the dream had been about.

It wasn't Vincent.

Chapter 5

"*D*o you smell that?"

"No. What?"

"There's something stinking in here," Sarah said.

Pointing my nose in different directions in the living room, I audibly sniff.

"Say, I do smell something. Like __"

"Like something dead."

"Yeah. It's not real strong, but I definitely smell it," I agree.

"It doesn't smell much right now, but it will in a couple of days."

"You sound like you know what it is." I was mildly surprised.

"I think it's a rat."

"A RAT?! What's a rat ... dead or alive doing in here?"

"Don put down some traps up around the rafters," she explained rather nonchalantly, I thought.

"Sa-Rah! Why didn't you tell me we had rats? I hate those things."

I couldn't help feeling put out that they hadn't found it necessary to inform me of this problem.

"They're just tree rats," she said laughing as if it were a good joke.

"Actually, it's really weird because we've never had that problem before. Not in all the years I've been in this house." She shrugged her shoulders.

"Do you think it matters to me whether it's from a tree, or a sewer? A rat's a rat!"

"Okay, okay, relax. I'll let Don know we caught something and he and Timothy can climb up there and get it down."

"Wonderful," I said, only slightly mollified.

"But, seriously Alexis, this is the tropics. And, you know by now that these types of things are just a part of living here."

"Okay. I've learned to live with the occasional lizard   skittering in and out of the house. I've even gotten used to the mosquitoes and have actually come to love the Iguanas.

But, rats? No way. It ain't happening. I refuse to get used to sharing my living space with rats. Period."

Sarah threw up her hands in mock exasperation.

"You win. No rats. It's not a big deal. We can get rid of them."

"Good," I said with a sigh of relief.

"Say, how was your date with that guy ... what's his name?" She asked.

"Vincent." I suspected she was changing the subject, and I let her.

"Yeah, Vincent. How did it go?"

"Great."

"You like him?"

"He's nice. Yes, I like him."

"Well, I think he's cute as all get out."

"He is cute, and he's nice; the chemistry is great,

and we have quite a bit in common."

"But?"

"What, but?"

"I hear a 'but' in there somewhere."

"I guess there is. The problem is ... I don't know why. Then again, we did just meet so there's no hurry about anything."

"That's true. Just remember though, really good guys aren't all that plentiful around here."

"Really good guys aren't all that plentiful anywhere," I replied thinking about my dream.

"When are you seeing him again?"

"Tonight," I answered.

"Thata girl. Just remember what I said."

"Yes, mother."

Vincent and I had chosen a new restaurant in Charlotte Amalia that serves native food.

High on a hill overlooking Havensight Harbor, it provided a romantic if rather dark view of the ocean, and the lights in and above town, which were breathtakingly beautiful.

Vincent ordered a traditional Virgin Islands meal for me, and although the food tended to be heavy, I enjoyed every bit.

There were appetizers of conch fritters that turned out to be similar to hush puppies with bits of the shellfish fried inside.

There was the not very tasty sounding, but absolutely delicious boiled fish cooked whole with herbs and spices in a Creole sauce. Fungi, a simple dish of cornmeal, okra and spices made into patties were a new taste treat while vegetables, and rice and peas were the perfect sides.

We washed it all down with Mauby, a delicious drink made from boiling Mauby bark with spices. Amazing.

After eating I felt heavy as lead, but was completely satisfied. Since arriving on the island I had tasted many of the dishes, but the Conch and Fungi were new to me.

"Oh, that was delicious!" I sighed.

"Did you really enjoy it?"

"Can't you tell?" I asked, glancing at the empty plate being removed by the waiter.

"I'm glad you liked it," he said simply, but looking pleased.

"Loved it. That fish was amazing; I'd like to know the exact herbs and spices used in the recipe."

"Some of the herbs would be hard to come by in the states, but are readily available here. I'll get you the recipe."

"You can cook too? Incredible. Well here's the deal; you get the recipe, and I'll cook the dinner."

"Deal. Where would you like to go now?"

"I'm following you."

"Well, one of my favorite bands is playing in town tonight, so we could do that."

"Sounds great," I replied, realizing again that our love of music and dancing makes us quite compatible.

"Do you mind if I make a stop on the way?"

"Of course not."

"Good. I need to drop off a package to my Aunt Eleanor."

"Not a problem."

On the drive to his aunt's, Vincent and I talked about West Indian culture and life on St. Thomas.

I mentioned Market Square and although noncommittal about its history, I learned that he was very knowledgeable about slavery and could even recommend a popular book on slavery in the Danish West Indies written by an islander.

As he talked, I thought of my ancestor, the slave girl and wanted badly to tell him of my own connection to the island's history, but how could I without having to lie about how I would know.

I could tell him I had researched my ancestry, but I didn't want to lie, so I didn't say anything.

Finally, Vincent pulled into the driveway of a small frame house on the west end of the island.

As we went up the narrow walk, he yelled out the greeting that many people here used when approaching someone's home... "Inside!?"

From somewhere inside came the answering call ... "Okay, comin!"

A couple of minutes passed before the door opened and a middle-aged woman, much taller than Vincent, looked out at us.

What struck me immediately was the glow that seemed to envelope her. From the moment she opened the door and we entered, I felt this incredible warmth emanating from her that made me feel strangely comforted and just plain ... good.

Once inside I saw that she was studying me as well. There followed a startling moment of recognition that was so powerful, it was actually physical.

I recognized her uncommon kindness, wisdom and strength and wanted to sit down and stay forever. She in turn gave me a beaming smile that I can only describe as soulful.

"Come. Sit. Busta, whare yuh mannas? Tell meh, who yuh fren?"

"Auntie this is Alexis … Alexis, Aunt Eleanor."

"Pleased to meet you," I said, as the woman settled her considerable bulk into an easy chair.

She was a big woman, but solid, and hovering not too far beneath six feet I guessed. She favored Vincent in skin tone and features and wore her pepper and salt hair in fat braids that she had wound attractively around her head. She was an imposing figure.

"You a state sida." It was a statement.

"Yes, I'm originally from Chicago."

"An somwhare de weatha is warma den Chicago," she said, speaking so fast, it was an effort to unravel the sentence.

"Atlanta," I finally said, just when Vincent was about to translate for me.

"I lived in New York, you know. When I was a young woman and he was just a little papoose," she said, throwing her hand in Vincent's direction.

I quickly covered my mouth with my hand to hide my smile, while Vincent, poor dear blushed furiously.

I also realized that her dialect seemed to have dissolved into thin air. All of a sudden, she sounded more like a 'State Sida' than me.

"Here's the package from mother. She said to give her a call in the morning."

"I'll do that, yes I will." She turned to me again and asked, "You ever had Bush Tea?"

"Not that I can recall," I answered.

She pointed to the package in her hand.

"It's good for whatever ails you.

A good strong cup of Bush is one of nature's best raw remedies."

"I'll remember that," I said.

"Well, we have to be moving along," Vincent broke in. "Alexis and I are going to town for awhile," he said.

"Oh." She turned to me.

"You come back to see me," she said.

"I will, thank you," I replied.

"Come any time. We have a lot to talk about."

I snapped to attention, met her steady gaze and clearly understood her meaning. She knew.

I don't know how, but she knew about the veil because … because she's like me, I thought.

I had recognized her as a highly spiritual person, but my thoughts and assessment hadn't gone farther than that.

She saw my look of confusion and urgency and

gently said …. "It's okay, we'll talk."

She patted my arm soothingly and I calmed down immediately. I looked at Vincent and caught him looking from one of us to the other with a puzzled expression.

"Vincent," she said, "You bring this pretty young lady back to see me, now."

"I will."

As we walked to the door I turned, said goodnight and ... "I'll see you soon." She nodded.

As we drove toward town, I broke the silence. "Your aunt is very nice ... and __"

"Strange?"

"No, I wasn't going to say that.

I think she's wonderful. How in the world did she know I had lived in a warm climate? Did you tell her?"

"No, not at all."

He paused then added, "They say she can see things, you know."

His embarrassment was obvious, and I felt he was only telling me something so personal because he figured I would hear it from someone else, sooner or later. After all, the nature of small town living was the difficulty keeping secrets.

"She seems to have taken a special interest in you. I'm surprised. I've never seen her respond to a stranger, especially a ... someone not from the islands," he added.

"She seems ... well, very special," I said again.

"Tell me, does she always talk in and out of dialect like that?"

"She did that in deference to you," he said. "Something else I've never seen her do."

"Well, I think she's just awesome," I repeated. "I hope you don't mind if I take her up on the invitation to visit."

"That would be great," he answered with a quizzical expression. "I'm glad you two hit it off. She doesn't get out much anymore.

It'll be wonderful if you could stop by sometime."

"Good," I said. "I look forward to seeing her again."

The rest of the evening was fantastic.

The music was great and we danced until we were near exhaustion. I met some of Vincent's friends, and like many small communities, I could tell that I was the object of great speculation.

At least his willingness to introduce me gave me confidence that he wasn't involved in a serious relationship with anyone else … maybe.

When he brought me home, we sat outside the house and talked quietly for a while before he left.

Vincent talked about his dreams and ambitions for the future, which included building a house on land he already owned. He had designed the house already and from his description, it sounded beautiful.

For my part, I was silent about the future, which was a total mystery to me. These days I usually had little to contribute when it came to future plans.

Our kiss goodnight was more intense, more passionate than the night we met, and I felt an unspoken urging for an invitation to come inside that, with some difficulty, I ignored.

As attractive as I found Vincent, I knew the time wasn't right for further intimacy.

That night I dreamed again.

Chapter 6

"*S*o, how was your date with Vincent? Did you have a good time?" Sarah asked.

"It was great as usual," I said, noncommittal.

"And?"

"Oh no, you don't. And ... nothing," I said, with finality.

"So, you're not talking?"

"There's nothing to talk about. When there is, Sarah dear, I'll let you know. Anyway, it's hard to concentrate on Vincent when I keep dreaming about someone else," I admitted in frustration.

"What's this?" She said, putting down the magazine she'd been reading and sitting up on the sofa.

"Someone else like who? What dream?"

I felt a compelling need to talk. To hear myself say aloud what was occupying more and more of my thoughts each day. "His name is Michael Metcalf and I met him during the time I lived in Boston."

"Boston? But, that's been ages ago. A couple of years or more, right?" She asked, practically quivering with anticipation at this surprising windfall of information.

"Yes, it's been quite a while. That's what's so perplexing about my sudden dreams about him."

"Well, you two must have been really close," she pushed her hair from her face and continued ... "Did you love him?"

"Get this, we had one date. We met while I was on a temporary assignment. He was vice president of the real estate division and I filled in for his assistant.

On the last day of the assignment, which was a little over three months, he asked me out to dinner.

I really liked him a lot but he was married. Legally separated, but still married and still very much involved, if you know what I mean?"

"Yes, I do," Sarah said, understanding. "Not good."

"You bet. Then, right after our date, I had to leave Boston and I never heard from him again. Now, all of a sudden I'm dreaming about him."

"You didn't answer my question, Alexis. Did you love him?"

"Did you hear me say we only had one date?"

"How many times you two went out doesn't have a thing to do with how you felt about him," she answered with impatience. "You just said you worked with him for three months."

Her statement was like a blow in the gut. I was silent as I allowed it to percolate.

Then, "You know, there was so much going on in my life at the time, I don't think I allowed myself to deal with how I really felt about him.

That, plus the wife thing was just too much to process. It was like another huge hill added to a mountain of challenges already confronting me."

"What are the dreams about?" Sarah asked.

"It's always the same. We're here ... on the island

walking on the beach and I'm so happy. For a long time, I couldn't see his face, then, one night I turned to the person walking beside me and it was him."

"Jiminy shit!" Sarah exclaimed. "What do you suppose it means?"

"Beats me."

"Maybe, you should call him," she suggested.

"Oh sure, I'll just pick up the phone and call him and say...'Hey there, Metcalf. Been dreaming bout you lately so thought I'd call you up.' I don't think so."

"It would sure get you talking."

"Again, I don't think so, Sarah."

"So what're you going to do?"

"I don't know. Just give it some time, I guess. Maybe it'll work itself out and the dreams will stop."

"I hope so ... for your sake and Vincent's."

"Well, putting my problems in the romance department aside for a moment ... did Don and Tim take care of that little problem with the rat? I still smell something. Is it in here or outside?"

"I think in here. You know Don is off island and I haven't been able to catch up with Timothy."

"Ohhhh," I groaned.

"Yeah, I know. It's really kinda bad today. Listen, let's just get it down ourselves."

"Get it down ourselves? Are you out of your mind?"

"It's no big deal. I'll just put on my rubber gloves," Sarah said.

She went to the kitchen and took the gloves out of the cabinet under the sink.

"Now," she said, coming back into the living room, "If I get up on the back of the sofa I can reach up between those low rafters, find it and get it out.

You get some newspaper, hold it open, and when I drop the rat into the paper, you take it outside to the garbage," she said authoritatively while I stood looking at her as if she had taken leave of her senses.

"Com'on Alexis, we don't have to wait for the men to get back to do something so simple. Get the newspaper."

I went ahead and obeyed because although unconvinced, the smell was turning into a stench. I got the newspaper and opening the pages held it directly underneath her.

The sofa didn't work, so after climbing precariously up on a ladder that always rested by the laundry room, I could see her feeling around between the rafters with her lips pursed in deep concentration. Finally she let out a cry of triumph.

"Got it! Get ready!" She yelled.

The next thing I saw was her hand coming up holding something big; much bigger than I'd thought.

I guess I'd been saying rat but thinking mouse. It looked huge. But, before I could really get a good look, she let it go and it was sailing down towards me.

There I was, looking up and realizing ... belatedly, that what was coming directly at my face was a squirming, wriggling, revolting mass of worms.

This registered in my consciousness about the same time the quivering mass hit the newspaper.

I flung the paper as hard as I could in one direction and ran screeching to the top of my lungs in the other.

Somehow I ended up outside yelling ... "Maggots!!!

AAHHHHHHWWWWWW!!!" while doing a jig.

Imagining that some of the parasites had gotten into my hair, I beat my poor head until it was sore.

It was a minute or two before I realized that Sarah was with me outside and was screaming as well.

Finally, our chorus was spent and dwindled down to some hoarse gasps, and moans. Breathing like a marathoner, Sarah said weakly:

"We've got to go back in there and clean up that mess."

"No," I said, as I leaned down with my hands on both knees struggling for breath.

"Alexis, we have to clean this up. Thanks to you those maggots flew all over the room. They're in the sofa and everywhere. We have to clean them up."

"Thanks to ME?!" I said indignantly.

"I don't recall you mentioning that the d__, that the rat would be covered with maggots!" Finally, I whisper in horrified fascination …why are they so big?"

"Probably because they've been having a picnic; and gorging themselves on the rat for the last few days."

Then added, "I don't know why I'm being such a ninny about this. In Japan, they cook and sell maggots as delicacies from push carts on the street."

"Oh, please," I said, grabbing my stomach and swallowing the bile that bubbled up in my throat. I think she's serious.

"If you're an islander, Alexis you've got to be tough. You can't go belly up at the sight of a few worms."

"Excuse me," I said sarcastically. "In case you haven't noticed, I'm not out here by myself."

"I was influenced by you," she said defensively.

"I'm not going back in there and mess with that … that mess," I said with finality.

Just then we heard the sound of loud, hysterical barking accompanied by terrible thudding noises. It sounded like all hell was breaking loose inside.

We glanced at each other and jumped for the door at the same time. Sarah made it through about a fraction of a second before me, but I was right on her heels.

Inside we froze at the sight of poor Buddy throwing himself frantically against the closed glass doors; and so hysterical, he was actually foaming at the mouth.

Sarah ran and opening the door dropped on her knees in front of the huge beast, and making little soothing sounds tried to calm him down.

Our screams had thrown him totally into defense mode.

When he saw we were okay, I could swear that dog smiled as he began to wag his stump of a tail furiously. Humbled by this display of devotion, I knelt and joined in the rubbing, petting and cooing.

Feeling a little ashamed of my hysteria, when we got Buddy calm, I agreed to help Sarah clean up. It was a nightmare.

She located the rat still covered with quite a few maggots, and took it outside. I don't know how because I wasn't looking, but she separated the rat from the maggots.

The rat went into a plastic bag and then in the trash can sitting by the road and the maggots went into a tin pail that she half filled with kerosene.

Then we set about finding the ones inside that had gotten away. It took us the better part of an hour, but once they were recovered and in the pail, she set it on fire.

By this time I was in a mild state of shock so I excused myself, and not caring about the military business, took a half hour shower.

I shampooed my hair until I felt satisfied that nothing could possibly be alive in it. Then, although it was early afternoon, I went to bed … with mom's dire warnings ringing again in my head.

Before I drifted off to sleep, I thought about the rats at the hotel in Harrisburg, and how they had sat on the floor staring at me with their red eyes.

I remembered reading something about Satan being able to command all manner of living things, including the beasts of the earth, and thought that the rats in the house, like those in Harrisburg and the dog on the highway, might not be coincidental.

I felt the one today might just be the tip of the iceberg. I resolved from that point on I would be tougher.

He wouldn't find me so easy a target in this area again.

The following morning, Sarah and I apologized to each other for our hysteria the day before, and then casually avoided the living room.

She had found several maggots in the sofa. The pillow covers had been laundered, pressed and put back on the pillows all nice and clean.

Still, I felt I could never sit on the sofa again with any peace.

I was late that morning for the meeting Angie and I had at the start of almost every day.

Our morning meeting was where we reviewed all pending events, which helped us stay on track and on top of everything.

I told her the story about the rat, and she howled with laughter. When she finally finished, after a good three minutes, I reminded her that as a resident of the island, she wasn't immune to such occurrences.

That sobering thought dampened her mirth, and she finally cooled out.

Turning our attention to work, we were going over the agenda for the next few days when I had a shock.

"What's this?" I asked.

"What?"

"This Bank of Boston appointment; when did this happen?"

"Oh, yesterday; a woman from the bank called and said an executive was here on business, and while on island wanted to look over resorts for a possible conference next year.

She asked if we could do a site inspection."

"What's the executive's name?" I asked, feeling cold all over. Without looking up from the legal pad she was writing on, she answered ... "Lynn Kennedy."

I slumped with relief. The bank was huge and this was probably a totally different area from Metcalf's.

It still, however had shaken me up.

"I'm going to need you to do the inspection for me," she added.

"Oh no," I said, noticing the time. "Why so late?"

"I don't know," she said, looking up.

"The woman I spoke with just said the Kennedy woman would be tied up all day, but still wanted to do the inspection. I of course, obliged. Why? Did you have plans this evening?"

"Yes, I did. I was going to visit Vincent's aunt. The one I told you about that's such a character."

"Every time I plan to go see her something comes up and I can't go."

"Well, don't look at me like that. I'd do it myself but I have those eighteen travel agents coming in today, and I have to have dinner with them … unless you want to trade?"

"No. It's okay," I said. "I'll just keep trying to get to her. Brief me on the bank's conference plans."

Kennedy was scheduled for five-thirty. At five I freshened up and took a sales kit from the file. The kit would give her information on the property, basic rates, plus some great photos, but I felt that any final decisions would be based on her impressions of the resort while on the tour.

I had rehearsed how I would ask about Metcalf. If he were still at the bank, which I doubted, the Kennedy woman would definitely know him. If still there I would totally surprise him by sending a greeting.

I asked the front desk to call me as soon as Kennedy arrived and asked for Angie. By ten of six she hadn't shown and I was getting fidgety, not to mention hungry.

Finally, Janelle at reception called to tell me the client had arrived.

"Is she standing there at the front desk now?"

"No, she just sat down on one of the sofas."

"What does she look like?"

"A good looking redhead wearing a green suit," Janelle responded

"Great. Thanks. I'll be right out," I said. I picked up the sales kit and left the office wearing one of my biggest, brightest smiles.

When I entered the lobby I spotted her immediately and went over ... "Miss Kennedy?"

"Yes," she said turning around to face me.

I introduced myself and extended my hand.

"I'm sorry, Angie has been detained, so I'll be conducting the site inspection for you."

She stood; a tall, attractive woman a little older than me.

"That's just fine, we were detained as well."

"We?" I asked, stupidly thinking I'd need to go back for another kit.

"Yes, my colleague and I. Oh, here he comes now," she said, looking over my shoulder.

He?

Chapter 7

I heard him before I saw him, and recognized his voice immediately. For the second time in my life, I felt the floor trying to get chummy with me.

With a will I didn't know I possessed, I forced myself to stay on my feet and although I was right on the edge of oblivion, I dug my nails into my palms and simply refused to go down.

We sat in the softly lit bar our voices rising and falling in syncopation with the others around us. I picked up my glass and took a sip then, placing it carefully back on the table asked;

"Is this a coincidence?"

"Of course it isn't, he answered. "It's totally not a coincidence."

"How? Why?" I asked in confusion.

"Brenda," he said, bluntly.

Metcalf placed his hand under my chin and tilted my face up so he could look into my eyes.

"Why did you run away from me?"

"It wasn't you I was running from."

"If not me, who? What?"

"Long, long story."

"Why wouldn't you tell me? Maybe I could have helped."

"No, you couldn't. Plus, you had other priorities. Somehow, I didn't imagine I would be one of them."

I knew I sounded churlish, but I couldn't help myself.

"Well, you imagined wrong."

"You were ... and probably still are ... obligated, Michael. Regardless of that legal separation you dangled in my face."

"My being here, Alexis, on this particular island, at this particular time, with you ... isn't coincidence," he said, with deliberate slowness.

"We spent one evening together years ago, yet as soon as I find out where you are, here I am. Doesn't that tell you anything about my priorities?"

I was about to speak when he abruptly stood and walked around the small table.

Pulling me abruptly to my feet, he looked down into my eyes and said ... "You're as beautiful as ever."

Then, he kissed me as slowly and thoroughly as if we were in my boudoir rather than a very public place.

I was so stunned and bewildered, and so needy, I melted against him in absolute surrender, and at the same time was happy that we'd met away from the job.

Given the fact that I was totally confused about his sudden appearance and what it might mean, I wasn't prepared to allow my actions to dictate any type of public conclusion about a relationship.

When he released me, I took his hand and led him out on the deck of the restaurant partially out of embarrassment and partially out of a need for some fresh air to clear my head and to cool down. One part of me was excited and happy about all of this, while the other was leery and on guard.

Once outside I suddenly felt exhausted. Everything was happening so fast, I realized I needed to catch up mentally and emotionally.

"How long will you be here?" I asked.

"Lynn is leaving in the morning, but I'm staying another day or two. That is, if you want me to."

"Is it up to me?"

"Yes."

"Would you mind very much if we called it a night?" I asked. "I've just realized how tired ... and confused I am."

"No, I don't mind As long as you promise to see me tomorrow. It's been a long day for me, as well. Will you drop me at my hotel?"

"Of course I will, and yes, I'll drop you." I responded.

He held onto my hand as we walked back through the restaurant and bar, but he didn't kiss me again.

We made arrangements to meet the next day, and when we parted for the night, he simply hugged me, got out of the car and walked away.

As tired as I was physically, when I got home I couldn't relax, and later, couldn't sleep. I was glad Sarah had gone out otherwise I'd be bending her ear with the numerous questions that plagued me.

I lay in bed staring into the darkness listening to the nighttime sounds and wondering how I had managed not to faint when I had turned and seen Michael Metcalf walking towards us.

When the world stopped spinning, I'd no idea how long we had stood there staring at each other. After a bit, I remember trying for a semblance of composure and making some mumbled apology, about what I don't know, but luckily he'd taken charge of the situation.

"Well, well, well! If it isn't Alexis Ashley! I guess it's true ... it is a very small world. How are you?"

He extended his hand.

"My … this is a … surprise," I said slowly, taking his hand and giving it a quick shake. "I'm fine, just … fine … just fine."

"I take it you two know each other?" Lynn Kennedy asked as she looked from one of us to the other.

"Yes, we do, believe it or not. A while back, Miss Ashley filled in at the bank for my assistant while she was on maternity leave," he coolly explained.

"You mean Rodney had a baby?"

"Very funny, Lynn," he said laughing. "This was before Rodney's time."

"Just kidding. It's just that Rodney acts like he's been at the bank since the doors first opened," she laughed.

"Well, he hasn't. Miss Ashley worked with me for several months and did a great job … if I recall. How on earth do you happen to be living on an island in the Caribbean?"

He stared at me with an intensity that made my legs go rubbery. "It's a long story," I replied, finally getting something of a grip on myself.

"But, it's getting late, and I'd like you to see the property, including the grounds while the sun is still up. Shall we begin?"

"Good idea," Lynn said.

I started by showing them the nightclub and restaurants in the main building working my way up to the third floor. I took them through the ballroom, the movie theater, and most importantly, through some of the conference and meeting areas.

Lynn Kennedy was totally involved in the tour. Michael was involved with me. I knew he didn't hear a word I was saying.

And as for me, half the time I didn't know what I was talking about. I was doing the tour totally by rote.

We left the main building and continued on to the section of the property with the guest rooms, and examined a suite and a regular room as well as, The Presidential Suite.

Then, it was on to the fitness center, tennis courts, the pools and the rest of the recreational center and grounds.

Even with the help of the little golf cart, it took us quite a while to see everything. I guess I did all right because when it was over Lynn seemed impressed.

She asked all the key questions clients ask when they're seriously considering using your property.

When I drove to the bell stand to get them a taxi, Michael and I found an opportunity to make a date for later. I gave him the name of a restaurant and we agreed to meet in thirty minutes in the bar.

I was so nervous and in such a tizzy on the way to meet him, I nearly ran my car off one of the winding roads.

It was a relief when he hadn't objected to leaving so soon after arriving at the restaurant, but on the way home I kept wondering exactly what it was he wanted. And why he had really come.

"Well, how was I supposed to know he would head straight for the Virgin Islands?" Brenda asked, all righteous indignation.

"But, since he did," she added slyly, "Seems like there must be some pretty powerful emotions at work."

"Well, the least you could have done was to tell me you talked to him.

When *did* you talk to him?" I asked.

"A couple of weeks ago I went to Boston for a two-day refresher course on new innovations. While there, I simply picked up the telephone and called him. We only talked that once and for just a few minutes, but apparently that was enough," her voice brimmed with mischief.

I thought of Sarah's advice that I call Michael and wondered if Brenda and I hadn't shared some kind of telepathic exchange. It just seemed so weird that she would almost simultaneously do what Sarah and I had so recently discussed.

"But, what made you call?" I persisted.

"I just didn't like the way he never acknowledged your message when you left Boston, and never contacted you. From what you'd told me about him, something about that just never seemed to add up. I needed ... closure." Suddenly serious ... "To be totally honest, it was if I was compelled to call him."

"You needed closure? You're nuts. So, why didn't he ever call?"

"I'll let him tell you."

"Oh no, Miss Butinski. You tell me."

"No. I'm going to let the two of you work it out from here."

"Do you think we can handle it?"

"I don't know. You've managed to screw things up pretty well till now."

I laughed because after all, she was right.

It was Friday and I had called Angie at home to let her know I would not be coming into the office.

I quickly outlined the meeting with Lynn Kennedy and promised to seal the deal with a follow-up phone call on Monday followed by the "Thank You" letter and kit. I didn't mention Michael Metcalf.

I then woke Sarah up and told her about his being on island. She screeched for a full minute, before running around throwing things in an overnight bag. She would spend the weekend at Don's, she declared.

I tried to tell her that was hardly necessary, but she insisted on giving me the house for the weekend ... just in case, she said, with a series of winks and blinks. I threw up my hands in exasperation.

Shortly after Sarah left and I was getting dressed to meet Michael for lunch, Vincent called.

He had called me at work to invite me to lunch and had been told I wasn't coming in. He took a chance, he said, and tried me at home.

His call was something of a shock. In the maelstrom of emotions that arrived with Michael's sudden appearance, I had actually forgotten about him, which I guess spoke volumes about how deeply my feelings for him did ... or didn't run.

I explained that a friend from off island would be visiting for the weekend. He seemed disappointed, but to my relief, didn't let it get out of hand.

He simply said he'd check with me the coming week. I felt guilty, but reminded myself that Vincent and I had only been on a couple of dates, and had made no commitments.

After setting myself straight on that score, I turned my attention to my wardrobe and decided on a white and mint green cotton, sun-back dress; white high-heeled sandals and a straw hat with a white and mint green band around the crown.

I had let my hair grow out natural and wore it loose around my shoulders.

It was a relief not to have to spend all those unproductive hours first, having my hair styled and then all that time under hair dryers for my hard to dry hair.

That, plus the money saved made it likely I would keep my hair natural forever.

On top of which, going natural made me feel closer to my roots, and free in a way that was difficult to explain; so it was all good as far as I was concerned.

When finished dressing, I looked at myself in the mirror and was satisfied. I had managed to keep the weight off that I'd lost while waitressing at The Depot, which was a blessing since the islands were the land of swimsuits.

I picked Metcalf up at his hotel in my little island car, which was something that looked one step away from the junkyard, but was deceptively sturdy and perfectly capable of maneuvering unpaved roads, steep hills and cow paths. I had chosen a restaurant at a bed and breakfast hotel on Government Hill.

The little cafe on the second floor gallery had a spectacular view of the harbor, excellent food and just the right amount of privacy to allow for intimate, uninterrupted conversation.

After ordering we sat and just looked at each other for a long moment.

Finally, I broke the silence.... "You know, this is positively surreal. I didn't think I would ever see you again, and here you are sitting across the table from me. It's more than a little unnerving."

"Is it so unnerving that you wish I hadn't shown up?"

"No. I didn't mean it that way.

I guess I mean ... after not bothering to call or get in touch in all this time, you suddenly show up saying you found me ... when I was never lost. What's that all about?"

"But, you were lost ... to me. I didn't have a clue where you had disappeared to," he said.

"I left you my mother's telephone number and address, Michael. If you had wanted to get in touch, you could have called. She would have told me if you had."

"Did you leave that information with me?"

"No. You know I didn't. I left it on your answering machine at the office."

"Think about it," he said quietly.

"Are you telling me you never got the message?" I almost whispered.

"I'm telling you exactly that," he responded.

I felt a rush of emotions so powerful, I almost couldn't contain myself. I took a couple of deep breaths, a sip of water and tried to slow down my racing heart.

I suddenly felt so stupid ... so defensive for never once giving him the benefit of doubt.

"Let me explain. When my assistant returned from maternity leave, everyone was a little over zealous in their assurances of how well you had filled in for her.

"Apparently, the green-eyed monster reared its ugly head, and you probably called and left the massage right in the middle of it all.

Sharon recognized your name and when she took my messages off the machine she simply never gave that one to me," he concluded.

"How do you know that's what happened?"

"During our conversation, Brenda mentioned you left contact information for me. Of course, I was curious why I hadn't received it.

I knew how to reach Sharon, who had been my assistant at the time, so I called her. She confessed.

She deliberately hadn't given me the message. Then, apparently, after seeing how I felt about you, she'd been guilty about the deception, but unfortunately had never gotten up the courage to tell me what she'd done.

I suspect that had something to do with why a short time later, after being with me for so long, she suddenly quit. "

If I'd had any idea," I said, shaking my head in amazement, "I would have called you until I reached you, or called your home. It just never occurred to me," I said.

"I can't tell you how many times I've wished you had tried to reach me, but I can't blame you for not knowing your message wouldn't get through.

Neither of us is at fault."

Then, I remembered why I had left him in the first place, and grabbed firmly onto that fact.

"Well, maybe never receiving my message was a blessing. You must know I was reluctant to get involved with you because of your wife.

The commitment or at least the attachment between you was obvious."

"I knew you were put off by that, and I hate to

admit that in my arrogance, I figured that like most women I had dated you'd get over it."

I was startled by his admission and must have shown it.

"I know, I know. You don't know how many jackasses I've called myself.

Anyway, your response to my relationship with my wife was a wake up call.

You helped me understand that I was using her as a shield; as a way of protecting myself from intimacy, commitment…. the possibility of disappointment and yes, heartache.

It hadn't worked with Jennifer and I didn't want to take the chance again. We've been divorced for quite some time now.

I knew that night how I felt about you, but you left so quickly I didn't have a chance to really think about it, or get the chance to articulate those feelings.

I'd given up hope of ever seeing you again. Of course, I could have hired a private investigator, but I didn't know about the message and decided if you didn't want me in your life that badly, I should respect your wishes.

Brenda was a blessing; when she told me about the message, I made it my business to get down here and try to salvage what I believe is something special," he concluded.

Outwardly calm as I listened to this, on the inside my emotions were raging. I wanted to cry, sing and dance all at the same time.

Now that he was free, I could honestly face how I felt about him – had felt about him all along. I could finally admit to myself that I had been waiting for him … only him.

I started to laugh, but it came out a sob.

"Let's go." He stood and threw a bill down on the table.

Just then, the waiter arrived with our food. He saw us about to leave and putting it down asked, "Is something wrong?"

"No. We're leaving." Then he seemed to think better of that, and asked ... "How long would it take you to wrap that up?" He pointed to the food.

Sensing the possibility of a big tip if he came up with the right response, the waiter rose to the occasion.

"About sixty seconds, sir. Consider it done."

"Make it fifty," Metcalf called to the retreating figure.

We're a tangle of arms and legs, lips and hands shifting from one rhythm to another as easy and smooth as a river gliding sensuously towards a waterfall.

And like the lazy river, we begin with slow, languorous movements; gradually picking up speed; going faster, and then faster until we reach the precipice where we hang breathlessly for a pulsating second before crashing together in a torrid eruption over the edge.

Hardly catching our breaths the heat raises again and moving in measured cadence we take our time delighting in each caress; each sensation; each fevered sigh until our hearts pound fiercely as we abandon measure and restraint and wildly race down that ancient path toward release once again.

A short time later …

"Now, do you understand why I've come?" he whispers, his lips pressed against my hair.

"I …" I can't yet speak.

"You knew. You were simply afraid," he says. Then he chuckles. "So was I."

Sometime in the night we realize we're hungry, and go to the kitchen where the containers of food still sit where I left them unwanted on the counter.

I heat it all in the microwave, and we fall ravenously on the meal.

My senses are so heightened I can taste every spice, every bit of seasoning and can't recall food ever tasting so delicious.

There's grilled lobster, broiled salmon, Caesar salad, rice and peas, fresh broccoli and asparagus, baked potato, fried plantains and banana pudding. It's a feast.

We eat out on the moonlit deck covered only by a shared sheet. Later, back in bed ...

"I want you to come back with me to Boston."

"I don't know about that," I answer slowly.

"Actually, I'm thinking of leaving Boston."

"And the bank?"

"I'm not really with the bank in the capacity you remember. I still have an office there, but I work with them now only as an outside consultant."

"Do you still have your real estate businesses?"

"Still do. But, for some reason I've been feeling the need to move on; leave Boston and start fresh somewhere else. It's strange because I've always loved Boston ... it's my home.

But, sweetheart we can live anywhere. Anywhere you want ...except, maybe here. The islands wouldn't be an ideal place for the business.

I realize you have a job and a life here, but I want us together. I can even stay while you tie things up."

"I can't leave," I say, reluctantly returning to reality. I'm sorry," I say, dropping my head so I don't have to look at him.

"I don't understand. Why not?" He asks, sitting up, the hurt in his voice making me miserable.

"I know you well enough to know that a job isn't what's holding you here. What is it?" He asks, lifting my chin and pushing my hair out of my face so he can see my eyes.

"It's just not time for me to go yet," I answer, knowing he won't understand. I certainly don't.

"Not time to go? What does that mean?"

"I have ... I have a few more things to do here before I leave, that's all."

Which is news to me; I just know that Michael or no Michael, I can't leave yet. He's quiet, then...

"I want us together, Alexis."

"We will be together. Just not right now.

I promise we will; we've been apart this long, a little longer won't hurt. Wait for me?"

He answers by pulling me back into his arms, and covering my face and body with kisses.

The next day Michael wants to visit some of the Virgin Island beaches he's heard so much about. I tell him to prepare himself for some awesome beauty, and take him to a small, but lovely beach located on St. John.

He agrees that Trunk Bay is even more beautiful than he could have imagined.

After swimming and romping in the water like children, we amble along the water's edge talking and making plans.

I close my eyes and remember us walking a similar beach in the dream and half expect the man to appear with the work, but of course, he doesn't.

I understand that he was only symbolic of my job at that time, and the force that was gently guiding me to this place.

And just like in the dream my heart feels ready to burst with love and joy. I want to pinch myself to confirm that this is all really happening, but I only have to glance at Michael's strong profile to confirm that it isn't a dream, but the real thing.

He leaves late Sunday afternoon and I feel inconsolable. We have shared a glorious moment in time and waving goodbye knowing the miles that will separate us is almost too painful.

How quickly and completely I have come to rely on his love.

He made me promise that as he searches for a location outside of Boston and makes preparation to relocate, I will prepare to leave St. Thomas.

I promise, hoping it is a promise I can keep.

Chapter 8

Shortly after Michael's visit, I had finally gotten to visit Aunt Eleanor. It was a Saturday afternoon, and when I called, she seemed happy to hear from me and promised to fix us some lunch.

After eating an amazingly delicious meal and at her suggestion, we had gone out and sat in comfortable chairs on the front porch that was coolly shaded by two great old mahogany trees.

She had been about to say something and had turned her head to look at me when she stopped abruptly.

"It … It's," she managed, still staring at me. Then the glass of lemonade she'd been holding slid smoothly out of her hand and crashed to the floor.

Her eyes rolled back as her head fell back on the chair.

"Aunt Eleanor!"

I ran to her and grabbed her wrist. I could definitely feel a pulse. I put my finger to her throat and felt the same pulse beating a little unsteadily, but it was there.

I thought she might have fainted, but I wasn't sure. My heart was in my throat.

It could be something worse, so I ran in the house to find a telephone and call an ambulance.

I had just picked up the telephone when I heard her calling me weakly from the porch. I ran back outside and she was sitting up looking dazed, but at least conscious.

"I'm sorry. I do that sometimes. I was just so … I just can't believe it's you."

"Yes, it's me, Aunt Eleanor. Alexis," I said softly.

"No," she said, vigorously shaking her head.

"It's you. Oh, my good Lord, you're the one. I didn't even realize __," she cut herself off.

"Let me get you inside. Should I call someone?"

"No. I'm fine. It was just the shock. It kinda just hit me," she said, brushing off my attempts to get her into the house, or call for medical attention.

"I tell you I'm okay. Sit down, we must talk."

"You're sure you're okay?" I queried again.

"Positive. Right now, we need to discuss what you've been going through."

"You know about that? I don't understand … any of it," I said, with notes of desperation and defiance vying for first place in my voice.

"You don't have to understand … yet. In time," she said, rocking in her chair and acting like she hadn't just scared me near to death by fainting.

"Until then, you must be patient. You're an instrument child, and as long as you obey as you have been, everything will work of its own accord."

"An instrument to what end?

What does that mean? Why do I have to see all the terrible things I've seen?"

Then, at her prodding, I had poured out my story. Starting with Boston and my satanic housemate, I'd worked my way around to the slaves and the demons.

When finished, she nodded her head, continued rocking and had finally given me what she probably thought was a complete explanation for everything.

I, on the other hand, felt it explained little.

She had simply said that I had been chosen by the Father for a special assignment.

After emphatically telling her I didn't understand, she sat quietly for a few moments and had finally looked up and said, "In here," she placed her hand over her heart, "You know much already.

You're the student and life is teaching what you must know in order to do what is needed.

You have become familiar with the various forces at work in the world; good and evil, mortal and immortal; natural and supernatural.

You have met yourself coming and going. What you have learned is essential to your success; it gives you a clear understanding that will serve you well," she concluded.

I had no idea what she was talking about.

"All right, I admit I do have some limited understanding of what's been going on, but my question is … what's the bottom line?

What is it specifically that I'm supposed to learn? And, exactly how am I supposed to use it when I've learned it all?"

She sighed and for a few moments seemed deep in thought. After a bit, she took one of my hands, closed her eyes and spoke in a soft, singsong.

"You were gifted from the womb. I see the veil and its many mysteries. I see gifts you have already met, and those you have yet to encounter … and command.

I see the years of your youth and the elevated level of consciousness. There has been denial and fear; a learned response.

Regardless, the powers have always been with you … even before your first earthly breath."

She shifted and I saw her hands clench in her lap as if she was seeing something painful.

"The earth is poised on the brink of many, many changes and massive turmoil that will bring with it great chaos and destruction."

"Oh no," I breathed.

"It is destined," she continued. Some of the children were pruned from the garden especially for these times, which are nearly upon us; the veiled babies."

"Whoa! Wait a minute," I said, getting it for the first time. I held my hand up in an attempt to stop her, but at the same time couldn't help thinking that mom was right about the veil figuring into what was happening with me.

"You're not, by any chance suggesting that I'm one of the children who were ... pruned to deal with this coming chaos and these disasters?"

When she didn't answer, "But, I'm just an ordinary person ... I mean, I'm not really saintly, or strong, or anything. As far as being chosen, I do things that the Bible ... things that I know to be wrong, but I'm just one little person, and not a particularly strong one."

I rush on eagerly giving an accounting of my sins.

"I curse like a sailor – or I used to. I don't go to church like I should and I'm not exactly like … pure."

I mean ... I don't think … I'm just not strong enough to do whatever it is I think you're suggesting!"

"Oh, yes my child. You have been chosen as a Spiritual Guide; a Warrior Guide; a Leader of Men," she added. "About this there is no mistake," she said softly.

"I say too much, but you must accept this.

You have been led from one experience to another growing wiser and yes, stronger each leg of your journey. When the time comes, you will do what is required.

You will use the weapon that is yourself for the sanctified purpose for which you were born," she said, looking me in the eye now.

"Aunt Eleanor, I don't mean to be disrespectful; I just wish you could be more specific? I mean, how will all this work? How is it tied into the veil? And were you a veil baby? Will __"

"Stop. I've told you all that I may. It's not my place to speak further. And yes, I too was born in the caul."

We sat quietly while I swallowed my additional questions, and tried to process what I'd been told. It was startling, then again, it wasn't. I had known there were supernatural forces at work in my life. After a point, that was clear ... but this?

My heart fell at the thought of what she saw coming. I looked at her badly wanting to question further, but understanding that I couldn't. Plus, I didn't want to push her beyond her strength.

She had laid her head back again, closed her eyes and seemed to be sleeping.

"What about you, Aunt Eleanor? I asked.

"When this ... whatever it is ... when it happens, will you be a spiritual guide, as well?"

"Me? Nooo! I'm not strong enough. Who knows how far a distance I have yet to travel. I think not far."

She looked beyond me and murmured,

"I see now that I have only waited for you."

"You're scaring me," I said.

She leaned forward and took my hand again.

"There is no need to ever be afraid. Draw on your strength that is great in its proportion and know that you are never, ever alone."

It was difficult to understand and accept what she was telling me. It all sounded so impossible. But, hadn't my life been impossible these last few years, yet I had continued to live it, with hope, which is what I must continue to do.

"When will all of this happen, Aunt Eleanor? I mean the changes? When will all of this destruction begin?"

"It already has," she said, cryptically.

"Until the new century is attained, it will all seem as isolated incidents. But, after the world has passed through to the new millennium, there will be an acceleration and intensity of destructive forces. While still in relative youth, the next century will bear witness to a great confrontation."

I was confused, but since that condition was nothing new I tried to remain calm and not push. I could see Aunt Eleanor was far from well. But, exactly what kind of destruction was she referring to.

I stood and walked to the edge of the porch and looking out over the green hills, it was difficult to imagine anything upsetting the serenity of the scene.

"Can I ask about my dreams? They're so real sometimes. Do they have any special meaning?"

"Your dreams are often of things to come, but may also be of times past … depending on what the dream seeks to elicit," she replied.

I frowned and recalled a recent dream. I'd had it only once, but it had been frighteningly real and I'd never been able to put it entirely out of my mind.

"It's funny what you said about destruction and chaos. I had a dream recently that for some reason was really scary.

But even in the dream, I didn't understand why it was so scary, which was all very strange: It was raining, but the rain wasn't falling vertically like it would normally fall, but horizontally and was so thick you couldn't see through it.

And, there was this horrible roar that was really, really deafening. I kept asking the people around me what was going on, but they seemed too frightened to speak.

After what seemed a long passage of time, I was standing at a window looking out and I was crying like my heart would break. I couldn't see what I was looking at, but I can still feel my sadness.

What do you suppose that was all about?" I asked.

As I talked, there had been a quickening about Aunt Eleanor as her body tensed and she sat up straight in her chair and staring into space …

"Hurricane," she finally whispered.

Chapter 9

"*S*o, what's up with all the talk about hurricanes lately?"

"Well, it is hurricane season," Don, who was lying on the floor with his head propped up on Buddy's side, answered.

"But, don't go getting any ideas about us having one," Sarah added. "We were hit hard some years ago, but that was like the storm of the century.

It was called, The Hundred Years Storm. It'll probably be another hundred years before we get another one that bad," she said.

Then, their attention was drawn back to the television screen and the rented movie. The conversation about hurricanes had passed, but as I stared blankly at the screen, my mind lingered on the subject, and I wondered.

The dreams were coming with greater frequency, but unfortunately, none of them were any clearer than the first one.

If they were indeed about hurricanes, as Aunt Eleanor seemed to think, maybe it was one from the past.

If I could have visions of the past when awake, surely I could have them while asleep, so I'm thinking it was a past hurricane.

I continued trying to make sense of them until finally giving up and deciding to let whatever it was take care of itself.

Hurricane preparations had begun at the resort. Oil lamps, candles, flashlights, rain slicks, transistor radios and other supplies had been ordered months before and added to the hotel's inventory.

Some of the locals, including Vincent, with whom I still had an occasional lunch talked about the big hurricane from years ago and I learned a lot from the conversations.

This year, the National Weather Service hadn't predicted a very active season, so nobody thought the Virgin Islands would see much activity. I hoped they were right.

I still stocked up with extra bottles of water because supplies could become contaminated, or worse, become non-existent. I had canned foods, candles, a transistor radio and an oil lamp. Sarah, who had stocked up as well, felt we were adequately prepared.

"When should it hit St. Thomas?" I asked Angie, who had been listening to the radio in her office all morning.

"Sometime late tomorrow," she replied, tracing her finger along the lines of the hurricane-tracking map.

"So, everybody who felt we wouldn't get one this time was wrong. Right?"

"Yep."

"Great," I said.

"Who I really feel sorry for are the tourists. They're pretty scared," I added.

"As well they should be. We did inform everyone that there was a level four hurricane heading our way.

Of course, at the time it wasn't on a direct course for St. Thomas like it is now."

"Plus," I added, "They probably didn't understand what a level four hurricane meant. I'm sure the ones that did had their airline tickets changed and are long gone. The ones that didn't __"

"Are still here and stuck," Angie cut in.

"So, are we all; we're in the direct line of a class four hurricane and there's no way off the island.

All the flights leaving today and tomorrow are jammed, even after a couple of airlines added flights. When is the last flight out?"

"Early tomorrow morning. If the hurricane stays on its present course and speed, it'll be here sometime late in the evening."

"If it wasn't so darned scary, it would be exciting," I said.

"Anyway, when you come tomorrow, bring your toothbrush. All the managers and the professional staff will be riding it out here so we can help out with the guests. You're better off here anyway.

The hotel is big and strong enough to withstand a level five, if necessary. This hurricane won't be much of a problem," she said.

"Sure, I'll be happy to stay and lend a hand. Sarah is going to stay at Don's, and although she invited me to come with them, I think I'd rather have stayed home."

"Well, no need for that. We'll get through this together."

As I walked back to my office, I thought of the dreams, and acknowledged that Aunt Eleanor had been right. The dreams had been about something that was coming. And it was here.

Because everyone was doing everything possible to prepare for the storm, I felt positive about the outcome. I had called mom, Jason, Michael, Gail, and Brenda and told them what was happening.

I asked mom to communicate with other friends and relatives, particularly after the storm was over. I assured all of them that I would be staying at the resort and would be safe.

I warned them that one of the first things to go out on the island would be communications and asked them not to panic if they couldn't get through for a while.

They believed me, but every one of them was angry with me for not leaving the island sooner. How could I explain, running away just wasn't an option.

"Hi honey, guess who?"

"I know who. How are you, my love?"

"Wonderful! An incredible thing happened. The hurricane missed us! I mean we got some of it ... winds up to ninety miles an hour and lots of rain, but it changed direction at the last minute, so we didn't get hit full force," I told Michael.

"I know. I've been keeping up with it through contacts at the National Weather Service and the Coast Guard. It's no surprise that I've had trouble getting through to you.

Listen, I'm sending a ticket. I want you on the next flight to Boston."

"Don't worry, sweetheart. I'm fine, and it's over. Let's keep things the way we planned. You just keep looking for our future home," I added.

All the long distance lines were backed up, probably with people calling loved ones in the states, in other parts of the Caribbean and elsewhere.

I explained to Michael that I was on my cell phone and still had to call mom and Jason. I ended the conversation promising to call as soon as the lines were back to normal.

As I hung up, I thanked the Lord once more for delivering us from what could have been a terrible disaster.

"So, this one is a level one?"

"Yes," Angie replied. "But, don't worry. It's not much more than a tropical storm and they don't expect it'll escalate beyond that.

As a matter of fact, they think it'll lose some of its strength before it even gets to the VI."

"You know what I find amazing?" Nobody, I mean nobody that I've talked to felt we would even get a hurricane this season, and then we have two in two weeks."

"True, but this one's no big deal. Of course, the hotel will be taking the same precautions as before and we're asking managers and professional staff to stay and help, but it's just to keep the guests calm."

"Well, at least we should try to keep Ron from walking the roofs this time," I said laughing.

Can you believe that? The man is up on the roof of the main building after the hurricane started last week checking for weak spots."

"He should check the one in his head. That sort of thing should be left to the engineers. I think Ron sees himself as a sort of cowboy ... you know, rough 'n tough," I said.

"I've got his rough 'n tough, although you have to admit, he has chutzpah," Angie laughed.

"Exactly. And you also have to admit that he's wildly popular with the staff. So, when is this one expected to hit?"

"Early tomorrow evening, so bring your jammies again. We'll check in for the night as soon as we get here in the morning."

"I don't think I'm staying this time, Angie. I only did before because it was supposed to be really bad, and we had a lot more guests.

We know this one's just going to be a little blow and there aren't that many guests this time. There'll be enough staff to help with the guests without me staying."

"You sure? I'd feel better with you here working with me. Plus, you still don't need to be alone, little blow or not."

"I'm sure. I'd really rather stay home."

What I didn't mention was that I'd heard a lot of the staff – especially the younger ones – were planning to stay at the hotel and party.

They knew this was little more than a tropical storm, so they intended using the hotel as party central.

I didn't want to end up having to baby sit a bunch of immature adults, or find myself in a position where I'd be expected to break up parties and drinking and everything that came with that.

On the way home from work I stopped at the store to pick up two more gallons of water, some batteries, a good novel and some more lamp oil.

The telephones would probably go out if the winds reached eighty miles an hour and the electricity would be turned off regardless.

I wasn't sure why. But, I could watch television and listen to the radio until it did, then I would settle down with my transistor and my novel, which I could read by lamplight.

I had already filled a five-gallon water bottle that Angie insisted I bring home from work.

This way she said I would have a little extra water for bathing and cleaning, if it came to that. I laughed at her, and took it just so she would relax.

The next day, I only went in to work for several hours, but since everything was under control, I left even earlier than planned.

Once home, I again called everybody in the states and told them that a hurricane was headed our way, but that it was basically only a fast-moving tropical storm that would pass in a couple of hours, and was practically no threat. I went through the same conversation I'd had with each of them two weeks earlier, only this time I wasn't trying to hide my nerves. I was perfectly calm.

I cooked and ate a late lunch-early dinner and watched television. Most of the programs however, were preempted for assurances by the governor that everything was under control.

He assured us that the U.S. government and FEMA was standing by ready to send in medics, medical supplies, food, water and whatever else that might be needed in the event things turned bad.

The governor had been on television during the last hurricane, so I knew the drill.

He had on these army fatigues, which I thought was a little hokey since he wasn't in the military any longer, but I had read him a while ago, and had felt an intelligence that was piercing in its sharpness, and also knew there was a good heart beating under that shirt.

I was surprised I could actually read someone on television. It was the first time I'd tried. While reading him I had laughed aloud.

Outwardly he sometimes appeared arrogant and egotistical, but there was an entirely other side to him.

Not that he was goody-goody, but at his core was a kind, caring man who would go to extreme lengths to protect his people and his islands. He was very possessive of both.

I knew he had a firm grip on the helm and felt confident with him in charge.

Finally, I switched the set off and turned on the radio. All the stations were playing religious music with local ministers coming on to pray and ask for our safe deliverance. I gave a heart felt 'amen!' at the conclusion of each prayer.

Sarah called around four to make sure I was okay and to give me some instructions about the house; and I could hear Buddy barking gleefully in the background.

Like so many others, she hadn't bothered to board the windows again, since she'd had it done and undone just two weeks earlier. It seemed foolish, she'd said, to do it all again for such a small storm. I agreed, and assured her I felt perfectly safe.

We talked a while longer, and hung up. I turned off the radio, picked up my novel, settled down comfortably and started reading.

I awaken with a start. The house is pitch black, and aside from heavy sounding rain, everything is quiet.

I turn on the lights and I'm relieved the electricity is still on. Glancing at the clock on the dresser, I see its seven-thirty. The last thing I remember is turning the *radio* off and starting my novel.

The novel is lying open on the bed where it apparently fell from my sleeping hands. I smile at how tired I had obviously been then stop short.

There's the nagging feeling that there's something I should remember. I sit up on the side of the bed straining to recall what has slipped my mind. Then in a flash, it comes to me.

I jump to my feet and run for the door. Opening it, I see it's too late; the storm has begun.

The rain is coming down hard, and the wind is picking up as I stand there. I force the door shut and go back to my room where I feel my stomach tightening in panic.

"What do I do now?" I ask aloud.

Chapter 10

I pick up the telephone and feeling extremely grateful to hear a dial tone, I force myself to remember the telephone number to one of the most popular radio stations on island.

Before turning the radio off, the announcers had continuously cautioned that the shelters were all empty, and that people who live in unsafe housing like trailers, or live close to the shore, should go to them despite the prediction of a light storm.

While the phone rings and rings, I turn the radio back on. The news is on and I hear that the hurricane has escalated to a level two; still lightweight, but there's a problem … a big one.

Finally, someone answers and I ask to speak to Anesia (Nesie) Dawkins, one of the islands' few female disc jockeys.

I know she is one of those who are most concerned about the populace taking the storm too lightly.

After an interminable wait ... "Hello, Anesia here," she says in her authoritative, no nonsense contralto.

"Miss Dawkins, you don't know me, but I have something of grave importance to share with you and your audience."

"I'm listening," she said, with an impatient edge to the voice.

"First, I'd like you to understand that I am not crazy, high on anything, and I'm not playing a joke. What I'm about to tell you is real ... and it's serious."

I pause and take a deep breath, thinking about everything I'd just seen in the dream. I wondered how to convey that the devastating hurricane I'd seen … had been seeing in the dream was the one now approaching the island?

I continued, "Despite information from the National Weather Service, this hurricane is going to be a killer. It will be the most deadly, the most devastating storm the Virgin Islands has experienced at any time ... at least on record.

You must warn your listeners. They have to go to shelters ...now; while there's still time!"

Tears had started pouring down my cheeks, and to my horror I hear myself sobbing into the telephone.

There's a moment of silence on the other end, then ... "Who is this? I need to know to whom I'm speaking. What's your name?"

I struggle to control my emotions.

"Who I am isn't important. I … I'm ... a … spiritualist," I reply, accepting, embracing the role for the first time as I try to pull myself together.

"I'm not saying this to cause panic or alarm. I want to help you save lives," I say, much calmer.

"The NWS can't see what's going to happen with this storm. It's deceptive and if we don't move fast, hundreds maybe thousands will die. Please, Anesia, believe me," I plead.

"I know you say you're a spiritualist, but at least tell me how you came to believe this information," she insists.

"It was revealed to me by the Father … in a dream. I know how that sounds, but please understand it is real. I'm not some nut, and I'm not hallucinating.

This is a bad one, and if you don't warn the public, it'll be on your head and your heart for the rest of your life," I quietly conclude, and hang up.

I turn the radio up. There's religious music playing, and it continues for a few minutes. I'm just trying to decide what to do next when the music is interrupted.

"I have something I want to share with all of you listening. When I finish what I have to say, call friends and relatives who may not be tuned in and pass the information along.

If I'm wrong, I probably won't be working at this station tomorrow. If I'm right, maybe some of you who might not have been here tomorrow, will be around to hear my show another day."

"Well, all right!" I jump up and down ecstatically. I know this will make the difference.

"Thank you, Father."

"I just received a call from a woman identifying herself only as a spiritualist. She wants me ... no, she's begging me to tell you that the hurricane we're about to experience is going to be the worst in the history of the VI.

She said it's going to be highly destructive and will have the potential to claim a lot of lives.

I don't know if I believe this woman, but I'd just as soon err on the side of caution.

What about you?" She pauses, as if giving them a moment to think about it.

"If you feel, or know you may not be safe in a strong hurricane where you are, please put together the items the Red Cross has asked you to bring and go to a shelter.... NOW!"

I can hear someone trying to talk to Anesia in the background. It sounds like they're arguing. Probably the station manager asking her if she has lost her mind? But, she doesn't give up the microphone or stop talking.

"Way to go! Stick to your guns!" I yell.

"If you have the materials close at hand and haven't boarded your windows, you might want to go out now and throw up a few pieces of wood.

We still have some preparation time, folks. Let's make good use of it. Again, I've received a call from someone identifying herself as a spiritualist …" And she continues the warning, listing the locations of all the shelters on the island and on St. John.

After discussing some possible last minute preparations, she went back to the music and the ministers for a while.

I figured she was probably catching serious hell from the station manager as soon as she switched off her mike.

But, she had done the right thing. She would see.

Then, I start to call people I know, like Sarah and Don, Vincent, Sammy and Aunt Eleanor, who knew it was me that called the station. She told me I'd done real good and said she was proud. She also chuckled because it turned out that I hadn't had to wait very long to see one of the many ways the Father would use me.

Aunt Eleanor and an elderly neighbor are staying at her house during the hurricane, which surprises me. I had assumed she would be with her sister, Vincent's mother and the rest of their family, but she explains that she always stay in her own house.

I still try to convince her to go to her relatives or to a shelter, but it's like talking to a wall. I know her house is sturdy, so I finally bow to her wishes.

I tell everyone except Aunt Eleanor that I'm calling around because Anesia has suggested her listeners call friends and relatives and spread the word.

After that, I call a few more stations and tell them the same thing I'd told Anesia, but while some of them hear me through, not one of them say one word to their listeners.

Then, Anesia is back on the air repeating the information. This time there's urgency in her voice.

"Time is running out. Let's get busy," she says, and explains over and over that once the hurricane hits full force, the National Guard, Coast Guard, police and nobody else will be going out in an attempt to rescue people.

They will be forced to wait either until the eye is passing or until the storm ends, so till then it's every man for him self.

I'm gratified to hear her say the shelters, which had so recently been empty, are filling with people.

Around the time I finish my last call the electricity abruptly goes off. I pull out an oil lamp, light it and get my transistor out.

Sticking the plugs in my ears I turn it on and continue listening to updates. A few minutes later, I pick up the telephone and sure enough it's dead.

"Thank you Father."

When the storm hits full force, I'm so grateful.
I'm grateful I acted when I did; it's even worse than my dream. The wind, which has been a high-pitched whistle, suddenly shifts and becomes a relentless and deafening roar.

The house seems to shake from the foundation to the roof. Judging from the force of the wind, I'm sure this must be the granddaddy of all hurricanes. Because the sound is unbearable, I keep waiting for it to abate. It doesn't. If anything the wind steadily increases and just keeps roaring and roaring.

For the first time since awakening I think about myself. Until now I'd been so concerned with everyone else, I hadn't given a thought to my own predicament.

I realize that I am extremely vulnerable.

Staying home alone and not boarding up the windows has been a terrible mistake, but there is nothing I can do about that now.

All the disc jockeys are acknowledging that the storm is on us and are now warning against going outside saying,

"Anything not done now won't get done," and "Okay, everybody, let's just hunker down and ride it out!"

As the panes in the glass doors rattle, and the sounds of chaos outside elevates to a screaming crescendo, my heart races along with the wind.

I have never experienced anything even close to this, and spiritual guide or not, I'm thinking my number could just as easily be called as the next guy.

Maybe I've already completed whatever task I was assigned to do. Maybe it was simply warning the populace about the storm.

Listening to the radio helps to keep my mind off the horrible crashing, ripping and tearing sounds coming from outside.

It's impossible to see anything out of the windows, but what little I can see is incredible. The rain is coming down on a slant; more horizontal than vertical, just like in my dream, and I finally understand it is because of the wind's tremendous force.

Then, I hear a sound in the distance that makes my blood run cold, and understand exactly what forces will wreak havoc on the island. My fear slides rapidly into terror, and I begin to tremble.

As my breathing becomes more rapid and shallow, I acknowledge that I am losing control.

I grab the flashlight and frantically rush through the house to the kitchen where I yank open drawers in a vain search for a paper bag. There are none.

Going back to my room I stretch out on the bed and try to do what I had on the drive to Boston when I'd heard about the bridge washout –stop hyperventilating.

I discover it's a lot tougher to think pleasant thoughts when it sounds as if your house is about to become airborne.

The sound comes again. It is like the mighty roar of a train gathering speed as it comes closer and closer and faster and faster, until with a mighty crash, it's upon you. It is a separate and distinct roar from the ceaseless howl of the storm's regular wind.

As a child of the Midwest, I recognize the sound of tornadoes and know that with them comes incredible destruction.

They are coming at intervals and at least to this point, have all mercifully passed the house.

As I lie listening to the hullabaloo I forget my fear as I am moved by the storm's power and force and the majesty and wonder of the Father's power. It is truly magnificent. I calm down and pray.

When I finish, I resolve that if this is my time I will go joyfully, fearing nothing, just as Aunt Eleanor taught me. I'm still a little afraid, but feel nothing close to the terror I had felt before.

Going back to the radio, I'm horrified as those who either hadn't heard Anesia's warnings, or hadn't heeded them call the station begging for help as their homes are destroyed around them.

I cry while continuously praying for all of our deliverance. Anesia and the other disc jockeys are taking turns at the mike in their all-night vigil, and are advising people as best they can, but as the destruction on the island intensify, so does the people's circumstances and their panic. Their screams for help are wrenching:

"Sun Station ... hello."

"Please, I need help! My house is almost gone and I have three small kids. Can you send the National Guard?!

Another caller …"We have over forty people here! All the other trailers are gone! This is the last one still standing and it's about to go too! Please, we need help ...fast!"

One that is most frightening:

"I have two babies, and the roof of my trailer is gone! The walls are starting to cave in! Please, please help us!"

And …"This is Frank George! I hope my neighbor Rudy Edwards is listening. Our whole house is going, Rudy! Be ready to open the door … we're going to try to make it to you! God help us!"

And, on and on it went.

The calls are all the more terrible because there is nobody to send to these people … nobody allowed to risk their lives by going out at the height of the storm.

All evening I'd heard these horrific ripping noises outside all around the house; sometimes close, sometimes distant. I couldn't identify the sound until the roof above me begins to break up. The noise, I finally realize is galvanize on the roof being ripped off by the force of the wind. Now I understood why everyone is asked to stay indoors once the storm has begun. Sheets of galvanize from hundreds of rooftops are flying through the air like giant razors.

Suddenly, there is such a hullabaloo above me, I know the roof is caving in or being blown off. Getting into the bathtub with a mattress over you for protection is presumably safer than staying in an open room.

I don't have a bathtub, so with my heart pounding I race across the foyer to Sarah's room while the noise above swells to a screeching pitch. I don't look up, I just run.

Once I reach her room, I pull her king-size mattress off the bed and drag it to her bathroom, where I intend using it as a shield over the tub.

The mattress is too wide to make it through the door, so I settle for using it as a kind of tent as I lie on the floor underneath it between the bedroom and bathroom.

From the sounds of shrieking wood, shattering glass, the increased noise level, and the water flowing in under the bedroom door, I know we have lost some of the roof, but I'm still covered in this part of the house, so some of it at least is still intact.

I have my bible and a flashlight. I don't hesitate flipping through the book to find words of support and smile as the book falls open on Psalms and the perfect scripture to calm my fears:

> *He that dwelleth in the secret place of the most*
> *High shall abide under the shadow of the Almighty.*
> *Psalm 91: 1-2*

At approximately one-thirty in the morning the radio abruptly goes silent. The Sun Station had been the last radio station able to broadcast in the Virgin Islands.

Now, it too is gone and I feel completely isolated. I pray for those at the station.

The eye of the storm settles over the island around two-thirty in the morning and the deafening roar finally, mercifully abates.

I have felt a painful pressure in my ears all night, which doesn't cease with the noise. I pray that my eardrums aren't damaged, which I understand is sometimes the case.

Although the eye brings a period of calm, I stay put because I know the storm will begin again soon. In the quiet, I turn the radio back on and look for stations broadcasting outside the Virgin Islands.

I pick up an all-night news station in Puerto Rico. Earlier, I had heard the station's announcers joking about the hurricane and how it would miss their island, but give some of the other's a good drenching.

Now, they solemnly report that before communication with St. Thomas was lost, they heard that the island was taking a direct hit.

I turn the radio off. I don't need them to tell me what I already know.

Suddenly, there's a pounding out front. At first I think it's something falling apart from damage, but the knocking is coming too evenly spaced.

I slowly crawl from under the mattress, go to the bedroom door and open it a crack. My worst fears about the house are confirmed; at least half the roof is gone and rain is pouring in.

The knocking starts again, this time followed by a shout. Grateful that all the walls are still intact, and that someone is alive on St. Thomas other than me, I run to the front door and open it. Timothy, our neighbor falls into my arms.

I get towels from the linen closet where everything is still relatively dry and lead him into the bedroom. There is a long, bloody gash across his forehead, but otherwise he seems okay. While he dries off I take antiseptic and bandages from the medicine cabinet, and dress the wound.

"Wow!" He says, touching the bandage after I finish. "That's a real professional job. Thanks."

"Don't mention it." After a pause, I ask,

"You lost your roof, Tim?"

"I wish. I lost the whole damned house!" His voice breaks on a sob.

"Do you believe that shit?"

"The whole house?" I ask dumbly.

"I think it's somewhere down the hill. The wind picked it up, spun it around and swept it up out of sight. I could hear it breaking up."

"A tornado, I think. How did you get out?"

"When it started to shake real bad and the roof started lifting up around the edges, I ran outside to the tool shed, which is built of concrete.

I watched as the entire house lifted from its foundation and spun around in the air like it was a doll's house. Then, I couldn't see it anymore."

His voice is trembling so badly, I know he's in shock. I make him lie down on the mattress, and cover him with a blanket.

"I'm so sorry, Tim."

"So am I, but I'm happy to be alive. For a while there, I didn't think I was going to make it."

"That's the attitude," I say, feeling grateful that he can see the blessing in his situation.

"I don't know if this house will stand what's left to go through. You think we should try to make it down to the Crenshaw's?" I ask.

"No. From what I could tell when I was coming here, it looks like their house might be gone. Let's stay where we are, and hope the walls stay up."

I'm getting into the tub, which I have softened with towels and sheets when suddenly, the hurricane hits again, this time from the opposite direction.

Tim and I spend the next several hours 'hunkered' down riding out the storm, which feels like it will never end.

Somewhere along the way I know we will be alright, but there's no way I can explain knowing it, so I say nothing.

I just thank the Father for Tim's life and continue to pray for all the lives still in jeopardy.

By five in the morning, the worst seems over. The wind suddenly dies down to a bearable howl for the first time since the storm began ... except for the period when we were in the eye.

It is still too bad to go outside, but going into the living room is pretty much the same as outside since the glass doors and windows have blown out and a good deal of roof is gone.

We stick our heads out of the windows a bit and peer out at a world that's so strange it seems we've landed on another planet. Before the storm, the foliage everywhere had been so dense many houses went unseen from the roads, and many areas looked like jungle.

Now, the trees that are still standing hold leafless arms eerily up to a rainy, dark sky.

There isn't a leaf left on a tree, neither is there a bush, or a plant with leaves intact. In fact, there are few bushes left. It is indeed an alien landscape.

We stare in mesmerized silence at the changes only a few hours have made to our world.

Around six a.m. the darkness rolls away, and we know that although we can't really see it, the sun has come up. Now, the destruction is clearly visible. It looks just like my dream.

All along the mountainside are gutted or roofless houses. Some are in rubble, while others are completely gone, only the foundations remaining.

And like the dream, I can't stop the flow of tears streaming down my cheeks.

Squalls come and go all day keeping us from going outside, but on a distant road on a hill across the way, we see a steady stream of pick-up trucks loaded with people heading down to town.

"Where do you suppose they're going?" I finally ask Timothy.

"They've been coming down like that all morning."

"They're either injured and are being brought in for medical attention, or like me they've lost their homes. If they're homeless now, they're being taken to shelters," he answers and I feel my heart will break.

When night arrives again it is even stranger than the day. The island is completely dark and eerily silent; the only sounds are the military helicopters with searchlights that circle overhead through the night.

Their presence provides us some assurance, or at least creates the illusion, that we're not alone.

By the following day the weather has calmed considerably and we finally venture out.

We find pieces of Tim's house scattered around halfway down the hill among an astounding amount of other debris. We don't find any of the contents.

I desperately want to get to the hotel, so I leave him to make his way back up to the house.

My little island car is completely demolished, so I walk carefully over rubble down to the main road.

Most vehicles on the road are pickups, so I hitch a ride on the back of one through streets that are obstacle courses of downed power and telephone lines, and debris of every kind imaginable.

Quite a few people are out in search of loved ones, and I recognize the look of shock in their glazed eyes from my own mirrored reflection that morning.

Reaching work I discover that everyone has made it through ... but only barely.

All of the tourists and employes o the basement of the main building and hadn't realized it was disintegrating. By the time they did, they were trapped.

I heard that many became hysterical when being led from the basement and saw that the building above them was practically gone.

I hug and kiss everyone ... Angie, Ron, Marian and Freddie and Felicia, who no longer pretend they're not a couple.

By the time I make it back home, Don and Sarah are there and are mourning the damage to the house.

Sarah still manages to wring a laugh out of us when she climbs upon a waterlogged table and does a perfect Scarlett O'Hara imitation.

Scarlett is determined to rebuild her beloved Tara and Sarah repeats the last iconic lines of the movie ...

> *'"I'll think about it tomorrow ... at Tara. After all tomorrow is another day."'*

The good news for the day is that Don's house came through with only minor damage.

We are also happy to hear that none of the other islands had been hit as hard as St. Thomas.

In less than forty-eight hours the Sun Station is back on the air giving assessments of the damage, connecting people on and off island with loved ones, and offering advice on various types of assistance.

But, even as the island attempts to return to normal, it pauses to mourn its dead that are miraculously few, and to celebrate its heroes, which are many.

One of these is Anesia Dawkins whose decisive actions are believed to have saved many lives.

She is often heard exclaiming that people should credit the mysterious woman who called in and told her about the severity of the storm.

Everyone is quick to remind Anesia that the woman had not wanted to be identified; and that she could have played it safe and not said anything to her audience ... as many in her position it was discovered, had done.

There is talk of an award.

A small loss of life on the island is good news. My heart is heavy, however because Aunt Eleanor suffered a heart attack during the storm and because she couldn't be reached with medical assistance, she didn't make it.

At first disbelief followed by raw, searing pain. It is impossible to believe I have lost her so soon.

I think I might drown in my tears, but remembering her words about not having far to travel, I understand she had known her time was near.

I realize too that my grief is selfish, and try to find solace in what I know is her joyful home going. I am thankful for having her, no matter how brief the time and know that she will always be with me.

Only military aircraft carrying medical personnel and supplies can land on the island, and with no telephones we are essentially cut off from the world.

I worry because I can't let everyone on the mainland know that I'm okay.

The damage to the hotel is so profound that after getting all the tourists on military flights off island, it joins many other government and commercial buildings and closes.

I immediately volunteer with the Red Cross, which keeps me busy and doesn't allow time for worrying about everyone off island worrying about me.

It is the general consensus that the recovery from the storm might prove worst than the storm itself. We are faced with months of no electricity or telephone service.

Without electricity there is no water because the pumps for the cisterns run on electricity, which means no showers and no toilet flushing.

Generators become the new world order. The buildings, homes and apartment complexes that didn't own one before the storm have one now.

Generally run only several hours a day because of their fuel consumption, the generators afford us a window of opportunity to cook, clean, bath, and yes ... flush the toilets.

We all agree it will be a very long recovery.

One night after the storm I dream of a beautiful, sunny island with lush green foliage and colorful houses with roofs intact dotting the hillsides, and huge cruise ships lining the harbor.

When I awake I realize the island is St. Thomas, and I am so happy that despite the severity of the storm and the tremendous destruction, like Tara, the island will rise again.

Six days after the hurricane I'm walking a bit despondently up the hill to the house after working that morning with the Red Cross. I glance up and see a man standing at the top, arms folded, looking down at me. I raise my hands to shield my eyes from the sun and squint.

Then with a loud whoop of joy drop my bag and race up the hill at high speed.

At the top Michael sweeps me up into his arms and around and around we go while I am kissing him, laughing and crying ... all at once.

He explains that through some connections he was able to hitch a ride on a military flight out of Miami.

"I didn't trust the media reports of a low fatality rate. I had to see my baby for myself, with my own eyes. I had to know for sure that you're alive and well," he said, almost crushing the breath out of me with a big, bear hug.

More good news, Michael has a cell phone that can reach the mainland; a feat that many of those on the island haven't been able to accomplish.

He goes down the hill, retrieves my forgotten bag and we walk arm in arm into the house and out onto the roofless deck. While I call home, he takes a tour of the house shaking his head with each step.

The moment mom hears my voice she breaks down. Sylvia, who has come to stay with her, comes on and she too starts to cry. Pretty soon we're all bawling. I'm crying because for once, Sylvia is so glad to hear from me she has no recriminations. Maybe, just maybe, there's hope for us.

I take full advantage of Michael's generosity and talk with Jason, Gail, and Brenda before I relinquish his telephone. I give them telephone numbers of people I want them to call for me that include Bo and Jacoby, both of whom know that I am on the island.

When Sarah arrives, she calls her friends on the mainland and there are more tears.

I am happy beyond measure. That night Michael stays with me and we talk far into the night. Much has changed somehow since that conversation with Aunt Eleanor, his last visit and the hurricane.

So, although we sleep together and hold and kiss each other, I explain that it can't go beyond that until we take part in the ceremony that will allow the Father's final blessing of our union.

Not entirely understanding, Michael is accepting and I laugh as he seriously makes plans for the wedding to take place on the island within the next few days.

While Michael is on an errand the following afternoon, I feel a sudden need for solitude and decide to take a walk to the top of a steep hill close to the house.

While in deep thought, I sadly survey the leafless trees and destroyed homes in the valley and on the hillsides.

It begins almost without notice. I shake my head to clear a slight dizziness when a sudden nausea claims my attention. I wonder in a detached way why this is happening here, and now.

Suddenly, the sky brightens until it is almost unbearable to look up. The sickness abruptly dissipates and I realize that the time has come. I am so eager after the years of waiting for all the answers, I'm quivering with excitement.

I am surprised when I feel myself gently lifted high above the ground. I look down and realize I'm floating above where I see myself still standing looking down at the valley. I haven't moved; I'm there and here.

Then, I rise on into the sky and feel the most marvelous sensation of flying, and such an astonishing sense of release, I wonder if I have transitioned.

Thoughts of death are dispelled as I travel to the far reaches of the earth where all that is destined to come is revealed to me: I see natural destruction in the magnificent explosions of mighty volcanoes; mighty earthquakes; rivers and oceans over-running the land; twisting tornadoes; and storms of raging wind and rain.

In the aftermath of many disasters, I see water where there was land, and valleys where there were mountains. I see unnatural destruction brought about by manipulative, evil entities and the mayhem they visit on mankind by the use of man's own hand.

I see hatred, avarice and strategic violence that will take tens of thousands, millions of innocent lives around the world – all for the imagined sake of fanatical dogma, but in reality is Satan's evil manipulation.

I see wars, plagues and famines. There are huge ruins that were once pulsating cities and towns; parentless young roaming the streets as wild and directionless as equally dispossessed animals.

I see a world in chaos.

As I travel, a voice inside my mind speaks of my journey and completes the circle of experience and understanding. In the blink of an eye I see my lives rush past my face like a gust of wind.

I see the rebellious slave girl on the auction block; the grief stricken slave woman fighting so valiantly for her child; the mysterious person at the dinner party in the Newport mansion, and others; not ancestors as I had imagined, but various incarnations of myself.

I am astounded at the many times I have lived, which provides understanding of time's continuum. I see myself from the first birth … all fearless fighters and yes, leaders.

I see the evil that cast its net for me in Boston, and vainly plotted my destruction by planning to use me for its own seditious purposes and in so doing defeat the Father's Will.

I see the faces of those I have met along the way: lovable Bo, whose speech is now strong and sure, as he protected me from the storm; Brenda, fiercely enveloping me in friendship; and Gail, with one hand on her gun, hugging me with the other.

I see Richard smiling back at me with a gentle kindness camouflaged by indomitable strength; and Jacoby, his wisdom and knowledge fixed clearly on his intelligent countenance as he counsels me; and there is Sarah, with as yet undisclosed skills and abilities reaching out to me with steadfast love and acceptance.

I see the veils covering all their faces at birth and understand that we are charged with raising a mighty army united in spiritual battle against the forces of evil. We are the leaders.

I see countless others marked by the veil who will soldier in the Father's army, and with the passage of time, many others that will join us in the fight.

Among these, a young girl whose disfigured face was transformed to equal the beauty of her spirit by the touch of my hand. I smile because I see that over time she will become as another child to me.

At the time of reckoning the Shofar will blow sounding the call to battle and they will converge from all corners of the world, armed with understanding, acceptance of our unified purpose and God's amazing grace.

Our task is formidable but I am undaunted because the end of the turmoil will mark the dawn of a new beginning for mankind; a time of peace and harmony for those who, during the greatest, most inconceivable trials have and will choose the light over the darkness.

Slowly, I return to the hilltop and float back down into my body. I am startled at the powers I feel surging deep and potent within me.

The voice inside grows faint and I feel rather than hear the last ... *"Know that the greatest power is love."*

And just like that, it is gone.

"Alexis?"

I turn and smile as Michael, my love and my chosen partner joins me on the hill.

"Are you all right?"

"Yes, why do you ask?"

"You were so still. You seemed almost frozen in place."

"I was just wondering where our new home will be," I reply.

Sweetheart," he begins slowly, and I know he is struggling with telling me something. Then, I smile in understanding.

"I've chosen a place that will be ideal for me to relocate the business, but I'm afraid you won't like it," he continues, and then takes a breath.

"The city is __ "

"Atlanta," I cut in softly.

He looks at me in surprise. "How in the world did you know?"

"It just came to me," I honestly answer.

"And you don't mind?"

"No, I don't mind. You're right. It is the ideal place and add, "Michael, not today but soon, we need to have a long talk."

I must give voice to what he is already feeling.

He nods his agreement confirming to me that he does indeed have a divine suspicion.

The sun is casting a lovely, softening glow over the island and as it slowly sets in a beautiful concert of colors, Michael takes my hand and we start back down the hill.

My heart is filled with joy as I accept my destiny. There is joy in the knowledge that I have completed the first leg of my journey toward that destiny; and the greatest joy … finally understanding it all at last.

I will journey on confronting the difficulties ahead with confidence and courage for my Father is with me.

This is after all, my purpose. Why I am here.

And I smile because I know that at last, I am ready.

EPILOGUE: *Somewhere In Georgia*

High in the Georgia Mountains, a large house has been under construction for some time much to the curiosity of the far-flung and sparse community.

The size and strength of the structure has caused great speculation; it is much too large for a single-family home, and it is strangely reminiscent of a fortress.

During the construction contractors busily worked on the building during the week, but the weekends always belonged to a small group of people who arrived wearing what the locals described as citified clothing, but driving vehicles built for rugged terrain.

It is Saturday. The group arrived the previous evening and has been up and working around the building since first light.

Among them there is an elderly woman who spends most of her days rocking in an old rocker on the front porch while she watches the others as they work. On rare occasions she will join in a little gardening.

There are two couples. The first is a tall, handsome, well-built man and a petite woman of serene beauty with a startling streak of white in her long black hair.

There's a good looking younger man and a pretty blond woman with just the slightest shadow of a scar still discernible above her top lip. They are an odd assortment, but even the casual observer can sense their closeness.

On this particular morning, the two women are working peacefully in the garden.

The woman with the white streak in her hair abruptly stops and stands up, the trowel in her hand and her chore apparently forgotten as she stares off into the distance with fervent intensity.

The young woman stands and moves to the woman's side where she quietly waits. After a time, the woman shakes her head, wipes at the tears flowing freely down her cheeks, and whispers a prayer.

"What is it?" The young woman asks softy when the prayer is finished.

"We are passing into a new season. I see devastating fire and smoke ... great clouds of smoke, people running and ... Oooohhh," her voice breaks.

"Such tremendous loss of life; although I don't know the time, or place, it will happen soon. Soon."

"Well, just think the others will be here, all by tomorrow ... for the dedication of The Refuge and the services," The young woman says seeking diversion.

"Yes, we will all be together," the woman sighs, but nothing will appease her sorrow, which appears great.

She sees beyond the devastation, and knows that what is coming will be the catalyst that brings a gradual acceleration and a final unraveling.

But, her faith is as sure as the wind and the sun and she knows the fight will continue as it has these past years and that they will press on until the light swallows the darkness.

Just then, the men come from behind the house pulling a wagon with a large stone sign.

The woman smiles and nods as she gazes approvingly at the natural beauty of the stone and the simple words chiseled in its center:

THE REFUGE
SEPTEMBER 9 2001

*"That I may publish with the voice of thanksgiving,
and tell of all Thy wondrous works."*
Psalm 26:7

www.ingramcontent.com/pod-product-compliance
Lightning Source LLC
Chambersburg PA
CBHW060157260626
47160CB00001B/301